ENIGMA OF THE MISSIONARY

A Novel by

Jacques Oscar Lufuluabo

W0009705

Author's website:

www.joloscar.com

To those who are gone but continue to live in my heart.

To the memory of my mother and father.

ENIGMA OF THE MISSIONARY

GENESIS

A cruel silence sinks its claws into the night. On the border with the world of the dead, it branches between mounds and cypresses, expands along faded walls, and echoes, like the howl of a wounded beast, to cry out the anguish of a hundred thousand souls. Where tombstones rise vertically to raise marble walls, the stunning absence of sound suffocates every hope and has the power to kill. All that remains is a framed face, a voiceless image in a world of darkness and silence.

Between the subdued light of the candles, the hooded man bows his head. He pays homage to death and wonders why his name does not appear on any headstone. He is dead. He knows he is. Yet, his heart throbs furiously, rebels, and hammers his chest with growing fervor to remind him that the death of the soul does not coincide with the physical one, to remind him that he is alive and a final task awaits him before the end arrives. He is the only one who can bring justice to those who still claiming it. And this, ultimately, is the only reason that keeps him from indulging in the embrace of eternal sleep.

While waiting to find peace, he would like to shout his despair at least, but he cannot open his mouth. Perhaps he has clenched his jaws too long and too hard, or perhaps the body is suffering in a manner all its own, with a language unknown to him. In any case, he resigns himself, swallows, and instead of spitting out the suffering that devours him, he swallows it despite himself, sucking it up where it hurts the most.

A twinge in his stomach comes suddenly, as direct as a well-placed right. The face, already streaked with tears, hints at a grimace of pain, but he is on the verge of vomiting, and, for a moment, he understands nothing more. He sees the world spinning around him. To avoid falling to the ground, he is forced to bend forward. He spreads his legs to distribute the weight, brings one hand to his chest, rests the other on the icy slab, and only then realizes that he is screaming at the top of his lungs.

He screams. He cries. Again alone, abandoned in a world he hates, he screams and cries in the night.

It is the last weakness he allows himself.

Shortly after, he wipes away the tears. He thinks the time for crying is over, and it is time to act. The real culprits are out there, unpunished, and soon they will pay.

He has been waiting for this moment for years. Every sacred day he has prayed that it would never come, but he knew it would come sooner or later. For him, there is no hope anymore; love and life are dead. Revenge is all that remains.

Now he is no one. Neither dead nor alive, he is a voice that cries out and demands justice.

He has a mission to fulfill, and he will carry it out.

CHAPTER 1

It's retirement day. The Postal-Banking Solutions office struggles to contain everyone, partly because an air-conditioning breakdown in the middle of July makes the environment unlivable. There is a foul, rarefied air, with the smell of sweat mingled with evaporated perfumes, heavy breaths, and the foul mood of those present. An unknown number of people swear loudly. Some take it out on the staff beyond the counters, and some share the sense of discontent by propagating their complaints in the air. Still others, after hours of waiting, give up and put off until the next day.

Teresa, on the other hand, stands quietly, waiting for her turn to come.

Intent on avoiding the hubbub, she had come before opening time but found the Postal Bank already filled with people packed to the entrance doors. So, as soon as she got inside, she hurried to grab the queue number she now uses as a pastime. She turns it over in her hands as her eyes bob up and down, undecided whether to stare at the illuminated scoreboard or the long line in front of her.

She has been exhausted for a while now. Before she can get her own money, much more time will pass. She would like to imitate the many who leave in annoyance, but she just can't put it off. She needs that money.

Therefore, she hints at a grimace, resigns herself, and rests her back against the wall.

When her gaze passes through the glass window, she cannot hold back a sigh. Her eyes stop and stare at a bar across the street. A frozen juice would be nice now. In her purse, however, there are only a few pennies left, miserable coins that match her false hobo clothing.

In her threadbare clothes, dull in color from too many washes, Teresa wears old shoes with worn-out soles. She repeats to herself that in summer, the feet need to breathe; she jokes about it, even though those shoes have accompanied her throughout the winter. She already knows that she will wear them the next winter as well, but at the moment, she does not want to think about it. She will, when the cold weather returns to freeze her bones. For now, the warm weather has granted a respite, and she can pretend to be just a person like many others.

Intent to step into the part, she looks around to convince herself of her fantasies. However, a boy sitting not far away casts shifty glances at her and smiles as if to mock her. It is an insult to Teresa, who, despite her age and shabby appearance, is an energetic woman capable of getting respect. After all, she is a former policewoman and knows how to deal with certain people.

At another time, she would have stepped forward to put that greenhorn in his place, but now she is uncomfortable. Caught helpless, unprepared for outside gazes, she has the impression that those eyes have managed to break through an impenetrable armor and catch hidden emotions.

Therefore, although the boy keeps looking at her, she forces herself to ignore him. She turns her head as if to disappear, crosses one shoe over the other, places one hand on her tattered skirt, and with the other, brings a finger to her right pupil. To make sure it is always in its place, she taps the fiberglass prosthesis that has allowed her to hide her handicap for years.

The loss of an eye is why she left the police force and enjoys a privileged pension. A bloody accident on duty, one of many that can happen to those who wear a uniform, but for Teresa, it marks the boundary between before and after: until the age of forty-seven, she was a police inspector, a mother, and a wife; then the decline, life fell apart.

In the short time that memories take hold, the world around her seems to fade away. She is almost on the verge of shedding a tear when pride takes over. *"You can't give it up to a pimply-faced kid,"* it rants at her from who knows where.

Determined to confront him, she then turns back.

He is already on his feet, perhaps ready to run away. Yet, he does not seem willing to give in. In a brash manner, he waves her forward.

She does not let him repeat it. She sets off determinedly.

As soon as she is in front of him, she starts to speak, but the boy anticipates her.

"Sure it took you long, huh? I was just about to leave."

"I beg your pardon?" Teresa is confused and does not understand.

"Come on, lady! Sit down, or someone else will take the seat."

She lets herself fall down. "Thank you," she manages to say.

Bewildered by the unexpected gesture, she stays to watch the boy walk away and thinks back to the movie she had created in her head, with insults and mockery to which she had the most appropriate responses ready. Feeling like a fool, she shakes her head and raises her eyebrows. Then she smiles, amused at the misunderstanding and relieved by the discomfort of just before.

Soon, however, the unpleasant feeling returns to assail her. She again has the impression that she is being watched. She wonders if it is just her fixation or if two eyes in that room are on her.

Maybe it wasn't the boy who put that sense of nervousness on her. Maybe someone is really following her moves. Or maybe her paranoia now leads her to imagine something that is not there.

In any case, she cannot help but look around.

On the hunt for any detail that jars with the environment, she carefully scours the area. She scrutinizes the faces of those beside her and those she barely glimpses in the distance, yet no one seems to dignify her with attention.

"Stop it! You're being ridiculous," the little inner voice that won't compromise scolds her. *"It's no use looking for the solution out there when the problem is you."*

Fortunately, the display finally flashes her number, and she has no time to think about it further. She runs to the counter.

"I withdraw four hundred euros," she says, handing the clerk her ID.

The woman carries out the transactions without saying a word. With a weary air, she hands her the cash from under the glass and glances at her with the hint of a greeting.

Teresa puts the money in her purse, lets it sink into the bag, and heads for the exit.

About to cross the threshold, she thinks back to the sensation she perceived earlier. She turns to cast one last glance. Not noticing anything suspicious, however, she feels ridiculous and steps outside.

It is now past eleven o'clock. In the humid air of Rome, the smell of melted asphalt spreads. The desire for some coolness brings attention back to the bar. The feet stop for a moment eager to turn, but it is only a passing hesitation. When they resume their initial direction, Teresa leaves behind the illusion of a few hours ago.

Now, she has enough money. If she were really an ordinary person, she would run across the street to quench her thirst in that city oasis of umbrellas and coffee tables. Unfortunately, she belongs to the category of people who break the mold of normality because they are incapable of living in it and who, precisely in order to lower themselves into the habit of the ordinary, resort to the semblance of ritual gestures behind which hide their pettiness. Like the primal need that from the first light of dawn has taken hold of her and presses more and more, in the requirement to be satisfied. The same need that took her out of the house. The same one that all morning has sustained her inside the Postal-Banking Solution office and that, for years now, seems to give her existence a modicum of meaning: gambling.

She is a gambler, Teresa. She bets and bets big. And like all players who hazard and rely on fate, she needs calm and steady points and constant reassurance. All of which she can find in the bar below her house, the usual gathering place where everyone knows her and where she can blend in with others. There, she is truly an ordinary person because the rules change and the roles are reversed. The oddballs are not the regulars but rather people passing through who stop to enjoy a cup of coffee.

The venue is close by. It is just a couple of miles away. However, public transportation leading straight to the destination is not there. Teresa should have to take two buses that would make a very long round trip, and she cannot wait any longer now. So, she sets out on foot, ignoring her fatigue, thirst, age, and even the blazing July heat.

With her bag tightly clutched on her arm, she proceeds in the shade of the trees lining the road. Then, when even the last one disappears, the only shelter that remains is the linear and narrow tracing of the ledges. To escape the sun, she is forced to rub the walls of the buildings like a poker card, but she does not care; as she walks, she daydreams. She has time to hope, believe, and convince herself that victory will soon come.

Of course, she knows the truth well, but she tries in all sorts of ways to hide it from her own eyes.

"You have the worst vice," she told herself repeatedly. On several occasions, she even tried to quit, or at least pretended to try, to feel at peace with her conscience. Dissatisfaction, however, always got the better of her. In the unbridgeable void enveloping her life, everything lost meaning. Her affections, friendships, and old habits are now indifferent to her. The only thing that can still give her a thrill of excitement is the risk of gambling.

As she nears arrival, fatigue returns to assail her. Her clothes are soaked with sweat, and her legs seem to want to give in to the effort, but the compelling need continues heedlessly to push her forward. So, she quickens her pace, turns the corner, and here, at last, is the bar.

As soon as she is inside, she rushes to the counter. She rests her elbows to keep from falling down.

"Claudio, give me a drink," she says to the bartender.

"Hello, Teresa. What are you having?"

"Just some water. Frozen."

As the man fills the glass, she already feels resurrected by the cool air from the air conditioners. She wipes the sweat from her face, gobbles all the water in one gulp, and hurries to ask for more. In a state of semi-apnea, she drinks three glasses in a row. "Ah!" she sighs. "That is what I needed."

"Rough day, huh? It's hot as hell."

"Yeah!"

The venue houses five slot machines at the entrance and as many in the back, but seeing that there is not a free one, Teresa buys a dozen *Scratchers* and goes to sit at one of the tables in the back. She takes out her lucky coin and places it close to her lips as if to kiss it. She quickly takes to scratching the patina off the paper, looking for the win. In that gesture, between fear and the desire to believe, she feels a shiver run through her body, a grip that starting from her stomach, forces her to hold her breath in moments of uncertainty.

In the brief interval, the mind races madly. Dozens of thoughts overlap, from the many dreams relegated to the corner in time to the illusion of how a hypothetical future would erase the suffering of the past. Thoughts shattered shortly after when a series of losing numbers shows itself to Teresa.

At this point, she throws away what has become a mere piece of paper and lets go, almost relieved. Absurdly, even defeat has taken on a definite purpose in her sick world. Because winning

– in the true sense of the word – would mean having to change. Even if for a moment, she would be forced to face reality, and she just does not know how she would react to the situation. The fear of finding out is great. It is the exact counterweight that balances the desire to exult. And this is what allows her to go on, to keep losing and losing without giving up her illusions. Because at the end of the day, as the line between dream and reality thins almost to the vanishing point, she feels life flowing through her and is certain that she still exists.

However, time runs fast. The bar begins to get crowded, and everything suddenly changes.

"Excuse me, ma'am..." A man points to a nearby table. "Are you waiting for someone?"

"No. It's free," she replies, taking her bag off the tabletop.

Soon after, four people sit beside her. Workers on their lunch break, joking and laughing, fill the sense of emptiness that reigned until just before.

What comes from outside is a breath of real life.

Some of those faces are familiar to Teresa. People she sees every day and whose normalcy she envies. She would like to be one of them, free to laugh and joke, but that world to which she aspires seems to reject her like an old shoe.

The sudden sense of dissatisfaction dampens even the desire to play, forcing her to step aside. She leaves the bar without saying a word.

Outside, the heat has risen again. Fortunately, her building is just ahead.

However, rather than hurrying, halfway there, she slows down, takes one last step and stops altogether. The inkling of being watched overwhelms her, but this time it is not just an impression. For a split second, her eyes catch a detail she struggles to focus on.

With the road semi-deserted, it takes her a short time to notice a guy on the other side of the roadway. He is in the car, and Teresa cannot get a good look at him. Not least because he is wearing a pair of sunglasses and has his head half-covered by a hood.

Convinced that he is looking in her direction, Teresa wonders if it wasn't him at the post office.

Her paranoia is probably taking off again, but there is no escaping it now. She has to figure out who this guy is and what he might want from her.

Unfortunately, she has just enough time to set off. The man starts the engine and drives off at speed. Within seconds, the vehicle pulls away, turns onto a side street, and disappears from view, leaving the road again in silence.

***

Having been back home for half an hour, Teresa still cannot banish the image of that guy.

Who the hell was he?

To accompany the unanswered question is a film of faces that floods her mind.

She struggles to think of anyone who might resent her, but too many cases have passed through her hands during her career.

Certainly, she has not imagined the man in the car. However, this is not enough to figure out who he was and what he was looking for, assuming he was really looking for something. Who knows! Perhaps, when she noticed him, he was already about to leave. It could be pure coincidence, a chance event to which she would have given more weight than she should have.

Of all the solutions, this is surely the most likely, but by now, the worm of doubt has crept into her mind, and she cannot get rid of it.

Making matters worse is the fact that she is at home.

Teresa hates that environment, with all that it represents. It encloses the sufferings of a lifetime and forces her to recall memories she would like to erase from her mind.

Unfortunately, she has no money to move elsewhere: she has already sold the bare property to pay off her gambling debts.

"It is the sentence for your mistakes," scolds the familiar little inner voice. *"You have to pay the bill."*

She rolls her eyes in the air, lets out a sigh of resignation, and goes to the bedroom. After a tiring morning, sleep is the best remedy. It will help her not to think.

She does not even remove her shoes. She drops onto the bed, ignoring her rumbling stomach. Soon, her eyelids grow heavy, and her head releases the ballast that anchored her to the floor. She is about to drift off to sleep when a sudden thought abruptly wakes her up. "It's tomorrow!" she exclaims, opening her eyes wide.

She had put it out of her mind. Her 60th birthday is less than a day away.

Still lying down, she stares at the ceiling. An invisible force seems to push her down. With the impression that any second now, everything will come crashing down on her, she gets up with difficulty and pushes herself up to the dresser. From one of the drawers, she pulls out a cardboard box bound by a blue ribbon.

Contained inside are photographs that she keeps with manic care, neatly stored in plastic wrappers to escape the wear and tear of time. There are ten of them. And tomorrow she will receive one more.

Twelve years have now passed since her daughter, Angela, left home. Teresa has waited patiently for forgiveness, continuing to hope for her return, and a part of herself has not stopped believing.

The truth, however, is quite different.

The first two years spent wondering if she was alive or dead were not enough of a punishment. In the end, Angela found a more subtle way to punish her. With simple photographs. One for each birthday, to show her a life she will not take part in.

Aware of hurting herself, she pulls the first in the series, the only one accompanied by writing on the back, out of the box.

In the shot, Angela is smiling, holding a baby in her arms.

"This is my son, your grandson. His name is Pier Giorgio," was her

last words.

Words written down, never spoken, but which echo in Teresa's head every year like a divine retribution.

To escape the pain, she lifts her gaze. With a violent lash, the mirror slams her image into her face, that of a woman she despises.

"Why did you leave me alone?" she asks as if her daughter could hear her voice.

She already knows the answer, but she does not have the courage to admit it. It is too heavy a truth to carry on her shoulders.

So, she continues to pretend she does not know. For her misfortunes, she blames an adverse fate that someone else has written for her. However, no matter how hard she tries to deceive herself, her eyes betray her. Unable to go along with the lie, they let a tear drip down. She chases it away with a dry gesture, and while she continues to stare at her face, time seems to rewind.

The wrinkles that mark the years disappear from view one by one; she sees herself as young again, still in her 40s. She stands in front of the mirror, making herself beautiful and feels like a lucky, happy woman.

From the dining room, she can hear the voices of her children bickering – the youngest whines.

"Mom, Mom," she hears her son calling.

She is about to answer when an indistinct sound suddenly shakes her. She would like to remain clinging to that happy memory, a reflection of what has been. The noise, however, becomes more insistent and definite. The images blur. Finally, the trill of the phone breaks through completely, brings her back down to earth, and everything fades away.

Regretting the pleasant feelings that have returned to caress her soul, she is on the verge of tears but refuses to give space to her emotions. She goes to the living room to answer the phone.

"Teresa Graziani?" asks the voice on the other end.

"Yes. Who is this?"

"Best wishes!"

"But who is speaking?"

"What does it matter? Aren't you happy that someone is still thinking about you?"

She tries to associate a face with that voice, but she is certain she has never heard it before.

"I've prepared a special gift for you."

"Who the hell are you?"

"You know who I am. You've seen me."

The guy in the car! How does he know her number?

"Who are you?" she repeats. "And what do you want from me?"

"Don't be impatient. We've introduced ourselves for now. We'll get to know each other better."

Other people in Teresa's place would be overcome by fear. She, on the other hand, who is afraid of life more than death, is just curious.

"I would say that you already know me well while I know nothing about you," she says. "Why don't we talk about it face to face?"

On the other side, however, there is only the continuous *tu-tu-tu* signaling the end of the call.

HELL – ACT I

July 3, morning

Built in the immediate post-war period, in the aftermath of Italian unification, Vittorio Emanuele II Square is the largest square in Rome – over six hundred thousand square feet of neo-Baroque style. Once an esteemed and genteel place, it is now referred to as the Capitoline Chinatown by locals since the fine stores have disappeared to make way for Chinese competitors.

Entirely surrounded by porticoed buildings, located between Termini station and Porta Maggiore, it has long hosted the celebrated Esquiline multi-ethnic market, which was even covered in the *New York Times*. Now that this has been moved indoors to the adjacent street, the square lets people admire its gardens inside. Palms, plane trees, cedars and magnolias guard the *Trophy of Marius* - a fountain from ancient Rome - and the *Alchemical Gate* - the only remnant of Villa Palombara and a frequent source of legends.

In short, the square owes its fame to a wide variety of reasons. However, it will soon be talked about for a completely different reason – nothing to do with art or food. Soon the newspapers will have bread for their teeth: and there will be talk of death.

This is what goes through the man's head as he waits for his prey.

Stopping at the back of a colonnade, he glances listlessly at his watch, smokes a cigarette, and stares at a doorway just ahead. He looks like anyone else there.

He wears ordinary clothes: a pair of jeans, a white cotton T-shirt, and a light, short-sleeved sweatshirt. With the zipper fully deployed, he keeps the hood pulled up to conceal his head while tall and squarish sunglasses camouflage his face.

However, being seen does not bother him that much. No one knows his intentions.

It is ten past eight. Although the sun has already warmed the streets, the morning freshness is still in the air. Those who can take advantage of it to shop. And in a few minutes, the woman will also walk out the main door.

By now, he knows her habits well. She likes to eat fresh foods and is a methodical person. During the week, on fixed days, she goes to the covered market, always around the same time.

Today she is strangely later than usual.

He will certainly wait as long as necessary. He just wonders if some unforeseen event has not compromised his plan.

To quiet his doubts, he pushes to the roadside, outside the arcades, where a peddler displays secondhand books. Feigning curiosity, he grabs one from the stall, brings it up to face level, and lifts his eyes up.

The apartment he is interested in is on the third floor.

Twenty minutes before, the shutters were closed. Now the window panes reflect the sun's rays. A sign that the woman is in the house.

Satisfied, he then returns to his post.

While waiting for her to come out, he watches the streetcars crossing the square, people sitting at cafe tables, elderly people sitting in the shade of trees, and people taking their dogs to do their business. He looks around him and feels a strange sensation. He feels alive.

Excited with anticipation, he is almost displeased when he

sees the woman pop up.

Nearing forty, she still retains a youthful air, although her beauty is beginning to wither. Unaware of what awaits her, she is advancing in utter indifference. She passes him, crosses the street, and heads toward the market.

He stays to watch her as she walks away. He makes sure she does not turn back. Then he reaches the car, a black Panda parked about twenty feet further.

The back seats have been pulled down, increasing the capacity of the trunk. Lying there is a metal locker, lightweight and equipped with casters. Its size slightly exceeds that of a dishwasher. To make it easier to load, he has mounted a folding platform in the trunk, but for now, he does not need it. He pulls it out without difficulty.

The rubber wheels with swivel mounts are good; the cabinet is very manageable. Lined with cartons to avoid the gaze of curious onlookers, it appears as two stacked boxes.

While he walks, he takes the keys out of his pocket.

He smiles, thinking how easy it was to get them. It was enough to visit a few Internet sites. He had no idea that one photo was enough to create a duplicate. The most challenging part was finding the right person to commission the work.

The wooden door is large and heavy. Helping himself with his back to keep it open, he slides the cabinet inside, reaches the elevator, and goes up to the third floor.

No noise is heard on the stairs, and at this hour, the man who lives in the apartment opposite is at work. So, without hurrying, he pulls out some gloves, puts them on, and inserts the key into the lock.

Once inside, he goes to the living room to prepare the necessities.

From the cabinet, he takes some gauze, a cutter, some rope, tape, a bottle of chloroform and arranges everything on the table.

Now he just has to wait for the woman to return.

She is not one to stock up endlessly. She buys just enough

from time to time. It usually takes her about ten minutes, fifteen at most. Also, she always takes the same route. She cuts through the gardens so that she avoids going around the square. And since, from the apartment, the view is great, he doesn't even need to lean out the window. He should see her soon.

Nonetheless, the minutes tick by slowly. At least until the woman emerges from under the palm trees, goes through the railing gate, and crosses the street.

When she sets foot in the house a little later, he is still in the living room, but his presence passes unnoticed. From behind the wall, he catches a glimpse of her walking into the kitchen; he hears her fiddling with groceries; he sees her enter the bathroom with the clear intent of freshening up: she is slipping off her sweaty T-shirt.

The woman is not wearing a bra underneath, and only a pair of shorts remain to dress her body.

With the gauze already soaked in anesthetic, he advances without making the slightest sound. He stays to spy from the corridor.

Water is flowing from the sink faucet. The woman gathers her hair and ties it with a rubber band. She soaps her face and neck, and part of her chest. For a moment, she pauses to look at herself in the mirror; she brings a finger to her nose as if something is bothering her, perhaps the unwanted gift of a mosquito. Then, when she leans forward, she begins to rinse her body, throwing water on her face an inordinate number of times. Clearly gratified by the sense of refreshment, she grabs the towel without opening her eyes. She passes the cloth to dry her forehead and cheeks until the cloth descends to her neck, and the reflection in the mirror returns into view.

Now, however, she is no longer alone. Her image has been joined by his. He is behind her back, smiling with amusement.

The woman's eyes widen, she jerks and makes to scream, but a hand over her mouth prevents the sound from spreading. An arm encircles her neck to impede movement. Gauze with anesthetic obstructs breathing.

"Good," he says softly. "Be good. Rest."

She continues to emit sobs. In an attempt to extricate herself, she pushes back, flails her arms, and kicks madly, but the gestures soon drop in intensity. She is on the verge of unconsciousness. Her body rebels a few more moments, then yields to the soporific's effect and surrenders in his arms.

Lifting her off the floor, he goes to the living room and lays her on the sofa.

She should sleep for quite a while. At least long enough to get to his destination. In any case, he doesn't want to take any chances. He seals her mouth with duct tape to prevent any eventuality. After putting her shirt back on, he grabs her legs, pulls her thighs close to her torso, slides the rope under her back, and ties her tightly. Then, he returns to lift the helpless body, this time to lower it inside the cabinet.

Before closing it again, he throws in what he brought with him. He makes sure he has left nothing out. Finally, certain that everything is okay, he leaves as he came. Or almost. Now the trolley is far less maneuverable, and it squeaks.

As the elevator opens the doors, he turns to cast one last glance. His work in that house is not yet finished. He will have to return to finish what he started.

CHAPTER 2

Teresa no longer knows what to think. A full three days have passed since her birthday, but the photograph she has been waiting for has not arrived.

The fact worries her seriously.

At first, she had thought of a simple delay in correspondence. Now, however, she is terrified at the thought that something bad has happened to Angela. Among the thousands of questions she continues to ask herself, she wonders if this is not another prank on her part, a new way to get back at her.

She feels as if she is reliving the time when she had not heard from her.

Haunted by the image of her daughter, dying in a hospital bed or victim of who knows what accident, she can no longer close her eyes and feels broken. The need to give a logical explanation for what is happening prevents her from letting go. She fears that at any moment the phone will ring to confirm what she already suspects. *"Your daughter is dead,"* she will be told. And, as much as she is ashamed to admit it, at this point a part of herself almost hopes so, because the uncertainty is consuming her bit by bit. Not knowing is worse than death itself.

In that helpless state, she keeps one elbow resting on the table, her forehead sunk into the palm of her hand, she despairs and cries. She would like to ignore the pain as she has done so far, but she can no longer find the strength to react.

The photographs in front of her seem to have a hypnotic power. Taking her eyes off the images is impossible. And on the hunt for any clue, she does not stop moving her gaze from one to the other.

The first five film Angela in the company of her son; only the locations and dates change. In the later ones, however, she disappears from the scene and Pier Giorgio is the sole protagonist.

For the umpteenth time, Teresa returns to wondering if the detail might have some hidden meaning. By now, that is all she hopes for: an answer that will make sense of the events of a lifetime.

From her daughter's escape, she tries to find a why to her merciless gestures, wondering what Angela feels, what she thinks, and above all, what she wants to prove. Striving to understand her, to really know her, Teresa has made up her mind to be a mother. She was not when she should have been, and now regret and guilt devour her.

She hears the little voice of conscience buzzing.

"You always found an excuse to put her in second place," it tells her. *"First because you were working too much. Then, because you had lost your job. You always found a way to play, but there was never time for her. Not even when Piero..."*

"Enough!" she shushes it.

Those last words, she does not want to hear. It is a wound that is still vivid, the kind that does not heal, and to ignore it completely, she goes back to thinking about Angela.

Teresa remembers how difficult it was with her. On the few occasions when she tried to act like a parent, she could never get her right. Like the time when she had bought her a latest fashion dress, intending to surprise her.

"I'm not wearing that stuff," had been Angela's reply.

"What the hell! You dress like a scarecrow," she had raged. "You look like a tomboy."

"You could have given birth to me as a boy. You can't imagine what a favor you would have done me."

Teresa had never been able to stand her daughter's way of dressing, especially in recent times: clothes that were too loose and lacked shape. However, on that occasion, seeing Angela with tears in her eyes, she had merely put the dress back in the package and changed the subject. "Never mind," she had said. "Rather, what did you want to talk to me about this morning?"

"Nothing."

"You said it was important."

"It was! But I don't want to talk about it anymore. Not with you."

Angela was like that. She changed her mood from one moment to the next, and you had to catch her at the right time.

Teresa unfortunately always chose the wrong one. Yet, since Angela left, she even regrets those episodes made up of quarrels and misunderstandings. She would like to have a second chance. And if she cannot give in to the evidence, it is because she needs to keep believing. After a lifetime of failure, her daughter represents her last chance.

"You can't leave me," she says, grabbing one of the photos.

She had almost gotten used to that situation. The annual assurance that Angela was okay was enough to keep her hope alive.

Instead, she is now forced to think the worst.

As she continued to sift through dramatic scenarios, she wondered if the mystery man might have something to do with it. She had repressed him from her mind, but his words resurfaced with force.

"I have prepared a special gift for you," he said over the phone.

Could it be that he was alluding to this? That he harmed Angela?

The idea hardly convinces her. It lacks a logical connection. And making it implausible is a big question mark. How would he have found her?

This should be enough to dismiss the hypothesis. Instead, Teresa goes hunting for a rational explanation that makes it plausible. She wants to force two jarring puzzle pieces together. Because no matter how absurd, that is the only lead she has.

After all, she knows nothing about the guy. Whether he is a clown or a crazy maniac is impossible to determine. He never showed up again.

To get an answer, she will have to be the one to find him.

She knows it is madness, that it amounts to looking for a needle in a haystack and will almost certainly be just a waste of time, but now the fact is irrelevant. She must do something to avoid thinking, or risk going crazy.

CHAPTER 3

July 4, morning

Her world is no longer the same. It once appeared large, boundless. Now, instead, it has shrunk to four bare walls and the pungent smell of disinfectant, to the sight of syringes and the comings and goings of white coats, to phrases of circumstance and looks of pity. Only a glimpse of real life penetrates through the window as if to mark the boundary with the past.

She is a fragile woman with a broken soul. Alone in that hospital bed, she weeps at the thought of what awaits her: continuous suffering while waiting for a certain death. This is what frightens her. It is not the inevitable denouement but the length of time that separates her from the end.

One day after another, that protraction becomes more and more painful, ravaging the body and wearing down the spirit. Liver cancer with cirrhosis has reduced her to skin and bones. She now eats little or nothing. Because of constant bleeding, she often goes into mental confusion. She spends her nights contemplating the ceiling because even medication can no longer make her close her eyes. All treatment has proved futile: the tumor has grown again, and now the metastases are also creating breathing difficulties.

She is tired of so many tribulations. She would like to end it once and for all. But no one is willing to help her. What she thinks and feels does not interest a single soul. The law considers assisted suicide something abominable.

Those who make the rules should be in her place. They would certainly see the issue differently. There is her lying on that bed. It is she who has an IV needle stuck in her arm. And she is the one who should have the last word.

Instead, she has no say in the matter.

However, today her crying is different from usual. As the tears trickle down, a gleam of joy spurts from her eyes. An unexpected event has rekindled a spark of hope, perhaps proving that divine mercy does indeed exist. Therefore, she sketches a smile and passes a hand to dry her face.

A voice suddenly bursts into the room.

"Good morning, my child," she hears.

The hospital priest is on the threshold. As usual, he came early in the morning. By now he is the person she is most familiar with. He visits her several times a day. Each time with the intention of convincing her that God is there, that nothing happens by chance, even if the first person to doubt it seems to be him. He never addresses her by saying her name. Always just appellations — daughter, sister, my dear — to keep the feelings beyond a safe line.

"Good morning, Father Giulio."

"Shall we say a prayer?" This is one way, among many, to ask her how she is doing. She is not a believer, and he knows it well. But he is evidently convinced that sooner or later, she will give in to the pain, to the need to cling to hope.

"No, thank you," she replies, emphasizing that that moment has not yet come. "I have a favor to ask of you."

"Tell me. If I can be of any help to you…"

"Yes. I'd like you to make a phone call for me."

"Are you having trouble with your cell phone? I forgot mine in my room but give me time to go get it and I'll bring it to you."

"No, Father, you don't understand. You should make the

call."

Bewildered by the unusual request, the man frowns. "And who do you want me to call?"

"My mother. I'd like to let her know I'm here. So far I've kept her in the dark, and I don't think it's appropriate to continue any further."

"What? Your mother is alive? I was convinced you had no relatives left. Why didn't you inform her right away?" The priest looks annoyed and relieved at the same time. "In any case, I'm glad you reconsidered before..." Discomfort, in the face of death, forces him to dose his words. He leaves the sentence hanging.

"Before it's too late? Don't worry, Father Giulio, you don't have to feel guilty. Keeping silent doesn't change things."

"Anyway, you should be the one to call her. Don't you think?"

"Please. I asked you because I lack courage. I already know. I would hang up before I heard her voice."

"Um... I see! Then it's okay, I'll take care of it."

The woman smiles, turns around with difficulty and grabs a note from the bedside table. "I thank you. I knew I could count on you. Here is the name and phone number."

The priest waves the note in his hands. He seems to want to add something else. Finally, however, he hints at a condescending expression, casts one last glance at her, and exits without saying anything.

She is relieved. She has paid her last tribute and will perhaps now be able to find the peace she seeks.

As the minutes tick by, she keeps her gaze fixed on the door and waits. Unable to decipher the emotions that run through her, she closes her eyes and takes a deep breath. She regrets the many things she would have liked to do and has kept putting off over time. Convinced she had a whole life ahead of her, she never thought life could be so mean, ruthless, and as short as a blink of an eye.

However, it is late now. Late for everything. She knows it

well.

With this knowledge, she clenches her fists, fills her lungs almost to ripping them open, returns to raising her eyelids, and gasps.

A man has appeared in the room.

Motionless just over the threshold, he looks at her and smiles. He seems to have appeared out of nowhere. She did not even hear him coming.

This is the second time she has seen that face. The second within a few days. On the first occasion it was only the face of a stranger, but now he has revealed his true nature. He has returned for her, to fulfill the promise he made.

Relieved by his presence, she says nothing. She merely returns his gaze and smiles in return.

CHAPTER 4

July 4, afternoon, 12:45 p.m.

The nightmare of the past few hours has not loosened its grip, far from it. The negative inkling that fueled Teresa's uncertainties suddenly materialized.

Sitting in the backseat of a cab, she still cannot come to terms with what is happening.

"Please go faster," she says to the driver as they travel along the eastern beltway.

"I'm already speeding. The speed limit here is…"

"Please, it's urgent."

Understanding the situation, the man does not dare to refuse; he sinks his foot on the accelerator. "Do I continue on to the ring road?" he asks a moment later. "It increases the route a bit, but you certainly arrive earlier. On Nomentana Street there are traffic lights and it's busy at this hour."

"Yes, go ahead. And speed up if you can."

Teresa knows the area well. The taxi driver does not aim to run the meter. That is the shortest route, at least in terms of time, and she wants to get to her destination as quickly as possible.

The cab takes the Tiburtina ring road; skirting the Verano municipal cemetery, it turns onto Scalo San Lorenzo's Avenue and goes up Regina Elena Avenue. The Umberto I Polyclinic is less than two hundred yards away.

Teresa lays her palm against the window, holds back a tear and thinks back to the phone call she received a half hour earlier.

"Hello? Mrs. Graziani?" she heard.

Thinking of the mysterious man, she has kept silent for a few seconds until she realized that the voice was different, warmer and quieter.

"Yes. Who is this?"

"Good morning, ma'am. I am Father Giulio, one of the chaplains at the Umberto I Polyclinic. I am calling on behalf of your daughter."

Another long silence followed: time for the words to reach the brain, time to convince herself that she had heard correctly, time to process it all. Then the panic. "My daughter? The polyclinic? Oh my God! What happened?"

"I'm sorry I have to be the one to tell you. She is hospitalized here with us and unfortunately… well, that is… she is in critical condition. I hate to give bad news, so I will get right to the point. According to the doctors, she doesn't have much time left." The man let a few moments pass. He must have expected some kind of reply, but in response, he has found only silence. "Your daughter asked me to inform you," he added. "She would like to have you near her."

Teresa has hurried to hail a taxi to rush to the hospital, and now that she is close to arrival, she is terrified of what awaits her. Twelve long years have passed since her eyes met those of her daughter. Twelve years spent wondering if she would ever see that look again, if that day would come. Never did she think that day would also be the last.

She barely knows Father Giulio's voice, but it is already clear he is a no-nonsense guy. Of course, turns of phrase would not have changed the situation, and yet, she already feels that she detests that man she knows nothing about. At the moment, she has no one else to blame. All she can pour her helplessness on is the voice of a stranger.

The priest told her the ward number. In her haste, however, Teresa hung up before he could provide her with the room number. So, as soon as she sets foot inside, she rushes to the front desk and asks for Angela Brunetti.

The attendant does a search on the terminal. "Um!" she mutters, performing the search a second time. "I'm sorry, but no one with that name comes up."

"Can you try Angela Graziani? Maybe she used my last name; who knows!"

The woman casts her a biased glance. She opens her mouth to speak but reconsiders. Between pointing out to her that the documents exist for a reason and avoiding the hassle, she must have opted for the second option. She types the name without replying.

"Nothing. No mention of her. Are you sure she is admitted here with us?"

"You called me! You are the one who has to tell me," Teresa rants.

"I'm sorry, ma'am. I don't know what to tell you."

As the attendant makes to walk away, Teresa does not know whether she should be relieved. Assuming it is just a bad joke, she thinks about the mysterious man, about his phone call, until Father Giulio jumps into her mind. In the agitation of those moments, she had forgotten him. "Wait!" she says, calling the woman back. "Could you..."

"Excuse me, but if you haven't noticed, there are other people too. I can't just type in random names to make you happy."

"No, no, of course! Just do me a courtesy. The person who called me introduced himself as Father Giulio. He said he was one of the chaplains. Could you have him call?"

The other is already on the verge of retorting, but when she hears the priest's name, she changes her attitude, hints at a smile, and in a conciliatory manner, lifts the telephone receiver. "Hold on a moment."

Teresa remains staring at her despondently. For a moment,

she had really believed that this was a set-up. Instead, she must surrender to the facts. A confirmation about the priest's existence is a tacit validation of his words.

"He'll be here in a few minutes. In the meantime, if you would like to take a seat." The woman points to a waiting room a few feet ahead.

"No, thank you. I'll wait here."

More people approach the counter to ask for information. A succession of people visiting friends or relatives. Relaxed faces, some duller or fatigued, but none ridged with grief or anguish. Teresa envies them. Evidently, the sick people they have come to visit will get out of those walls on their own two feet, sooner or later.

Caught up in that reflection, she does not notice the time passing. Finally, a voice calls her attention.

"Mrs. Graziani?" she hears behind her back.

When she turns around, she finds before her a portly fellow with a few extra pounds at belly level and under his chin. Over his clothes, he wears a white lab coat like the one used by doctors. However, a black suit, with the classic crew-neck cut and white clerical collar, is enough to distinguish his qualification.

"Father Giulio?"

"Yes, we spoke on the phone."

"And you said that my daughter was admitted here to the hospital. At the reception, however, her name does not appear."

"What do you mean? I don't understand."

"If you don't believe me, ask the lady." Teresa points to the woman behind the counter.

This one pulls the shoulders up and spreads her arms wide. And lifting her chin, she nods to the priest in further confirmation.

"No need," he downplays. "Maybe someone made a mistake in registration. But no problem, come with me. I'll take you."

"Are you sure that there is no mistake in person? How do you know it's my daughter?"

"She is the one who asked me to call you. She gave me your number," he replies, pulling out a note. "Here, see for yourself."

Seeing that on the piece of paper is her own call sign with the phone number, Teresa sighs and closes her eyes for a moment.

By now, there is no longer any doubt. Her daughter is there. And she is dying.

CHAPTER 5

Rejoiced by the closure of a case he had been working on for some time, Massimo Nardi has decided to make an exception to the rule by taking a slightly longer lunch break than he should. It is a beautiful day, sunny and not too muggy, and before returning to the police station, he wants to treat himself to a little extra to end the meal on a high note. So, having set foot outside the restaurant, he leaves his car parked alongside, walks up Province Avenue, and, at the height of Bologna Square, takes refuge in the best ice cream shop in the area, where he occupies a small table outside.

"Good morning. What can I get you?" a waiter greets him.

"A cream ice cream with strawberry syrup."

"Anything else?"

"Just that, thank you."

Good ice cream is all he wants, and they make really good ones there.

While waiting to be served, he enjoys the sense of contrast emanated by the environment. It seems to create both agreement and dissonance between old and new. Behind him, there is a focal point of university nightlife, a splash of freshness and modernity, while just ahead opens up XXI April Avenue, which with its Federici Palaces, reminds him of Ettore Scola's film, starring Sophia Loren and Marcello Mastroianni, and transports his memory back to the 1970s.

He loved the Rome of that period. Even though he was just a child then, he remembers it as if it were carved in his mind. There are images, smells, and tastes that time does not erase. After all, rooting deep within is the power of a city.

Unfortunately, today's Rome is a chaotic, messy Rome, amalgamated by social hardships, submerged realities, and ambiguous interests. Yet, in this matryoshka of jarring worlds, life goes on undisturbed. Nardi wonders whether it is the urban center that conforms to its inhabitants or, rather, the other way around, but he has no time to give himself an answer. The waiter reappears with a tray in his hands.

"Here you go." The man places a coaster on the coffee table, lays the bowl of ice cream, and withdraws.

The wet glass lets a few drops drip down. It already conveys a cool effect. Massimo grabs the teaspoon and begins to taste the dessert. The coolness and strawberry flavor flood his palate, and when a breath of wind joins that moment of pleasure, the sun seems to caress his skin. Nevertheless, he cannot let go. A nagging woodworm keeps buzzing around his head.

He then sinks a hand into his jacket pocket and drops an object on the table. It is a silver necklace with a small crucifix on it. Someone had delivered it to his office a couple of days earlier, and he cannot help wondering what significance it might have. The sender was anonymous; every attempt to trace it back to anyone was in vain.

This is not the first time he has received an anonymous missive. It had happened before on two or three occasions when he stuck his nose where others did not like it. Back then, however, these were threats, warnings whose purpose was obvious. That chain, on the other hand, means nothing. And this is why it seems to conceal a far darker insidiousness.

For the umpteenth time, he grabs it in his hands and turns it to one side and the other. He wants to force the mind to recall an image, a face, or an event of some kind, but there is nothing to be done. Probably, in his head, that memory does not exist and he is just wasting time.

Forced to remain in doubt, he stows the choker in his jacket pocket and goes back to enjoying the ice cream. The teaspoon sinks into the cream two or three times, then the sound of the cell phone adds to the surrounding buzz.

When he looks at the display, he sees the call from the police station. It is almost certainly the Deputy Cataldo.

"Hello?" he answers listlessly.

"Chief, Chief, this is Cataldo. Sorry to spoil your lunch, but we've had reports of a probable murder."

As he imagined. The deputy has the power to show up when he least expects it. Usually at the most inopportune times, but for once, perhaps, he got the right one right.

"Okay. Tell me everything," Nardi replies, getting up from the table.

As Cataldo brings him up to speed, he gets the bill and pays his due.

Seeing the waiter already intent on cleaning the tabletop, he waves to him to wait. Before saying goodbye, he goes back to grab one last spoonful from the bowl of ice cream. Then he crosses the square and heads in the direction of the car.

CHAPTER 6

"I don't know why she wanted to keep you in the dark. I'm sorry you found out about it this way. If I can do anything..."

"Sorry, Father Giulio, but I'm not in the mood to talk. I just want to see my daughter."

The priest seems used to dealing with such situations. He falls silent without flinching. He merely nods his hand and takes to lead the way.

Teresa lets herself be guided along the corridors. With each step she takes, she feels her heart lose a beat. She gasps for breath, swallows hard, and her mouth is kneaded. She is thirsty. What's more, she doesn't touch food since morning. But this has little or nothing to do with her contracting stomach or her legs that seem to want to give out at any moment. She would like to cry; however, she cannot. The thought of what awaits her inhibits muscles and nerves. Only the brain runs wild: sweeping away the succession of past images, it anticipates an imminent future scene.

Taking an elevator, they go up to the fourth floor. They turn down a couple of aisles until they reach the gastroenterology department.

It is visiting hours, and the doors are open. Among the coming and going of people, there are also those pausing in the hallway, perhaps eager to leave as soon as possible. About thirty feet ahead, a glass room separates the hospital staff from the rest of the ward. White or green uniforms move in and out; there is a glimpse of the excitement. Doctors and nurses, and auxiliaries talk agitatedly to each other. One sniffs a sense of uneasiness in the air.

Teresa casts a look that is not at all interested. She has much more on her mind.

Father Giulio must have noticed it, too. With a confused expression drawn on his face, he turns to peer back. "We have arrived," he says a moment later. "Your daughter's room is around the corner."

Teresa comes to a sudden halt. She feels her breath failing. Assailed by dizziness, she rests one hand on the wall to keep from falling to the floor.

The man hurries to support her. He places an arm around her waist and pulls her close to him. "Come on, ma'am! I know it's a difficult time, but be strong."

"Thank you, that's better now," she replies, drawing in a breath and returning to stand on her own legs.

"Would you like to sit down for a moment?"

"No, no, let's go. It's past."

The priest seems undecided about whether or not to leave her, but finally detaches himself from her and starts walking again.

Around the corner, men and women from the medical staff crowd in the hallway. They stand in front of the first room, where a uniformed officer is stationary in the doorway, motioning for them to keep their distance.

"What are you all doing here?" Father Giulio looks around confusedly.

"Is this her room?" Teresa asks.

"Yes, but I don't understand..."

Teresa does not listen to another word. She runs forward, makes her way through the crush, and rushes toward the door. When the officer stops her from going any further, she is now unable to contain her anxiety. "What happened?" she shouts. "What are the police doing here?"

"Please, ma'am, stand back. You can't go in."

"I want to see my daughter!"

"I'm sorry, but I can't let you pass. This is a crime scene."

"What are you talking about? Where is my daughter?"

The policeman does not respond.

Inside the room is another man in uniform. Standing with his back turned just over the threshold, he obstructs the view.

"Come on, what's going on?" asks Father Giulio, turning to the staff.

"Father, she is dead! Someone killed her."

"What?"

"It's true! A nurse came in and found her dead."

On hearing those words, Teresa feels herself missing for an instant. Next, a sudden rush of adrenaline sends her brain into a tailspin, inhibiting reason to make way for instinct. "Step aside; let me pass," she tells the officer. And seeing that this one doesn't obey the command, she pushes hard. "I'm the mother. Get out of the way!"

The man grabs her by the arms, forcibly restraining her. The colleague inside the room comes to his rescue and tries to reason with her, but when she hits him, the policeman pins her facing the wall.

"Ma'am, don't force me to arrest you," he says.

"Let go of me! You can't stop me from seeing her!" she cries hysterically.

"Please, please, officer, have some regard," Father Giulio interjects. "She has just lost her daughter. She's clearly upset."

"If I leave you, will you promise to calm down?"

Teresa seems to ignore the offer. Unwilling to listen to reason, she continues to fidget. "I don't want to calm down! I want to come in."

The man is at his wits' end. Determined to put an end to the situation, or perhaps with the intent to frighten her, he makes to pull out the handcuffs.

"What's going on? What is this commotion?" intrudes a voice at that instant.

"Nothing serious, Inspector," replied the officer. "The lady is the victim's mother. She's just a little shaken up."

"Come on, come on, let her go!"

Teresa recomposes herself, annoyed. When she turns around, ready to pick up where she left off, she notices something familiar in the newcomer's face. However, her eyes are watery with tears, and she struggles to focus on the man.

"Teresa Graziani?!" she hears him say, in the tone of someone who has just seen a ghost.

At the sound of his voice, she recognizes him.

"Oh, Massimo! Thank goodness!" she replies, relieved. "Let me in, please. I need to see her."

"Teresa?" repeats Nardi, still half in disbelief. "You're not going to tell me she's yours..."

"Please, let me pass," she interrupts him, with crying returning to disfigure her face.

"All right. Just don't touch anything. Not even the body."

Teresa rushes toward the room, but the man at the door insists on blocking her passage.

"Chief... Are you sure?"

"Don't worry! She is my former colleague. She knows the procedure."

The officer decides to step aside, and Teresa takes to advancing.

Now that access is cleared, fear returns to grip her.

She proceeds on tiptoe — small steps, pained and full of terror. Once inside, she sees what remains of her daughter — a skeletal body lying in that hospital bed. With her head resting on one shoulder, her face turned to the window, and her long hair falling over one cheek and chin, to look at her face Teresa is forced to go around. In the meantime, she cannot avoid the sight of the needle stuck in her arm, the small tube going back up to the IV at her side, a syringe, with the plunger depressed, hanging from the plastic bag like a guillotine blade. Someone has killed her, and it is already clear that that is the cause of death.

Teresa takes the last steps. When she is on the other side of the bed, her eyes suddenly open wide, and she brings a hand to her mouth. Nardi hurries to catch up with her. He raises an arm as if to bar her way. Perhaps he fears that, overwhelmed by pain, she might pounce on her body and try to hold her close.

Instead, she lets go in his arms, turns to him, and, in a small voice, says, "This is not Angela."

"I beg your pardon?"

"This is the first time I've seen this woman. I don't know who she is, but she's definitely not my daughter."

"What do you mean? Just a moment ago, you were sure it was her."

"So I was told."

"Were you told? Who are you talking about?"

Teresa turns her gaze to the hallway and lifts her finger to the door. "The priest. He was the one who called me. He said Angela was admitted here and was dying."

"Come, let's get out of here. You need to catch your breath, and I need to clear my head."

The two stop in the hallway, where Father Giulio watches the scene motionless.

Nardi wastes no time in asking for explanations.

"So, Father. Would you like to let me know how it went, too?"

"I merely made a phone call. I was just trying to make myself useful."

The priest begins to narrate in detail the unfolding of events. To safeguard his good name, he repeatedly emphasizes his own extraneousness regarding the incident. He informs how the woman explicitly asked for her mother. He goes to show the note with the phone number when he realizes that he handed it to Teresa upon her arrival.

"Oh, yes," she confirms. "Here it is."

Nardi frowns for a moment, reading quickly. "All right,

Father Giulio," he then concludes. "You go ahead. If I need clarification, I know where to find you."

The corridor has now been cleared. Additional police units have arrived on the scene, and routine checks are being made.

As hospital records give a name to the victim – Silvia Rigoni – a hypothesis takes hold.

Given the woman's critical condition and desire to end her life, the idea is that an Angel of Death may be behind the act, the typical killer who kills out of compassion.

At this point, everyone is presumed guilty.

Hospital staff are questioned with extreme care, starting with the nurse who found the woman dead.

Teresa continues to linger in the ward, both to provide answers and to receive them. There are still dark points to be clarified, but although the tension has not completely vanished, she is herself again. So she patiently awaits in silence, waiting for someone to give her an explanation.

After about ten minutes, Nardi reappears and advances in her direction. For the first time since his arrival, Teresa takes a good look at his face and realizes that time has not spared him either.

At their last meeting, he was a carefree person, while now, two deep wrinkles between his eyebrows give his face a severe air. They seem to say that life has held some surprises for him, too. Over his shirt, he wears a beige cotton jacket and a classy watch on his wrist; however, a slightly unkempt beard and a few misplaced hairs reveal a certain carelessness. In contrast, his eyes are as they used to be: curious and watchful, always on the lookout, with that touch of mischief and irritation.

In spite of the situation, Teresa is pleased to see him again. And from the look in his eyes, she gets the impression that he also feels some emotion.

When they exchange a smile of understanding, the old colleague makes to say something, but an officer's voice calls him back to duty: "Chief! Here is something you should see."

"Eh! Unfortunately, this is not a good time to talk," the

inspector apologizes.

"Go, don't worry." Teresa remains watching him as he turns and walks away to re-enter the room.

Convinced that the worst is over, she now considers herself a stranger to what is happening. Or at least partially. She continues to wonder why anyone would go to so much trouble to terrorize her to death.

Shortly after, she hears Nardi's voice saying, "Graziani! You should probably come and take a look."

"To what?" she asks, stepping forward.

"Does that ring a bell? It was in the nightstand drawer."

Noticing that Massimo is clutching a piece of paper between his fingers, she squints to sharpen her eyesight but has to move a few more steps closer before realizing it is an ID card.

The document is old and already expired several years ago. What matters, however, is the holder. On the space reserved for the call sign, "Angela Brunetti" is printed.

She goggles her eyes, brings a hand to her mouth, and stifles a startled cry.

"Do you understand what it means?" Nardi waves the document in the air. "There is no Angel of Death here, and nothing is due to chance. Someone wants to play with you. And if he set up this whole stage, there must be a reason. Do you have any idea who it might be?"

"I actually had one before. And I think it's more than just an idea."

"I mean, what kind of trouble are you in?"

"I don't know yet. But maybe it's better if we go to the police station to talk about it. I have to tell you everything from the beginning."

HELL – ACT II

The darkness thins out imperceptibly. Everything is shrouded in a sense of haze. Between indistinct flashes and fragmented memories, the mind is unable to channel information. Grasping a thought is complicated and exhausting.

The woman does not understand. And she doesn't have the strength to ask why. She can only feel her heart beating, her breathing steady, the annoying buzzing in her head, and her eyelids vibrating in an attempt to lift.

In a constant flicker, the eyelashes sway more and more. They let sudden flashes of light filter through. Finally, the eyes open fully, but the pupils rotate wildly and do not focus. The view is blurred. Everything appears hazy.

She tries to bring a hand to her face, but cannot move.

She continues not to understand.

She has the impression of awakening from a long hibernation.

What has happened? Where is she?

As she shakes her head in search of an explanation, she tries to regroup her ideas.

Ciphered answers come to the mind like the tiles of a mosaic – brief flashes of images that slowly seem to dispel the sense of torpor.

Eventually, a memory manages to take shape.

She was crossing Vittorio Emanuele II Square. And she was holding grocery bags.

Yes. Now she remembers. She was returning from the market.

"And after that?" she asks herself. "What happened next?"

Of the subsequent events, the woman remembers that the day was hot and she was sweating. She wanted to freshen up.

She recalls the sweet pleasure of freshness on her skin.

That's right. She was in the bathroom. She was rinsing herself. After that? What else did she do?

The memory keeps reeling. Then, unexpectedly, a jolt. Everything suddenly resurfaces.

"Oh my God!" she bursts into a mask of terror.

In her head, her own image materializes, facing the mirror, with the man's face behind hers. In a split second, she relives the scene. She sees herself with that bandage on her face obstructing her breath. She remembers the strange, sweet smell. She realizes she has been drugged.

"Oh, Jesus Christ! Help!" she begins to shout.

In the meantime, she tries to stand up, but cannot lift herself up. She thinks she is still numb from the anesthetic until she realizes she is bound.

She is sitting in a chair with armrests. Her wrists are secured to the supports with tape, as are her ankles, which are anchored to their respective front legs.

"Help!" she shouts again. And flailing madly, she screams out over and over.

Yet, no one responds or appears in sight.

Not even the man shows up.

She is alone.

Now that her mind has resumed functioning, she remembers having lived through that experience before. She has only a blurred image, but she is almost certain that the man has nurtured her in some way. On a couple of occasions, she must have regained consciousness, only to plunge back into darkness.

Now, however, she is awake; she is alone. She intuits that if she wants to escape from there, this is the right time. And she has to rely only on herself.

Trying to master the panic, she starts looking around.

There are no windows. The place is bathed in the half-light. A soft glow penetrates from the bottom, probably from some opening behind her.

She is in a passageway, a wide corridor. There are doors on both sides, all closed, and from their size, one would not guess that of a dwelling. Rustic walls, crudely painted, suggest some kind of shed.

Corroborating the hypothesis is the sour, pungent smell, mixed with the stench of cut grass, that fills the nostrils. The air is imbued with a mixture of strong and barn-like odors.

In any case, nothing about her surroundings can come in handy. The only solution is to manage to unbuckle the tape to disengage a hand.

With all her strength, she rotates her fist and wiggles her wrist, prying with her forearm. The tape, however, has been wound several times, and the grip is too firm. So, she bends as far as she can, intent on bringing her mouth just close enough to sink her teeth in.

The inability to rotate her arms makes the operation difficult. She is forced to flex her torso to the side. And she pushes with such vigor that she feels a stab in her hip while her ribs seem to crack. Assailed by a cramp, she would like to surrender to the pain. But resigning now would mean the end. She would not have the energy for a second attempt.

Therefore, with tears in her eyes, she makes one last effort. She pushes until her teeth run aground on the plastic bandage, and before the muscles give way completely, she manages to rip part of it away.

The split has lifted two small flaps into the air, but when she tries to bite into them, her torso makes a sudden jerk and violently returns to an upright position. A whiplash to the back sends the body boiling.

Despite this, the pain is overwhelmed by the eagerness to break free. She shakes her hand like a crazed beast. In the frantic pushing and pulling, the rubbing wears down its skin and makes the back of her hand bleed; the fingers tangle with each other; a sprain in the wrist gives the impression that the bones are on the verge of crumbling. Eventually, however, the arm lifts, and she is free.

With labored breathing and a pounding heart, her forehead is beaded with sweat. She would like to give herself a moment to catch her breath, but she cannot afford to waste time. She hurries to untangle her other hand.

She is on the verge of unraveling the binding when she senses in the distance an oncoming of footsteps.

The man is back. And he is getting closer and closer.

The sound becomes more distinct one moment after another.

She speeds up. In her haste, her nails sink into her flesh. By now, it is just a mad flailing. She realizes it is all in vain. Her legs are still bound to the chair, and time is up: the man is behind her. Although he does not speak, she senses his presence and hears him fumbling with something.

She starts screaming and continues until a hand appears before her eyes.

Again some gauze lays on her face to cover the nose and mouth. Again that smell. Again the darkness comes back to swallow everything.

CHAPTER 7

July 4, afternoon, 3:00 p.m.

Massimo and Teresa have remained silent most of the way. Won over by curiosity, he has tried to ask her a few questions, but a succession of monosyllabic answers convinced him on putting it off. A sudden frost has fallen between them, with wary glances that seem to search the other's eyes for something elusive.

The vehicle has already traveled down Liegi Avenue. At the height of Ungheria Square it turns onto Gioacchino Rossini Avenue, turns onto Guido d'Arezzo Street, and stops in the internal parking lot of the Salario-Parioli police station.

"So?" he asks, just to break the silence. "Is it as you remember it?"

"I mean, a lot of things have changed."

"Well, it's also been quite a while."

Having walked through the main hallway, they ascend to the upper floor.

Massimo, however, has smelled Teresa's discomfort and does not want to rush her. Instead of going straight to his office, he stops in the corridor and casually offers, "I feel like a coffee. What do you say? For old times' sake."

"Maybe a chamomile tea would be better, though... that's fine."

As he turns his back to her, intent on tinkering with the vending machine, Nardi wonders if the embarrassment he tries to avoid is not his own. The former colleague's presence reminds him of a distant past he does not like to recall.

At that time, he was still happily married, while today, he is a lonely man living with regret. In addition, an inconvenient truth has suddenly resurfaced. A secret, jealously guarded for years, that inextricably binds one to the other.

A steaming glass passes from his hand to hers. Teresa is about to take a sip when Massimo winks and hints at a funny grimace. He used to make that gesture to her whenever they were in the mood to confide in each other, and now, who knows why, it came to him naturally. She responds with a tired smile, drinks her coffee, and finally nods her head as if to say she is ready to talk.

"Come, let's go to my office." Laying a hand on her back, he points to the room at the back.

Once inside, he closes the door, walks around the desk, and drops into the chair. "So, sit down and tell me all about it."

"I don't know where to start."

"First of all, explain to me what your daughter has to do with this."

"Yeah, well, that's…" she hesitates. "I'm embarrassed to talk about it with you."

"Come on! It's not like I'm a stranger."

"Maybe it would have been better. Talking to strangers is easier, at least when you have to admit your mistakes. I've made too many, and, alas, you can silence your conscience only up to a certain point. Sooner or later, it makes you pay the bill."

"Oh! I can understand you; rest assured. I have my sins to pay for, too."

"Like everyone. Talking about it, though, is always difficult. Especially for a mother who has to acknowledge that she has failed."

Toward Teresa, life has been anything but tender. Massimo is aware of what happened a decade earlier. Although by that time she had already left the service, the story of Piero – the youngest son who died in an accident – was known to everyone at the police station. He can well understand her continuing to lay all the guilt on herself; however, he wonders why on earth she goes back to dredge up the past and what it has to do with what happened at the hospital.

"However, I don't have much choice," she continues. "The truth is that I'm scared, and I need help."

"That's what we're here for, right? Tell me all about it. But first, speaking of which, have you called your daughter yet, to see if everything is okay? Do you want to give her a ring?"

"She is the real problem," Teresa replied, bursting into tears. "I don't know anything about her now. I haven't heard from her in 12 years. You have to help me find out what happened to her."

Massimo does not know how to act. Convinced of knowing his former colleague like few others, he had attributed that guilt to Piero's death, but suddenly he realizes there is a black hole dividing them: years and years of which he knows nothing about.

In an attempt to console her, he gets up, walks around the desk, encircles one of her shoulders, and hands her a paper handkerchief.

"What happened?" he asks.

Teresa wipes her face one last time, after which she starts explaining the events since it all began. She talks about Angela's escape, about the photographs she sent to her every year, and about that one photo that she waited for and never arrived. She talks about the mystery man, his appearance and the phone call she received. She talks like a runaway train. She pauses for a few moments only when her face turns purple and she is forced to catch her breath.

Nardi, meanwhile, has returned to his seat. He listens in silence to every word until Teresa's voice, reduced to a series of sobs, disappears altogether.

"And about that guy?" he then asks. "Would you be able to

describe him?"

"Unfortunately, no. I told you, he was in the car, wearing sunglasses, and a hood was covering his head. And I barely saw him for a moment."

"You saw him for an instant; you don't know what he looked like, but you are still convinced that what happened was his doing."

"By all the saints! I certainly didn't imagine the phone call. And it all started from there. First, the picture doesn't arrive, and then the priest calls to tell me my daughter is dying, and Angela's ID comes out of nowhere... Doesn't that seem strange to you?"

"As a matter of fact, yes. I'll request a check of the phone records. Maybe something will turn up. In the meantime, I'll have some research done."

"You will keep me in the loop, won't you? Any news, no matter how bad, I want to know. I can't live in doubt anymore."

"Okay. But before I let you go, I need to know something."

"Tell me."

Nardi hesitates, tapping a pen on the table. He feels some discomfort asking her that question and would like to avoid it, but he cannot. "Have you managed to put stop gambling?" he asks. "Or do you continue with the usual life?"

"What does that have to do with anything?"

"Well, I don't think I have to explain it to you. If not for that, you would still be a police officer today."

Teresa lowers her gaze. "I never stopped," she babbles. "Anyway, I have no debt. That's what you want to know, right?"

"Good; I wanted to hear you say that. You know, every lead has to be considered. Anyone with a reason to be mad at you is a potential suspect and..."

"Come on, Massimo! I know this job. I don't need lessons on how it works. I assure you I've thought and rethought about it, but no one came to mind. The only person I can imagine is the guy on the phone call."

"Um... All right. Then I'll call someone to drive you home."

"No thanks, it's not necessary. I'll take the bus."

Teresa gets up and walks to the door.

"Be careful!" he resumes. "Whoever is behind this will show up again. You don't kill a person for nothing."

Without replying, she waves a hand to give a final goodbye and closes the door behind her.

Leaning back in his chair, Nardi crosses his legs, joins his hands behind his neck, and lifts his eyes into the air. He tries to think about what to do.

Soon, however, he hears a knock.

The door swings back open, and the deputy's little head appears in the room. "May I, Chief?"

"Come on in."

"Here is the first information about the victim."

"I thank you," Nardi says, grabbing the file. He has always appreciated Cataldo's efficiency. One phone call from the hospital, and he wasted no time. "I also need you to research Angela Brunetti, the woman whose ID we found."

"Do you need anything in particular?"

"No, bring me what you find. If I need something else later, I'll let you know."

As soon as Cataldo retreats, Massimo gets up, reaches the window, and glances at the street.

Teresa is leaving the police station. He watches her as she walks away, and as her image shrinks, the memory plunges into the past.

She had always had a cursed gambling habit, but for her husband, Sergio Brunetti, money had never been an issue. As long as he had been willing to pay for her weaknesses, everything had gone smoothly. The complications had begun with the divorce. When he had turned off the spigot, she had taken on debt in a big way. And unfortunately, she had done it with the wrong person.

The Pariolino, as he was called, was a man who, from the neighborhoods of upscale Rome, under a facade of legality, ran his criminal activities. The authorities had only ever stopped him for petty crimes, although who he was and what he did was no secret to anyone. Money laundering, drugs, prostitution… he had his hands mixed all over the place. He was even rumored to have contacts with the local mafia, which was probably why he kept getting away with it.

Not that Teresa had gone knocking on his door, but the person she had turned to was connected to him.

She discovered it later when *The Pariolino* had tried to leverage her business sense with a simple proposal: wipe out her debt in exchange for information.

As far as Massimo knew, Teresa had refused.

At that time, he idolized his colleague. He had learned the tricks of the trade from her. Yet, on that occasion, the trust had wavered. He had wondered if that refusal had really happened. Because despite the large sum of money she owed, there had been no specific retaliations for her defaulting.

He had struggled to find various justifications for that preferential treatment. Perhaps the man had other plans for her, maybe thinking she could be useful in the future. Perhaps, the fact that Teresa wore a uniform had been enough of a deterrent. Or perhaps, that "no" to the exchange of information had never happened. How things had really turned out, Nardi could not know.

At any rate, that apparent truce had ended several months later when a police raid had sent five *Pariolino's* men to jail, blowing up a huge deal. The operation had grown out of an already ongoing investigation, of which Teresa herself was in charge. Thus, a week later, the showdown had come. The man had decided to make her pay with due interest.

On an ordinary evening, she was returning home when a guy attacked her from behind. Nothing seemed to tie him to *The Pariolino,* but that he had sent him was obvious.

The stranger had lunged at Teresa with a bat. He had beaten her to the point of shattering some of her bones, while a blow to the face had caused the loss of her eye. Had it not been for Massimo, who happened to be passing by, she probably would have left her skin behind.

Years have passed now, and yet, Nardi remembers as if it were yesterday. As he looks beyond the glass, he has the impression that he is watching the images of that evening flow by.

He remembers that Graziani, his superior officer, has already left the office. When he, too, is about to set out, updates arrive on the case they are working on, so he decides to drop by her place. They are on friendly terms. The house is on the way, and it is not the first time he shows up uninvited.

It takes him a short time to reach the area, but a few blocks from the building, a fight at a corner forces him to stop the car. Someone lying on the ground is subdued by an attacker's blind fury.

"Hey, stop it! Stop it!" Massimo gets out of the car to rescue the unfortunate. He advances until he realizes that the one curled up on the asphalt is Teresa.

"Stop! Police!" he then intimates.

The other ignores the call. He continues to sink blows without heeding Nardi's presence.

Massimo would like to intervene but is unable to come forward. He is petrified.

All he can do is bring his hand to the butt of the gun, draw the weapon from the holster, and point it forward. "I said stop! Don't make me shoot."

At that point, the man stops, drops the bat, and finally gives the impression of surrendering.

Then, it is time for a moment.

The stranger abruptly turns around, shouts something, and raises an arm toward Massimo, who, panicked, lets off a shot.

A bullet in the chest sends the guy to the ground. And Massimo watches the scene in astonishment. When he finally decides to advance, he looks around and brings his hands to his head.

That memory is interrupted by the image of himself crouching over Teresa; and of her, who, almost unable to open her mouth, finds the strength to say, "Do as I said."

The mind returns to the present; the street below reappears in view. Teresa has now disappeared, and Massimo moves away from the window.

Behind him, Cataldo's voice asks for permission to enter. The deputy advances into the office, hands over the requested information, and leaves soon after.

Nardi then reaches the desk. Leaning back in his chair, he grabs the first file, the one on Silvia Rigoni, and for a moment, thinks back to *The Pariolino*. If he had not died several years earlier, he would now be the main suspect in the case. A disappointed smile accompanies the gaze as it settles on the papers.

The file gives the particulars of the woman, a social worker assigned to the Juvenile Court. By then, she had not practiced for several years, probably since her illness had taken hold. A report lists the cases followed up to that time; however, since these are juvenile practices, much of the information is cloaked by official secrecy. Nardi's eyes hop listlessly here and there between useless details and a string of unknown names. About ten minutes pass. A yawn and then another seems to announce an imminent surrender. Instead, shortly after that, interest returns.

Angela Brunetti's name is mentioned among the foster care cases.

Unfortunately, everything stops there. A first and last name is all there is. In any case, it is enough to understand that the choice of the victim was anything but random. There is an unknown connection between the two women. And if it does not encapsulate the solution to the case, it must certainly represent an essential piece.

Massimo wonders what this might be about. Anxious to satisfy his curiosity, he closes the folder, grabs the one concerning Teresa's daughter, and begins to read.

The first thing that jumps out at him is a complaint report. A case of rape dating back twelve years seems to suggest a hypothetical answer. Perhaps, on that occasion, Angela had become pregnant. Who knows? Maybe she had given the child up for adoption, and Rigoni had followed the practice.

Otherwise, the document does not say much – a chronology of events accompanied by a rough description of the attacker. The only distinguishing feature is a tattoo on his arm: some kind of spider.

In her narrative, Teresa did not mention the affair. Massimo wonders if she has just overlooked it or is unaware of it.

The following pages contain information of little interest, nothing that appears of any use. Eyes scroll quickly between the lines. They pause from time to time to rise thoughtfully into the air. Finally, they widen, as if to catch the last part of the text in a single glance.

Angela Brunetti is reported to be deceased. And the demise dates back to the previous year.

According to the papers, following an attempted suicide – a jump from the third floor of a building – she had been in a coma for five years. Her body had continued to struggle. But in the end, there was nothing they could do. The doctors had declared her brain dead.

CHAPTER 8

July 4, afternoon, 6 p.m.

Teresa Graziani lives in the Trieste neighborhood. The building is located behind Villa Chigi, enjoys a pleasant greenery view, and stands in a quiet spot, secluded from the more commercial area.

Nardi often passes nearby, but that street he has continued to avoid for years. Now that it is under her house, he has the impression that time has rewound like a film.

Stopping in front of the doorway, he hesitates to push the intercom button. He looks around him, continuing to stall, and wonders if there are words that can lighten the weight of a shocking truth. What he has to say to her, he certainly could not say over the phone. Yet at the thought of having to look her in the eye and make her aware of the bitter discovery, he feels a sense of helplessness.

However, there is no point in putting it off any longer. Sooner or later, he will have to report to her what he discovered.

Eager to shake off the burden, he decides to ring.

The intercom begins to croak shortly afterward.

"Who is this?"

"It's me, Massimo."

"Do you have any news?"

61

"Can I come up?"

"Oh, sure! Sorry. Come on up."

The click of the lock echoes through the air for a moment. He takes a deep breath for courage, pushes forward the door and takes the elevator up to the third floor.

When the doors open, Teresa's eyes are there staring at him. Standing still in the doorway, she looks at him with a frightened look. She has already realized that something is wrong.

Caught off guard, Nardi remains motionless inside the cabin. And feeling caged, he seeks the strength to speak.

However, he does not have time to open his mouth. Teresa turns without a word and goes back into the house.

He frowns, moves forward, and closes the door behind him. Following Graziani into the living room, he wonders if her strange behavior is due to fear of receiving bad news or the dread of getting confirmation of what she has suspected for some time.

"At last it came," Teresa whispers as she turns around.

"What?"

"The photograph. The one I've been waiting for. It has arrived."

Massimo is displaced for the second time.

"There was a delay in the correspondence," she continues. "Back home, I found a package. The letter was inside, complete with an apology from the postal service. It was damaged and they had sent it back to the Central Post Office."

"And inside was the photograph?"

"Yes, I told you."

Nardi doesn't understand. Who could have sent it?

"I couldn't get it out, though," Teresa resumes. "I was about to do it when I saw a bloodstain and lacked courage."

"Blood? Are you sure?"

"Well, I certainly didn't analyze it, but I would say yes."

"Okay, give it to me. I'll take care of it."

On one side of the room, placed in front of the sofa, is a small living room table. It houses a letter wrapper, the commercial kind with a brownish color, a letter opener, a light blue ribbon, and a half-closed cardboard box.

Teresa grabs the package and hands it to Massimo.

The opening at the top end immediately shows the envelope inside. It is split in two.

The paper is torn, but it is not a clean cut. Rather, it looks more like an accidental tear. A piece of the photograph emerges from the split, damaged in turn. Settling himself on top of the small table, Nardi removes the right side of the envelope, tilts the other side, and shakes it until the two halves of the picture slide out.

Teresa is right. What conceals a part of the image is indeed a bloodstain. However, he is well aware that it cannot be Angela's.

"Well, it does really look like blood," he says then. "But, who knows, maybe the postal employee got hurt while bagging it. That can happen."

"Of course! It can also happen to win in the Super-Enalotto. I'm still waiting for my numbers to come up, though." Clearly, Teresa discerns in the event an aura of mystery and bad omens. With a pained look, she puts the two sides of the photograph together and stands staring at it as her eyes glaze over. "Strange, it's an old photograph," she then whispers. "And in the frame is Angela."

"Why, who should be there?"

"Oh, right! I forgot to tell you," she replies. Leaning forward, she opens the box on the small table and hands Massimo the ten photographs. "Here, look for yourself."

He flips through them carefully. He struggles to notice any detail that distinguishes them from each other. "Five and five," he finally says.

"That's right. In the early years, there was both Angela and her son. Then she disappeared. In the other shots, the little one always appears alone. Now, however, there is Angela again, or rather, only her. The child is not there. That's why it seems strange to me. And also because, as I said, that picture is old."

Looking inside the box, Massimo notices the envelopes with

which the photographs were sent. "I see you've kept just about everything."

"Yes. They mean a lot to me."

"May I take a look?"

"Go ahead."

Even the old papers highlight the strange detail. Although the sender is never listed, two types of handwriting stand out among the addressee headers. Whoever sent the last five letters is certainly not the same person who sent the first.

In any case, that dilemma is of very little importance compared to what he came for. And by continuing to remain silent, he is not only postponing the inevitable but also raising false hopes.

"The handwritings are different," he then points out. "Did you notice that?"

"Yes, I noticed."

"And you never wondered why?"

"Of course! But it's useless. There is no answer."

"Or maybe, you refuse to see it."

"What do you mean?"

"Teresa, I don't know how to tell you. Unfortunately..." Massimo cannot find the words. "Come, we'd better sit down."

"No. Speak up! What do you have to tell me? That's why you're here, right? What did you find out?"

"Well, here's... you don't know how sorry I am, but as it turns out, Angela is dead."

"Uh? What are you talking about? There must be a mistake."

"She has spent the last five years in a coma."

"That's not possible. I would have heard about that."

"I know it's hard to accept, however..."

"It can't be," she interrupts. "Otherwise, who would have sent the photographs?"

"Exactly! Think about it. Why is she not in the more recent ones? And how come the handwriting is someone else's? It was not your daughter who sent the last five."

"This doesn't make sense. Who would have done such a

64

thing? And more importantly, for what reason?"

"There! That's the right question. That's what we'll have to find out."

Nardi's words begin to make their way into Teresa's head. Sitting on the sofa, she rests an elbow on the armrest and lets her forehead sink into the palm of her hand.

Massimo dares not speak. Motionless before her, he observes her bitterly. He has said as much as he had to say, and any other words would be useless.

Silence falls in the room. A couple of minutes pass before she returns to lift her face in tears. "But then… where is Pier Giorgio?" she asks, sobbing. "What happened to my grandson?"

"Unfortunately, I don't really know, but I will do my best to find out. I promise you. By the way, I already have a lead to follow up."

"Huh? What lead?" Teresa passes a hand to dry her eyes and changes her expression.

"Out of curiosity, was Angela already pregnant when she left home?"

"No. Why?"

"So, you don't know who the father of the child is."

"Of course not!" she replies impatiently. "I don't understand what you're getting at. What else is there that you haven't told me?"

The annoyed tone of the reply chases away all doubt.

Of what happened to her daughter, she is totally unaware.

"Well… Here…" Massimo stalls. He has already inflicted a severe blow, and now the courage to go on fails. He would like to keep the rest of the story to himself, but he cannot refrain from revealing the whole truth. Therefore, in no uncertain terms, he makes up his mind to say, "There is a report of rape dating back to that time. Someone abused Angela."

"What?!"

"You know the woman killed in the hospital?" he continues. "She turned out to be a social worker. She used to follow juvenile cases, and it seems she also handled your daughter's

65

case. Given the timing, it's logical to think that the child was conceived as a result of that event."

"Oh, dear God!" Teresa widens her eyes and brings her hands to her mouth.

"I know it's a bitter pill to swallow. But now…"

Massimo interrupts himself, realizing that she has stopped listening. Dumbfounded, she stares blankly and falls silent while flickering eyelids seem to hold back crying with difficulty.

He waits patiently for a few minutes. "Do you want me to leave you alone?" he asks. "If you don't feel up to answering more questions now, I can come back another time."

"What do you want to know?" she whispers.

"Has Angela ever confided about it? Do you know if someone was harassing her?"

"She never told me anything. Besides, I think I would have been the last person she would have talked to about it."

"About her friends, though? Do you happen to remember anyone with a tattooed arm?"

"I never met one. She didn't bring anyone home."

"And what about your husband?"

"My ex-husband."

"Yes, we understand each other. Sergio."

"What's he got to do with this?"

"Well, you must have talked about Angela's disappearance."

"Only in the beginning. I called him to inform him. By now, our relationship is limited to the divorce check."

"Do you think he might know something about it?"

"Um… no, I don't think so."

"Anyway, I'll have to talk to him. Maybe he knows details that you're unaware of."

"I doubt it," she replies in a choked voice. "But you're right. Better not to leave anything out."

Teresa goes to the window. Lifting her hands, she plunges her nose and mouth between her joined palms, sighs, and, shedding tears intermittently, looks out.

Nardi keeps himself on the sidelines. He resumes examining

the envelopes and compares the handwriting for clues.

After flipping through them to no avail, he arranges them on the small table next to each other. He notices a single element that unites those ten pieces of paper: the postmarks. They are all different, each belonging to a neighborhood in Rome, but never the same. He wonders if the sender tried to cover his tracks. He ponders over it. However, the hypothesis hardly convinces him. It would have made sense if a single person had sent them, but, in this case, it is more likely to be a coincidence.

As he sets aside that doubt, his gaze falls on the image of Angela lying there beside him – a snapshot capturing a moment in her life and a rip that seems to mark its end.

Massimo turns away for a moment. He looks displeased at his friend. He cannot imagine what she is feeling. And the inability to give an explanation for what is happening makes him feel useless. So he turns around again and casts another glance at the photograph.

That framing holds something familiar.

Convinced that some detail has captured his interest, he tries to figure out what it might be. Unable to bring it into focus, he is almost on the verge of giving up when his pupils come to a sudden halt. He arches his eyebrows and wrinkles his forehead, and rolls his eyes. "I knew I had seen it before!" he exclaims. "Now, at least one thing is clear."

"Excuse me?"

"I don't know how or why, but one thing is certain. I'm mixed up in this matter, too."

"What are you talking about?"

"Whoever killed the woman in the hospital planned every detail. He wanted me, one way or another, to have the case in my hands."

"What are you ranting about? Why should you get into it?"

"Do you recognize this one?" Nardi pulls the silver chain he received a few days earlier from his pocket.

Lifting his arm, he lets it dangle before Teresa's eyes.

She stares at it in disbelief and reaches as if to touch it, but hesitant fingers caress the surrounding air until the crucifix settles in her palm, and Massimo relinquishes his grip.

"As you see, I don't rant. I merely infer."

The necklace is the same one that contours Angela's neck in the last photograph. He did not notice it right away because the rip had removed part of the pendant from the image.

"Where did you get it?"

"I received it a couple of days ago, anonymously. I couldn't understand its meaning, but now it's all too clear."

"I, on the other hand, do not understand. What connection should there be between you and my daughter? This doesn't make sense."

"I think we will soon find out. If someone has gone to so much trouble, there must be a reason. And I doubt the sender wants to keep it to himself."

"You're convinced he'll return to show up, huh?"

Nardi swings his head in confirmation. "Anyway, I'm certainly not going to sit still and wait," he says. "I have to ask you to hand over the photographs, the letter envelopes, and the necklace. As you know, these are all investigative items."

Teresa does not object. She merely clutches the chain to her chest for a few moments. Then, turning her gaze away, she stretches her arm toward him and goes back to crying for the umpteenth time.

CHAPTER 9

July 5, morning

Nardi has spent a virtually sleepless night. Every time he was on the verge of falling asleep, a question came back to his mind.

At the wheel of his car, still half asleep, he feels assaulted by a tremendous migraine. He would like to ignore it, but the discomfort becomes more and more insistent. He rolls down the windows, hoping fresh air will wake him up just enough.

To avoid the chaotic traffic on Tuscolana Street, he has traveled through all the adjacent streets running alongside it, turning left and right when forced by the traffic directions. At the height of the Felice aqueduct, however, he is forced to re-enter that artery congested by the swirling flow of cars. He passes under the Sisto V arch of Porta Furba and travels another half mile, after which, turning back onto a parallel road, he continues straight for the rest of the way until descending back onto the main road.

A hundred feet ahead stands the Cinecittà Studios – *the Hollywood on the Tiber* – and directly opposite, in over five cubic miles of glass and concrete, stands the complex of buildings of the Polo Tuscolano, headquarters of the DAC, the Central Anticrime Directorate of the State Police.

It is from there that all operations on the national territory are coordinated, including those related to the Forensic Police.

The facility houses as many as forty-two laboratories, and Nardi has thought of visiting his old friend Marcello Stefanini.

As a rule, the services of the DAC are requested for heinous crimes or in cases of high dangerousness. Or, at any rate, for investigations whose complexity makes ordinary means inefficient.

Under different circumstances, Massimo would follow standard procedures. This case, however, involves him too closely. He is eager to find answers as soon as possible. Going through official channels would take time.

Parking his car in the clearing outside, he heads toward the pavilion that gives access to the facility. Beyond an armored glass window, a couple of officers conduct entry control checks. Nardi provides his ID, waits to be issued an ID badge, and walks toward the entrance turnstiles.

At the thought that more than 1,500 people work there, he lifts his gaze and rolls his eyes. Used to his small police station, he feels like a fish out of water every time.

Upon reaching the building that houses Stefanini's office, an outside staircase ushers him into the main lobby. He passes through an open space crowded with a large number of agents, each bustling in front of their monitors, and soon after is in front of the elevators.

As a faint sound announces the doors opening, he holds back a yawn, shakes his head, and rubs his eyelids. Now he could use a nice cup of coffee.

The colleague's office is on the fourth floor. From the hallway, he notices the open door and spots his friend inside with his back turned. He seems absorbed in reading something. Around him, four gray walls, a couple of archives, a computer, and dossiers on the desk show an environment devoid of any personal touch.

Massimo taps his knuckles on the door and says, "What's the mood around here? Busy as ever?"

Taken aback, the other gasps and turns his head sharply. As some papers fly from his hands, he says, surprised, "Hey,

Nardi!" Bending down to pick up the papers, he asks, "How are you doing?"

"Not very well today. My head is bursting."

"You work too much; I've always told you. Every once in a while, you should take a vacation like everyone else."

With a mutual smile, they exchange a handshake.

They have known each other for years. And ironically, it was Teresa who introduced them.

Since their last meeting, Stefanini has put on a few extra pounds. The lab coat he wears is not enough to hide them from view. Curly hair overhangs two round, bulging eyes, set off by the glasses he keeps resting on the tip of his nose. He has his usual funny face, capable of misleading. A good-natured air behind which lies a quick-witted mind.

"So, what brings you to these parts?" he asks. "I guess it's not a social visit."

"You're right. I could use a favor."

Stefanini hints at a mischievous expression and places the papers back on the table. "Go ahead."

"I know you already have so much to do, but..."

"Don't worry. That's what friends are for, right? Besides, you know me. I'm a curious guy."

"Do you remember Teresa Graziani?"

"Of course! Although it's been ages since I've seen her. How is she?"

"I would say worse than usual. I, too, had lost contact for years. Today, however, I find myself working on a case involving her. That's why I'm here."

"Why, what happened to her?"

"Nothing to her. It's about her daughter."

Avoiding going into too much detail, Nardi updates his colleague on the situation. He has brought the findings taken from Teresa's house and, as he finishes laying out the facts, lays them on the desk.

"Gee, that's bad."

"I am well aware that the case is not within the jurisdiction of

DAC, but I need answers as soon as possible. I was hoping you could help me out by having everything analyzed: blood, fingerprints, and biological traces in general. Anything that might provide a clue."

"Count on it!" Stefanini glances at the silver necklace and peeks through the letter envelopes and photographs. "Of course, it's a shame, though. In case of positive findings, contaminated exhibits will be of little use to you, at least as evidentiary value."

"Yes, I know, but it doesn't matter. Right now, I'm just interested in finding a lead to follow."

"I'll see what I can find out."

"Perfect! Then I won't take up any more of your time," Nardi concludes. "I owe you a favor."

"Oh, for that matter, you owe me more than one. But since it's about Graziani, I'll put it down for you this time. Be sure to say hello to her for me."

"I will. See you soon!"

As he walks back through the halls, Massimo thinks about what the next steps will be once he is out of there. He has been dreaming about a nice espresso all morning, the strong kind, so his first stop will be at the coffee shop. Then he will pop into the pharmacy to buy a painkiller. He can't do without that anymore, either.

***

Having passed through the turnstiles and reached the outer perimeter, Nardi walks past the parking area, leaving his car behind. He proceeds toward a nearby bar glimpsed on arrival. In his desire to give himself a break, he advances briskly, at least until his cell phone begins to ring. When he answers, his gait slows one step after another, and soon his feet come to a complete halt. Cataldo's timing strikes again.

Apparently, a more thorough search confirmed the initial hypothesis: Angela Brunetti's child turns out to be the result of the violence she suffered. According to the deputy's account, on that occasion, the woman had refused to have an abortion. Opting to give birth anonymously, she had disowned the creature at birth. She had spent the gestation period at a pregnant women's shelter community, whose former owner, Cataldo, was able to track down: one Antonio De Marchi.

Nardi wastes no time. Anxious to get results, he says goodbye to the coffee he was already anticipating, returns to his car, and an instant later is back on the road.

It takes him about twenty minutes to reach the place: a parallel to Prenestina Street at the height of Pigneto.

The man lives in a 1960s apartment building. The facade, adorned with plaster bas-reliefs, hints at a sophistication worn away by time and decay. Between scattered cracks and peeling paint, and falling pieces of plaster, everything is left to total neglect. Even the lock on the front door is out of order, and Nardi, after peeking at the names on the intercom, enters unceremoniously. After all, the flat number indicates the apartment on the ground floor, and separating him from the door is not even a flight of stairs.

After two rings on the doorbell, he waits several moments. He has to ring a third time before he hears the sound of footsteps on the other side.

When the door opens, an elderly man appears – wrinkles and a melancholy look mark his face.

"Antonio De Marchi?" asks Nardi.

"Yes. And who are you?"

"Inspector Nardi," he replied, flashing his badge. "Can you give me a minute? I need to ask you a few questions."

The man watches him for a moment, then sketches a weary smile and waves to come in.

Crossing the threshold, Massimo is hit by a stale smell. There is a stench of closed, old. In the living room, well-lit by the sun, he notices how a blanket of dust stands out on the furniture and convinces himself that a woman has not set foot in that house for a long time.

"Do you live alone?" he asks.

"Unfortunately! My wife, rest her soul, left a long time ago."

"I'm sorry. And you have no children?"

"It shows, huh?"

"Oh… Excuse me if…" Massimo stutters, thinking he had better keep quiet. "I didn't mean to be intrusive."

"Don't worry. What did you want to know, rather?" With effort, De Marchi settles into a chair, points to the sofa, and waves for a seat.

Looking at the furniture and the layer of dust, Nardi hesitates but then chases away the thought and sits down in turn.

"This is a matter concerning the maternity shelter you owned."

The man, while remaining silent, frowns.

"I am investigating a woman you hosted years ago," Nardi explains.

"Oh, I understand! I don't know if I can help you, though. My wife was in charge of everything in there. I did little or nothing."

"Well, in the meantime, take a look at this," he replies, showing Angela's photo, copies of which he made before handing it to Stefanini. "Do you recognize her?"

De Marchi sharpens his eyesight and runs his fingertips over one temple. He seems to want to ward off an itch but instead realizes he is not wearing glasses. He turns to look around.

"Looking for those?" interjects Nardi, pointing to the table.

The other lifts his gaze into the air and snorts. "Ah, old age! What an ugly beast," he complains. "I have no head on my shoulders now."

Slipping on his glasses, he then resumes gazing at the picture. As he remains staring at it, he tilts his head slightly and stretches his neck, and brings a hand to cover his mouth. He seems to want to dredge up a remembrance that escapes memory. Eventually, however, he gives up. "I'm sorry," he says regretfully. "I don't recall ever seeing her."

"Um! All right. What about this other one? Does it ring a

74

bell?"

Silvia Rigoni's image immediately catches the man's attention.

"Yes, yes! If I'm not mistaken, she is a social worker. She used to come often to settle some girls there with us."

"Exactly. And the one I showed you was indeed one of them. But if you don't remember her, there is nothing to do. I doubt you can help me out."

Convinced that he has wasted a trip, Nardi begins to get up. De Marchi, however, extends a hand. "Wait!" he says. Turning his palm up, he wiggles his fingers back and forth. "Let me see it again for a moment."

Although he ignores the reason for the request, Massimo hands over Rigoni's photograph without question.

"No, no!" protests the other. "The one from before."

The man returns to rest his eyes on the image already squared off for a long time. On his face reappears the strange expression manifested earlier. He seems to be searching for something. And finally, after a few moments, he finds it. "There!" he exclaims. "I said so."

"What?" hastens to ask Nardi.

"Now I remember. I realized who you are talking about. From the face, I didn't recognize her; however, this necklace brought her back to my mind. I'm sure it's her."

"Was her name Angela Brunetti?"

"Oh my God, Inspector, you're asking a little too much of me. It's been years. It's already a miracle that she came back to my mind." The man smiles, amused. "You have no idea how many single mothers I've seen come and go. Imagine if, at my age, I can remember their names."

"Well, you recognized the necklace. Maybe, with an effort…"

"Yes, but it's different," interrupts De Marchi. "If what happened hadn't happened, I would have forgotten it like the rest."

"What do you mean?"

"I'm referring to the kidnapping of the child."

Nardi suddenly changes expression. Bewildered, he wrinkles

his forehead and arches his mouth.

The other is not slow to catch the astonishment on his face. "But why, don't you know?" he hastens to ask.

"I have no idea what you are talking about."

"I thought you already knew the whole story."

"Apparently not. You tell it to me."

"You know, to me, that was just another expectant mother. And honesty, if that incident had not occurred, she would have remained that way. When she came to us, she was still undecided about whether or not to recognize the child, so the social worker, as required by law, applied to the court to suspend the adoption proceedings. I think a couple of weeks passed before she decided once and for all to give him away. To everyone's surprise, however, that very night, the deed occurred."

"Meaning?" Nardi understood all too well. Nonetheless, what he thinks, he wants to hear it uttered from the man's mouth.

"I told you. One night, I didn't know how someone kidnapped the little one. A complaint was immediately triggered, but I think nothing more was heard of him. The girl spent a few more weeks with us, always thrown in a corner crying and nibbling on that little necklace. Evidently, whether she wanted the baby or not, she didn't know either."

"It's strange, though," Nardi replies, beginning to have some doubts. "Are you sure you didn't confuse the woman with another? There are no reports of that in our files."

"Maybe you've been looking in the wrong place."

"In what sense?"

"Well, we are talking about juvenile law. If a woman refuses to recognize her child, her name does not appear on the birth certificate. It is the civil status officer who assigns the newborn a first and last name. Therefore, in the complaint, you will not find a match between the two names."

"You're right! I hadn't thought of that," Nardi says as another question pops into his head.

If Angela's son was kidnapped, who is the child in the photograph?

De Marchi's statements have cast an aura of mystery over a story already tangled enough. Massimo wonders what else lurks in Angela Brunetti's past. He has a vague inkling that the surprises are not yet over.

Trying to get a complete picture of the facts, he poses a series of questions to which the other, unable to answer, replies with raises of eyebrows, and shrugs and swings of head.

"Well, I won't take up any more of your time," he concludes. "One last question, and I'll get out of your hair. Do you remember if anyone ever came to visit the girl?"

"Um! Let me think." De Marchi lifts his eyes in the air a few moments, rubs a hand on his cheek, and begins to tap his index finger over his mouth. "Now that you ask, I guess so. It seems to me that a boy used to visit her frequently."

"A boy?" Like a flash, a perverse thought crossed Nardi's mind. "I won't even try to ask you to describe him. However, do you remember if he had a tattoo on his arm?"

The man, in denial, responds with a wry grimace, but then his expression suddenly changes. "What a fool!" he exclaims. "I wonder why I didn't think of that before?"

"About what?"

"You know, my wife was a bit of a fanatic. Maybe she was too much so. She loved to see herself a few years younger, to the point that she never missed an opportunity to have her photograph taken. Likewise, she hated appearing alone. She always wanted someone to pose with her, even if it meant disturbing the guests."

"Are you saying you have a picture of that guy?"

"I don't know. It's possible. I'd have to rummage around a bit."

"Can you check?"

"I told you, Inspector, offhand, I wouldn't know where to look. I certainly kept them, but who knows where I put them."

"I see," he replies, disappointed. "Then I'll leave you my phone number. Please, try to find those pictures. It's very important."

"If you really need it, that's fine. It means it will be a good time to dust around."

***

The rest of the morning has been a slow progression of time. The investigation has taken a small step forward, but there is still no concrete lead to follow. While waiting for some update, Nardi has the impression that everything has become monotonous. And to make matters worse, he was not even able to enjoy lunch because of a headache.

Fortunately, at least, that seems to have vanished.

Now in his office, sitting in front of him, is Sergeant Ettore Lanzi. Nardi hopes that two fresh eyes will catch some detail he may have missed.

Lanzi is a young, open-minded man. That he is a bright guy is also revealed by his high forehead, shrewd gaze, and, above all, a wicked smile that does not leave him even when he is serious.

Transferred under his command a few years ago, he quickly proved his worth, managing to surprise him more than once.

All the while, the sergeant has been listening in silence, but by now, Massimo, having finished his tale, is silent in turn and waiting to hear what he thinks.

Lanzi raises an eyebrow and rotates his gaze in the air. "What can I say, Chief?" he then begins. "If someone has wanted to drag you into this, assuming that you and Graziani are both in the crosshairs, we should revisit the old cases. It will have to do with the period when you worked together."

"Yes, I thought so, too. However, something doesn't add up. What does the daughter have to do with this? The photographs started arriving ten years ago. And whoever sent them in the last five must have known her well. I, on the other hand, barely remember her. When I last saw her, she was little more than a teenager."

"Well, certainly, the connection is there. The problem will be finding it with the few clues available. We should proceed by exclusion."

"In what sense?"

"We need to revisit old files, draw up a list of potential suspects and skim through those whose feet you have stepped on. It is possible that some leads will come up."

"You may be right. I doubt it will do much good, but it's best not to leave anything out. I'll tell Cataldo to do some research later."

"If you want, I'll take care of it."

"No, no, you should inquire about the hospital records. They haven't let me know anything yet. Ask if they have finished viewing the tapes. And if not, tell them to speed it up."

"Okay, I'll get right on it." Lanzi gets up from his chair and starts toward the door. Soon after, however, he turns around. He shows some hesitation.

"What is it?" asks Nardi.

"Can I ask you a question?"

"Tell me."

"You and Graziani have worked together for years. Did you ever find yourselves overplaying your hand a little too much? I ask because, well, I mean who spends five years sending photographs before killing someone?"

"I know what you mean. And I would agree with you if it weren't for Graziani's daughter. As I said, she's the piece that doesn't fit. With her in the way, the list of names is pretty much reduced to zero."

The sergeant seems to want to reply, but the phone ringing interrupts the conversation. Nardi waves to wait and brings the handset to his ear.

On the other end of the line, Stefanini's voice resounds.

"Oh, Marcello, finally!" Nardi says. "What can you tell me? Have you discovered anything?"

"For the blood, you'll have to be patient for a while. In the meantime, though, I thought I'd fill you in on the rest."

"Come on, speak up! Don't keep me on my toes."

"On the previous photos, I did not find much, at least so far. But on the package sent by the post office, I detected an interesting element. From an external examination, it is clear that it was handled by several people. However, there were only three partial fingerprints inside. Two on the mailing envelope and one on the photograph."

"Well done. That sounds like good news to me. At least it narrows the field."

"Wait, I'm not finished."

"What else is there?"

"The fingerprints all belong to the same person. I did a database search, and a match came up."

"Are you being serious? And so, who is it?"

"I sent you an e-mail with the relevant file. But rein in the enthusiasm. As I said, the prints were partial. The dactyloscopy analysis revealed only eleven distinctive points so I can give you eighty percent certainty. But at least, now you have a first and last name."

"No problem, it's more than I expected. I don't know how to thank you, I'll take a look right away. If you find out anything else in the meantime, let me know."

"Count on it. See you soon!"

Putting down the receiver, Nardi lets go for a moment on the back of the chair.

"Well, Chief, is there any news?" Lanzi asks.

"You could say that – finally something to build on. In the last photo, fingerprints were detected. And they turn up registered in the records of the Data Processing Center."

"Do they belong to someone you know?"

"I don't know yet," Nardi replies, approaching the computer. "Now let's see. Our forensic colleague sent me the whole thing."

The file attached to the e-mail relates to one Sandro Donati. According to the reports, the man had been indicted years earlier on charges of murder. However, despite the circumstantial evidence against him, the suspicions had proved unfounded, and he had finally been cleared of all charges.

Nardi is absorbed in reading the dossier when his eyes fall on the corner of the monitor. Noticing that the clock reads 4:30 pm, he remembers making an appointment with Sergio Brunetti. They are to meet at five o'clock.

At first, he had thought of summoning him to the station. Then, however, on reflection, he changed his mind. Although they have known each other for years, they have never been close, and certainly, talking about his daughter will not be easy. Making him feel comfortable within the walls of his home, perhaps, will help him open up more easily.

Now that he finally has a lead, Massimo would like to hold back. In any case, he moves the cursor on the monitor and presses the print button.

The printer begins with a shrill sound and continues to drum. Nardi looks at it, and listlessly, he gets up from his chair. "Unfortunately, I have to leave now. I have to meet Angela Brunetti's father. Take the file yourself," he tells the sergeant. "And while I'm gone, try to find out everything you can about this Donati."

"Aren't official reports enough?"

"No. According to Stefanini, the fingerprint matches eighty percent, so he's not necessarily the right person."

"Oh, I see."

"Check to see if you can connect him to the case."

"What about the hospital surveillance tapes? Do I deal with those first, or..."

"No, no, never mind. This takes precedence for now. If anything, delegate the task to Cataldo. But, speaking of hospitals, see if you can clarify why, when Angela Brunetti died, they didn't inform the family."

"I'll get right to work."

"Okay. See you later!"

CHAPTER 10

Sergio Brunetti is a retired surgeon. During his career, he practiced in various parts of the world, always in clinics of excellence. Before leaving the profession, he was chief surgeon at Gemelli Hospital and a university lecturer. Teresa has never spoken to Massimo about how they met, and he has repeatedly wondered what glue held them together. In his opinion, they are two totally opposite people. Since their separation, the man has been living in a small villa on Aurelia Street, in a residential complex reserved for people like him: wealthy bourgeois who pay for their own peace of mind.

Out on the street, an intercom is placed at window height; it conveniently allows the button to be pushed from the passenger side of the vehicle. Nardi announces his arrival, waits for the gate to start sliding, then pulls into a tree-lined driveway. He has never been to this place. Scanning the house numbers, he proceeds slowly until he stops a hundred yards ahead.

Getting out of the car, he reaches the entrance. He raises his hand to knock, but the door opens before he can touch it.

"Hello, Massimo," Sergio greets him. "Come in! Be my guest."

"I'm sorry we have to meet under these circumstances," Nardi replies in response to the distraught look painted on the man's face.

After all, he expected it since he anticipated by phone the reason for his visit. He did not want a repeat of the scene he experienced at Teresa's house, that feelings might cloud rationality.

The foyer emerges into a spacious living room, lit by an entire wall of stained-glass windows. The decor, in a modern style, gives the room a touch of class. It exudes elegance in the same way as the person who inhabits it.

Sergio does not wear designer clothes; he wears a shirt with folded sleeves and old jeans. However, a distinguished bearing, a perfectly shaved beard, and neatly pulled hair are enough to give him a stately air.

"Have a seat," he says, pointing to the sofa. And as he sits down in an armchair, he looks at him in a strange way. Although the face hints at a sad expression, his gaze is cold, almost foreign. He seems to face his daughter's death with the professional detachment one would reserve for an ordinary patient.

Nardi returns his gaze without concealing a certain blame. Even though he feels some pity for him, he wonders how he can show such calmness. It is clear that he is in pain; the clenched hands, the contracted muscles in his neck and face, and his uneven breathing say so. Yet, he does not want to show it.

But this is not surprising after all. Sergio Brunetti has always been the kind of man who cares about appearances more than anything else.

On the phone, Massimo merely informed him about his daughter's death. For everything else, though – the rape, the existence of a grandson – he preferred to wait to talk about it face to face.

Undecided about the course of action, he wonders whether he should ask him direct questions or if it would be better to break the ice with a few sentences.

However, he has no time to decide – the other returns to

83

take the floor. "I still don't understand why you are visiting me," he says. "From what you explained, the death was a year ago, and the cause was already established. So, what does this have to do with the police?"

"Indeed, it is so. From the reports, it appears to be a consequence of attempted suicide. There have been recent developments, though. And they seem to link the matter back to the case I'm following."

"What does that mean?"

"The other day, there was a murder. The person who committed it shows some kind of obsession with Teresa. The matter is still to be clarified; however, it is clear that Angela is the key to the mystery."

"Explain yourself. I don't understand what she has to do with this."

Reporting the happenings of the past few days is now becoming a constant. Nardi is amazed to see how the facts, from time to time, take a different form: new details come to light; others are emptied of meaning and disappear. It almost seems as if the change of interlocutor alters the perspective from which to view the events.

After all, it could not be otherwise. At the beginning of the story, he was a mere spectator. Now that he has instead discovered that he is part of the game, he ends the tale with the impression that he is talking to himself. The mind is split in two, between one part that forces itself to report, and another committed to reviewing every piece of information that comes out of the mouth.

To ensure that the other remains lucid, he has limited himself to talking about the murder of the day before and the connection with the photographs sent to Teresa over the years. The gruesome details, those concerning Angela's past, he will tell him at the appropriate time.

"And how can I help you?" Sergio asks at the end of the explanation.

"Tell me about Angela. Teresa has already given me a fairly

detailed account, but I'd like to hear your side as well. Who knows, maybe you have knowledge of something she doesn't."

"Like what?"

"What do you think might have prompted her to leave home?"

"I wish I knew. I've wondered about it countless times."

"And about the relationship between her and Teresa, what can you tell me?"

"What do you want me to say? You know her well. Between playing and working, she certainly wasn't an exemplary mother. I tried my best to be close to our daughter, but a female presence was never there. It's normal that Angela felt neglected." Sergio sighs before adding, "With Piero's death, then… Well, never mind."

"I guess! That must have been difficult for you, too."

Massimo would like to bite his tongue. The words came out of his mouth unintentionally. At the memory of his wife, who died during childbirth, he could not restrain himself. He has never tasted the joy of feeling like a father, but he knows what it means to lose a child.

"I don't hate her if that's what you mean," Sergio replies. "Of course, it is true; if anyone is responsible for what happened, it's Teresa. And if hating her would serve to give me back my son, I would. I could tell you that I feel pity, but I would be lying. For her, I have only indifference now."

"I wasn't implying anything. I get you more than you know. But, going back to Angela, has she ever confided in you?"

"At one time, she used to do that. Unfortunately, in recent years it was getting harder and harder to communicate with her." With his eyes lost in the void, Brunetti swings his head. A deep breath fills long seconds of silence. "I always wondered if it depended on me," he resumes, "on something, I might have said or done. For a while, I thought it was because of the divorce, because I rarely saw her after I moved away. She often refused to even meet with me. However, I finally realized that the reason could not be that. She had changed much earlier."

"Let's go back to the photographs. They might have symbolic value or be related to particular moments in her life. Try looking to see if..."

"You're wasting your time. I doubt those photos can tell me anything."

Brunetti's response was too hasty. That he knows more than he lets on?

Peering into his eyes, Nardi tries to figure out whether the sudden outburst hides only an attempt to escape too much pain or something else. "You don't have to answer me now," he says, carefully studying his reaction. "I understand that it is difficult. In the meantime, please take a look at them and think about it. If you come up with something later, you'll let me know."

While the other merely nods in assent, he pulls the photographs from his jacket.

"They might bring back some memories," he encourages him. "Who knows!"

"Do I have to, huh?"

Massimo does not respond. With a lift of his chin, he twists his mouth to show his regret.

"All right, give me!" Sergio says. "Let's put an end to this."

Nardi is on the verge of handing him the pictures when he retracts his arm in a jerk. "Oh! There's something you need to know first," he points out, pretending to fall out of the clouds. "I'm so sorry. I don't know how I forgot, but between one thing and another, it had slipped my mind."

By now, it is time for straight talk. So far, he has kept everything generic, talking about photographs that showed Angela. But the baby also appears in the pictures, and he can no longer avoid the issue.

"What more is there?"

"It's useless to beat around the bush, so I'll just tell you. After she escaped, Angela had a baby."

"What?" Sergio's eyes betray a sense of astonishment. "Are you saying I have a grandchild?"

"Yep!" he confirms, returning to hand him the photos and

beginning to recount in great detail the events related to his daughter's past.

Brunetti listens in silence. Unable to bring himself to look at the images, he seems not to believe his own ears. Finally, in a hushed voice, he asks, "And where is he?"

"At the moment, we don't know anything." De Marchi's version of the kidnapping is still unconfirmed, and Massimo thinks better of keeping the information to himself. "The only proof of its existence is what you have in your hands," he says, knowing full well that he is lying.

The other frowns. With a questioning look, he hesitates for a few moments. Finally, he flicks through the images. "Is that him?" he asks as if seeking further confirmation.

"So it seems."

"And what do you plan to do to…?"

The sentence is left hanging in the air. Sergio opens his mouth and bends his torso forward to reduce the distance that separates him from the last snapshot. A strange expression appears on his face.

"What is it? Have you noticed something?" asks Nardi.

Brunetti is slow to respond. He runs two fingers over the paper. "This chain," he then replies.

"What did you say? The chain?"

"Yes! I had given it to her for her 18th birthday."

"And does it have any special meaning?"

"I wouldn't say so. Not for Angela, at least. Also, because I never saw it around her neck. I thought she got rid of it."

"Okay, listen! This necklace is the very one that was sent to me. And this photograph, besides being the last one, breaks the pattern of the previous ones. It must encapsulate a message of some kind."

"I understand, but…"

"It is important that you make an effort to remember. Think about the day you gave it to her. Did anything unusual happen? Every detail can prove valuable."

This time, Brunetti seems willing to cooperate. He lifts his eyes in the air and makes up his mind. "Um!" he mutters. "It's been an eternity. Let me think."

"Sure. Take your time."

Several minutes pass. Eager for the other to come back and speak, Nardi remains silent with his eyes on him. He hopes that at any moment, the man will provide some information useful to the investigation.

"It's all so blurred," Sergio resumes. "There's only one thing I remember. I think it was that day, but I'm not sure."

"What is it about?"

"She had cried because she fought with a boy."

"The boyfriend?"

"I don't know. It's possible."

"But did you know him?"

"Only by sight. When Angela came to visit me, sometimes he passed by to pick her up. I would catch a glimpse of him in passing, but she never introduced him to me."

"Ah, damn it!" bursts out Massimo. "You can't think of anything else, huh?"

"Nothing, unfortunately."

Determined not to throw in the towel, Nardi insists. "Do you remember if he had a tattoo on his arm?" he asks. But finally, seeing Sergio shake his head with a hint at a displeased expression, he leans back on the couch and lets out a sigh of resignation.

"But... wait a minute. Come to think of it; the last word is not said."

"What do you mean?"

"A detail came back to my mind. After Angela disappeared, that boy came looking for her here to me. I think a week or two later. He didn't know about her escape, and I didn't tell him anything. I had neither time nor desire to deal with such matters, especially with a stranger."

Massimo does not understand what difference that detail can make, but he listens patiently.

"He said he hadn't heard from her in days, that she wasn't

answering his calls anymore, and he asked if I could deliver a note to her. I guess he must have signed it."

"Are you saying you kept it?"

"I think so. It must have stayed where I put it. Only..."

"Let me guess. You don't remember it."

"Um! Give me a second."

As Brunetti rotates his head left and right to scour the room, Nardi crushes his thumbs together, shakes a leg, and wiggles his eyes to chase the other's gaze. There is anxiety in the air. And it increases when Sergio, patting his forehead, stands up and approaches the bookcase. "Yes, of course!" he exclaims.

Nardi continues to watch him in silence. With his back to him, the other reaches out a hand, grabs a book, and clutches it to himself. "You know," Massimo hears him say, "Angela loved to read. Ah! God only knows how much she loved it. And as it happens, a book is all I have left of her. Funny, huh?" When Sergio turns around, his lips disguise the pain with the hint of a smile. "Here should be what you're looking for," he says, starting to flip through the pages. "Yes, indeed! Here it is."

Massimo is already standing there waiting. However, he does not have the courage to look him in the eye. Without replying, he refracts his gaze on the note and holds out his palm.

What is evident from the message is only the torment of a young beau, but at least, among words like so many, there is a first and last name: Marco Rinaldi.

This is more than enough.

Now that Nardi has his answers, all he wants is to leave. Being in Brunetti's company, in that place foreign to him, makes him uncomfortable. Thinking of the many years that man has lived with Teresa, he turns an inquiring gaze at him. He wonders how far their confidences went and whether she ever let one word too many slip from her mouth.

For a moment, he feels as if the other's eyes can read him inside. Who knows? Maybe he knows, even if he doesn't speak. Is it possible that he is aware of his secret? That he pretends to ignore it?

Discombobulated, Massimo shudders and feels his breath getting heavy. The affair he thought was buried in the meanders of the past has come back to haunt him.

Shortly afterward, however, he recalls that at the time the event took place, the two were already on a collision course. Their relationship had been creaking for quite some time now.

The thought reassures him. Nevertheless, while he breathes a sigh of relief, he says goodbye and hurries to leave the house behind before emotion can play any more tricks on him.

CHAPTER 11

On the way back, Nardi cannot banish from his mind the image of Sergio and the expression carved on his face: a manifestation of repressed anguish in which he has seen himself reflected. Like him, Massimo has always tried to show impassivity, to hide his feelings from the outside world, but talking about the death of a daughter has made him feel disarmed. The memory of his wife haunts him. If he had opposed it at the time, preventing her from carrying a risky pregnancy, she would still be alive today. Instead, he has let petty selfishness prevail. He wanted a child more than anything, desire has blinded him, and by now, guilt is a traveling companion from which it is impossible to separate.

He would like to shelve those feelings in a lost corner of his soul; he tries to shift his attention to the investigation, but it is all in vain. He continues to blame himself the whole way.

It is only when he crosses the threshold of the police station that his thoughts vanish, and his mind becomes clear again. That place is his lifeline. He doesn't know why, but when he finds himself immersed in work, personal problems seem to separate from him, dissolve into a hazy blanket that hovers far away.

In the lobby, he crosses paths with the deputy as he emerges from his office hole.

"Ah, Chief, there you are! I've asked for updates for the hospital video footage."

"Is there any news?"

"Unfortunately, no. The surveillance cameras cover only strategic points. It is impossible to determine who entered or left that ward."

"I thought so," Nardi says. "Tell me, rather, do you know if Lanzi is in the station?"

"I saw him come up a couple of minutes ago."

"Did he tell you to research the old cases? Those carried on by Graziani and me."

"Yes. I have already started making a list. Then I'll see if I can cross-reference the data to minimize the names."

"Good," Nardi approves, starting toward the stairs. "Let me know when the job is done."

He hopes to be wrong, but he is already convinced that the attempt will be a washout. His instincts tell him that the solution lies elsewhere.

Reaching the upper floor, he spots Ettore Lanzi just ahead. Stopped at the side of the vending machine, he sips a drink.

"Can I keep you company?"

"Ah, it's you! I was wondering how long before you would be back. What would you like to drink?"

"One iced tea, please."

"How did it go with Angela Brunetti's father?" asks the sergeant as he orders the brew. "Did he provide any useful details?"

"I don't know if it's useful. We'll see. Apparently, Sergio Brunetti was the one who gave the chain to his daughter, for a birthday. And from what he says, on that occasion, she allegedly had a fight with a guy named Rinaldi, the one she'd been dating."

The mechanical screech of the automatic dispenser gets in the way of the conversation; meanwhile, a metal arm spits out the cup. Nardi grabs it and takes a few sips. "What about you?

92

Any news?"

"From the hospital, no. I asked why the family was not notified, but they could not explain. They merely said that an internal investigation will be launched. And from what I understand, the time frame will not be short."

"Oh! I can already imagine it. They will accuse each other. You'll see! It will be a blame-shifting."

"It would certainly not be the first episode of malpractice. I have heard often of poor devils, dead during hospitalization, who, through forgetfulness on the part of the doctor or nurse on duty, ended up in the cold room, often listed as unknown. And relatives would find out by accident, days or weeks later when they visited the sick person and found someone else in the bed."

"We will see if this is the case. Let's just hope the hospital gets a move on. In the meantime, though, I would say to track down the body. Let's find out who paid for the funeral, and we can get some answers right away."

"Yes, I thought so too, but I have already checked. Angela Brunetti arranged it when she was alive by entering into a prepaid contract with a funeral home."

"For crying out loud! It's macabre, isn't it?"

"Well, if nothing else, this confirms that hers was a suicide attempt."

"Yeah! Anyway, let's talk about something else. Did you find out anything about that guy?"

"With him I had a little more luck. Maybe your friend Stefanini got it right. Sandro Donati works as a letter carrier. It's a strange coincidence, no?"

"And what were you waiting to tell me?"

"I wanted to give you time to enjoy your tea," chuckles Lanzi. "You barely drank half of it."

"Then it is possible that we are on the right track. Any additional elements linking him to the case?"

"So far, I haven't found anything else about it. On the other hand, however, I found out something interesting. There is an ongoing investigation on that guy by the Postal Police. Nothing official yet; these are preliminary investigations."

"And how did you hear about it?"

"Since the situation concerned you so closely, I took the liberty of asking a few questions around." A stifled smile on Lanzi's face accentuates his sassy expression.

"Okay, never mind. I don't want to know," Nardi cuts it short. "Just tell me what he's being investigated for?"

"It involves subtraction of correspondence. Although it has nothing to do with our investigation, it might come in handy."

"Um, who knows? There might even be a connection."

"Meaning?"

"Come! Let's go talk in my office." Massimo downs one last sip and tosses the cup into the wastebasket at the side, and heads for the room.

Taking a seat across the desk, he motions for the sergeant to sit down. "Could it be that this is just a joke?" he mumbles to himself.

"What are you talking about?"

"I wonder if the two events could be unrelated. He would not be the first letter carrier with a mania for rummaging through other people's lives. Maybe this Donati has just been playing around with Teresa's life for the past few years."

"Are you implying that the person responsible for the hospital murder was not the one who sent the photographs?"

"It's a guess."

"To be honest, I find it a bit of a convoluted idea."

"Actually, it doesn't convince me either. Especially when I think about that damn chain. The fact that the bloody photo captures the woman with that very object around her neck is hard to think of as a coincidence. However, until we know more, best to keep every avenue open."

"Well, there's all the material available there." Lanzi points to a folder on the shelf. "The file sent by the forensic colleague and the information I was able to find."

Nardi begins flipping through the documents, lingering over

94

the file he received from Stefanini. Not having been able to examine it thoroughly because of his appointment with Brunetti, he picks up where he left off.

From what was written in the reports, a man had died as a result of a violent confrontation due to repeated blows to the abdomen with an edged weapon. The charge brought against Sandro Donati was based on solid evidence: tire tracks, which placed his car at the crime scene; DNA found on the victim's body and the handle of the knife; and overcoat fibers found under his fingernails. Law enforcement officials were convinced they had nailed the right man.

He had continued to profess his innocence, claiming self-defense. According to his words, it was the other who had attacked him.

And since the murder weapon also had the victim's fingerprints on it, experts had been unable to reconstruct the exact sequence of events. The lack of cameras made it impossible to determine who had actually acted first.

The fact that Donati had fled without even calling for help made him appear in a guilty light; however, when the prosecutor was now preparing to proceed, the case had deflated like a soap bubble. The news had hit the newspapers, and only then had an eyewitness come forward, supporting the version provided by Donati. Verification had confirmed the man's presence at the scene, and nothing left to doubt his word, so the charges had been dropped.

For a moment, Nardi questions the reliability of that witness who came out of nowhere. Soon, however, he lets go of all hesitation. There is no reason to question the work done by his colleagues. In all likelihood, feeding his doubts is only the urgent need to find a culprit.

Thus, continuing to view the papers, he examines the information found by Lanzi. Handwritten notes that, in addition to what the sergeant had already reported verbally, include the name of a chief inspector of the Postal Police and a telephone number.

"This Walter Persiani?" he asks. "Is he the one following the investigation?"

"Oh, yes, sorry. In my haste, I only jotted down the essentials."

"I guess."

"Aren't you going to call him?" incites Lanzi.

"Sure! I was just wondering if..."

"What?"

"No, nothing," Massimo concludes.

His objectivity is put to a hard test. He has the impression that he can no longer distinguish true from false. However, silencing any further doubts, he picks up the handset and dials the number.

As the phone rings, he closes his eyes for a moment and takes a breath, hoping to regain some clarity.

After a while, a voice answers from the other side. "Hello?"

"Good evening, I am Inspector Nardi," he replies. "May I speak to Chief Inspector Persiani, please?"

"It's me. Go ahead."

"I was calling because I heard about an investigation of yours. From what I understand, it would also involve a certain Sandro Donati."

"Gee, there's no official act yet, but I see the news is flying."

"Come on, don't take it badly! We are on the same side. Besides, we have a common interest."

"Meaning?"

"The man may be involved in a murder case. He is not yet a suspect, but I would like to know more. And since I have information pertinent to your investigation, I thought we could cooperate."

"Explain yourself further. What would a murder case have to do with our operation?"

"The link is a bloody letter. Donati's fingerprints were found inside. However, for now, it remains only circumstantial evidence, with a thousand possible explanations. There is a long story behind that envelope, but I don't want to bore you with the details. Suffice it to say that there are no elements to support an indictment. At least, as far as our case is concerned."

"Huh?" mutters Persiani, evidently intrigued by the last statement.

"I am referring to the man's fingerprints inside the letter. You are investigating the misappropriation of correspondence, aren't you? Well, that should be enough for you to apply for a search warrant, I suppose."

"What can I say? When luck knocks, it's foolish not to let it in."

"I take it that's a yes."

"Oh, you can count on it."

"Perfect! If you give me an e-mail address, I will send you the materials available to us."

"Sure. Ready to write it down?"

"Yes, go ahead." Nardi casts Lanzi a smug look and raises his thumb in victory. After that, writing a note, he concludes, "All right, then I'll be waiting to hear from you. Goodbye!"

HELL – ACT III

Standing still in front of a computer screen in an adjacent area, the man observes the framing of a cramped room. Twenty square feet or so, which he has adapted for his own purposes. Soundproof walls to prevent sound from propagating outside; an internal camera to allow him to watch the scene; a plexiglass plate abutting one side, hermetically separating a series of halogen headlights from the cell.

For now, he keeps them off. And in spite of a stone-cracking sun, light barely filters into that cubicle from a slit in the canopy.

In the half-light, he can barely glimpse what is happening inside. The camera lens returns an image in which the woman's body appears as one with the floor, an irregular elevation devoid of form. She is still motionless, but by now, the anesthetic should have exhausted its effect. Surely, she will open her eyes at any moment.

While waiting for her to come to her senses, he looks back. To implement his plan, he had to be patient for a long time. It's been five endless years. Now that the moment has arrived, he is anxious for it all to begin. He is curious to find out how his victim will react to looking death in the face, to feeling life slowly slipping away from her, aware that she can do nothing to

98

oppose the end. So far, reading the terror in her eyes has excited him, but not enough to quench the thirst for revenge that drives him.

Won over by impatience, he returns his attention to the monitor. The fact that the woman has not yet regained consciousness makes him suspicious. He wonders if she is faking it in an absurd attempt to study an escape route.

Although he knows there is no escape for her, the assumption is enough to put him in a bad mood. It is necessary for her to be awake in order for everything to be perfect. He has waited too long, taken care of every detail, to allow someone or something to ruin his plans.

For a moment, he is tempted to turn on the spotlights. He raises a hand to flip the switch but then holds back. It would spoil the surprise effect. And that's the last thing he wants.

Indisposed to the situation, he tries to find a solution to remedy the problem. He is undecided whether or not to go in and ascertain the woman's condition. Perhaps that is exactly what she is hoping for. Perhaps, the attempt to lure him to her is the ultimate gesture of desperation.

However, before long, the buzz of the audio speakers spreads through the air and sweeps away all doubt.

The body begins to move. Slowly, the woman's head sways from side to side, and her shoulders attempt to lift off the ground.

She is finally awake.

***

From the moment she opens her eyes again, her gaze is engulfed by the dark. The obscurity annihilates even the last shred of hope. Everything plunges back into the unknown.

She is tired and would like to continue sleeping, but the perception of danger forcibly shakes her out of her torpor. This time, it does not take her long to regain lucidity. Every memory resurfaces overwhelmingly and she, in fear, tries to scream. Out of her mouth, however, come only scraping, muffled sounds. She has a dry throat, struggles to move her jaw, and even her tongue feels heavier than normal. So she remains still, coughs, and while waiting for her sight to adjust to the gloomy environment, leaves it to her hearing to fill in the gap. Hoping to understand where she is, she tries to catch even the slightest sound, but it is useless. Around her is a stony silence.

At any rate, that place is not the same place where she was segregated last time. Of this, she is certain. Just as she is certain that several days have passed since the man seized her.

It is this consideration that keeps a glimmer of hope lit. She is still alive, and if he had wanted to harm her, he could have done so on several occasions, but he did not.

Now she is increasingly convinced that the fellow wants something specific from her. She wonders what it could be. And although every hypothetical answer terrifies her, she feels a desperate need for an explanation. Unlike the body, the mind she just can't keep in check.

To chase away those disturbing thoughts, she tries again to lift herself off the ground. Not least because now, mixed with the tingling sensation, a widespread pain indicates that the muscles are beginning to react. When she pulls her back up, in fact, despite the incredible effort, she manages to bring her torso upright.

Even the eyes begin to penetrate the darkness. Sitting on the floor, she then turns her head to look around. She has the impression that she is in a tiny, windowless room. If someone asked her to describe the place, she would not know what to say. She has no idea where she is or why.

Now on the verge of letting out a cry of despair, she notices a bright dot flashing just above. From the position she was in moments before, she could not see it. Only now does she realize that a camera is filming her.

"What do you want from me?" she shouts.

The LED continues to flash in total silence, but it is clear that he is watching her. "What is it that you want?" she repeats.

Convinced that she will not receive an answer, she bows her head resignedly and feels tears moistening her face when a microphone placed who knows where suddenly begins to croak: the man's voice spreads through the air.

"It is the penalty for your sins."

"What are you talking about? Who are you?"

"It doesn't matter who I am. It only matters who you are."

"What do you want? Please tell me. I will do anything, but let me go."

"Let you go? How can you think of that? You've reached the end of the line now; you're going to die. You know that, right?"

Those words paralyze her. A tremor runs through her from head to toe. Tension concentrates in a grip in her stomach, rises upward, and tightens a knot in her throat until fear bursts from her mouth in a kind of resignation. "Oh God, no!" she sobs.

To stifle the cry, she brings a hand to her eyes. Her forehead, however, cannot find support, and her head seems to fall through the air like a ripe pear. In that moment of anguish, she does not even realize it; she instinctively goes back to raising her hand. Only when she grasps nothingness for the second time does she feel her aching wrist.

Sensing that the limb has not yet regained feeling, she moves her arm and attempts to join her two palms together, but the grip goes awry. Bewildered, she then repeats that simple gesture. And feeling her left-hand crash against her chest, she wonders if she is drunk.

It is at that instant that the halogen headlights suddenly light up.

Blinded by the glare, she raises her arm in midair to shield herself from the bright beam. She closes her eyes for a moment. And when she opens them again, a blurry image reveals the chilling truth.

The right forearm is bandaged at wrist level, and the prehensile organ is gone.

With her eyes wide open, she lets out a cry of terror. She belts the bandage with her other hand to make sure her eyesight

101

is not playing tricks on her, and the moment her fingers grasp the bandage, her screams are exasperated, and she struggles madly. She cries, she screams, and she waves her arm in search of a part of herself that no longer belongs to her.

Lost in that hysterical fit, she struggles to realize that the floor has become damp. At first, she does not give the matter any weight. Sweat already covers every part of her body, and she is convinced it has soaked her clothes. Instead, when she lowers her gaze, she discovers that water is flooding the room and gasps for the umpteenth time.

The level is already a few inches above the ground and continues to rise.

Seeing the liquid mass growing faster and faster, she moves her head here and there to figure out where it is coming from. The pressure of the jet does not hesitate to point her to the outlet, and she pounces on it in a pathetic attempt to stem the flow. Unable to think, she places her hands against the exit hole, even one hand that is no longer there. And as futile as every gesture is, desperation compels her to try again.

Meanwhile, the microphone croaks again.

"What does it feel like?" she hears him say.

"Damn you!" she cries. "May you be cursed."

"Oh, I already am. If I weren't, you wouldn't be here now."

"Go to hell!"

"Don't worry; I will go someday, but not today."

The man's voice is supplanted by a mechanical noise coming from above. Outside, some sort of roll-up shutter begins to move, showing a small window in the ceiling. Beyond the glass, a clear sky appears to the eye as if indicating freedom at hand.

The water is now about three feet above the ground. Unwilling to give up, she continues to fight against the inevitable. She dives down to reach the relief valve and, this time pulls off the bandage that wraps around her wrist. She inserts the bandages inside the hole, pushes them in as far as she can, and, for a moment, the flow seems to slow. But soon, the pressure sweeps them away, and even the last hope vanishes.

She resurfaces, opening her mouth wide. The air penetrates violently to fill her lungs.

Meanwhile, the level has risen again. Just about a foot separates the surface of the water from the ceiling. No longer able to put her feet on the ground, she is forced to keep herself afloat while, with the last of her energy, she takes to hitting that glass that separates her from freedom.

She strikes again and again, with increasing force, but the glass is too strong. She can't even scratch it.

Finally, the spotlights go out, the outside shutter closes again, and darkness takes over the room again, enveloping even hope. She is now no longer afraid. Or perhaps, who knows, she is so afraid that she cannot now perceive it. Either way, she has stopped struggling. Around her, there is darkness, there is silence, and the only thing she can grasp is the little distance that separates her from the end. A few inches of oxygen to which her lips draw desperately. A few inches that mark the boundary between life and death. A few inches to let out a last cry.

CHAPTER 12

After a night's sleep, Nardi returned to work with a sense of relief etched on his face. He was shattered the night before, to the point of letting himself fall on the bed after dinner with his clothes still on. Plunged into a deep hibernation, he has slept for ten hours straight and now feels as if he has been rejuvenated by a few years.

Turning his gaze to the papers on his desk, he takes stock of the situation and thinks back to the bizarre way the matter began. A necklace, meaningless until a few days before, has dragged him into a multifaceted case. Between the murder of a dying woman, the photographs sent to Teresa, and the mysteries that have emerged from Angela's past, he still cannot find a logical thread that puts all the pieces of the puzzle together. In spite of the obvious connections, a few details always come out of place, like one too many pieces. Without taking into account the mysterious man Teresa mentioned. Will he be just a figment of her imagination, or is he really behind it all? And is it possible, if anything, that it is Donati?

He is absorbed in those questions when Cataldo enters the room. "Chief, Mr. Tancredi has arrived. Shall I let him through?"

"Uh?" Massimo asks, overthinking. "Who?"

"The person you were waiting for..."

"Oh, yes! Send him in, please."

He had forgotten it. Or perhaps, who knows, he may have unconsciously put it out of his mind so that he would not blame himself too much for his skepticism.

In the end, doubt outweighed the rest. At the thought that his colleagues might have overlooked something, he had preferred to summon Nicola Tancredi – the witness who had exonerated Donati – to hear his version of events in person.

As the man crosses the threshold, he surveys him to get an idea of who he has in front of him. It is a tall guy, just over 30, with an enigmatic gaze. The face, pale beyond measure, suggests a lonely person, the kind who spends most of his time holed up and who knows where far from sunlight.

"Please come in, Mr. Tancredi. Thank you for showing up on such short notice."

"No problem. Although I don't quite understand why you asked me to come."

"I would like to pose a few questions to you."

"What about?"

"It's to do with the testimony you gave some years ago. The one that led to an acquittal on a murder charge."

"Are you kidding?" retorts the other, annoyed. "Six years later, you want to start all over again? I was questioned by the police and by the judge. I said everything there was to say! You already have my statement, don't you?"

"Gee! I envy you, you know?" Nardi ironizes, suspicious of the brusque retort and the promptness of that answer. "I struggle to remember my birthday. Instead, you, just offhand, remember that six years have passed. Congratulations! You have a very good memory."

Ready to decipher the man's reaction, he tries to hide his watchful gaze behind the joking expression of someone throwing out a joke.

"I assure you that you have nothing to envy," Tancredi whispers, lowering his gaze to the ground. "Mine is a condemnation. Shortly after that event, I lost the woman I wanted to spend the rest of my life with. I could tell you not only the years but also the months and days, every single moment lived without her."

"Oh, so sorry. I couldn't imagine," he downplays. And realizing he has made a blunder, he hides his awkwardness by hastening to change the subject. "Please sit down and tell me what you remember about that story. How did it all unfold?"

Tancredi hints at a grimace of annoyance. Then, with the air of someone anxious to pull a bad tooth, he begins to report events. As he speaks, his face is crossed by a succession of contrasting expressions. Nonchalant for one moment, he appears shifty shortly after that; a steady, confident gaze is alternated with a sway of eyebrows and two eyes that dribble stealthily down and up.

Nardi watches him, puzzled. Intrigued by the ambiguous attitude, he does not know what to think. Not least because the man's account does not deviate one iota from what is already in the official record; he seems to have memorized a script to be repeated like a parrot. Strange that years later, he remembers every tiny detail perfectly.

That set of particulars hardly convinces him. However, as much as he trusts his instincts, he dares not counter. Not on the basis of mere impressions.

So, keeping his doubts to himself, he simply says thank you, stands up, and dismisses Tancredi with a handshake.

Before letting him go, however, he distractedly asks, "Why did you not come forward right away?"

"I beg your pardon?"

"I was thinking back to the dates. From the spreading of the news in the newspapers to when you decided to testify, a couple of weeks passed. How come?"

"Well, if I'm honest, I was afraid of getting myself into some kind of trouble. But I certainly couldn't let an innocent man go to jail."

"I see," Nardi concludes, sketching a smile and raising a hand to indicate the door.

***

Half an hour later, catapulted into an expanse of green, Nardi and Lanzi left the city's smog behind them. Trees and plants replaced the concrete facades of buildings, while the bustle of people's voices gave way to sheep, lambs and horses grazing quietly, chickens clucking and fenced rabbits watching silently.

What led them there was the note found at Brunetti's home, signed by Marco Rinaldi. Although it is a common name, it was easy to trace it back to the right person.

The man owns a farmhouse located just beyond the Grande Raccordo Anulare ring road. They went there in hopes of defining the contours of the blurred picture that is Angela Brunetti's past.

Having passed through the entrance, the car drives slowly along the last stretch of dirt road, continues on an expanse of gravel, and stops in the widening used as a parking lot.

Massimo impatiently gets out of the car to stretch his bones.

Closing his eyes, he then takes a deep breath to sniff the smells of the countryside mixed with those of the farm; wood and stones and hay warmed by the sun, fragrant flowers, the fragrance of grass mixed with the acrid and penetrating exhalation of animal dung. A mixture that invades the olfactory taste buds and that evokes in him pleasant memories of a distant childhood.

It is just after nine in the morning. The place, a modernized cottage, is still semi-deserted. Between its floral decorations and quiet state, it seems to doze off in nature. If customers stay on the upper floor, they must be in their rooms because only three attendants are visible, busy setting up tables outside.

Inside, behind the cash register, a girl reclining at the counter fiddles with her cell phone. When she notices their presence, she lifts her head slightly and shows a look that is not at all inviting. "Good morning," she simply says.

"Hello," he replies. "We are looking for Mr. Rinaldi. Is he here?"

"Who is looking for him?" The young woman's tone is that of an annoyed person, of someone who wants to be left alone.

Lanzi, stymied, shows his badge. "The police."

"One moment." The girl finally decides to put the smartphone aside and heads to the back.

While waiting, Nardi turns a glance at the sergeant. Sometimes he is too touchy. And that in their line of work does not help. He is about to point this out, but before he can open his mouth, he is interrupted by the appearance of a man. Emerging from the passageway from which the girl has disappeared, he asks worriedly, "Were you looking for me?"

"Are you Marco Rinaldi?" Massimo asks.

"Yes, that's me."

"Then yes. We were looking for you."

"And for what? Is there a problem?"

"Don't get worked up. We just need you to answer some questions."

"Well, sorry, huh! You tell me not to get worked up, but if you don't explain why you're here, it makes me even more agitated."

"We are investigating a person you were dating years ago. You, Mr. Rinaldi, could help us shed light on some aspects. We won't take up too much of your time; we just need a few minutes, and we'll get out of your way."

"Oh, Jesus!" The man brings a hand to his forehead and sighs, relieved. "For a moment, you scared the hell out of me. Who knows what I was expecting!"

In that liberating gesture, Nardi hasn't missed the other man's furtive glance outward in the direction of the waiters at the tables. Perhaps the employees are working off the books, or the business is not quite up to code. Either way, whatever it is, he doesn't care. It is quite another reason why he is there.

"Well, then, have a seat." Rinaldi wiggles his hands and points to the tables inside the room. "Can I offer you something to drink? A coffee or juice?"

"No, thank you," Nardi interrupts. "Do you mind if we sit outside, though?" He doesn't want intruders in his way. Besides, he will have to return to the city chaos soon, and while he can, he wants to enjoy the view and that odor-soaked air.

"You're welcome! Please!" Deploying a condescending smile, the man lifts an arm in midair.

Massimo cannot help but notice a dark spot located just above his wrist. "What happened to your arm?" he asks, pointing his finger.

"You mean this one? Oh, nothing! A burn."

"Ouch!" he merely exclaims, dropping the subject.

They take a seat at a table near the pool where no one can disturb them.

In his impatience for an explanation, the man quickly returns to the conversation. "Excuse my curiosity. You said it was someone I met. Who are we talking about?"

"Angela Brunetti."

"Angela?" Rinaldi lifts his eyelids and hints at a grimace of bewilderment. "And why are you coming to me? What has she done?"

"Strange question," Lanzi interjects. "Why do you think she must have done something?"

"Well, I can imagine that. You wouldn't have come here for nothing. Besides, knowing her, I wouldn't be surprised to find her in some kind of trouble."

"What do you mean by that? Explain yourself," urges the sergeant.

"Even though it's been a decade or so, I remember that she always liked to exaggerate. Yeah, I mean sex, drugs, and rock 'n' roll, so to speak. Sure, we were all a little wild, but she was going hard. She would do anything to get her mother riled up."

"Yes, we know they didn't get along. Do you happen to know if there were any particular reasons for that friction?"

Rinaldi arches his lips in a kind of indifference. "Mah! I never asked her, and she never told me."

Locked in silence, Massimo reflects on how Teresa's irresponsible actions contributed to create that situation. Increasingly aware of that truth, he wonders if he, too, in a small way, should not hold himself responsible. After all, he has always known about his friend's problem, her gambling addiction, and perhaps he could have been closer to her.

In any case, he doesn't want to think about it. To ward off the warning of guilt, he begins speaking, "Tell me, Mr. ..."

"However," the man interrupted him, "you still haven't told me why you are interested in her."

"She died," Nardi replies bluntly.

"What?!" The exclamation is punctuated by two wide, disbelieving eyes.

With a certain nastiness, Nardi reinforces the point. "That's how it is, unfortunately." A tactless confirmation, which is followed by a cold, succinct explanation of what happened. "She committed suicide if you really care to know. She died last year. But we are not here about that. We are only interested in clarifying some aspects of her past because of an ongoing investigation."

That cruel way of acting does not belong to him, and even he cannot explain what triggered it – perhaps impatience to get to the point. But more likely, pouring out underlying anger on the other man is just a poor attempt to shake off the negative feelings that run through him.

Even the sergeant must have noticed the anomaly in his behavior. He looks at him bewildered and says, "If you prefer, I'll take care of it."

"No need," Nardi admonishes him, annoyed with himself for losing his temper. "So, Rinaldi, tell me, how did you know Angela Brunetti?"

"We hung out with the same group of friends."

"And do you know if anyone might have had a grudge against her? Was there anyone bothering her?"

"Um! I would say no."

"And what was the relationship between you two? Were you

engaged?"

"Absolutely not."

"But what? What else is there?" prods Nardi, sensing something unspoken beyond those words. "Come on, speak up! From the way you remarked that *no*, it's clear you didn't tell me everything."

"Well, yes… actually… I used to chase after her. But having an affair was not part of her plans. Not with me, at least."

"You mean there was another one?"

"I think. Even though she kept denying it."

"Tell me about this alleged suitor. Were you suspicious of any particular person? Did you perhaps see her socializing with anyone?"

"No, none of that. Her attitude spoke for itself. There was nothing serious between us. There never was. She was quite forthcoming, however. On several occasions, we slept together. But then, in the last while, everything changed. She hardly let herself get close."

"And how did Angela justify that sudden transformation?"

"She didn't."

"Well, you must have discussed it, I guess."

"And how! The last time I saw her, we had a fight over this very reason. She kept denying that there was someone else; I was tired of being teased, so…" The sentence hangs in the air. The man changes his expression, and the eagerness of just before gives way to a shadowy, guarded mask. "Hey, wait a minute! You're not suspecting me, are you?"

"What is on your mind? Why should I suspect you?"

"And what the hell do I know?" shrieks Rinaldi, starting to fidget. "You know how some things go. One wrong little word, something that doesn't add up, and you get screwed with your own hands."

"Come on! Don't let your imagination run away. You can rest easy. Besides, I spoke with Mr. Brunetti, and he reported that you stopped by his house looking for his daughter, as she was no longer answering your phone calls. That speaks for itself. If you had been aware of her escape, that visit would not have happened."

As Nardi waves a reassuring smile, Lanzi is about to add to the conversation. Perhaps he has caught the inaccuracy in his statement and plans to correct him, to dot the i's. Either way, he doesn't have time to take a breath. Nardi glares at him, making sure he keeps quiet. His was certainly not an oversight. If anything, a half-truth, a small lie that might prove useful.

The fact that the man is uninvolved in Angela's escape does not exclude him a priori from what happened later. And if he is somehow implicated in that story, feeling safe could lead him to take a false step.

Fortunately, Rinaldi gives no sign of paying attention to that exchange of glances. Compounded by fear, he seems to ignore it. "Ah, okay!" he says, regaining his composure. "Sorry for raising my voice. But you know how it is."

"It's okay! No problem."

"So you also spoke to Angela's father."

"He was the one who gave us your name."

"Ah, that's it! Anyway, he didn't give you completely accurate information."

"In what regard?"

"I'm talking about the phone calls. Actually, after I went looking for her, we talked again. I had left a note there at her father's house, and a few days later, she got in touch."

Massimo glosses over the issue of the note. He knows that message never reached its destination.

"And what did you say to each other? Did she mention why she had left home?"

"No. She just told me that I should stop looking for her, that she didn't want to see me anymore."

"Um! I see," Nardi concludes as he stands up. "Then, I'd say that's enough. Thank you for your time."

He wishes him a good day. After that, with the sergeant at his side, he sets off in the direction of the car.

The building housing the animals is just behind the parking

lot, and the mixture of smells perceived upon arrival comes back to hit him. This time, however, instead of bringing with it pleasant memories, it merely accompanies a nagging thought: the spot noticed on Rinaldi's arm. Could it be that it hides something else? Perhaps, a removed tattoo?

CHAPTER 13

A couple of days have already passed without Massimo letting her know anything. The last time he showed up was to tell her the news of her daughter's death. Teresa can no longer bear the waiting anymore. She needs to know, to understand, and find a reason for this absurd situation. Feeling she is going crazy, she finally decides to leave the house to go to the only place where she hopes to find some relief from her anguish. She has taken refuge in the usual bar amid the rattling of slot machines, the virtual rustle of poker cards, and the constant clinking of tokens falling to plump up the cash registers.

This time she found a video poker machine loose, so, having changed some money, she started playing cards. Or at least that was the intention. In reality, she just watches the screen and pushes the buttons like a robot without any conscious involvement. And when she gets a winning combination, instead of taking advantage of it, she passes her hand in total indifference. All she does are automatic gestures: she inserts coins, pushes buttons, moves her eyes, and meanwhile thinks. Not even the game can distract her from her thoughts.

Massimo had promised to keep her updated. The fact he has not yet made her aware of anything annoys her.

She has tried to call him two or three times, but he has not returned her calls or bothered to contact her again. She wonders if he is too busy pursuing the case or has instead discovered something he does not want to make her aware of. And while both justifications are valid, she feels some resentment toward him. Because now, more than ever, she would like to hear his voice, even just to be told that there is no news.

Instead, she is forced to remain in doubt, to question who might have sent the photographs over the past five years and for what purpose; about what ties her former colleague to that dark mystery, about the uncertain fate of a grandson she has never met. If only she could answer these questions, she thinks, she would perhaps find some peace. But the truth is that she does not understand. Although in her head, she has been through that situation dozens of times before, she still cannot believe that Angela is really dead. Or rather, she refuses to do so.

So far, she has continued to ignore reality, shunning any emotion that might sear her. The decisive woman with a strong character has eclipsed her weak side for years. Now, however, that armor has shattered, and she cannot help but face loss; that of Angela, of Piero. All the grief, which over time, she has pushed away from herself, pours over her with the impetus of a hurricane. And with it, shame and guilt.

Overcome with emotion, she rushes out of the club.

"*Ah!*" the little voice so long ignored chases her. "*So you haven't forgotten, huh?*"

"No, no! It is not possible!" she shouts like a mad woman.

"*No? Yet until today, you have done nothing but justify yourself by blaming others. Piero died because of you, and the only thing you have been able to do is to pretend, to go on living as if nothing had happened. What kind of person are you? What kind of mother does such a thing?*"

"I will never forgive myself," she sobs. "I should have…"

"*I should have, I should have, blah, blah, blah. If you had listened to me, we wouldn't be at this point. I told you to get help, that gambling wouldn't do you any good. You never wanted to listen to me. Now it's too late to turn back. We are left alone, you and me.*"

115

As tears stream down, Teresa walks at a brisk pace with no definite destination. With her back to a sun now in twilight, she chases the long, intangible veil that is her shadow. It is what she would like to be in this instant, a dark blur incapable of remembering and suffering. Instead, memory hurls her into the past, recalling the day that changed her life.

The first thing she remembers is the scene in which she and Piero are preparing to leave the house.

Since leaving the service, the nanny's help has been increasingly sporadic. Dropping her son off at school and then waiting for him at exit time has become the norm.

"Hurry up!" she shouts. "It's getting late."

"I'm coming, Mom, I'm coming!" Piero is still finishing packing his backpack. He is at the end of the first year of school and, like the first day, he is looking for some special item to take with him to impress his classmates. "I don't know whether to take the magic box or…"

"Take whatever you want, but hurry up."

Teresa's words are echoed by the ringing of the doorbell.

Mrs. Roversi, who lives a few floors below, stands on the landing in the company of her son.

Teresa is not surprised to see them.

"Hello, Marilena," she begins, smiling.

"Sorry to bother you, Teresa. I know, it will just sound like an apology, but… Would you please accompany Giorgio again today? I had another setback, and as always I don't know who to ask."

"Don't worry! It's no trouble at all. It's not like they go to two different schools."

It happens a lot of times. Mrs. Roversi is a widow and, unlike Teresa, is not doing well financially. Not well enough to afford a babysitter.

Piero immediately turns up his nose at it, because a mutual dislike runs between him and Giorgio. Teresa knows this well. Fortunately, they do not attend the same class, and their relationship lasts only for the duration of the journey.

Therefore, to spare her neighbor further embarrassment, she hurries to push her son out of the house and closes the door behind her.

On the landing, Marilena does not stop apologizing and saying thank you. She continues until the elevator decides to arrive.

"Okay, see you later," Teresa cuts it short. She incites the little ones to enter the elevator and pushes the button for the basement.

In the parking lot, the car throws a few tantrums. For several days now, the door opener has not been responding properly. "Come on, open up!" she exclaims in annoyance, thinking she will have to have it looked at.

The vehicle seems to obey the command; the doors unlock. Then, she places the children in the back seat, makes sure they have their belts fastened, starts the engine, and drives off.

There is a clear sky outside, and the sun is already high. A wave of heat sweeps over the car as soon as it hits the road.

Teresa opens the windows wide to let the air circulate.

Piero, however, complains about the breeze, and Giorgio laughs and mocks him. Between jokes, the two take to bickering. And no one is willing to grant the last word. They continue bickering until close to arrival when she shouts to shut them both up. Stymied, she huffs and closes the windows. Luckily, the school is just ahead. Time to turn the corner for it to appear in view.

The gates of the building are already open, and the few children still standing outside are about to enter. Usually, Teresa lingers for a few minutes, having a word with the mothers who talk among themselves about more and less. Today, however, she runs away, anxious to go to the new casino that has opened a stone's throw away.

She has passed in front of it three or four times and has never gone in to take a look, so now she thought she'd pop in.

The only problem is parking at this time of day. She has to drive around a bit before finding a spot on an adjacent street.

Too bad it's not a shady spot, but it doesn't matter; on the way back, she'll be able to roll the windows wide open without much trouble.

When she steps inside, she is undecided whether to stop for a drink or to try her luck right away. Removing her doubt is the sight of a woman walking away from a slot machine. From her dissatisfied expression, she appears to have lost quite a bit of money.

Teresa rushes to take her place. It is her tactic. After a long string of losing plays, the odds of winning increase. Not that it always works. On the contrary! More often than not, she draws a blank. This time, however, she gets it right. All she has to do is insert a coin and pull the lever for the machine to start rattling and spitting out tokens in bursts.

The man sitting next to her turns to look at her. He smiles, but not to share her mirth. There is a hint of envy on his face.

However, she doesn't care. She rakes in the winnings.

"Hey! Look, those are mine," says a voice from behind her.

When she turns around, she is confronted by the young woman from just before, having a drink.

The girl wears indecent clothing. A tight mini-skirt reveals her panties at the slightest movement, while an almost nonexistent blouse brazenly displays a prominent bosom. She has all the connotations of someone who makes a living working the streets.

"Are you talking to me?" asks Teresa in a puzzled frown.

"Of course! And who else? That money is mine."

The woman has a foreign accent. Even from her appearance, she sounds Eastern European. However, she speaks the language well and has no trouble making herself understood.

"What are you talking about?" Teresa replies.

"I get up to get a drink, and you steal my place? I hadn't finished playing. After I put my money in it the whole time, you come and take it all? Forget it. Those are mine."

"Excuse me? Look, I don't know how it works in your country, but here the winnings belong to those who play. You

118

could have postponed that drink." Teresa starts to walk away.

But the woman does not seem to want to give in. She blocks her way, raises her voice, and insults her. And to Teresa's response, she retorts by throwing what is left in the glass in her face.

Teresa winces. For a moment unable to react, she then goes into a rage and can no longer contain herself. They come to blows. The glass flies into the air, smashing into a display case not far away, and as the two brawl, they continue to damage the casino. A couple of chairs fall over, bowls of snacks end up on the floor, and a few customers get tugged. Two employees have to intervene to end the scuffle.

Furious about the incident, the owner of the club called the police.

Teresa would like to be able to say that she is a cop, but she is no longer one. This is the first time she has been on the other side, and being forced to answer those she once called colleagues makes her feel uncomfortable.

The officers ask her and the other woman for their personal information, draw up a transcript reporting the events and the damage done, and finally ask the owner if he wants to press charges.

The man says he just wants to be compensated, but he is told he'll have to file a complaint. So, after wasting time filling out paperwork, it all ends for nothing: the owner decides to let the matter drop and everyone goes their separate ways.

Teresa has not yet blanched with anger. As she takes the adjacent alley to get to her car, she thinks she will never set foot in that place again. She wants to forget this bad adventure once and for all. Instead, as she approaches the vehicle, an aberrant scene appears before her eyes.

She cannot believe what she sees.

Piero and Giorgio are sitting in the back seat of the car, motionless, their eyes closed as if they were sleeping.

She jerks and brings her hands to her mouth. "Oh my God!" she exclaims, hurrying to open the door and yank her son out.

In a split second, she runs through the morning's sequences in her mind and wonders how she could have failed to notice what was happening. She had driven past the school pulling straight ahead, convinced that she had taken the two little ones to their destination. But they never got out. They remained silent even as she walked away from the car, perhaps because they had been reprimanded just before.

"Piero!" she shouts madly. "Wake up, Piero!"

Piero, however, does not sleep, and neither does Giorgio. By now, the two are not breathing; their hearts have stopped beating. She can only clutch her son's lifeless body, weeping, crying for help.

Later, investigations revealed that it was the failure of the opening system that had proved fatal. Trapped in that sort of furnace, where the temperature had exceeded fifty degrees Celsius, the children had asphyxiated to death.

Teresa had been accused of manslaughter, but what frightened her was certainly not the jail time so much as having to go on living.

In any case, in the courtroom, the lawyer had relied on several mitigating factors, from the state of apathy caused by the loss of her job to the handicap to her eye that, according to him, had prevented her from noticing the presence of the little ones on board. In addition, on expert opinion, he had argued the line of transient dissociative amnesia. So many excuses that, at the end of the judicial process, had been enough to get her acquitted.

The law, in short, had been lenient.

But life had not done the same. An already shaky family had reached the breaking point. Sergio, from then on, had not even wanted to hear of her. And Angela, although she had already been gone for several months, had never stopped making her pay, starting with that grandson named Pier Giorgio.

Now, continuing to wander aimlessly, Teresa thinks back to that name and how it immortalizes her guilt. Aware that she will never stop paying, she cries her eyes out.

CHAPTER 14

July 8, night

At the crack of dawn, a phone ringing breaks into Nardi's sleep. He is informed by the police station that his presence is required. The body of a woman has been found on Twisted Wall Avenue, the stretch of road that runs along the Aurelian Wall and connects Popolo's Square to Porta Pinciana. Two miles of asphalt that, separating the Pincian Hill from Villa Borghese, act as a watershed between the first and second municipalities.

Massimo has left his house in annoyance. The ancient wall from which the avenue is named is a natural barrier between the two jurisdictions. Had the incident occurred on the opposite side, the other district would now be working on the case, and he would still be in dreamland. A detail remarked even upon his arrival by the tree-lined docks placed in the middle to divide the roadways in the two directions.

Skimpy sidewalks, swallowed in places by guardrails, as well as the absence of parking spots, highlight a road intended for vehicular traffic. It is usually smooth, yet in spite of the hour, a column of cars proceeds in slow motion.

Law enforcement intervention has rendered one lane unusable, where several squad cars, forensic pickups, and unmarked police sedans are queuing up.

A couple of officers standing in the middle of the driveway diverting traffic to the left by waving drivers forward. Nardi, too, is urged forward as he tries to pull over. Only when he shows his badge the policeman waves him through.

He stops at the height of an indentation, where about thirty feet of lawn separate the wall from the road surface.

The recess in the wall further reduces the low light, and flashing beacons stand out against the walls and surrounding vegetation. White forensic suits stand out: men scattered here and there, busy taking photographic surveys and sampling the ground.

One of these provides him with a pair of latex gloves. He hurries to put them on and wiggles his fingers for an ideal fit. Then noticing a squad gathered about fifty feet ahead, he climbs in that direction.

Sergeant Lanzi is already on the spot. He comes to him with a pale complexion on his face. He even seems to have lost that grin that never leaves him.

"Chief, Chief, you have arrived!" he begins in an agitated manner. "You can't imagine! It is out of this world."

"Hey! What's the matter with you? I think I hear Cataldo talking. You've seen people killed before, haven't you?"

"Yes, of course! But I've never seen anything like it. And neither have you, I bet."

"What are you talking about?" Without waiting for a response, Massimo moves forward curiously.

Over the shoulders of his colleagues, he catches a glimpse of the victim's body, close to the wall and half engulfed in the bushes. However, he doesn't have a good view from that point, so he makes his way until he is only a few steps away from the corpse. Only then does the scene show itself in all its rawness.

He sees a woman with her hand severed, one eye gouged out clean, her rib cage quartered like a calf, and a cross marked with blood on her forehead. Completing the unnatural picture is the marked makeup on her face. One comes to think of a broken doll.

"Oh, for crying out loud!" he exclaims. "What the hell did they do to her?"

"Did you see how they reduced it?" reiterates Lanzi.

"You're right. It makes me shudder to look at her."

Stooping to the ground to examine the body is the medical examiner, a short, pot-bellied fellow. It is Dr. Padovani. For a moment, he lifts his gaze, drops his glasses to the tip of his nose, and arches his eyebrows. "Hey there, Nardi!" he greets. "They kicked you out of bed, too, huh?"

The two know each other well. On several occasions, they have found themselves collaborating on the same cases. Mutual esteem binds them together.

"We'd better talk about something else, doctor. I haven't been able to get a decent night's sleep for days. What about the victim?"

"From her body temperature and *rigor mortis,* I'd say she's been dead less than forty-eight hours. But if you'll be patient for a moment, I'm almost done."

"Take your time. I think we'll be here for a long time anyway."

Leaving the doctor to his work, Nardi turns back to the sergeant. "Have you identified her yet?" he asks.

"Not yet. She had no documents on her, and among the missing person's reports, there were no women matching the profile. We sent photos to the station, but so far, nothing."

"You will see! Soon a name will come up. Whoever killed her certainly didn't want to go unnoticed. An execution like this must be a message to someone. I just wonder who the recipient is."

"Maybe it's a gang dispute."

In recent times, turf disputes have escalated. In addition to the succession of robberies, two nightclubs have been set on fire, and three men have been killed for the same reason.

"Possible," Massimo replies, although the modus operandi does not match at all. "Are there cameras on this road?"

"Further on, at the height of the overpass. Unfortunately,

this section is covered by the curve."

"It is already something. At the very least, it will give us a way to narrow down our search. Up to Porta Pinciana there is no way out. The car must have gone over the bridge."

"Yes, but forty-eight hours is a long time, and the daily turnout here is huge. If forensics doesn't give us some useful clues, I doubt the footage will be of any use."

Nardi is on the verge of retorting when some flashes and cackles behind him get his attention. The woman's death has already made headlines, drawing the first reporters to the scene. "Keep them away from here," he shouts to the officers ahead.

"If you shriek like that, you'll end up feeling sick," says a voice behind him.

Dr. Padovani advances in all his awkwardness. As he slides the gloves off his hands, an expressionless face hints at indifference. After all, dissecting bodies is his job, and that gruesome scene must not have fazed him all that much, if at all. "I am finished," he says. He wiggles his glasses as if to reposition them, perhaps just to show a modicum of involvement. "You are dealing with a sadist. He enjoys watching his victim suffer."

"What do you mean?" Nardi asks.

"Well, judging from the *livor mortis* and the foam around the mouth, the cause of death is drowning."

"But how is it possible?" marvels Lanzi. "Then why would they have reduced her like that?"

"What do you want me to say, sergeant? The concentration of cadaveric lividity is all on the anterior part of the body. The rosaceous hypostases and other indicators speak for themselves."

"Sorry, doctor, I didn't mean to question your opinion. It just seems strange to me. That's all."

"I understand that. However, as for the rest, both the heart and the right eyeball were removed, but only later. The only exception is the amputation of the hand."

"Exception for what?" asks Nardi.

"That one is ante-mortem. Judging by the appearance of the wound, I would estimate between ten and fifteen hours ahead. Whoever did it cared about keeping the woman alive because they bothered to suture the wound."

"So... let me get this straight." Massimo struggles to find logic in the sequence of actions. "Are you saying that the murderer would first cut off the hand, then treat the wound, only to drown the victim a few hours later? And finally, unsatisfied, he rips the heart out of the chest and pulls out an eye. Have I understood correctly?"

"That's exactly what happened."

"But what's the point?" remarks Lanzi.

Massimo's hesitant expression joins the sergeant's request.

"Why are you asking me?" Padovani sketches a half smile. "That's your job, dear sirs, not mine. Perhaps, it will help you to know that the killer might have some smattering of medicine."

"Huh? Are you sure about that?" asks Nardi with renewed interest.

"Quite, but let's wait to draw conclusions. I'm not saying our killer is a doctor. We could very well be looking for a nurse, just a student, or anyone with a minimum of practice in health care."

"What makes you think that?"

"Pure deduction. None of the removals were performed surgically; however, the stitches on the wound were applied with some precision."

"Um! Interesting detail."

"That's all for now. The preliminary examination shows no evidence of sexual abuse, but I will be able to tell you more after the autopsy."

"All right, doctor. Then..."

"Oh! I almost forgot," Padovani resumes, bringing a hand to his forehead. "I wonder where my head is! This was inserted in the eye socket." He waves something in the air, a transparent sachet with some kind of marble inside. "It would seem important, considering where it was."

"What is it?" asks Nardi.

"It's a rolled-up piece of paper."

"Well, let's open it," incites Lanzi.

"I have already taken off the gloves. Wait just a moment, that…"

Massimo does not allow him to finish the sentence. Slipping the envelope out of the doctor's hands, he hurries to pull out the paper to unfold it immediately.

What appears to the eye is a strange note.

The text cites:

"Even if I testify about Myself, My testimony is valid, because I know where I came from and where I am going. But you do not know where I came from or where I am going."

"A Bible verse?" says Lanzi. "What the hell is that supposed to mean?"

"Oh, perfect!" echoes Nardi. "All we needed was a religious fanatic."

In that instant, a flash behind him catches him by surprise. A photojournalist has managed to sneak past the security cordon and is only a few steps away.

"What are you doing here? Who let you through?" Massimo asks angrily. And recalling an officer, he continues in his outburst, "Didn't I tell you to keep the press out? Get him out of here."

As the man is escorted past the demarcated area, a woman advances in the opposite direction.

It is the assistant prosecutor, Assistant District Attorney Amanda Mellis.

"Good morning, everyone," she says when she reaches them. "Sorry, I'm only coming now. I couldn't make it earlier."

Massimo hints at a sarcastic smile. She wishes him good morning, but as far as he is concerned, it is still night, and he would like to be under the sheets.

"Hello, ADA. Have they entrusted you with the investigation?"

"Yes, Inspector. I'm glad to find you here, too."

The woman has the power to understand him on the fly. She intuits what he means before he opens his mouth. With her in charge, he will not have to dwell on unnecessary explanations or make excuses to justify his actions. They are both practical and few-worded types, the kind of people who look at the results.

"So, give me an update. What information do we have so far?"

"The identity is still unknown. Only this was found on the deceased," Nardi reports, showing the note found. While the ADA is intent on reading, he adds, "Dr. Padovani has determined the cause of death was drowning."

"So the body was moved here at a later date," she emphasizes.

"Correct. It appears the murderer was in contact with the victim for several hours before killing her. He mutilated the body while she was still alive."

"Mutilated?" Mellis frowns and casts a glance. Perhaps out of sheer curiosity, or to see the situation for herself, she begins to advance toward the corpse.

"You'd better avoid looking," Lanzi warns her. "It's not pretty. Trust me and don't even look."

She seems not to hear. She pushes herself a few steps toward the body until, coming to a sudden halt, she gasps and brings a hand to her mouth to stop a gag of vomit. "Oh my God!" she exclaims.

"I told you," Lanzi remarked.

Then, as the woman recovers, Padovani gives her a detailed account of what the checks have ascertained. The sergeant updates her on the reports of the first officers who intervened at the scene. Massimo, on the other hand, wonders about the meaning of the note.

If this is the way the murderer intends to give manifestation of himself, reducing a woman to meat for slaughter, one wonders what they should expect next. The end of the verse speaks clearly: *"You do not know where I came from or where I am going."*

Assuming those words make sense, it means it is only the beginning.

CHAPTER 15

July 8, morning, 8:00 a.m.

It is just past eight o'clock. Rising portcullises and an opening and closing of gates, scattered voices, engines, and horns announce a city now awake. Nardi, on the other hand, struggles to keep his eyes open. He has been up for about three hours and has had little or no sleep. Sitting in his office, he drinks coffee – already his third of the day – but instead of relieving his eyelids, it only serves to increase his stomach acidity.

He has recently received some updates. Intent on sifting through the data at hand, he taps his index finger on the desk, stares at the papers, makes up his mind, and tries to examine the whole thing from new angles.

When he lays his eyes on a copy of the coded message, he begins to wonder again what meaning it might hide, but the ringing of the phone bursts in before he can formulate a guess. He lifts the handset instinctively. Still absorbed in his thoughts, he pulls it close to his ear and remains silent.

"Hello, Nardi?" he hears a moment later.

It takes him a short time to recognize the voice on the other end of the line. The police commissioner, Ignazio Nicolini, rarely calls him, and the few times he does get in touch, it is not to pat him on the back.

"Yes, Commissioner, I'm here. Go ahead."

"I just heard about what happened," rants Nicolini. "Why didn't you inform me? I had to find out from the newspapers."

Massimo casts a glance at the clock. It is twenty past eight. Surely the man has just stepped into the office. He imagines him, polished, with his pipe in his hands and fresh as a rose. He, on the other hand, has missed even the time to take a shower. Just thinking about it, he wants to tell him how much is on his mind, but instead, he just lies. "I was just about to call you."

"I hope you already have some elements of investigation."

"So far, we know little or nothing, unfortunately. I have received few advances from colleagues at UACV, but we are still on the high seas."

Given the heinous nature of the crime, the task of supporting them in the investigation falls to the Violent Crime Analysis Unit, the forensic section of which Stefanini is a member.

"Let's be clear, Nardi. This case must be a top priority. I want results as soon as possible. Find something to work on quickly, or the assignment goes to the homicide section of the Mobile Squad."

"Don't worry; we are already doing our best," he reassures. And thinking of Teresa, he hints at a grimace of annoyance. That investigation in which he is co-starring will have to wait, at least for a while.

"Also, take care!" concludes Nicolini. "Keep the press as far away from this matter as possible."

Putting down the receiver, Massimo furrows his brow, shakes his head, and snorts. He has enough headaches without having to deal with the commissioner's outbursts. Nonetheless, he curiously approaches the computer to look at the day's information.

The news is reported on the home page of all major online newspapers.

They were very careful not to publish the full photo of the victim. A close-up of the face is shown at a three-quarter angle to hide that missing eye from view. Despite this, the detailed narration, the broken doll's face, and the cross of blood on the

131

forehead are enough to elicit the desired effect.

Nicolini must be worried about the impact it will have on public opinion. And honestly, he cannot blame him. In his place, he would have reacted the same way.

"Am I interrupting anything?" Lanzi stands in the doorway of the office.

"Come on in. I was just about to call you. Stefanini sent me some preliminary reports. It's not much, but at least we can do a partial reconstruction." Placing some papers on the desk, Nardi waves for a seat. "Here are the latest updates."

As the sergeant sits down and begins to read, he stands up.

A magnetic board is fixed on the side wall. Massimo has a habit of writing on Post-it notes and pasting them on there. He finds it the most practical way to sequence the information and reorder it when needed.

Grabbing the notepad, he writes *Victim's name*, followed by a question mark.

Hanging the slip of paper at the top, he fills out a second one, entering the place of discovery and the surrounding areas. He pastes it a little further down and continues in this way, putting on paper the various data he has: sex, cause of death, state of the corpse, the time of discovery, and so on. Before long, about ten notes form a horizontal outline on the blackboard.

He is still finishing writing when Lanzi takes up the conversation. "Gee, not the slightest trace of blood was found between the corpse and the road surface."

"Yeah. He must have sealed the body in a plastic bag."

"We are dealing with a thorough person."

"I also find the deep footprints left on the ground interesting. About three hundred and thirty pounds in weight, according to the report. Hard to think of a curious fat man passing there by chance. The culprit must have left them."

"What about this?"

"The body was not dragged. If only one person carried it, he must have some strength. I would discard the female profile from possible suspects. And since the woman's weight must have been around one hundred and thirty pounds, I would say we are dealing with a man of about two hundred pounds. Of course, that's of little use for now, but, who knows, it might come in handy."

Lanzi agrees with a slight shake of his head. "It is possible. But we should focus on the message. That's the key to everything."

"Yes, I was thinking about it just before you arrived. Forensics will already be analyzing the fibers of the paper and the type of ink used, but as for the meaning, that's a whole other ballgame."

"What on earth could that mean?"

"Who knows," grumbles Nardi, grabbing the copy of the note from the desk.

Using a magnet, he locks the paper in the center of the board, pastes another Post-it note on it, and writes, "Gospel – John 8:14."

He reads the text for the umpteenth time.

"Even if I testify about Myself, My testimony is valid, because I know where I came from and where I am going. But you do not know where I came from or where I am going."

"Will he want to spread the word of Christ?" jokes Lanzi.

"There is little to joke about," he replies. "Those words scare the hell out of me. I wonder if we're not dealing with a serial murderer."

"What makes you think that?"

"That last sentence. It hints at some kind of evolution."

"Mah! I wouldn't take it literally. Sure, it may sound like a warning, but it seems early to me to jump the gun."

"I'm just speculating. If that's the case, though, we should ask ourselves what drives him to act. Who are we dealing with? A sadist? A sociopath? Why does he kill? Unfortunately, until we identify the victim, our hands are tied."

The noise from the street has become irritating, and Massimo, as much as he resents the air conditioning, approaches the window and closes it without a second thought.

"He may also want to deflect us," Lanzi says. "Maybe the intention is just to cover up a trivial murder. He may have orchestrated all this to muddy the waters."

"Um! I doubt it, given the modus operandi. His purpose does not seem to me to be to kill. He wants something more. He mutilated the victim when she was alive and again when she was dead."

"Well, yes, it actually suggests a kind of symbolic ritual."

Nardi's head makes a sudden jerk. He feels the muscles in his forehead contract; his eyebrows pull up. "That's right!" he exclaims, snapping his fingers. "Maybe that's where we need to start. Have a search done. See if the excised parts have any special significance in the history of Christianity."

"Do you really think there could be a connection?"

"Who would know?"

Lanzi is about to stand up when the deputy bursts into the room.

"What's wrong?" asks Nardi immediately.

As a rule, Cataldo usually knocks. When he does not, it is because urgency comes before good manners.

"News about the woman, Chief. In the case of the Twisted Wall."

"Has she been identified?"

"Yes, she is listed on file. From what I understand, there was a problem with the fingerprints, and it took longer than usual." Cataldo hands over the relevant file and adds, "If you want my opinion, someone made a mess at the central criminal records office and..."

"Okay, okay! Don't worry about it," he interrupts, with no interest in clarifying why the delay. "Go ahead, thank you."

As the man walks to the door, Massimo prepares to leaf through the documents. But then he returns to lift his face. "Oh, by the way!" he resumes. "Assign a couple of officers to research Christian symbols. And maybe pagan ones, too."

Cataldo appears confused. He motions that he does not understand.

In his haste, Nardi has spoken as if the other had witnessed the conversation just before. When he realizes this, he properly instructs the deputy, who, this time, gets the message and takes his final leave.

With Cataldo's entrance, Lanzi is back to getting comfortable. Clearly impatient, he points to the file and asks, "What does it say?"

"Let's see! Her name was Juliana Petrescu. Thirty-nine years old, Romanian nationality…" Massimo's voice thins until it fades completely. Only a few faint whispers accompany his eyes as they scroll over the papers. Then, having finished reading, he returns to say, "It seems she's been very busy."

"Why, what did she do?"

"She was a prostitute. At the age of twenty-eight, however, she was also arrested for extortion and fraud, serving a sentence of three years and two months. She would select wealthy clients and film them without their knowledge during sexual performance. After that, she would blackmail them."

"But someone didn't play along since they caught her."

"Yeah!"

"Are there any other reports? Does it say if she continued to prostitute herself?"

"No, that's all there is. Of course, it is possible that she continued to carry on her shady tricks. But in that case, if someone else fell into the trap, he must have kept his mouth shut."

"Maybe she fell victim to her own deception. The murderer might just be a client. Backed into a corner, he may have decided to get her out of the way."

"This brings us back to the inconsistency from earlier. The modus operandi does not match. Someone who feels threatened does not kill that way. Our man seeks attention, cries for revenge or ransom."

A nod of irritation appears on Lanzi's face. "I understand you have already opted for the serial murderer line," he retorts in a defiantly.

"Absolutely not! Never put subjective deductions before objectivity. To preclude the formulation of more valid hypotheses would be to depart from the truth. We will make all the appropriate checks, and if we find your theory is a match, we will act accordingly."

On hearing the superior speak like a textbook, Lanzi attempts to repair the misunderstanding. "Excuse me, Inspector; I didn't mean… It was not to contradict you."

"Don't stand there justifying yourself! Keep thinking with your own mind." An imperceptible smile contours Nardi's lips.

One of the characteristics for which he appreciates the sergeant is precisely his stubbornness. On several occasions, it has allowed him to look past prejudices or backtrack on bad choices. "Rather, tell Cataldo to contact the Romanian authorities," he resumes. "Let him inquire if there are any pending charges against the woman, if she had any relatives, and if anyone might have had a grudge against her for some reason."

"I'll go right away."

"Meanwhile, I will contact Mellis for a search warrant. I would say it is appropriate to drop by the victim's house."

Lanzi nods and walks away.

As he disappears over the threshold, Massimo's gaze falls down, settles on the papers, and lingers on the victim's last domicile: Vittorio Emanuele II Square. At the thought that it is only three or four miles from where she was found, he wonders if there might be a connection. He holds back the question for a few seconds but finally lets it go, picks up the handset, and dials the number of the assistant district attorney.

CHAPTER 16

July 8, morning, 9:30 a.m.

On the colonnades and cobblestones of Vittorio Emanuele II Square, the morning sun still glistens when the entry of three police cruisers draws the gaze of passersby. Even the unmarked police car in which Nardi and Lanzi are riding, slightly detached from the others, is clearly recognizable by its exposed flashing beacon.

The queue of cars completes half a circle of the square and stops double-parked under the victim's building.

Immediately intent on giving instructions to the officers, Massimo notices a forensic pickup truck coming up. In its wake is another car, from which, shortly afterward, he sees Stefanini pop out.

"Oh! Hello, Marcello," he greets him. "You're here early. I thought you were going to keep us waiting for a while."

"You were lucky. Today, Tuscolana Street was all clear."

Thinking back to the stressful traffic a few days ago, when he had gone to the DAC, Massimo would like to point out to his colleague that the lucky one among them was certainly not him. But instead, he simply says, "Good for you."

"We've been meeting a little too often lately, don't you think?" Stefanini's bulging eyes become even more prominent, accentuating his funny air. "Months and months without even a

137

phone call, and then we see each other days apart."

"Yeah! And since you'll have to join us in the investigation, I will have to put up with your face for a long time."

"Think about your face. When was the last time you picked up a razor? Is it just laziness, or do you do it to save money?"

Between them, they are wont to poke each other. A sense of rivalry, steeped in irony, due to each other's admiration for the other.

"How is it going with Teresa's case?" continues Stefanini. "Has there been any development?"

"Thanks to your information, we traced it back to a letter carrier. Beyond that, nothing much. However, the case will have to wait for now. The quaestor is breathing down my neck."

"Eh, I guess so!"

The conversation is interrupted by the arrival of Lanzi. The sergeant approaches and remains silent, but Nardi and Stefanini turn to look at him as an intruder.

"Excuse me, Inspector," he then says. "We are ready."

Nardi notices a slight discomfort on the subordinate's face. At first, he attributes the embarrassment to that unintentional intrusion. Then he realizes that the two do not know each other. He, therefore, provides the necessary introductions and becomes serious again. "Okay! Let's go do what we came here to do."

"You're right. Let's go in," Stefanini agrees.

"We'll go ahead," he replies. "If there is no danger, I'll give the okay for your people to go up."

From their information, it appears that the woman lived alone. The risk of finding someone in the house is highly unlikely. However, a search is always a leap in the dark; one can never know who will be found once inside. For all they know, the killer himself could be on the other side of the door, and Massimo certainly has no intention of being found unprepared.

Before going to the site, he obtained cadastral maps of the building to study the environment and block possible escape routes. Other than the front door, no other exits are apparent;

nevertheless, he has stationed a couple of officers on the side of the building should anyone attempt to climb over the boundary wall to escape from the backyard.

Lanzi pushes the intercom button a couple of times. He pushes buttons at random until, on the third attempt, a condominium resident decides to answer it.

"Police," he announces. "We should..."

The automatic opening clicks off before another word can be added. Perhaps the guy on the other side has already peeked through the window and noticed their presence on the street.

Nardi orders one officer to check the lobby and waves the others forward. The sound of footsteps bouncing between the walls spreads like an echo in the stairwell, but he does not care, not in such a situation. Although he acts with due precautions, he strongly doubts that there is a presence in the house. And anyway, at this point, the surprise effect is long gone.

Reaching the third floor, he rings the doorbell and takes the search warrant out of his pocket if someone opens up. When at the umpteenth ring, no one answers, he gives permission to proceed.

The lock, hitherto free of signs of forced entry, is knocked out by one of the officers.

Having finished the job, the man moves to the side and pushes the door forward.

A nauseating smell escapes from the apartment, overwhelming them. On instinct, Massimo brings a hand to cover his nose and mouth; however, he has no time to ask himself any questions. The safety factor takes precedence over the rest. The men enter and deploy to the various rooms, making sure that the dwelling is indeed empty. Only then does someone bother to open the windows to circulate air.

"All right! Bring up the forensic colleagues," he says, looking around.

"What the hell is that smell?" complains Lanzi.

Already absorbed in searching for clues with his eyes, Nardi had removed the question from his head. The stench that haunts the room has diminished, yet it is still clearly distinguishable. He knows it well. And he is on the verge of answering, but the words remain on the tip of his tongue. Stefanini anticipates him as he crosses the threshold. "Gas. Decomposition," he says.

"Ah, that's it!" Lanzi replies. "It seemed a familiar smell to me. But where did it come from? There is no dead body in here. Maybe it's a dead mouse?"

"I don't want to be wrong, but it seems to be coming from here." In the living room, an officer points to the sofa, where some decorating cushions are stacked on one side.

Nardi moves forward curiously and shifts the first pillow. Feeling the smell penetrate his nostrils, he hurries to lift the second. Blood stains daub the fabric underneath. In a split second, he hypothesizes various scenarios, but as he pulls the last pillow away, he is completely shocked.

"Oh, shit! He's been here!"

He did not expect it. The victim's hand is resting on the sofa, palm up, containing a crumpled paper.

"Perhaps this is where the crime took place," Lanzi suggests.

"Um!" Nardi is not convinced. "And then the killer would clean it up? Hardly."

"Well, that's what we're here for, right?" Stefanini pushes forward a few steps. "How about you leave it to the *experts*?"

There is a mocking tone in that last word — an apparent jibe aimed at Nardi.

Catching the subtle irony, he shrugs. "You're right, Marcello," he says, and turning to his team, he adds, "Okay, guys! Everybody out. We've contaminated the scene enough already. Let's let forensics do their work."

It is a meticulous operation that awaits the UACV men. Scanning every corner of the apartment for traces will take time. But the killer has been there, and he must have left signs of his passage.

At Nardi's order, officers from his unit clear the room, careful not to touch anything. They exit one by one. Only he and Lanzi continue to hold back in the living room.

"You better get out too," Stefanini says.

"Just show me one thing. Then I'll get out of the way."

"Uh? What do you want to see, Massimo?"

"That one!" he points to the slip of paper lying in the palm of the hand.

"Is that what I think?" asks Lanzi, leaning in for a closer look.

"I think so," Nardi replies, between a sigh and raising his eyebrows.

"All right! But I'll open it." Stefanini is already wearing a pair of gloves. Nonetheless, he makes use of tweezers to handle the find. He unfolds the card with the utmost care until a new message shows itself.

The style of the text recalls the previous one – another passage from the Bible.

It quotes:

"If your right eye makes you stumble, tear it out and throw it from you; for it is better for you to lose one of the parts of your body, than for your whole body to be thrown into hell. And if your right hand makes you stumble, cut it off and throw it from you; for it is better for you to lose one of the parts of your body, than for your whole body to go into hell."

"Right eye, right hand… He certainly didn't pick at random," Nardi says with a hint of sarcasm.

"I have satisfied you. Now let us work." Stefanini places the slip of paper in a transparent envelope and prepares to affix an identification number. "Up! Get out of here."

"Just a second," Nardi retorts. Pulling his cell phone out of his pocket, he grabs his friend's wrist and lifts it just enough to take a picture of the message. Then, turning to Lanzi, he waves to go and walks to the door without adding anything else.

Once on the street, he grabs his smartphone and rereads the text.

Like the previous one, except for the clear allusions to body parts, it tells him nothing.

If the murderer is trying to communicate, there are still missing pieces to make up the puzzle.

With a series of questions on his mind, Massimo shifts his eyes inside the square. As he sees the well-kept gardens beyond the railing, he recalls the old local market when that place was teeming with stalls and smells and noises. Back then, one only had to walk a few, move a step to go from one nation to another, from one culture to another. Now everything appears quiet, and there is no more clutter, but it is as if that square has lost what made it come alive. Regaining its former beauty, it seems to have lost its soul.

CHAPTER 17

Biological elements, fibers, and various findings have been collected in the apartment. It will take time for them to be analyzed, but initial investigations have allowed a partial reconstruction of the incident. The contamination of the scene by officers did not prevent the detection of several latent prints. The scattered, confusing placement seems to indicate a scuffle that occurred in the bathroom, where footprints were even found on a cabinet and a wall. The man must have caught the woman from behind. Everything suggests that he knocked her unconscious, lifted her up, and carried her to the other room since, from the bathroom to the living room, there is no trace of blood, and the male footprints become more pronounced while her footprints disappear.

Although forensics occupied the apartment for much of the time, Nardi's team nonetheless had its hands full. He and his men spent the last few hours hunting for information about the woman, knocking on apartment building doors and questioning nearby shopkeepers. Unfortunately, no one was able to provide relevant information. Some exchanged a few words with her – little more than a simple good morning or good evening – while others knew her only by sight or knew of her existence because of the name on the intercom.

The only one who was able to provide a useful indication was a food merchant who practices inside the covered market. Not that he revealed who knows what indiscretion; nothing personal about the victim. Their conversations were limited to this or that about his products. According to his words, however, she was a regular customer, showing up every other day, and the last time she set foot in there was five days earlier.

Five days the woman may have spent in the company of her tormentor.

Upon returning to the police station, it is almost noon.

Setting foot in the office, Nardi takes himself to the blackboard to update the information chart.

The sticky note at the top still reads, *"Victim's name,"* with a big question mark beside it.

He draws an X on the question mark and writes, "Juliana Petrescu." He relocates some Post-it notes to the most ideal position, corrects others, and then begins to fill in new ones.

- Residence, Vittorio Emanuele II Square; possible connections to the Twisted Wall?

- Priors for prostitution, extortion, and fraud.

- Last seen: 5 days before death.

- No evidence of conflicts with other condominiums.

- No forced entry marks on the lock. Interior environment apparently in order.

- Right hand found in victim's home.

- First message: found at crime scene (in right eye socket). Gospel, John 8:14

- Second message: found in the apartment. Gospel, Matthew 5:29-30. References to right eye and right hand.

Lanzi has followed the superior like a hound. Without detaching himself from him for a single moment, he stood watching him in silence. Sitting beside him, he whispers, "Could he have had the keys?"

He seems to be talking to himself.

"I beg your pardon?"

"I was thinking about the intact lock. Getting a copy of a pair of keys is certainly not that difficult, but it's also possible that the victim had a relationship with the murderer."

"Possible," Nardi agrees, adding the hypothesis to the board.

"In my opinion, we should not discard the argument of the blackmailed client."

A look of disappointment. In Massimo's eyes, returning to the subject is time wasted. Besides, with the new clues at hand, there is work to be done.

Lanzi intuits on the fly. He hastens to correct his position. "I get that you think the theory doesn't stand up because of the modus operandi. But maybe the guy was already out of his mind. Who knows? Maybe the woman secretly videotaped him, and when she tried to blackmail him, she triggered the spring that made him go completely off the rails."

This time the sergeant's words succeed in breaking through. On Nardi's face, a furrowed brow seems almost to swallow his eyelids, while his irises rise up to stare at the ceiling, and his teeth nibble on his lower lip. "Actually…" he admits later, "it seems like there is a certain logic to it. Although it keeps me a little skeptical, let's add it to the rest."

The file on Juliana Petrescu does not contain enough information to validate or disprove Lanzi's thesis. Nevertheless, the sergeant hints at a satisfied expression as if he has scored a point.

"The first thing to find out is whether or not she was continuing prostitution," Nardi continues. "I would say to start with the old clients. In the record, we have the names of the extortion victims, and they are not many."

"It would be wasted time. Those fell into the net once before, having their money taken out of their pockets. I doubt they are back to take the bait."

"Um! True, so what do you suggest?"

"Let's get the word out among informants. If she was in the business, someone must know."

"All right! You take care of it. Spread the word and see if

anything comes of it."

Nardi turns his back again. His gaze resumes wandering over the blackboard, hunting for hidden details, but nothing seems to rise to the surface.

He is almost on the verge of resignation when his attention falls back on the last line.

- Second message: found in the apartment. Gospel, Matthew 5:29-30. References to right eye and right hand.

"There!" he exclaims. "I had missed it."

"What?" asks the sergeant.

"It probably won't mean anything. However, who knows!"

"What are you referring to?"

"I was reflecting on the last verse. It mentions the eye, and the hand, while the heart is not mentioned."

"So what? Unless that guy wants to rewrite the gospel, he will have to make do with what is written on it. He is the one who chose to communicate by verse."

"Sure, but I wasn't talking about that. The fact that something is missing raises a question. Where did the eye and heart go? He made us find the hand again. Why is there no trace of those?"

"Maybe he just wanted to make the final twist, just for the sake of teasing us. And you have to admit, the note on the couch was a master's touch. Of the rest, bah! He must have gotten rid of them."

"It may be. Or, he took something out just to highlight something else."

"In what sense?"

"If you think about it, it traces the time stages of the crime. The mutilation of the limb occurred before the death. Then the removal of the other organs followed. It gives food for thought. It's likely that the killer attaches special significance to the hand."

"Um! Will it be related to the victim's past? To extortion? Yes, I mean, as if to say she put her hands where she shouldn't have."

The hypothesis appears to support the theory advanced earlier by the sergeant.

"Who knows?" Nardi comments without giving him satisfaction. "For now, let's add it to the notes and see. If more comes up, we'll think about it."

When a phone ring interrupts the exchange of views, he glances at the desk and hesitates to answer. He continues to ponder the latest remarks. The device rings for a long time before he decides to pick up the handset.

"Hello?"

"Nardi? This is Persiani."

"Oh, yes! Good morning!" he replied, tapping his forehead. The mailman had really slipped his mind. "Any news?"

"That's why I was calling you. I wanted to inform you that stolen correspondence was found in Donati's car."

"Good. Can anything relate to my case?"

"I don't know. We still have to compile the list of recovered material. However, he is currently being held here by us. You can drop by to ask him a few questions."

"Damn! You caught me at a bad time."

"Do you want me to call back later?"

"What? Oh, no! I wasn't talking about the phone call. Go figure! It's just that I'm grappling with a far more urgent investigation. The problem is time."

"Ah, I see! Then I'll let you do your work. If anything, I'll get back to you with any updates."

Nardi pounds a fist on the desk. A slight snort accompanies the irritated expression. At the idea that he cannot move, he thinks back to the commissioner's words. He has the impression of seeing him in front of him, pointing his pipe at him like a sharp blade. "I have no choice but to rely on you," he regrets. "Maybe, between confidences, try to get some useful information out of his mouth for my case."

The last words forcefully banish the image of the commissioner, bringing to mind that of Teresa, who seems to remind him what really has priority. The necklace received in an anonymous envelope; the woman killed in the hospital for the sole purpose of embroiling him in that story: everything reminds him how closely the affair affects him. A mysterious figure lurks in the dark, hovering over him, and is inextricably linked to the daughter of his former colleague.

He is about to break off communication when he notices Lanzi holding his arm out and pointing to his wristwatch.

"Excuse me a moment," he says. And bringing a hand to cover the handset, he asks confusedly, "What is it?"

"It's half past noon," Lanzi replies. "You have to eat, right?"

Massimo ponders this for a moment. "Hello?" he then resumes. "Are you still there?"

"Yes, of course."

"Maybe I can make a run during lunch."

"Good! Then I'll wait for you."

CHAPTER 18

The Postal Police Department is located on Trastevere Avenue, about twenty minutes from the Salario-Parioli police station. Wanting to get there as quickly as possible, Nardi sped along the route.

Or almost.

Before reaching his destination, his stomach had taken over. He had been skirting Castel Sant'Angelo when his eyes had swung up and down, jumping from the dome of St. Peter's to a little hawker kiosk on the road just ahead. On seeing fumes and vapors rising into the air, hands of customers grasping drinks and sandwiches, he had not been able to help but indulge in a brief pause. Time to drink a beer and devour a piece of focaccia as he repeated to himself that on a full stomach, he would work better.

Having arrived at the site by now, he crosses an iron gate and parks his car in the small clearing adjacent to the building behind a full array of police cars.

Inside, an officer escorts him to the chief inspector's office.

Walter Persiani, a puny man, rises from his desk and approaches him with a gracious smile upon seeing him enter.

"Good morning, Inspector. It's a pleasure to meet you in person."

"My pleasure."

As they exchange a handshake, Nardi thinks back to the commissioner's pressure regarding the Twisted Wall murder. He has little time, and Angela's case is not a priority. Therefore, he avoids further pleasantries. "Have you discovered anything new?" he asks.

"Only that the allegedly misappropriated material appears to be addressed to a single recipient. These are largely trade journals. Veterinary stuff, it seems."

"What do you mean by alleged?"

"Donati claims to have withdrawn the correspondence at the request of the person directly concerned, one Giovanni Ronconi."

"And you believe him?"

"He seems quite convincing. He didn't try to deny anything. On the contrary! When he realized what it was about, he urged us to contact the man in question. We are just waiting for confirmation."

"Um! That's a little strange. Don't you find?"

"Well, consider that the search of the residence led to nothing. Then the correspondence was found inside the car, stacked in the trunk. We thought we had hit the jackpot, but it was a washout."

"And what did he say? Did he explain why he was collecting mail for this Ronconi?"

"It appears that the veterinarian has moved. But he still owns the old home and continues to receive mail there."

"I understand. I don't care much about this matter anyway," Nardi cuts it short. "As you know, the case I'm dealing with is quite different, and the answer I'm looking for concerns only a specific letter. The one from which we traced to Donati."

"I know, Inspector. I'm the one who told you to come by, remember? He is now waiting in the other room, but only as a person of interest. Given the situation, no charges have been filed."

It couldn't have gone better. That means no lawyers in the

way to complicate things.

"Can I ask him some questions?"

"Sure, come along! I'll accompany you."

Leaving the office, they cross a short corridor. Persiani points to a room just ahead. The door is open, and he waves for him to enter.

Donati is quietly sitting in front of a table. He is a man in his early thirties. His shaved head, a hint of a beard under his chin, thick eyebrows, and a hard gaze hint at a person who is not at all conciliatory.

"Mr. Donati, this is Inspector Nardi. He would like to ask you some questions. Do you have any objection to that?"

"For me, you can ask whatever you want," the man replies grumpily.

"Very well," Nardi interjects. "You are free not to answer if you see fit. My investigation has nothing to do with what is happening here." He could have held the interview outside those walls as well. Questioning witnesses to hunt for clues is part of his job. Nevertheless, having the suspect in a room to himself, and querying him off the record, is a good way to play his cards. Discerning the lie will certainly be easier. That is why he bothered to repeat the magic little words – *you are free not to answer* – because often, what matters is precisely the unsaid.

"I have nothing to hide, "Donati reiterates. "Ask me these questions. Just make it quick. I want to go home."

"I'll try to be brief." Taking a seat on the other side of the table, Nardi begins to scan the man's face. "You see, what I'm investigating is a murder case. And one of the clues available to us, well, it does seem to lead to you." He pauses slightly. With his eyes fixed on Donati, he waits for his reaction. The other, however, merely observes him with the annoyed air he had just before. "Don't you care to know what this is all about?"

"I'm waiting for you to tell me. You said you wanted to ask me something, didn't you? Then speak up! Or do I have to guess for myself?"

"You're right. Excuse me," Massimo justifies himself. And

151

realizing that curiosity is not enough to move the man, he changes his approach. "I will try to be clearer. We found a bloody letter that connected to the case I was talking about. Well, prints were found inside. Yours, Mr. Donati. So, I would like to understand how they got there."

"What on earth are you talking about?"

"You want me to believe you don't know anything about it?"

"That's right. I have no idea."

"Yet, the fingerprints say otherwise."

The dactyloscopy examination yielded an eighty percent positive match, but this Donati does not know. Massimo plays the bluff. Not least because, given the man's job, a postal clerk, the margin for error is reduced by quite a bit.

"I'll tell you again. I don't know anything about bloody letters."

"Inside the torn envelope, though, were your fingerprints."

"I beg your pardon?"

"What language am I speaking? We found your…"

"No, no! First. Did you say a torn envelope?"

"Yes, why?"

"Ah! All right, then! I get it now."

"What do you mean?"

"It happened a short time ago. I was delivering the mail as usual, and I don't know how, that envelope got torn. I merely tucked it back in and sent it back. Those are the rules."

"And what do you tell me about the blood?"

"Nothing. I didn't pay any attention to it. If it was there, I didn't see it."

Donati's attitude is not that of someone who fears being exposed. He seems more like a dog ready to bite, eager to get to the point and clear up any doubts.

In addition, his version of events turns out to be plausible, and Nardi finds no reason to doubt it.

Lending credence to what he says is the evidence itself: partial prints on the outside of the envelope and on the top edge of the photo. If the sender was really him, they would have found more of them on the inside and the underside of the picture. It would be absurd to think that after using gloves, Donati then went back to touch the paper with his bare hands.

By now, it is clear. The one in front of him is not his man. So he gets back on his feet and hints at a grimace of resignation. He hoped to find out something, but that trail led nowhere.

"All right," he says bitterly. "There must have been a mistake. Thank you for clearing up my doubts."

Intending to take his leave, he glances at Persiani when the same officer who accompanied him on arrival appears across the threshold with a man in tow.

"Chief Inspector, this is Mr. Ronconi. He decided to drop by in person."

"Oh, good! You can go, thanks," Persiani replies. And turning to the newcomer, he adds, "Please come in. You didn't need to come all the way here. But anyway, thank you."

"No problem. When you called me, I was just a stone's throw away, so I came straight through."

Now convinced that the fact does not concern him, Massimo is not interested in witnessing the conversation. Regardless, he waits patiently, waiting for Persiani to get rid of those two. It would be rude to leave without a handshake.

"Finally!" Donati exclaims, looking relieved. "You tell them, Mr. Ronconi. These people don't believe me."

"Do you know each other?" Persiani turns a glance to Ronconi as he points to the other.

"Yes, why?"

"Some correspondence addressed to you, Mr. Ronconi, was found in his car. He claims to have picked it up at your request. Can you confirm this?"

"That's right! I moved out a while ago, but I haven't made the change of residence. You know, I still use the old house from time to time. But I rarely go there, so I asked Sandro to pick up my mail. I've known him for a long time. And it doesn't cost him anything since he delivers it."

"Are you satisfied now? Can I leave?" Donati asks.

"Certainly. Sorry to both of you for the inconvenience." Persiani recalls the officer, instructing him to do the bureaucratic paperwork, and invites the two to follow him. "One signature for the report, and you can consider the matter closed."

Donati does not fail to cast one last glare. Even as he leaves the room to turn into the hallway, he mumbles something unintelligible.

Nardi's mouth manages a smile from his comical attitude that's developed.

"What a strange fellow," he says when the man is too far away to hear his words.

"Oh, yeah!" admits Persiani. "There are quite a few around."

"I'm sorry. Apparently, I just wasted your time."

"Don't worry. Although he was able to provide justification this time, our investigation is still open. And among the subjects we are keeping an eye on is him."

"Well, in that case, I hope you find what you are looking for."

"If there is any news, I will let you know."

"Thank you." Feigning gratitude for his willingness to keep him informed, Massimo bids farewell and heads for the exit. At this point, he no longer has any interest in knowing the developments in that operation. If Donati is guilty of anything, it is certainly not about his case.

CHAPTER 19

July 8, afternoon, 3:00 p.m.

After making a trip for nothing, Nardi is running out of patience. By nature, he is an optimistic type of person, but at the moment, he can only see the negative side of what is happening. Fatigue prevents him from thinking clearly. He struggles to keep his eyes open; the headache has resumed hammering him, and he just wants to go home to enjoy a good night's sleep. But the day is still long, and the bed will have to wait.

He doubts any new information has come to light in his brief absence. At any rate, upon returning to the police station, he goes to the deputy's office, and discharging his discontent on him, he grumpily asks, "Did you do the checks I asked for?"

"Which ones are you referring to?"

"What do you mean, *which ones?* Come on! Are you sleeping in here?"

"You have given me several assignments," Cataldo points out. "If you specify which one you're talking about..."

"You're right," Nardi interrupts, realizing he was out of line. "I'm so sorry. I have a migraine that's driving me crazy."

"Don't worry."

"By the way, do you happen to have an aspirin?"

"No, sorry."

"Patience. I'll deal with my headache."

"However, if you were referring to what you had asked before you left, I prepared a short file for you."

"Um! Help me out. What did I ask you?"

"You were interested in the symbolic meanings on…"

"Ah, okay! I got it. And where is it?"

"In your office. You can find it on the desk."

"Thank you. I'll go take a look."

The deputy hints at a smile, but pretending is not his strong suit. Embarrassment can be seen on his face. He is clearly hurt by the unwarranted rant.

"Sorry again about earlier," Nardi repeats, leaving the room.

Reaching his own office, he drops into his chair. A widespread pain moves from one side of his skull to the other, and he huffs in annoyance and raises his hands to his forehead, and closes his eyes. He stays like this for about twenty seconds until a soft knock at the door alerts him that he is not alone. When he lifts his eyelids again, he sees the sergeant standing firm on the threshold.

Without opening his mouth, Massimo waves to come in and recomposes himself.

"How did it go at the Postal Police?" asks Lanzi, stepping forward and making himself comfortable. "Discover anything interesting?"

"Forget about it! It was just a waste of time. The letter carrier readily admitted that he had handled the letter. He had nothing to do with the rest of the matter."

Briefly summarizing what happened, he explains how Donati's fingerprints had ended up on the letter and how he had convincingly justified the incident, enough to oust him from the list of suspects.

"Too bad!" Lanzi hints at a grimace. "It seemed like the right track."

"Yeah, I thought so, too."

"If you had known earlier, you would have enjoyed your lunch in peace."

Feeling like a fool, Massimo pretends to ignore the sergeant's words. Convinced that he was stealing time from the investigation, he had eaten in a hurry, with a sense of guilt, and now the thought infuriates him.

"About the other investigation," Lanzi continued, "while you were away, I talked to a couple of informants. I told them to get the word out and keep their ears open. If Juliana Petrescu was still in the prostitution business, something will come out."

"We'll see! In the meantime, we'll make do with what we have. Did you find out anything about Silvia Rigoni?"

"I had the juvenile court contacted to get some information, but for now..."

"Okay, okay! I understand. We will have to wait."

With the Angela Brunetti affair set aside, Nardi dives back into the case of the Twisted Wall.

Glancing at a file lying in plain sight on his desk, he thinks it must be the one the deputy was referring to and begins to leaf through it curiously. "Cataldo got us some material," he says. "Symbolic meanings related to the parts removed from the victim."

"Did you find any connections?"

"Give me time to read."

"Oh! I thought you had already done that."

"Here, take a look at it too," he replies, pushing a couple of papers to the other side of the desk. "Let's see if we can find a key to decipher those messages."

Both unaware of what they are looking for, they begin to view the papers.

Absorbed in the reading, they remain silent for about ten minutes until Nardi speaks up. "On the hand, the interpretations are varied. It is seen as representing strength, dominance, and power but also as a sign of loyalty and trust. In divine art, instead, it is traced back to God and would stand for the hand of justice."

"Certainly, positive values do not fit the profile. But even if we want to consider the rest, we're back to square one."

157

Ignoring the retort, Nardi frowns and focuses his attention on the next paragraph. "This is interesting," he says. "The hand of Fatima. An ancient symbol widespread among Middle Eastern cultures. You know it? It is often seen on costume jewelry stalls. A hand with an eye in the center."

"And why should it concern our case?"

"Well, the last verse does mention those two body parts."

"Ah! Because of the eye and hand? But it doesn't seem like much of a clue. It's easier to think of these randomly."

"Apparently, the symbol has been adopted by monotheistic religions. Muslims, Jews, and Eastern Christians... all connect it to the number five, like the fingers of a hand. In fact, the amulet is known as *Hamsa*, which in Arabic means precisely five. And every religion links the number with relevant themes."

"I am not following you. Where is all this supposed to take us?"

"First of all, there is an analogy with the Bible," Massimo replies, standing up. "I suppose there is a reason if he uses it as a means of communication. Anyway, what interests me most is the number five." Moving to the side of the room, he points his finger at the blackboard, indicating the Post-it note with the last verse, and says, "Matthew, chapter five, verses twenty-nine and thirty."

"Ah, all right! I'm beginning to understand."

"Perhaps the key to interpretation is not in the text, but in the ciphers."

"It could be. There are two cheat sheets, though. And on the other one there is no trace of the number five."

Nardi turns to look at the blackboard, reading the first message.

"Even if I testify about Myself, My testimony is valid, because I know where I came from and where I am going. But you do not know where I came from or where I am going."

John 8:14

"Um! You're right. Also, this doesn't even refer to any body part. Did you find anything on there? Anything that would support the theory?"

"No. The heart is mentioned here, and even it is given multiple meanings. But there is no mention of numbers."

"And as a symbol, what would it mean?"

"Oh! From what it explains here, the Bible is full of it. It seems that the word is rarely used to refer to the organ in the physical sense. Mostly, it would express understanding, memory, knowledge and feelings… the meanings are many. In essence, it is supposed to represent man in his totality. It is saying everything and the opposite of everything. I don't think it serves much purpose."

"Let's see if we have better luck with the eye." Nardi returns to his seat and grabs the papers to pick up where he left off. "Mhmm. This also has archaic origins," he says, beginning to read aloud. "Among the ancient Egyptians, the eyes of *Horus* were considered the two boats on which the sun god *Ra* and the moon made their journeys between day and night. The symbol of the *eye of Ra* was attributed with the god's powers, particularly that of awareness, knowledge, and transformation. The amulet was seen as an omen of new life and rebirth."

"Yes, all right," interrupts Lanzi. "Interesting for a history lesson, but it doesn't seem very relevant to the case."

"Who knows! The fact that it talks about rebirth… Anyway, the most common interpretation seems to be the divine eye that sees everything. Even the Bible speaks of it as the eye of God and…" Leaving the sentence unsaid, Nardi arches his eyebrows and stares at the page with renewed interest.

"What is it?" asks the sergeant.

"This is interesting," he replies. "Here, it talks about Christian iconography. From the Renaissance on, the eye was depicted inside a triangle in reference to the Trinity. The equilateral triangle would be the geometric equivalent of the number three, the universal symbol of perfection."

"I don't think we're on the right track. The first note quotes John, chapter eight – the second, Matthew, chapter five. The number three does not correspond to either one or the other. Besides, you said it yourself! The opening verse does not make the slightest mention of any part of the body."

"Do you think it's a waste of time?"

Lanzi merely sketches a half-grimace.

Nevertheless, Nardi persists. "Maybe it may seem a little absurd," he says. "However, eight is the sum of three and five."

"But come on Chief! Adding up random numbers doesn't get us anymore."

"I know it sounds silly, but the guy is crazy. To get inside his head, we must be crazier than he is."

"What do you want me to say? I would understand it if…"

For no apparent reason, Lanzi goes silent all of a sudden. A half-closed hand grasps his lips while his eyes zigzag in the air.

"If…?" Nardi urges.

"You know what? Maybe you have a point. I hadn't thought about it, but we left out a significant detail."

"Meaning?"

"We did not take into account *where* the first note was found. That verse doesn't mention body parts, but it is still true that the murderer took care to have us find it inside the eye socket."

"Right! And since he left the other one in the center of the hand, just like that amulet, it's possible that the hypothesis is well-founded."

"Who knows?" Lanzi frowns and hesitates. "But even if so, what could those numbers indicate?"

"Maybe these are just the first pieces to solve the puzzle. Three, five, eight…" Unable to follow up on the reasoning, Nardi feels ridiculous. At the moment, it is idiotic to seek an answer to that question.

Seized by discomfort, he then observes his colleague surreptitiously and begins bow his head when coming to his rescue is the ringing of the telephone.

He hurries to pick up the handset with fear that the caller may hang up before time.

"Hello?" he asks, relieved.

160

"Oh, Massimo! At last! Where have you been?"

Teresa has caught him off guard. Over the past few days, she has called him several times, but he has always been careful not to answer. He did not feel like telling her that the investigation had not made a single step forward. Moreover, seeing her or even hearing from her forcibly brings him back to that distant memory that, if he could, he would erase from his own past. For a moment, he is tempted to hang up. Instead, searching for a congenial tone of voice, he says, "Hello, Teresa. Sorry, I haven't been in touch. I've been pretty busy and haven't found time to call you."

As his former colleague's voice rings out on the other side, he thinks back to that arrogant, in some ways bizarre, letter carrier and almost feels a sense of gratitude. After all, it was not all wasted time. At the very least, he now has something to talk about, even if it is only a lead that ended in a vacuum.

HELL – ACT IV

The darkness of the night has fallen to engulf the rooftops of the city. It breaks against the light of street lamps on a deserted and apparently motionless street. Only the fleeting appearance of a cat, the leaves of the trees, and the clothes being spread out stirred by the wind break its sense of stillness. Except for the pair of lovers holed up inside a car.

Protected by the darkness, they continue to exchange loving effusions for several minutes. They feel safe, convinced that they are alone. They do not imagine that he is there, not far away, and keeps his eyes fixed on them.

As he watches them from the cockpit of his Panda, he feels a certain restlessness. He already knows that he will have to wait longer before he can act, and he is beginning to grow impatient. He has been tailing them all evening, from the moment they went out to dinner. At first, he followed them to a restaurant in the suburbs, an inconvenient location to reach. The perfect place to avoid unwanted encounters. Clearly, a choice made by the man, who, unlike his date, has a wife to answer to.

Determined not to lose sight of them, he occupied a table across the room and ordered like any other customer while waiting for the romantic dinner to end. Outside the restaurant, he then resumed tailing them on the way back, and now, after a brief stop in the downtown parts, they are back where they started: all three of them under the woman's apartment.

Judging in hindsight, he could have spared himself the stalking. However, he had to make sure the couple returned rather than spend the night in some hotel room. Otherwise, he would have been forced to put it off until another time. But it doesn't matter. Everything is proceeding as planned, and that's what is important.

Finally, the doors of the vehicle open. The two of them get out.

Lying on the seat, he remains still, merely following them with his gaze as they reach the doorway just ahead. Quickly the woman seems to almost disappear before his eyes, as his attention focuses entirely on the man. Ready to hunt, he studies him like a feline. He is the one who is his prey.

His prey is a well-groomed, good-looking fellow. He's long past fifty, yet he seems to keep himself in better shape than many 30-year-olds. Perhaps he is going through a midlife crisis, and that relationship is an attempt to escape a gray life. Or, a more likely hypothesis, he is just one of those people who cheat on their wives, heedless of the consequences, convinced that there would be none. After all, he is used to keeping his foot in two stirrups; he is a lawyer. And lawyers, it is known, are all the same: they lie by profession. They lie to others and also to themselves. But most of all, like any husband, they lie to their wives when a mistress is involved, even though they always return to them in the end.

As he sees him disappear inside the building, he thinks about this. That guy cares about family tranquility. He never spends the entire night away from home. As much as he loves to have a good time and indulges in his escapades, he always returns to the fold. So, he will wait for him on the way out. He will let him satiate the pleasure of meat one last time, after which he will be his.

He glances at his watch. In spite of the late hour and the empty street, he pulls up his hood. By now, it's something of a ritual. And by the way, he doesn't want to run the risk that carelessness will nullify his efforts so far. The police are certainly on his trail, and he cannot afford any mistakes. He already made a mistake once, a long time ago. He won't do it a second time.

After all, that is the cause of it all, what drives the yearning for justice: a wrong choice. It was enough to mark the course of his life, and he will never stop regretting it.

Sooner or later, he will have to answer for that mistake, but not before each of the responsible parties has paid their own price. Unlike them, he does not fear the moment he will have to be held accountable; on the contrary, he looks forward to it. In the silence of the night, he even has the impression of hearing its call. It is a sense of guilt that echoes in his head in the form of an accusation. And for everything to cease, he hopes to put an end to it as soon as possible.

Oppressed by that torment, he does not notice how fast the hands are ticking until his gaze falls back on the clock and he remembers what he came for. It has been a long time now. The man could come out at any moment. So, he turns the key to start the engine, gears up, drives forward to where the lawyer's car is parked, and stops double-parked to obstruct its passage.

Lying on the seat on the side is a small bag with everything needed. He takes out the gauze and the bottle of anesthetic and leaves the rest there.

Before moving, he rotates his gaze around himself. Although he is on a dead-end street frequented only by those who live there, he still wants to make sure he is alone. Someone could always come back late.

Seeing that no one appears, he decides to get out of the car. He casts one last glance upward, looking for any onlookers. After that, he covers the short distance that separates him from the man's car, leans against the hood, and stands waiting for the other man to show up.

Above the streetlights, it is total darkness. Not even a lighted window indicates any sign of life. Still, a sense of insecurity continues to keep him on edge. Having to act in the open exposes him to the unexpected, and he would have preferred to avoid it, but it is the option that best suits his purposes. The only one capable of pulling the wool over the police's eyes.

Not at all happy with the choice, he wonders if the wait will have to last long.

Time seems to dilate.

About ten minutes pass before the click of a lock breaks the silence. The clanking sound spreads through the air, followed by the creaking of the door.

Standing still with his back turned, he avoids turning around. Although he wants to, he limits himself to peeking out of the corner of his eye. Finally, he catches sight of the man emerging from the building. He then turns the display of his cell phone towards himself, extends the camera's lens just enough to frame him, and observes him as he approaches.

Seeing him advance casually, with a smirk contouring his face, he wants to tell him what awaits him. If only he imagined that he was going to meet his death, his expression would be quite different. Oh yes, he would really want to anticipate his fate. Instead, he merely takes a picture to capture that instant. Who knows! Maybe he will show it to him later, reminding him that he has taken more from life than he should have.

Feeling his anxiety rising, he looks around for the umpteenth time. He tilts his cell phone, framing the buildings behind him. Some windows are open, but not the slightest hint of light escapes from inside. Therefore, he turns off the camera, pulls the phone up to his ear, and, taking to speaking in a low voice, pretends to be engaged in conversation.

He lifts one shoulder to support the smartphone so his hands are free. He pulls a pair of gauze pads out of his pocket. He soaks them with anesthetic and stands ready to act.

"Excuse me! Can you please move?" he hears shortly after. "I need to get out."

On his part, there is no response.

"Hey, I'm talking to you!" the other insists.

He ignores him by continuing to simulate the phone call.

The man approaches and, annoyed, raises his hand and snaps his fingers a few times. "Did you hear me? If you could do me the courtesy of getting out of my car and moving yours, I'll get out and let you have the spot."

"Huh? What?" he exclaims, trying to appear surprised. "Oh, I'm sorry! I didn't hear you. I'll move right away."

That is all he wanted: to induce his victim to step forward so that he would turn his back to the car door.

Satisfied, he then pretends to head toward the Panda, giving the lawyer just enough time to turn around. Bent over the door, his prey is about to climb aboard. That is when he grabs him around the neck. Pulling him to himself, he lifts the blindfold to cover his nose and mouth.

However, this time he has to deal with a man, a robust one at that, and the advantage of surprise does not seem to be enough to overwhelm him. On the contrary! He is caught unprepared by the alertness with which he sees him react. In fact, without giving in to fright, this one almost manages to wriggle out of the way and tip him back to the ground. He is just in time to place a foot on the side of the car, leverage his leg and push himself back. With all his energy, he goes back to tightening his grip, clutching his opponent with a calf to keep him from playing any more tricks. "Come on! Be still," he says, slurring his words because of his strained abs. "You'll see that in a few seconds, it will all be over."

Though unable to move, upon hearing those words, the other takes to writhing and moaning and tries to shake off that hand that presses overwhelmingly against his mouth. Soon, however, his strength leaves him. Unable to resist any longer, he slumps down.

Although he sees him unconscious, he continues to put pressure on the bandage. The man may be faking it, and he does not want to take the risk of finding out.

Meanwhile, he takes the opportunity to recover from the strain and, letting go of the tension, catches his breath.

When he finally decides to move, he drags the lawyer's body up to the Panda and lays it inside the trunk.

Retrieving the bag from the front seat, he pulls out the duct tape, tears off a piece to apply on the mouth, and wraps his wrists and ankles. Then he spots one end of the rope sticking out of the bag. He thought he would not use it – last time, it proved to be an unnecessary precaution – but instead, he pulls it out. The man was about to overpower him, and it is best to be cautious.

He ties him properly before spreading a heavy cloth to cover the body.

Having closed the tailgate, he climbs into the car and lifts his gaze one last time. He sees nothing suspicious, and yet, he continues to wonder if anyone might have witnessed the scene. A question that accompanies him as he drives off into the night.

CHAPTER 20

On the day of the murder, everything happened too quickly. Between finding the body, searching the victim's house, and taking statements from neighbors, there was no time to stop and think. So, the next morning, Nardi decided to go to the Twisted Wall in search of clues. With a fresh mind and a hint of tranquillity, he hoped to catch some missing aspect of the story, but it turned out to be a vain hope. Returning to the crime scene proved to be just a waste of time. By now, he has been there with Lanzi for over half an hour, and nothing new has turned up.

Casting a glance through the bushes, Massimo thinks back to the chilling scene he faced, to the woman's battered body, and wonders what could drive a person to such ferocity. No guilt, assuming there was any, would justify such an end.

The greatest fear is the belief that the culprit will strike again. That is certainly the work of a madman, and madness knows no limits or inhibitions.

Even the choice of location shows a kind of recklessness. Opting for such a busy area, lacking shelter from prying eyes, exposed the killer to no small risk.

"What do you think? Why would he have brought her here? I doubt he chose a random place."

"Who knows!" Lanzi looks around. "Maybe he just wanted to make sure the body was found quickly."

"Um! I don't think so. There is a constant flow of cars here. It's too exposed, even at that time of night. He could have chosen a less visible location and played it safe. If he preferred to take the risk, he must have had a good reason."

"Perhaps it has a special meaning for him. To know for sure, one must be inside his head."

Unable to come up with a rebuttal, Nardi turns to observe the road leading up the hill. "Let's try to look in the section where the cameras are. The car must have passed through there."

"What should we be looking for?"

"Who knows? Maybe nothing," he replies, starting toward the car. "But since we're here, we might as well check it out."

"If you say so..." mutters Lanzi, walking in tow. "To me, we're just wasting time."

Once aboard, they begin to climb up the roadway. They advance to the height of Porta Pinciana, where the sergeant, driving the vehicle, slows down almost to a stop. "And now?" he asks.

Without looking for anything specific, Massimo turns his gaze here and there. "Mhmm..." he mutters, glancing at a pair of cameras not far away. "I wonder if there's anything useful in the footage?"

"So, what do I do?" urges Lanzi. "Do I go straight or turn?"

From there, the road forks, then branch out further like a spider web.

"Well! Maybe you're right," he resigns himself. "It's useless to waste any more time."

"Shall we go back to the police station?"

Nardi feels a certain languor in his stomach. That idle searching has stirred his appetite. Moreover, it is almost lunchtime: the clock on the dashboard reads twelve twenty. "Shall we have a bite to eat first?"

"Sure. I know a café where you can spend very little. It's just a stone's throw away, and they make delicious sandwiches."

"Well, okay then. If the food is good, let's go there."

***

Lanzi was no joke. The place is just a few blocks away. From the open space where it is located, you can see the arches of Porta Pinciana and the upper part of the Twisted Wall.

It is a beautiful summer day. The few outdoor tables are all occupied. Convinced they have to settle for an indoor seat, they are about to go inside when a young couple gets up and pays the bill.

They hurry to take their seats.

As soon as he is seated, Lanzi looks at the menu and tries to strike up a conversation about food. Nardi, however, is absorbed in his own reasoning and pretends not to hear. Thus, while waiting to be served, they remain silent.

Irritated by how slowly the investigation is proceeding, Massimo would like to find an instant answer to all his doubts. He continues to ask himself questions he already knows he cannot answer, which puts him in an even worse mood. It makes him feel like an idiot.

He perseveres for a few more minutes. Then, determined to put an end to the useless expenditure of energy, he begins to look around for any entertainment.

Attention falls on a group of tourists, about thirty feet away, stopping at the side of the road. Rome is always full of them, especially this time of year, and recognizing them is easy. The way they dress, the sun hats, the backpacks on their shoulders, or a map of the city in their hands make them almost folkloric, at least in his eyes.

Entertaining them is a tour guide, a woman who won't stop talking. Among the many voices, hers is like a continuous hum. Convinced that since their arrival, she has not been silent for a moment, he wonders if the place is hiding something singular because nothing of what he sees seems to merit such a detailed description.

Won over by curiosity, he starts listening to her. At first, he struggles to understand what she is talking about. Then he realizes she is referring to the Twisted Wall and its history. As the woman continues in her narration, he is amazed at the amount of information he is unaware of. He must have passed through there hundreds of times, yet all he ever saw in those ramparts was a pile of tufa and bricks degraded by time. And it certainly never occurred to him to wonder why that name.

Apparently, in ancient times, a subsidence at the base had brought down an entire block of the wall, giving part of the structure the crooked, leaning shape that earned it the designation of the *Leaning Wall.*

Built in the time of Emperor Aurelian, many nicknames have accompanied that wall; however, tickling Massimo's fancy is one in particular: *Evil Wall*, an epithet affixed to it between medieval times and the early 1800s because of the succession of violence and misfortunes.

According to the tour guide, that area has always had a reputation for being cursed. The land in front would house a kind of deconsecrated cemetery, where for centuries, the executed, the unrepentant dead, actors and acrobats, thieves and murderers and prostitutes were buried, ending with the murder of two Republican Carbonari, convicted without evidence or trial, guillotined by the papal executioner. According to popular rumors, their ghosts would wander near the walls every night with their heads under their arms.

Between history and legend, it was said that the body of Emperor Nero – the antichrist, according to early Christians – was thrown there and that his spirit continued to roam there in the company of evil spirits. The area is supposed to house a kind of gateway to the afterlife, created precisely to plunge him into hell.

Thinking back to the biblical verses, Massimo wonders if the choice of location is not related to those stories. Perhaps it is an additional message from the killer. After all, the similarities to

Christianity, the heinous way in which the victim was killed, as well as the fact that she was a prostitute make it all plausible.

The unexpected insight seems to push him toward an imprecise goal. As if he had made who knows what steps forward, he feels closer to the culprit. Without even realizing it, he tries to put a face to him, wondering what past he may have behind him. In his mind appears the faded figure of a lonely, fragile child, perhaps born of an incestuous relationship. He imagines him as someone who has been discriminated against and mocked for years, who has finally found a way to say enough is enough. Furthermore, the heinousness of the crime, that mutilating of victims both alive and dead, juxtaposes the pleasure of torture with an absolute quest for dominance, but at the same time suggests an outlet, a kind of revenge.

The imagination has now taken to traveling on its own, and what goes through his head only contributes to distancing him from reality. The only sensible hypothesis is the one that would explain why the killer chose that place. Massimo turns his gaze to his colleague. Determined to ask his opinion, he begins to speak, but just then, the bartender arrives.

"Sorry for the wait. What can I get you?"

"It's about time!" exclaims Lanzi. "A sandwich with smoked salmon, arugula, and cherry tomatoes."

"And for you?"

Caught up with everything else until just now, Nardi did not even glance at the menu. "Huh? Yes, just a moment."

"Listen to me, Inspector. Try the salmon one. I've had it before and, I guarantee you, it's delicious."

"Hmm! All right. Then bring two of those."

"Inspector? Are you policemen?"

"So they say. I hope it's not a problem," Nardi ironizes.

"I don't mean to pry into your business, but… Are you by any chance here because of that incident yesterday?"

"Why?" Nardi changes his attitude. The smile slides off his face. "Do you know anything about it?"

"I don't, but…"

"But what?"

"Well, here's… There's one person who may have seen something."

"What does 'may have' mean? And why didn't you inform us right away? Anyway, never mind. Who would that be?"

"An immigrant. He hangs around there at night. We know each other now, and he has confided in me, but to go to the police, he didn't want to get involved. He is without a residence permit, and, as you can imagine, he is afraid."

"What did he say to you?"

"Only that he saw someone at the place where the body was found."

"Do you know where we can find him?"

"Is he going to get into trouble? I mean, the fact that he's not in compliance…"

"We are not from immigration. I don't care about his papers. I just want to know what he saw."

"Ah, good! Because I would have felt bad. I'll call him right away. He's right over there." The man turns, takes a few steps forward, and whistles. "Hey, Faruq!" he shouts.

Across the street, an itinerant seller, a tall, slim African man, tries to entice some tourists to buy his wares. Hearing his name mentioned, he answers the call with a nod.

The bartender returns to approach the table and waves his hand. "Come here for a moment."

The peddler looks around to make sure he is not letting a good customer slip through his fingers, and he begins to advance. He carries a shoulder bag crammed with items, wears bracelets and necklaces to show off his merchandise, and lets souvenir T-shirts dangle from one arm.

Perhaps he thinks the friend has provided him with potential buyers because he approaches with a sly expression. An expression that disappears as soon as he reaches them when the bartender, turning to speak again, says, "They are from the police."

The man suddenly stiffens.

173

"Don't worry; they won't give you any trouble. They just want to know what you saw."

"That's right! Don't worry!" confirms Massimo.

Stepping forward, Faruq stands there looking at him in silence and hints at a shy smile as if asking permission. He seems to be pondering what to do.

"Take it easy," Massimo repeats, intent on putting him at ease. "I'm only interested in knowing what you know. Come! Sit down."

The other obeys with a submissive attitude. He reclines in a chair without saying anything.

"So… Is it true that you saw someone on the night of the murder?"

Faruq's eyes jump from Nardi to Lanzi to the bartender. He hesitates a few more moments. Then he shakes his head in confirmation.

"Can you describe him?" Nardi asks eagerly.

Yet another exchange of guarded glances. A sigh. And finally, the mouth opens. Faruq decides to break the silence. *"Too dark. Him look like shadow."*

The man knows little of the language but speaks just enough to make himself understood.

"But did you see him leaving the body?"

"No. Me see car that park and he go on grass. Me think him pee."

"What about the car? Did you get a good look at it?"

"Yes, I saw good. Car small. What's calling? Panta, Banda? No, no, Panda! All black."

"Are you sure?"

"Yes, yes! Me remember well, no mistake. Front light is off and me think is scooter. Then me understand is car."

"That is, it had a broken light?"

"Broken light, yes. Right light off, but other one on."

This narrows the field quite a bit. If the information is accurate, it will be easy to identify the vehicle from the video footage.

"I thank you. You have been very helpful." Massimo pulls

out his wallet and hands Faruq a twenty-euro bill. "Here! Drink to my health."

"Me no drink."

"Bravo, you do well. Alcohol kills."

Faruq is certainly not an informant, so much as a person with knowledge of the facts. As a matter of procedure, Nardi is supposed to bring him to the station for a deposition, but he already knows it would get him in trouble, and he has no intention of going back on his word. He will say he received the tip from a confidential source, so he will not be required to reveal his identity. After all, this is not the first time he lies, and it certainly won't be the last.

CHAPTER 21

Four days. That's all it took for the killer to strike again.

Nardi had predicted it. He knew that more blood would be shed. He was just waiting for it to happen after Juliana Petrescu's murder.

He expected it, in other words, but certainly not like this: same place, same time – a real slap in the face for him and the entire police force.

Having gotten out of the car, he has the impression that he is witnessing a bad replica of a show already seen. The gloomy environment and that stench of death hovering in the air, the high walls towering over the scene like a silent witness. Everything appears identical. A surreal atmosphere into which he ventures with small steps while continuing to look around perplexed. Apparently, the guy he is chasing is far crazier than expected. He knew he could not stop him in time, just as he was sure the man would shed more blood. However, he did not imagine that this one would go that far. After what happened, surveillance in the area was intensified, patrol cars doubled, and yet, it was not enough to stop him. He risked getting caught just to throw down a gauntlet.

Unfortunately, Faruq's help was of little use. Although video footage confirmed that the suspect was driving a black Panda with a broken front light, the license plate had been adequately concealed. In addition, in all shots, the driver kept his head bent over the steering wheel to hide his face. There was no way to trace the vehicle, let alone the person driving it.

The autopsy on the first victim did not help much either. Besides confirming what the medical examiner had expected, it determined that what was found in the lungs was fresh water, tap water, to be exact. Based on hardness, between calcium and magnesium concentration, and the remaining chemical parameters, forensic analysts were able to determine its source. Despite this, the attempt to confine the investigation to a specific area soon proved to be a vain hope. The Peschiera aqueduct is the largest in Rome, and about seventy percent of the water poured into the capital's water network every day comes from there.

Every road seems to lead to a dead end in this case! That's not all. To add insult to injury, Massimo's gaze falls on the marker tapes placed to mark the area. New ones have been put up to replace the ones from last time, which are now scattered on the ground, useless. The culprit must have torn them off as he passed by, and who knows if it was the victim's own body that dragged them along.

Just ahead, Stefanini is engaged in conversation with some forensic men. He points to the right and left, giving directions on what to do.

"Have you discovered anything?" Nardi asks as he walks past him.

"Hey, about time!" his friend exclaims when he sees him. "No, nothing new so far. The footprints on the ground look the same, and so do the tire tracks. But beyond that..."

"Okay. I'll let you work," he cuts it short, moving straight ahead. He's not really in the mood to exchange useless chatter. It's the second murder in a short time, and being told what he already knows irritates him even more.

To increase the nervousness, the presence of those vultures of the press. Even keeping them at a distance, escaping them is virtually impossible. In seeing them lurking with their cameras, Nardi has the impression they are ready to open fire on a target. Those lenses conceal prying eyes, and they all point in one direction, the same direction he is heading towards.

On the prosecutor's side, there are Lanzi and a third man. Seeing all three of them with their backs turned, he wonders if they are analyzing the crime scene or trying, in turn, to disentangle themselves from the intrusiveness of the reporters.

As he approaches, the first voice to reach his ears is the sergeant's. Judging by the tone, he sounds annoyed.

"…my opinion matters little. I know! It just doesn't feel right, though."

"It is useless to keep talking about it. It's decided by now," Amanda Mellis replies. "And it's not my choice anyway."

"Choice of what?" intrudes Massimo.

Taken by surprise, the three turn around simultaneously.

The man to the deputy prosecutor's right, a stocky guy with a pockmarked face, lifts a hand just enough to show his palm. The hint of a greeting. "Hey there, Nardi! Long time no see."

"And you? What are you doing here?" Nardi asks in wonder.

"I see no one has informed you, huh?" the other replies in a sarcastic tone.

"Informed me of what?"

"We of the Mobile Squad are taking over. By now, the serial killer thing is no longer a wild guess, and the police commissioner, well, you can imagine."

"Inspector Paolini will be in charge of directing the operation." Prosecutor Mellis lowers her gaze and hesitates for a moment. "However, you and your team will support him in the investigation," she clarifies. "Having handled the case from the beginning, your help will be useful."

Guido Paolini is an old acquaintance. He was once sergeant at Nardi's precinct and for years took orders from him until their paths parted. Nardi remained in charge of an area police station, while the other, seconded to the Mobile Squad, had quickly risen through the ranks and made a career. Now they are two peers, but only on a hierarchical scale. And Paolini knows this well because he has never missed an opportunity to point out the gap between them.

"You can always call the Chief of Police," he jokes, with a mocking smile across his face. "Who knows, maybe you can persuade him to change his mind."

"Don't worry! As far as I'm concerned, there are no problems. You are at the helm of command. Message received, loud and clear."

His surrendering manner catches everyone a little off guard, starting with Lanzi. The sergeant stares at him strangely, seems to want to retort, but dares not add anything else. Amanda Mellis, too, lets her astonishment shine through. Knowing him for the stubborn fellow he is, she should have expected a reaction of a completely different kind; however, an outburst would not have changed the situation. Regardless, the biggest disappointment is on Paolini's face, who evidently feels defrauded of a victory. From his stinging words just before, the intent to humiliate him was clear, but if he hoped to enrage him, he was left high and dry.

Of course, at another time, Massimo would have taken badly to seeing himself sidelined. Now, however, he is almost relieved. Not having to direct the investigation means no pressure from the police commissioner. This will allow him to devote more time to the case that involves him personally: the affair related to Teresa's daughter. Someone wanted to pull him into that game, and he still does not understand why.

Paolini can think whatever he wants. If the belief that he has taken the upper hand makes him feel better, he will let him believe it. After all, Massimo has no grudge against him. And in spite of everything, he pities him in some way.

"So, how do you plan to proceed?" he asks calmly.

"Well, we are talking about a serial murderer. I suggest starting with a profile analysis and assessment of the modus operandi."

"I suppose he used the technique of the previous crime."

Nardi has not yet looked at the corpse.

Breaking away from the group, he moves a few feet ahead, where Dr. Padovani, bent over the ground, is intent on examining what remains of the victim.

"There is a small variation." Paolini's voice reaches him from behind. "The killer has again removed the heart and the right eye. And he drew in blood the cross on the victim's forehead. Only this time, instead of the hand, he cut off the tongue."

Another puppet is added to the collection. That is what goes through Massimo's head as he looks at the body. It would look like a marionette lying on the ground, seated. With its back resting against the wall and its legs spread apart, the jaw dangles in the void like a facial appendage.

"The tongue instead of the hand. Mhmm. We'll have to figure out why. If he has not changed the system, we will likely find it at the victim's house."

"Apparently not," Lanzi interjects. "According to his wife, everything in the apartment appears fine."

"His wife?! So we already know who he is?"

"Just like that. Does that surprise you?" Paolini persists in his mockery. "Yup! You'll see! You'll enjoy working with *us*. A little efficiency will be good for your team, too."

Same provocative register. That "us", pronounced with sufficiency, is a demonstration that the colleague is not willing to give in.

Even Mellis does not miss the touch of sarcasm. "Well...! I can see you're very confident, Inspector Paolini." She speaks while pointing her gaze away. "I hope you can do your job as well as you say."

Lanzi lets out a laugh. As if trying to hold it back, he immediately brings a hand to his mouth. The other, however, has already begun to look at him sideways. He also casts a sullen glance at the deputy prosecutor. However, he finally seems to have run out of jokes. When he makes to retort, it is clear that he does not know what to say.

Massimo took advantage of this and took the floor, "About

the identity of the victim, would you rather I try to guess?" This is a provocative question in response to the jab from just before. "Should I discover things a little at a time, or do you plan on informing me too?"

"Get an update from Lanzi. He's already up to speed on everything," Paolini mutters, stepping aside. "I have other things to take care of." With a mask of anger contouring his face, he walks toward the medical examiner and, in an unconvincing manner, attempts to show himself unconcerned about the incident. "So, what do you tell me, doctor? Do you have any news for me?"

Amanda Mellis casts a glance at Nardi. Hinting a giggle, she shakes her head and lets out a sigh. "Well, I'd better go too," she comments resignedly, turning away.

"That guy is insufferable," Lanzi complains immediately afterward. "Why the heck don't you talk back to him in the same tone? He should be kicked to the curb."

"Ah! It's not worth it. I know him well. He just needs to show off. When he doesn't fall into ridicule, he can even be likable. So tell me about the victim."

"It's about a lawyer. Carlo Pietrangeli. And by the way, just so you know, the fact that they identified him quickly is just by chance. So much for efficiency! His wife had reported him missing a couple of days ago."

"Stop thinking about Paolini and tell me what else we know."

"There is an interesting detail. It seems Pietrangeli used to hang out with a high-class prostitute."

"A prostitute?!" Nardi exclaims. In his mind, the image of Juliana Petrescu resurfaces. "Are you sure about that? Where did the information come from?"

"It was discovered by colleagues who dealt with the disappearance. After some research, they found his car parked under the woman's building. Testimony from neighbors allowed them to link him to her."

"My, I dare not imagine how the wife must have taken it."

"She probably would have told him to go to hell. Or maybe

not. Who knows what her reaction would be."

Prosecutor Mellis' voice interrupts the exchange of words. "Nardi! Lanzi! Come and take a look." Frantically, she waves her hand, inciting them to hurry.

"What's up?" Massimo asks as soon as he joins her.

"We have another note." Padovani is now standing, talking to the other two. "This one was lodged in the eye socket as well."

"What does it say?" Paolini's tone has changed. He lets a sincere interest be perceived, an involvement reflected in his facial features.

Massimo, too, feels his anxiety rising in the few seconds of waiting. And judging by their attitudes, the sergeant and the deputy prosecutor are no exception. The only one who maintains his usual apathetic air is Dr. Padovani, who, having carefully unrolled the note, reads aloud:

"There is a time for everything. There is a time to be born and a time to die, a time to heal and a time to kill. There is a time to be silent and a time to speak."

"Have you figured out anything?" Turning his head to the left and right, Paolini looks for suggestions in the eyes of his interlocutors.

"I don't think there's much to understand," Lanzi replies. "If only they were his words… Those texts lend themselves to a thousand interpretations. To find logic in them, one must be crazier than he is."

"However, if he was so meticulous in getting them to us, they must mean something," prosecutor Mellis points out. "What do you think, Nardi?"

"I agree. Besides, let's remember the first verse, especially the final part. How did it go? Ah, yes! *But you do not know where I came from or where I am going.'* Whoever the killer is, he is making his painting and is only at the beginning. It is too early to see it."

"I suggest we focus on more practical things," Lanzi says. "Where did the tongue go? He made us find the hand, didn't he? It seems strange to me that he doesn't do the same now. He may have chosen another place, maybe because the lawyer's wife was in the house."

"It's a sensible idea," agrees Paolini. "Taking a look at the office won't cost anything. Do we already know where he worked?"

Lanzi wastes no time. "I'll check it right away," he says, moving away from the group.

***

According to the medical examiner, the cause of death matched the first murder: drowning. And as in the previous case, everything indicated that the man was still alive during the amputation of the tongue. So if the slightest doubt about the serial killer theory still hovered in the air, the modus operandi swept it away. Those deaths bear the same signature.

By now withdrawn from the scene, Amanda Mellis issued the writ to proceed without raising objections: seven o'clock has already passed, and everything is within the time limits on house searches.

Guido Paolini is the first to step into the lawyer's office. With the shutters barred on the windows, the room is bathed in half-light. "Shine the flashlight," he tells the officer standing in the doorway.

Busy fixing a copy of the warrant on the door, the man suspends what he is doing to obey the command.

However, when he is about to point the lamp forward, Nardi abruptly makes room for himself, goes inside, and pushes the switch on the wall.

It may be because of stress, the flood of questions piling up in his head, or maybe it is just tiredness. Nonetheless, in recent times, this letting impatience overcome him is happening more and more often.

As the room brightens, the grim expression painted on Paolini's face takes shape, his eyes watching him askance.

"Take it easy! I'm not going to steal your thunder," he hastens to say. "I just want to get to the point."

The colleague mumbles something unintelligible and, as Lanzi and Stefanini enter the office, turns away.

Massimo meanwhile looks around.

A very normal waiting room houses a small sofa and a couple of armchairs, abstract paintings on one wall, and a desk in the corner probably reserved for a secretary. To the right is a short hallway with two doors to the side and one at the end.

Paolini has already started to walk it.

Massimo is not slow to follow. And imitated by the other two, they proceed in single file.

The first room is the bathroom, while in the adjacent one, wall shelves filled with filing cabinets create a small archive. The last one at the end houses the lawyer's office instead. Inside the office, three leather-upholstered chairs, a wall bookcase, and a large desk surround a computer monitor and a series of folders scattered on the shelf. A couple of pens, and more or less useless furnishings, complete the picture of an office like many others, where the presence of the police turns out to be the only element out of place. In fact, nothing abnormal jumps to the eye. There is nothing here that deserves attention.

Paolini quickly shrugs off responsibility for a failed attempt. "Don't feel bad, Lanzi! The idea wasn't bad. It was worth a try."

Nardi shakes his head and hints at a smile. That man has not changed one iota since their last meeting. Had it been a conquest, he would have been quick to credit himself for it.

Still standing in the doorway, the sergeant advances a few steps. "I still stand by my opinion," he retorts. "All right, this may not be the place, but I'm convinced he wants us to find that damn tongue again."

"And you're not wrong!" sentences Massimo.

"Did you find out anything?" asks Stefanini.

Nardi points a finger forward to indicate the desk. "His trophy. Nicely packaged."

Confused among the objects scattered on the shelf, a glass

container holds the cut tongue. And there beside it, yet another message.

Leaning forward, the UACV colleague examines the container more closely. Then, gloves in hand, he grabs the note by one end and brings it up to his eyes.

"What does it say?" asks Lanzi.

"Let's see right away."

This time, the text quotes:

"Even ships, though they are so large and are driven by strong winds, are still steered by a very small rudder wherever the pilot wants to go. Likewise, the tongue is a small part of the body, but it makes great boasts. Consider what a great forest is set on fire by a small spark. The tongue also is a fire, a world of evil among the parts of the body."

Silence falls in the room. Moments of awkwardness, during which everyone seems to wonder about something undefined.

Massimo notes a similarity with the message of the first murder. He doubts it could be a mere coincidence. "A behavioral pattern is beginning to emerge," he then says.

"What are you talking about?" Paolini is only the first to open his mouth.

Everyone is staring at Nardi in curiosity.

"For both murders, he made us find two notes – one before, one after. The ones found at the crime scene seem to be a kind of warning for what is to follow. The others, however, have a common element."

"What do you mean?"

"The message left in the first victim's house mentioned the hand and eye. Now it refers to the tongue. Almost a self-celebration of the deed done."

"Mhmm... Interesting," Lanzi interjects. "It will help us profile."

"What about you, Marcello? What do you think? Do you agree with me?"

185

"I actually hadn't considered that. That would suggest an organized killer, someone who doesn't act on impulse but chooses his victims carefully."

"Surely, our experts will be able to draw a more detailed profile and give us an idea of the person we are dealing with." Guido Paolini takes center stage again, assuming a superior attitude. "At the Mobile Squad, we will call daily meetings with the investigators and analysts of the homicide section," he says, turning to Nardi. "And since we'll be working together, you'll have to be present as well."

Massimo merely shakes his head in a nod of assent, and as Stefanini calls his team back to him, he leaves the room without adding anything else.

While the forensic team takes over the premises, Lanzi and Paolini join him in the waiting room, where he continues to look around for who knows what.

Looking at the doorway, he reflects on the fact that this time, too, there are no signs of forced entry. Just as in Juliana Petrescu's apartment. And as much as it is not that difficult to get a cast of a key, the hypothesis that the killer knew the victims is perhaps not to be dismissed.

Paolini, a few feet away, orders one of his men to canvass the neighborhood for any witnesses.

Curious to know what direction the investigation will take, Massimo patiently waits as long as it takes for the agent to walk away. "Hey, Guido!" he then starts. "So? What do you think of this story?"

"Uh?"

"Have you got an idea yet?"

"Bah! So far, the only connection between the murders is that both times there was a prostitute involved. Maybe he wants to punish them for some reason."

"However, in this case, the victim is not the prostitute, but the lawyer."

"Hmm! True. Anyway, it's not certain that prostitution isn't involved. Perhaps the lawyer wasn't there for sex."

"What do you mean?"

"Maybe he was involved in some shady business himself."

"You think so? I don't think that's why he was killed. We should check if there are connections between him and Petrescu. If the killer chose him, there must be a common element, something that made him the ideal victim."

"We'll see," Paolini concluded, heading for the exit. "We'll talk about it again at the meeting. Hopefully, we'll have some more information by then."

CHAPTER 22

The morning announces itself shyly. With a reddish sky on the horizon, the sun seems to be delaying its appearance. Nevertheless, the already high temperature portends a more sultry day than usual. During the night, Teresa kept turning over in bed precisely because of the humidity. Or at least, so she thought. Waking up in a puddle of sweat, she took a refreshing shower, but getting the sweat off her has not been enough to rid her of her thoughts. It's the ones that suffocate her, the real nightmare.

Even now, as she sits on the couch under the breeze of the air conditioner, she feels bombarded by the questions that have been constantly accompanying her for days.

What really happened to Angela? She needs to know. By now, it is evident how her death hides something dark. The impossibility of seeing a glimmer of truth beyond the fog shrouding that mystery makes the rest all the more oppressive. The thought that her grandson is somewhere out there, alone, she cannot resign herself to the idea. Trying to imagine him in the company of who knows what stranger, she thinks back to the face in the photographs and how she has watched him grow up, year after year, never feeling the warmth of his affection. In a selfish longing, dictated more by guilt than by feeling, she would like to have him close, hold him in her arms, and make up at least in part for her shortcomings. Instead, she has no idea where he might be.

She breathes a sigh of relief at the ringing of the phone – a handhold to cling to in order to escape from the worries that nag her. Without delay, she lifts the receiver and brings it to her ear.

"Hello?"

There is no response on the other end. Only the faint sound of breath in the background.

The image of the man glimpsed outside the bar, the hooded guy, appears in the mind. She remembers his phone call well. And convinced it is him, she shrieks angrily, "Who are you? What the hell do you want?"

"Um! Yeah, hello, Teresa. How are you?"

This time she is the silent one.

Surprised and unsure, she doesn't know whether to react well or badly.

"It's me. Sergio."

It really is him. She hadn't heard his voice in years, not since the day she had dragged him into court to demand alimony. On that occasion, determined to make him pay for leaving her, she had made sure to squeeze as much money out of him as possible. The judge had been favorable, recognizing her the right to maintain the standard of living she had sustained during the marriage, and she had tasted the flavor of revenge, if only for a fleeting moment: by then, with her son dead and her daughter missing, life had fallen apart for her.

"Can you hear me, Teresa?"

She was certain that she hated that voice, hated the man it belonged to, and had continued to believe that until a few moments ago. But now, a chill down her spine, a twinge in her stomach, words choked in her throat, and everything seems to say the exact opposite. No use denying it; part of her still feels something. She does not know what it is, but it is a feeling that exists. She can feel it.

In an attempt to decipher it, she thinks back to the day they met, the early days of their life together, and how he, then, made her feel important and wanted, unique.

Things had changed with the birth of Angela.

Giving way to a caring father and husband, the lover capable of making her head spin had disappeared bit by bit, and she had felt neglected. Nevertheless, she had kept silent. At first, convinced it was a passing phase, she had continued to keep silent afterward, when unexcused absences, silly excuses, feminine scents on his skin, and lipstick stains on his shirts swept away all sorts of doubts that he was cheating on her.

At the mere recollection, ah, such anger! The impertinence with which Sergio shoved his love affairs in her face seemed like an invitation to take the first step, a way to walk her to the door so she would be the one to ask for a divorce. Convinced that she would have lost him forever if she had spoken, she had limited herself to looking away, cowardly pretending not to know.

In revenge, she had paid him back with the same coin. A night spent with Massimo in a hotel room. A night of simple sex. A night they had both regretted the next morning. He had returned to his wife's arms with his head bowed, and she had found solace in gambling.

But the greatest wound had nothing to do with betrayal. For the sex, who knows, Teresa could even have closed her eyes by continuing to pretend. Instead, what had happened that nefarious evening when she had seen herself attacked... no, she had not been able to ignore. She had woken up in the hospital, half dead and with a blind eye, and Sergio was not there for her. Perhaps busy enjoying himself in some hotel room, he had only shown up the next day. In his defense, he later claimed that he had been in the operating room until morning, but she had seen the lie in his eyes.

"Hey! Are you going to answer or not?"

Sergio's voice is heard again. Teresa has the impression that an eternity has passed since she picked up the phone. In reality, a fraction of a second was enough to see the past flash before her eyes and, now as then, she lacks the courage to speak. She has nothing to lose now, but for who knows what reason, she is afraid.

"What's up?" she finally manages to say.

"Oh! So you are here."

"Have you come back to life that you're contacting me again?"

"Well... I saw Massimo the other day. He told me about what's going on, and I thought we should talk about it."

Teresa is increasingly perplexed. Twelve years have passed since the day Angela left home. In all that time, not a phone call from Sergio, nor a sharing with her of his concerns, assuming he had any. Not even that time in court had he deigned to ask a question about it.

Their daughter was the only bond that could unite them, and her death has now broken even that. So why this sudden change?

"You want to talk," she says – a dismissive sarcasm in her voice. "After years of silence, now you want to speak? Go ahead, speak! What else have you been hiding from me?"

"Excuse me? No, nothing. What are you thinking?"

"And why this surprise?"

"Hmph! Maybe I made a mistake in calling you."

Sergio seems to be about to end the conversation, and she realizes that she does not want to. Suddenly, it is as if all the resentment accumulated over time has dissolved into nothingness. It seems absurd to her, and yet, she feels that she still loves him.

"Wait!" she hastens to say. "I'm sorry if I reacted badly, but your call... threw me off."

"Yes, I understand you. I feel a little uncomfortable myself."

"What did you want to tell me?"

"To be honest, I don't know either. I was wondering what you and Massimo talked about."

"What do you mean?"

"Well, yes! For days I couldn't think of anything else. First, a phone call tells me Angela is dead, then he shows up here and tells me about a case that's supposed to be about her disappearance and that you've been receiving her pictures for years; he tells me about a grandson I didn't even know existed. You can imagine how I feel. I need to clear my head. What is going on?"

"Oh! You don't know how much I wish I knew," she sobs. She feels two tears streaming down her cheeks. Sergio is the last person she would have thought to confide in, but he is the only one who can truly understand her.

"Come on, be strong," he encourages her. "Tell me all about it."

It is clear that Sergio's interest, that invitation to open up, is aimed at the present. Teresa, on the other hand, can no longer hold back. She needs to get out what she has never been able to say. "Why did you wait so long? If you had returned to me right away, we would still be a happy family today."

"I don't follow you. What are you referring to?"

"To what I should have told you years ago. You don't know it, but the silence has taken everything away from us."

CHAPTER 23

Upon arrival at the police station, it is after nine o'clock. Stained-glass windows from the building across the street reflect fierce rays of sunlight into the office, a glint that is annoying, but to say the least, forcing Nardi to pull down the Venetian blinds. Grabbing the directional rod, he turns the slats just enough to create some shade, then sits at his desk and starts the computer. In the short wait, he twists his mouth and snorts. Work has again started ahead of time, and his habit of keeping odd hours is not enough to compensate for the lack of sleep. He has not been able to get a good night's sleep for days now.

"Patience," he thinks as he pulls his cell phone out of his pocket and lets out a resigned sigh. On the display is the photo taken a few hours earlier of the recovered notes. After taking a quick glance at it, he types a few buttons on the PC keyboard. The search engine returns a table of contents with the verses that interest him. Before grabbing the notepad beside it and jotting down all the information on paper, he makes a quick examination to compare the texts. Getting up, he then approaches the blackboard, sticks the Post-it notes next to the rest of the material present, and rearranges the order, juxtaposing the new messages with those of the first murder.

- First message: found at crime scene (in right eye socket). Gospel John 8:14

- Second message: found in the apartment. Gospel Matthew 5:29-30. References to right eye and right hand.

- Third message: found at crime scene (in right eye socket). Bible, from the book of Ecclesiastes 3:1-7

- Fourth message: found in the lawyer's office. Gospel James 3:4-6. Explicit reference to the tongue.

The initial hypothesis seems to stand. Three, five, and eight could hide a key to understanding.

A somewhat forced interpretation; he has to admit it. And even assuming there is some truth to it, it will be difficult to understand where it might lead. In any case, it will be worth passing the information on to Paolini. Who knows! Maybe the computer analysts will be able to get something out of it.

Letting go of the issue of numbers, he shifts his gaze to the third verse, on one passage in particular. Some words have been reversed from the original, which quotes verbatim, *"a time to kill and a time to heal,"* not vice versa. The killer ends the sentence with *"kill"*, and he wonders if beyond a subliminal threat lies a more subtle meaning.

"The press didn't waste any time indulging itself, huh?" Lanzi enters the office waving a newspaper in the air. Without paying attention to him, still standing beside the blackboard, he drops onto the chair. "They wallow in stories like that."

"What are you talking about?"

"Still haven't read it?"

"Read what?"

"Look at this!" The sergeant shows the front page of the newspaper. "They've renamed him *'The Missionary'*, just to give him some more publicity."

"Well, we could use it too."

"Uh?"

"Why not? We don't have a face or a name. A nickname is better than nothing."

"Oh, yes! It's really a lovely nickname. And who are we

194

supposed to be? The Holy Inquisition?"

As a smile emerges on Massimo's face, the phone starts ringing. Still amused, he grabs the receiver and brings it to his ear. "Yes, hello?"

Replying from the other side is the chief inspector of the Postal Police.

"Oh, hello, Persiani! Go ahead."

"Good morning, Nardi. I wanted to inform you that Sandro Donati has been removed from the list of suspects."

"Ah, I see."

"Although the investigation continues, we feel it is pointless to continue with him."

"We were both wrong. What can we do? It happens."

"I'm sorry I can't help you with your case."

"Don't worry about it. It's my problem," concludes Nardi. "Have a good day!"

He ends the call without delay. Whoever sent Teresa the photos has nothing to do with Sandro Donati. Having cleared up the misunderstanding, anything that might concern him has lost interest. Thinking about that man now irritates him quite a bit. The many clues converging on him portended victory. And feeling the solution in his grasp, Massimo savored it until the facts forced him to admit his mistake.

He would like to banish the image of the man from his mind, but instead, that gruff manner and cocky tone seem to chase after him and mock him.

Lowering his eyes to the desk, he casts a glance at his dossier, still there in plain sight. As soon as Stefanini had sent it to him, he had rejoiced. The fact that the fingerprint belonged to a murder suspect had seemed like a godsend to him. Then everything had collapsed like a house of cards when, on reading the file, he had discovered that those charges had been dropped; when Donati had provided plausible explanations and a witness to support him regarding the blood stain and the theft of the correspondence; when Nicola Tancredi, confirming the version he had given at the time, had put an end to all doubts.

"So, what do you think? Do you also think prostitution has anything to do with it?" he hears someone say.

"Huh?" he startles.

Coming back to reality, he sees the sergeant still intent on reading the newspaper. He had been silent the whole time, so much so that Massimo had almost forgotten he was there.

"Paolini is right," Lanzi continues. "That is the only obvious link between the two victims. What else could connect a lawyer and a prostitute?"

"I don't know. And there's not much we can do anyway. I'd say let the Mobile Squad handle it."

"But come on! What's wrong with you? I don't recognize you anymore."

"What do you mean?"

"Easy! First, you hear that they're taking the case away from you, and you don't say a word. Now you're washing your hands of it. Well, it seems strange to me. It's not like you."

"Yes, I know. It's just that I have other things on my mind. Right now, I'm more interested in the investigation of Angela Brunetti. I want to find out why someone went to the trouble of involving me in this matter."

"Ah, that's it! I knew something was wrong. So, what do you want to do?"

"Uh?"

"You said you want to carry on with the other case, right? That's fine with me. But where do we start? It doesn't seem like we have much to go on."

"Alas, it's true! I was just thinking about Donati. That lead is now a dead end. De Marchi, on the other hand, hasn't told me anything yet. The photograph he spoke of…"

"Who is De Marchi?"

"The former owner of the maternity home. I told you about him, didn't I?"

"Ah, yes! I remember now. You mentioned him when you first presented the case to me."

"I guess he didn't find anything. Then I'll make sure. Anyway, he was right about the kidnapping of the little one. Cataldo checked it out. And as far as we know, Angela Brunetti had no other children. So, who is the child in the photos?"

"Good question. Another thing not to forget is the woman who was killed in the hospital. The fact that she was really the social worker… If anyone could give an answer, it was her."

"Yes, it gives you pause."

"Maybe we should focus on the identity of the child," Lanzi suggests. "He could be the key turning point."

"Well, I'll try to hear from Stefanini. Who knows, maybe he's discovered something." Nardi lifts the receiver, dials the number and stands by. "Hey there, Marcello!" he exclaims after a few moments. "Any news on Graziani's daughter?"

"As a matter of fact, yes."

"What?! And what were you waiting for to tell me?"

"If it had been up to me, I would have done it already. I wanted to tell you when you arrived at the Twisted Wall, but you passed me by like a train. Then one thing after another, and there was no time."

"Okay, sorry. I was in a very bad mood. So, tell me! What did you find out?"

"A few interesting things. I had the letter envelopes examined by an expert calligrapher, who compared them with the signature on the document found at the hospital. The expert concluded that the handwriting on the first five matched the hospital document. The others, however, were probably written by a man. Hard to say for sure. But I think you will be more interested in the results of the biological analysis. When I received the results, I requested Angela Brunetti's medical records from the center where she was admitted, and the blood on the envelope may match."

"I beg your pardon?"

"So at least it seems."

"Let me get this straight. What do you mean 'might'?"

"Well, that's it… To be sure, we'd need a DNA test, but unfortunately, we don't have any samples to make a comparison."

A long silence follows Stefanini's words. Massimo reflects in bewilderment. As far as he knows, Angela has been dead for a year. Is it possible that she is still alive? While he is asking himself this question, a strange idea crosses his mind. "Tell me one thing. The tests you did on the blood, if it had belonged to a son, would the result have been the same?"

"Um! Maybe. But not necessarily. Why?"

"No, nothing. Never mind," he concludes. "See you soon!"

After he hangs up, he pauses to consider the possibility of mistaken identity. He wonders if the body should be exhumed. And as his eyes stare into the void, he imagines Teresa's reaction. It is impossible for him not to think of her. Such news, should it be a failure, would give her the death blow. Better to keep her in the dark until he knows more.

Slightly tilting his head, he repeats to himself that this is the best solution.

When he finally lifts his eyes, he sees Lanzi watching him silently. Returning the gaze, he leans back in his chair, lets out a sigh, and begins to bring him up to speed.

***

Ettore Lanzi left Nardi's office without saying a word. Understanding his superior's motives, he merely masked his disagreement by feigning indifference.

In reality, the idea of having to shelve the investigation of the Twisted Wall does not appeal to him at all. He had never dealt with heinous crimes before and had not imagined they could have such an effect on him. To his surprise, this case fascinated him from the beginning, and he is not willing to give up on it just yet. He has been working on it for days. Although he tried to keep his enthusiasm in check to avoid showing it, he has been working harder than usual, combing through criminology texts and psychiatric and sociological treatises.

Of course, he does not claim to replace profilers; however,

he feels a special attraction to this dark and twisted world of serial killers. Who knows? Maybe this is his calling, and this might be the right opportunity to prove himself. Moreover, blowing the solution of the case out from under Paolini's nose would be a great satisfaction.

After reaching his desk, he sits down, pulls his chair forward, and opens a drawer. He pulls out the folder where he has placed the information he had gathered up to the day before. The most recent data stops at the autopsy results and the negative video surveillance report about the black Panda and its driver. Intent on updating the file, he turns on the PC to print out the latest reports. However, his gaze is caught by the many notes he has written by hand.

Questions and conjectures that have crossed his mind over the past few days continue to pique his curiosity. Such as the attempt to place the killer in a specific category.

At first, because of the removal of the body parts, he had assumed it could be a fetishist. But he was clearly wrong. Otherwise, the fetish capable of satisfying his sex drive would have remained unchanged; it would not have gone from the hand to the tongue.

Although come to think of it, those are the parts the killer later got rid of. The eye and the heart were not found in either case and perhaps it is onto these that the man projects his fantasies.

Ettore had read an article on the subject. It explained that the phase of greatest pleasure, in cases of fetishism, was revealed after the crime has been committed when the murderer felt the need to relive the excitement of the murderous act.

He wonders again if this could be the case, but before he can ponder any further, his attention falls on Juliana Petrescu's photography, and his imagination begins to travel to other shores.

He is reminded of the way the woman blackmailed her clients. And although everything seems to suggest otherwise, the hypothesis he put forward at the beginning keeps running through his mind.

Is it possible that this is just a set-up? Sensational murders for the sole purpose of covering up one like so many others?

***

The sun has quickly changed its angle. For several minutes now, it has ceased reflecting on the glass windows of the building in front. With the Venetian blinds still down, it is the bright computer screen that outlines the contours of the room. Left alone with his thoughts, Massimo is lost in a kind of oblivion. His back curved in the chair, causing his chin to protrude forward as if it wanted to rest on his chest. With his elbows resting on the armrests, his hands clasped together to support each other, and his eyes turned toward an indefinite point, his entire body is left to itself.

He has the impression that everything around him is crystallizing. Everything stands still. Even time has stopped flowing. Only the image of Teresa continues to haunt him in the remote meanders of his mind. With her, he has a debt he can never repay. A debt he wishes he had never incurred.

Tormented by remorse, he turns his gaze to his desk, where a silver frame holds a photograph of his wife. Despite her smiling face, she seems to blame him from beyond the grave. Not even to her has he ever revealed the uncomfortable truth that has haunted him for years.

Unable to rebel against an oppressive past, he gives in to his memories: his mind goes back in time to that damned night that changed him forever. He sees himself there on the road as he gets out of the car, as he orders the man to lower his bat, as the image of Teresa curled up on the asphalt comes into his view.

"Stop! Police!" he is shouting with his heart in his throat.

But the man does not listen. He keeps hitting.

Blocked by a fear he has never felt before, Massimo is petrified. He cannot move a step. Not even his hand belongs to him anymore. He feels it resting on the butt of the gun, drawing the weapon from its holster and rising into the air to point the barrel forward.

"I said stop!" he repeats. "Don't make me shoot."

His cry is one of desperation, driven by the hope that everything will come to an end. It has nothing to do with rules. It has nothing to do with the law. Not even the safeguarding of his colleague is so important in that instant. He just wants to push that suffocating fear away from himself.

The attacker drops the bat, but turns sharply and raises an arm. Sniffing the danger, Massimo no longer understands anything. Panicked, he does not even feel his finger pull on the trigger. He can only hear the detonation of the shot. He sees the man's feet rise from the ground, as his body falls back, and Massimo does not know how to act or what to feel. He fired without meaning to. And it is the first time he has ever shot anyone.

Suddenly the fear is gone. But in its place, it seems to have left a void in his mind and soul. Massimo does not feel anything anymore, only the adrenaline dropping, the breath becoming regular, and the heartbeat slowing a little at a time. Lost in a trance-like state, he advances slowly, looking around, until reason regains control. Then, desperately, he puts his hands to his forehead and stands there, searching for a weapon that never existed. The man was unarmed. And now he is dead, shot through the heart.

"Mas-si-mo" he hears slurred.

Teresa's bleeding face brings him back to reality. He sees her head rise slightly from the asphalt, only to fall back down soon after. She beckons him back to her with her gaze, or what is left of it: she can barely raise an eyelid.

He hurries to bend down to the ground and pull his cell phone out of his pocket. He puts a hand on her shoulder. "Hold still," he says. "I'll have someone come right away."

"Take... take mine."

"What are you saying?" Not understanding the meaning of these words, Massimo acts as if nothing has happened. He thinks the blows to her head must have confused her. "Stay down," he insists. "You'll be okay."

"The gun," she interrupts. "Take my gun." She barely moves her chin to indicate the body beside her, as her eye jumps from her own jacket to the man's hand.

"What? Are you crazy?" he shouts as soon as he understands.

"Do as I say."

"But why? We just have to explain how it happened and..."

"Do it!" she repeats peremptorily, with the little breath she has left in her body.

He falls silent. Consciousness makes room in the chaos. He shot an unarmed man. And the fact that he let his fear get the best of him will not be enough to resolve the matter.

He would like to object to that reckless idea, but instead, even before he realizes it, he clutches his colleague's weapon in his fist, wipes it clean with a handkerchief to pull away his fingerprints, places it on the man's hand and presses his fingers against the grip.

That last image hurls him out of his memories.

In the office, time has started to flow again, but he is still torn between the past and present. He thinks back to how Teresa has continued to cover for him since day one, starting with the report in which they both had reported false.

According to the official version, the man had pounced on her for no apparent reason and, after beating her, had taken possession of the gun. Then, before he could fire, Massimo intervened, saving her life.

Since then, they haven't spoken about that story. And until two weeks before, he was convinced he had put it behind him.

Now, however, resurfaced with overbearingness, the past forces him to look back and face his demons again. Since the day he went to the hospital for Rigoni's murder when their paths crossed again, everything has become uncertain. And the doubt that this secret is no longer so safe never ceases to nag at him.

CHAPTER 24

July 12, afternoon, 7 p.m.

Sitting on the couch at home, Sergio reflects on his life with a guilty look on his face. Throughout the day, he kept thinking about Teresa's words. He did not imagine that he had been such a source of pain to her. On learning that she had always been aware of his betrayals, he was stunned. She had never said or done anything to suggest this to him, and he had never been aware of anything. It is clear that he was wrong in believing that he was hiding these love affairs in the best possible way. Just as he was wrong in interpreting Teresa's behavior, her sudden mood swings and her slow mutation into an absent wife.

At the thought of having helped shape her, he feels mixed emotions; pity and guilt and anger, and who knows what else. He wonders how things would have turned out if he had only known. Surely life would have taken a different turn.

He now realizes that he is the one who drove her down the deplorable path of gambling.

Despite this, he fails to justify her for what happened later. On the contrary! The thought that she has been brooding the pain within herself, continuing to keep silent, irritates him even more. If only she had spoken up... Who knows? Maybe Piero would not have died in that car, and Angela would not have done what she did.

What he has discovered should make his judgment less harsh; instead, absurdly, it was easier to remain impassive before when he ignored the truth. Perhaps it is because he refuses to believe that a simple word could have changed fate. Perhaps it is because of that feeling of partial guilt. Or perhaps it is because blaming her to escape his conscience is the most convenient way. He can't give himself an answer, and deep down, come to think of it, he doesn't even want to know which one it is.

The only thing he knows for sure is that Angela is dead, and the police are investigating in search of her son, his grandson.

He was curious how far they had gotten with the investigation, but Teresa had not been able to tell him much. And Nardi, who promised to keep him updated, still hasn't contacted him.

His business card is on the table, and he will call him in the morning. But in the meantime, he needs to do something.

So he gets up from the sofa, walks over to the bookcase, and grabs an old folder from a shelf. With a sigh, he runs a hand over to graze its cover before returning to his seat and beginning to leaf through it.

It is a photo album that belonged to Angela. A suitcase of memories that he dips into whenever he feels the need to feel close to her.

In most photos, the daughter's face appears cheerful, surrounded by a carefree air. These portray the exact opposite of how she looked at home. Some pictures show her alone, others in a group, but in each one, she looks like a different person, a free woman. At this sight, he swings his head and hints at a sad smile. He would like to forcefully snatch her from those inanimate images and bring her back to life, so that he can hold her in his arms again. Instead, as happens every time, he can only stare at her face, brush against the glossy paper that separates him from her, and surrender to the memory of what was.

In these few moments, his eyes have become moist. To prevent a tear from falling, he passes a wrist to dry them. Then the cell phone begins to ring, breaking the silence, almost as if trying to make a dent in the memory.

The device comes out of his pocket. Just in time to turn it off.

Meanwhile, a noise behind him catches his attention.

Sergio turns and looks in the direction of the entrance. He tilts his head to lend an ear.

He thought he heard a metallic click but sees nothing unusual. Wondering if the sound came from outside, he brings his torso forward and leans in to take another look, but sees nothing. The only thing moving is the hands of the clock on top of the cabinet. Noticing that it is a quarter to eight, he thinks it is almost time for dinner. Now he doesn't feel like going to the stove anyway. So he turns around again and continues flipping through the album.

HELL – ACT V

July 12, afternoon, 7:10 p.m.

Inside the house not a single lamp is on. Outside, the sun begins to set. In this hidden intimacy, between dim lights and dumb shadows, a chiming of hands shatters a silence hungry for silence.

Tick-tock is the cadenced sound that echoes through the room. Tick-tock, tick-tock is the noise that rips through a palpable sense of anguish in the air. Tick-tock, tick-tock is the rhythmic passage of time. This sound is a sweet and bitter lament that marks the approach of an end and the opening of a new chapter.

The man sitting on the sofa is leafing through a photo album. He stares at the pictures, unaware that he is being watched. It is clear from his slow and calm action that he does not perceive the intrusion of his gaze.

While spying on him, he stands still in the hallway. Hidden behind the door that leads to the living room, he leans his ear toward the front door to catch any suspicious noises. He makes sure that everything is quiet outside as well.

This time he could not avoid video surveillance, and the last thing he needs is to be caught early.

As for the surveillance, it matters little. The cameras are closed-circuit, and the guard is an airhead old man who spends most of his time sleeping instead of keeping an eye on the monitors. If and when he alerts the police, he will already be far away. Besides, he covered his face with a bandage before entering the residential complex, and the glasses and hood will do the rest. From the video footage, they will only be able to outline the contours of an anonymous man.

The neighbors, however, worry him. The car is parked right in front of the house. It could attract attention. And if anyone had ever seen him pass by, they would certainly have been alarmed. At the sight of a masked-faced stranger, they would have already called for help.

When in doubt, he waits a few more minutes. He continues to listen.

Finally, convinced that he has gone unnoticed, he turns his gaze back toward the living room.

The other is still there, looking at the photographs. In a repetitive, almost ritualistic action, he touches them with trembling fingers, pulls them close to him, lets a kiss fly through the air, and carefully stows them away. From time to time, he seems to want to bring his hands to his face to dry his eyes. Instead, each time, he freezes. Perhaps afraid that a tear might spoil the paper, he rubs his face with his arm. Obsessive gestures from which a deep torment shines through.

Watching that scene, he is not surprised. He knows his story well. A brilliant career as a doctor, then made meaningless by pain. The pain of loss. The most unjust. Brunetti is a man defeated by life – a survivor. To understand what anguish pierces his soul, he does not need to look at him. Because if anyone is capable of understanding that sense of despair, it's him. He knows very well what demons can arise in the face of helplessness, in the face of an adverse fate. Rebellious and furious, they shake the body and the mind, and the spirit until they tear them apart. So either you find a way to control them, or they control you.

Oh, yes! He can totally understand him!

That's why he's sorry, because he knows that this time he will have to be more energetic than usual. If he had a choice, he would go out the way he came in and run far away, but he can't. He must stick to the plan. Allowing sentiment to interfere would vain what he has done so far. Moreover, it might arouse suspicion. He cannot risk the police catching up with him. Not before he has completed the whole thing.

He must do what is necessary. He has to do it for her. He swore it on her grave.

At this thought, he feels his head bow. His eyes fall to his chest, and stare at the 358 printed on his sweatshirt.

That cursed number. He is the one who had it printed on the fabric. To remember where it all began. To remember where it all has to end. To make sure he will go all the way.

He only has to look at it to find the determination he needs.

Without further hesitation, he lifts the hand in which he clutches the bag, pulls out the gauze and the anesthetic, and begins to advance into the room.

When Brunetti notices his presence, he gasps and turns his head sharply. For a split second, their eyes meet in the air. Astonishment, in that lapse of time, is when the pain of one is absorbed in the pain of the other.

CHAPTER 25

Determined to find some clues, Nardi has spent the entire afternoon researching. As Lanzi suggested to him at the beginning, he has started to review old cases that he and Teresa had worked on together. On the other hand, although the investigation centers on Angela Brunetti's past, the former colleague remains one of the central figures in this dark affair. She is the one who received the photos. And any connection that links her to her daughter and the mysterious sender must include him as well.

Cataldo had already looked at the material days before. Nevertheless, given the impasse and the lack of anything else to work on, Massimo decided to dig deeper.

Unfortunately, very little turned up.

Not even sifting through the most recent papers yielded better results. Much of the information is irrelevant, and some of it relates to matters that are now established. Others, while clarifying some gray areas, are not enough to move the case in any direction. Like the autopsy report on Silvia Rigoni, which says essentially nothing.

What killed her was a lethal dose of cyanide. And the syringe found lodged in her IV was the murder weapon. Full stop.

As for the clues that could lead to the murderer, there is

nothing.

So many files crowd the desk. Among these files is a copy of the report of Teresa's trial.

Massimo had requested it by curiosity. He found unusual the similarity between the names of her son and grandson: Piero and Pier Giorgio. He had wondered if this detail was purely coincidental or if it concealed something more.

In the end, it turned out that Giorgio was the other deceased child in the car. A discovery that still does not say much.

There could be many reasons for this strange pairing of names.

Maybe Angela wanted to honor the memory of her brother and his little friend. Or, given her relationship with her mother, it is easy to think that she just wanted to spite her. Indeed! This is the most likely hypothesis. Otherwise, why bother to mention it on the back of the only photo with an inscription?

"This is my son. Your grandson. His name is Pier Giorgio."

At first, it had seemed to Massimo that these were words like so many others, devoid of any double meaning. But looking back now, it is clear that contempt seeps out of that message.

What wrong suffered could have caused Angela to harbor such hatred?

The question hovers in the mind until Lanzi's sudden arrival sweeps it away.

The sergeant bursts in like fury. Opening the door wide, he barely crosses the threshold. "He's struck again!" he exclaims agitatedly. With one foot in the room and the other in the hallway, he is already ready to dash off. "Paolini just warned us."

"Hey, take it easy! I can hear you fine. No need to shout," Nardi replies listlessly, if not almost indifferently. "What's this all about? Another corpse at the Twisted Wall?"

"No! There was a report of a kidnapping."

"What does that have to do with our case?"

"It seems that the intervening patrol found something in the dwelling."

"And what would that be?"

"I don't know. All I know is that the kidnapped person is Sergio Brunetti."

"What?" Massimo jumps to his feet in amazement.

"That's right!"

"What the hell does he have to do with it?"

"Don't ask me. I know as much as you do."

"Have Paolini and the others arrived at the site yet?"

"They were going."

"Okay, then let's not waste any time. Let's go!"

***

Upon their arrival, Nardi and Lanzi find a small crowd of onlookers on the scene. Attracted by the flashing lights and the commotion, people have clustered in the street just outside the residential complex. Even the outside gate, set to close automatically, seems to tell those on the other side that something is wrong: the sliding sash is wide open.

As the car pulls into the driveway inside, Massimo looks around in disbelief. When he had gone to that place a few days earlier, he did not think he would return here. And certainly, not for the reason he is here now.

Crazy! He was looking for answers about Angela's past, and now he finds himself hunting a serial killer.

He still does not have a clear picture of what happened. However, unless the intervening officers made a huge mistake – which he doubts – it is now obvious how the facts stand. He thought he was investigating two separate cases at opposite poles, while now everything is converging on a single thread. The photos sent to Teresa, the necklace sent to him, the murder of Silvia Rigoni, the victims of the Twisted Wall. Behind every mesh of that mysterious web is the same hand.

Guido Paolini is in front of the villa talking to two policemen, and Massimo, getting out of the car, goes straight to him.

"Well? What do we know?" he asks as soon as he reaches

him.

"Hey, Nardi! I just got here, too. I've been here for a minute. These are the officers who responded to the call. Apparently, it was the neighbor who raised the alarm when he saw a Panda with a masked man behind the wheel driving away."

"Have the traffic cops been alerted yet?"

"Yes, but..."

"And have you set up checkpoints?"

"I'm capable of doing my work, thank you!" protests Paolini. In a fit of anger, he waves his hand in the air. "Anyway, yes, I did! But I don't think it will do much good."

"Why?"

"It's our fault," interjects one of the two officers.

"Huh?" Massimo looks at him with a questioning frown.

"Yes, I mean... The door was open, the house was empty. We thought it was a petty thief."

"Stop it! It's nobody's fault," Paolini silences him. And turning to Nardi, he adds, "Unfortunately, by the time they warned us, half an hour had passed. By now that guy can be anywhere."

"There's got to be a way to track him down!" he says. "Maybe from the roadside video surveillance or some report."

"We're doing what we can. I was in contact with the police station on my way here, and checks are already underway. They are also trying to trace Brunetti's cell phone, in case he had it with him."

"Simply put, all we can do is wait and cross our fingers and hope it's not too late," Nardi grumbles.

"But are we sure this is our guy?" interjects Lanzi, who had been silent until then. "There are hundreds of Fiat Pandas around. And then, the covered face! Who's to say he wasn't really a thief?"

Seized with doubt, Massimo stares at the sergeant for a moment, then turns toward Paolini, waiting for an answer.

"Thief, my foot!" shouts the officer instead, seeing himself being dragged in. "A thief doesn't leave two eyes on the table."

"Two eyes?!" Nardi echoes.

"That's right," Paolini confirms. "Come on! Let's go inside."

Passing through the door, Massimo sees that the forensic team is already searching for clues. When he reaches the living room, he finds Stefanini in the middle of the room.

The friend immediately notices his arrival. On seeing him appear, he approaches him. "Another souvenir to add to the collection," he says, shaking his head to indicate a spot behind him.

Nardi looks ahead, but a forensic technician, busy with a photographic survey, blocks his view. So as not to interfere with his work, he simply takes a few steps away.

From a plastic container, the gruesome image of two eyeball's visible. They seem to be screaming for help, staring him in terror. He averts his gaze in disgust, also because Sergio's frightened expression comes to mind.

With a grimace of annoyance, he lets out a resigned sigh and begins to look around.

The living room is a bit upside down. The clock on the cabinet overturned, and a couple of pillows lay on the floor, along with photographs scattered here and there.

"It's really strange," he says in a dumped voice as if talking to himself.

"What?" asks Paolini.

"This change in modus operandi. In the other cases, he acted in two stages, making us find the removed parts only after the crime was completed. This time, however, he not only reversed the sequence of events, but what he left behind belongs to the other victims, or so I hope."

"Uhm! Yes, that's right. What do you think that means?"

"Simple!" says Stefanini. "We're not dealing with a serial killer."

"What do you mean?" Paolini looks surprised and puzzled. "Why would you think…"

"That's right!" interrupts Massimo. "Serial killers don't behave that way. There may be an evolution over time, but not so sudden. And above all, not so radical."

"You're thinking what I'm thinking, aren't you?" Stefanini gives him an understanding look.

Nardi shakes his head slightly. "I guess so," he says, putting a hand to his mouth and frowning thoughtfully. "If you're referring to Teresa Graziani... well, yes, I think we have the same thing on our minds."

"I thought so! You know what that means, don't you?"

"That it's a tough nut to crack."

"At this point, we must also include the murder of Silvia Rigoni."

"Yes, I had already thought of that."

"Guys! What the hell are you talking about?" interjects Paolini, unable to understand the argument. "What murder? And who is this, Teresa Graziani?"

"Huh? Oh, you're right!" apologizes Massimo, realizing that he has pushed him out of the conversation.

With Marcello, they are on the same wavelength, but Paolini doesn't know anything about that story. So he starts to tell him about the series of events related to the other case. Without going into too much detail, he reports just enough to highlight the connection that brings the two investigations into a single investigative thread.

"Wow! This changes everything!" Paolini exclaims at the end of the story. "At least now we know that Brunetti's kidnapping is somehow connected to that affair."

"Yes, but the role of the other two victims, the lawyer, and the prostitute, is unclear," Nardi replies.

Then he is about to add something, but Lanzi's voice reaches him from behind. "Hey, Chief!" he hears him say.

The sergeant, who has remained somewhat aloof, leans forward and waves him over. "Come and take a look."

"What is it?" Massimo asks as he steps forward.

Ettore Lanzi waggles a finger to point at some photographs on the floor. "Look at these. They all capture Angela Brunetti, and they look quite old to me. They might be useful to understand what…"

"Oh, shit! Here's another one!" A cry, Stefanini's, silences everyone in the room. The intensity of the exclamation must have surprised even him; he puts a hand to his mouth as if to chase it back. Then, in a calmer tone, he adds, "Maybe someone dropped it without noticing."

After such an outburst, there is no need to call on his colleagues to join him. A moment later, they are all behind him, all looking in the same direction.

Hidden behind a table leg, yet another note.

The verse quotes:

"If in spite of this you do not listen to me and still resist me, I will fiercely resist you. I will discipline you seven times for your sins. You will eat the bodies of your sons and daughters."

"What the hell is he trying to prove with these messages?" erupts Massimo. "This guy is neither a sadist nor a sick in the head. He has a definite plan. And I don't understand what it is. Ah, the rage!" He punches the table with his fist. "Damn it!"

"Hey, take it easy, or your blood pressure will skyrocket," Stefanini says, putting a hand on his shoulder. "Taking it too hard won't help."

He is about to answer when an officer rushes in. "They traced it," he warns. "They were able to track the cell phone signal."

CHAPTER 26

Amid screeching tires and overtaking other vehicles, the police cars zoomed through the streets of Rome until they left the city and the approaching evening behind them. The race continued at a brisk pace for another quarter of an hour before slowing down on the last stretch of road: a treacherous dirt road full of curves, bumps, and sudden potholes.

The cell phone signal has led them into the open country.

Once out of the vehicle, Nardi looks around for signs of life, but all he sees are a few ramshackle farmhouses, trees, bushes, and fallow land.

"Well? Where is he?" he asks.

He looks at Paolini, who, in turn, turns his head toward the unmarked car behind him.

In the driver's seat, a plainclothes policeman clenches the radio microphone in his fist: he is in contact with the station. "This should be the place," he confirms shortly after. "It's the last point where the signal was detected."

"And where is he?"

A question, Nardi's, that is lost in the void.

"Come on! Up, up!" Stefanini urges the others. "Let's wake up! Take a look around."

As the officers scatter in search of some clue, a rustle of

216

bushes echoes nearby. Some animals, disturbed by their presence, scurry away.

Several minutes pass before anyone speaks. One of the men waves an arm in the air, calling his colleagues to join him. "Found it! The cell phone is here."

With the screen smashed, the cover pulled off, and the battery removed from the compartment, an old Samsung phone lies in three pieces in the grass. Next to it, tire tracks continue on the ground for about thirty feet, until they disperse into the gravel of a mule track that climbs a small hill.

"He went this way." Paolini immediately starts moving forward.

"Wait!" says Nardi, grabbing him by the sleeve of his jacket.

"What is it?"

"Better to split up. You never know." Eyeing Lanzi and Stefanini, he motions for them to follow. "We'll go around to the other side."

Paolini does no objection. With an expression of total indifference, he turns and begins to climb. "Eyes open, the rest of you!" he exhorts, calling the rest of the men to him.

For a moment, Massimo watches the group of officers walk away. But then his gaze moves on, ahead of the march, to look up, left and right, where the sky outlines the contours of the high ground. He wonders if the body of Sergio Brunetti is waiting for them on the other side.

Then Lanzi's voice shakes him.

"Well, Chief?" he asks impatiently. "Shall we go?"

"Huh? Yes, yes, of course! Let's go through there." Massimo points to a place where the hill gives way to a hollow. And as he sets off, he turns to Stefanini. "Hey, Marcello... you're armed, right?"

"Sure. Why do you ask?"

"Well, you know how it is. I wouldn't want to find out at the last minute that you left your gun to gather dust."

"Sst! Come on, funny man, let's go. If we are lucky, Brunetti might still make it out alive and in one piece."

"Sorry for worrying about your skin. Anyway, you're right; let's hurry."

For the entire climb, the path is flanked by a dense row of elms and field maples. Only as the slope diminishes does the presence of the trees become gradually more sporadic, and piled blocks of stone give shape to a dry stone wall: it delimits the area of a small road that flows into the widening of an old farmhouse.

It appears shabby, probably abandoned.

Nardi looks around, looking for signs of life, but the only movement is that of the windblown vegetation. Then he glances off into the distance. Paolini and the rest of the group are still out of sight.

"I'll check the back," Lanzi says, walking to one side of the building.

"Okay!" he replies. And turning to Stefanini, he asks, "What do we do? Do we try to get in?"

The colleague raises his palm. "After you."

Massimo starts to move forward when the sergeant hurriedly reappears.

"Did you hear?" he asks.

"Hear what?"

"Some noises. They came from inside."

"I didn't hear anything. And you, Marcello?"

Before the other can answer, a movement in the bushes attracts attention. The silhouette of a man can be seen hurrying away.

"Hey, you! Stop!" yells Massimo. Seeing that the man doesn't stop running, he draws his gun. "Stop!" he repeats. "Police!"

Lanzi and Stefanini were faster. With weapons in hand, they jumped into the chase without even intimating a halt. Massimo takes off in hot pursuit, but only has time to cover a few feet. He stops at the call of a voice, a cry for help that echoes through the air.

The other two turn around as well.

"It must be Brunetti. He's still alive!" cries Stefanini.

Nardi hesitates for a moment. He turns his head back and forth, looking at the cottage, at the fleeing man, and the cottage again. "You go after him. We'll take care of it here," he says to Lanzi. "Sergio! Is that you?" he calls as he starts walking back. "Can you hear me, Sergio?"

But there is no answer from inside the building.

The door is old and falling apart. Of the rusty hinges, only the bottom one supports the right door leaf, which hangs slightly forward. And the lock is practically missing.

He glances at his friend next to him. When he sees him raise his thumb to indicate that he is ready for action, he pushes the door forward, and it opens effortlessly.

In a long, wide hallway that leads inside, thick cobwebs cover the walls on both sides and dangle from the ceiling, and their almost total absence in the central area indicates a recent passage by someone.

Just ahead, the corridor branches off. Part of it continues straight ahead, ending a few feet further on a staircase leading down, while to the right and left are two narrower passages.

Nardi does not know which way to go. "Hey, Sergio!" he repeats for the umpteenth time. "Can you hear me? Where are you?"

"Help!"

This time the call comes loud and clear.

"It's coming from below," says Stefanini.

Without wasting any time, the two of them sprint to the stairs and begin to descend.

"Help, help! Somebody help me!"

Brunetti's cries become more and more desperate.

"We are here, and we're coming." Massimo has certainly not forgotten the unfortunate fate that befell the other two victims, and he wonders what scenario he should expect.

He is surprised when he reaches the bottom of the stairs because the area seems deserted.

The staircase leads to a damp basement, a sort of cellar where small porthole-shaped openings allow light to filter through. But except for three metal cisterns leaning against the wall at the bottom, there is nothing else.

Or so it seems.

It is a matter of a moment – time for Sergio to shout again.

Guided by the sound, Nardi's gaze falls downward, to the foot of the tanks, where a movement is seen through a metal grating on the floor. It is Brunetti's fingers wiggling.

"He's there!" cries Massimo, rushing forward. "Oh, shit!" he then adds, chilled by the spectacle before his eyes.

Sergio is trapped in a pit dug into the ground. The grate above him prevents him from getting out, but it does not prevent the water from getting in. Vessels are pouring their contents into the pit.

"Oh God, help me!"

"Hang in there. We'll get you out now."

When he and his colleague try to lift the grate, they find it blocked by two padlocks. He glances at the tanks, looking for some kind of valve, but sees nothing to stop the flow of water. The tanks are anchored to the ground, and it is practically impossible to move them. Besides, there would be no time: the pit is almost completely submerged, and Brunetti's lips press against the metal in search of air.

"Be careful. Get down!" Impossible as it may be, Massimo motions for him to cover himself. Then he points the gun forward, shows Stefanini one of the padlocks, and says, "You blow that one off."

Soon after, the guns fire simultaneously. The padlocks splash away. And while the shots still echo, they rush to lift the grate.

When the water begins to overflow from the pit, Brunetti is now outside, safe.

***

By now, the evening has long since fallen. What illuminates the area are the flashing lights and headlights of cars, flashlights that move here and there in the hands of police officers.

In the back of an ambulance, Sergio Brunetti sits on a stretcher with a blanket over his shoulders. In addition to several cuts on his hands from friction with the grate, he has a bad wound on his forehead. Paramedics are attending to him.

"Does he have much longer?" asks Nardi, eager to ask him some questions.

"We're just finishing his medication. Just another minute."

He lets out a sigh, more like a snort, and as he waits, he casts a glance in the direction of the cottage. Stefanini and the forensics men are searching the interior for some clues. He hopes that at least this time they will find something useful.

"Of course, it was lucky that you arrived in time." Paolini's voice reaches him from behind.

"Yes!" he replies, turning to his colleague. "And I don't like it."

"Uh?"

"I don't see this guy relying on luck."

"What do you mean by that?"

"I don't know. It's an impression. I think we're missing something."

"But come on! He just made a mistake. Like everybody else, after all. They always make some mistake sooner or later."

"That's the problem. He's made too many mistakes, and all at once."

"Isn't it rather that you overestimate it?"

"Mah! Maybe," he concludes, unconvinced.

Returning to turn around, he waits for the paramedics to step aside.

Brunetti is still half trembling, but at least he got out without serious injury. Seeing him again in that pit, looking for a breath of oxygen, he thinks back to the other two victims. He cannot imagine what they might have felt in those last moments without even a hope of rescue. Perhaps that is why the fact that Sergio has been saved is not enough to satisfy him. Having had the killer in range and not being able to catch him annoys him more than ever.

Not even Lanzi, with his rabbit-like running, could catch up with him. Unfortunately, the man had already planned his escape, making sure to leave his car parked on the road behind the hill.

"That's it!" says one of the paramedics, stepping aside.

"Are you done?"

"Yes. But I don't know if..."

"Don't worry. Just a few quick questions," Massimo interrupts.

However, before he can take a step, he sees Paolini carrying himself expeditiously in the vicinity of the ambulance. As usual, he wants to run the show.

"Are you ready to tell us how it went?" he asks.

Brunetti does not answer.

Paolini calls his attention a few times but to no avail. Seeing that the other one does not react, he turns to Nardi with a puzzled expression.

"Hey, Sergio!" he interjects. "Are you all right? Can you talk?"

The man's eyes, however, are lost in emptiness. His arms crossed, he stares straight ahead, trembling and silent.

"That's what I was trying to tell you," says the paramedic. "He's in shock."

Undeterred, Nardi insists. "Did you see his face? Could you describe him?"

"I told you. He is still in a state of trauma."

Massimo cannot restrain a gesture of annoyance. "Damn it!" he shouts. And continuing to grumble to himself, he starts walking in the direction of the farmhouse.

CHAPTER 27

At nine o'clock in the morning, in a conference room at police headquarters, all the officers assigned to the Twisted Wall investigation are present. Although the meeting is already on the agenda, Brunetti's foiled murder has added additional aspects to be examined, and there is a certain electricity in the air.

Standing in front of the others, intent on reporting the events of the previous evening, Guido Paolini gesticulates almost triumphantly, barely holding back a smile in an ill-concealed expression of self-satisfaction.

Nardi, who has stayed in the doorway to escape the air conditioning, keeps his arms crossed and his eyes fixed on his colleague. He watches him curiously, trying to figure out what on earth he has to cheer about. The fact that the killer failed to carry out his murderous plan is only half-victory. The man is still on the loose, and he certainly won't stop on his own. On the contrary! The anger and frustration of the unsuccessful attempt will probably make him even more dangerous.

Among other things, he continues to have doubts about the killer's latest moves.

The uncoordinated action, the prematurely found verse, the carelessness in covering the tracks... He fails to frame these superficialities as mere unforeseen events due to chance, even though Sergio's testimony at the hospital seems to prove him wrong.

According to his version, after breaking into the house and attacking him by surprise, the man had been distracted by the unexpected intervention of a neighbor, who, because of the noise, had gone to knock on the door. To prevent Sergio from answering and calling for help, the assailant had nearly suffocated him by pressing his head against a pillow. When the neighbor had retreated, the other must have become agitated because he had chloroformed him in a hurry. This had prevented the anesthetic from working all the way through, and Sergio had awakened earlier than he should have in the trunk of the car.

At first overcome by panic, he remembered his cell phone in his pocket, turned off. He had had just enough time to turn it on and dial the police number before the car came to a stop. There was still the sound of the call on the other end of the line when the tailgate opened wide, and the blindfolded guy appeared in front of him.

Socking him in the face, the man snatched the phone out of his hand to throw it to the ground and stomp on it forcefully. After that, grabbing the jack from the spare tire compartment, he knocked him unconscious with a blow to the head.

Sergio had awakened in that underground prison, with the iron grating above him and water dripping down.

In short, even according to him, the killer's carelessness was justified by the unexpected visit of the neighbor. Still, Massimo cannot shake the doubt that it is all part of a twisted plan.

Absorbed in these thoughts, he had followed the meeting as if he were somewhere else. He is sure he heard the names Teresa Graziani and Silvia Rigoni mentioned, but he has no idea what was said about them. Only distant voices reached his ears.

When he turns his attention back to what is happening in the room, he sees that some people are turned toward him and watching him.

"...yesterday there was speculation about a connection

between the Twisted Wall murders and this other case being handled by Inspector Nardi," he hears Paolini say. "However, the latest elements at our disposal seem to support a completely different hypothesis."

"What do you mean?" asks one of those present.

"I'm talking about the photographs found in Brunetti's house. One of them turned out to be very revealing. A picture that shows him in the company of Carlo Pietrangeli."

"The second victim? I mean, did they know each other?"

"Yes! As it turned out, Pietrangeli was his lawyer and a long-time friend."

"So, if I understand you correctly, you are suggesting that we go ahead with the serial killer theory, ignoring the connection between Brunetti and the investigation into his daughter. Right?"

"Not really. I mean, as far as the daughter is concerned, yes. Pretend I didn't tell you about that. But as far as the killer is concerned, there is a small change. It seems that the kind of murderer we are dealing with is quite different from what we thought." Paolini raises his hand and points to the profiler sitting in the front row, motioning for him to intervene.

"That's right!" confirms this one. "Serial killers may choose people at random, or they may plan it down to the smallest detail, but always for the purpose of satisfying their murderous impulse. They certainly do not base their choices on the personal relationships that might exist between the victims. If anything, they look for a symbolic link that binds the victim to themselves."

"In short, we pick up where we left off," says Paolini. "The only exception is the man we're hunting. We are not dealing with a serial killer. So, whether he's acting on his own or a hired killer, it's reasonable to assume that he has a specific list of targets."

"It would be appropriate to conduct further verification on Juliana Petrescu," suggests another of the investigators. "If that is the case, there must be some connection that places her in the triangle as well."

"Colleagues are already looking into it. We will also try to hear from Brunetti as soon as possible. Maybe he can give us some guidance on the matter. So... if nobody has any further questions..."

These last words are followed by a few headshakes and raised eyebrows. Some people start making small talk, some put the ringer back on their cell phones or even start making calls, and some just get up to head for the exit.

As the room quickly empties, Nardi is still there, standing by the door. He waits for his colleague to come in.

Paolini is finishing gathering some papers. When he finally gets ready to leave, he flashes a smile and says, "You really came to punch out, huh? You didn't say a word."

"Would it have done any good?"

"Uh?"

"I've already told you how I feel. There are too many things wrong with the way that man acts. It's almost as if we were dealing with two different people."

"But come on! You know what I think instead? That this guy panicked at the exact moment you went to see Brunetti. Of course, you were there to talk to him about his daughter, but the killer couldn't have known that. When he saw you, he probably thought you were there for him. He must have thought he had been discovered or would be soon, and so he anticipated the timing. Doesn't that seem like a logical explanation?"

"Yes. But beyond logic, there is instinct, and mine tells me that something is wrong. In any case, you're running the operation, so there's no point in us talking about it any further. I salute you!"

CHAPTER 28

July 13, morning, 10:00 a.m.

Leaving the offices of the police headquarters, Nardi decided to go for a walk to think a bit in the fresh air. First heading towards the Quirinale Palace, he then turned back towards Nazionale Street, where he began pacing the sidewalks from one side to the other. Between the gleaming storefronts of those nineteenth-century buildings, the bursting white of the Altar of the Fatherland in the background, and the grayness of the cobblestones on the pavement, he walked a couple of miles. Finally, tired of wandering, he stopped to enjoy a cup of coffee.

Sitting at a small table in a bar, under a still lukewarm sun, he glances distractedly here and there. The bustle of the passers-by appears as a blurred image, one among many already cluttering his mind, silhouettes without contours, reflecting thoughts governed by uncertainty. He continues to wonder if the two cases are actually connected or if he is making a blunder. Because he has to admit, Paolini's hypothesis is just as valid: his visit to Brunetti's house could have been misinterpreted by the murderer.

Unlike his colleague, however, he does not rule out the possibility that a single perpetrator could be behind this tangle of events. After all, if Carlo Pietrangeli was Sergio's lawyer, a longtime friend to boot, it is likely that Teresa and her daughter also knew him. In that case, everything would acquire a meaning.

Immediately intending to ask her for confirmation, he probes the breast pocket of his jacket to find his cell phone, but at the thought of hearing her voice, he feels his arm grow heavy and fall back down.

The stain of the past resurfaces from nowhere. Suddenly, Nardi sees himself back on that cursed street as he arms the lifeless hand of the man on the ground. Pressing his fingers against the grip, he had let that piece of metal speak instead of truth and justice, turning his own life into a lie.

That is why solving crimes has become a kind of drug.

It is his temporary anesthetic.

And no matter how many crooks he puts in jail, sooner or later, the effect wears off, and everything starts all over again.

Seized by discouragement, he forces himself to return his attention to his work. He pushes the memory of that scene out of his mind and, with it the idea of making the call.

In order to validate his own theory, he goes back in search of a missing piece, a detail that can irrefutably associate those investigations with each other.

Of course, there is no lack of similarities. Starting with the symbolism and the theatrical staging: Bible verses on the one hand, photographic shots on the other, both designed to mock the recipient. But this is not enough to dismiss alternative leads.

It is clear that whoever sent the photos to Teresa wants to make her suffer slowly; otherwise, he would not have waited so long. And to assume that the attempted murder of Sergio is part of this machination is plausible. But if it were true, if the episodes were the work of a single perpetrator, why would he have acted as he did? Why lure Teresa to the hospital, making her believe that the murdered woman was her daughter, and then cut her off from everything else without implicating her in any way in the murders related to the Twisted Wall case?

In search of an answer, the mind begins to retrace the entire history of Angela Brunetti. A succession of flashbacks takes

Nardi back to the events of the past few days. He thinks back to Silvia Rigoni, who became a scapegoat for the sole reason of having handled the adoption procedure; to Mr. De Marchi, who had shed light on the baby's abduction; to Rinaldi, who took the existence of another man in her life for granted. He thinks back to the necklace he had received and the moment he had seen it portrayed in the bloody picture. He even thinks back to Sandro Donati, to the anger he felt for that absolute failure.

Finally, the sight of a passerby distracts him from his thoughts.

The man catches his attention for no particular reason. He seems to be just another person. But Massimo is convinced that he has noticed something important. So he begins to follow him with his gaze as he walks away, now with his back turned. He minutely scrutinizes his physique, his clothes, his hairstyle, and the way he walks. He tries to figure out what has struck him, but nothing he can grasp is worthy of interest, at least not until his mind jumps back in time and takes him back to just a few moments ago.

Suddenly, he sees the man before him again, the image of his face at the exact moment he had first noticed it. Because of the light, that face had seemed ambiguous to him, for the features that outlined it were lost in the shadows.

This detail paves the way for a whole new set of thoughts.

He thinks back to Tancredi, the witness who had cleared Donati of the murder charge. And who knows why? A doubt creeps back into his mind. Maybe it's because he doesn't want to give in to the evidence, or maybe it's because he remembers when he had summoned him to the station: it had seemed strange to him to hear him parroting an incident from six years before.

In any case, since he knows the place where it happened, he tries to visualize the scene. Thanks to what he had read in the minutes, he is able to focus on the exact spot of the scuffle, as well as the spot from which Tancredi had watched as a spectator. But try as he might, it is all to no avail. Though he knows the exact time – four-thirty in the afternoon – establishing the angle of the light is beyond him.

Nevertheless, he does not decide to drop the bone. His stubbornness forces him to continue, probably in search of something that does not exist. He imagines witnessing the clash between the two, a scene in which Donati and the other man appear as dark silhouettes, but it is a mere fantasy.

He begins to feel like a fool and is about to let go of these thoughts when a detail suddenly occurs to him.

He remembers the date on the file: February 12.

How is it possible that he didn't figure it out right away?

That time of year, that time of day, it is practically dark. And from that distance, Tancredi could not have distinguished one face from another, not on that dimly lit street.

It is easy to guess why the detail escaped the attention of colleagues. Blame the staggered timing. Tancredi came forward about two months later when daylight saving time was already in effect, and the days had long since lengthened.

Now, however, it is clear that he lied.

This means that Donati's alibi does not hold up. The man has escaped a murder charge thanks to a false statement. And it does not matter that that crime has nothing to do with the case of Angela Brunetti. It is enough to bring him back into the picture.

Massimo has not changed his mind. He still finds it absurd that a person would wear gloves to avoid leaving fingerprints and then make the stupid mistake of touching the object with his bare hands. But this reasoning has already led him to underestimate the problem once. At the Postal Police headquarters, he had settled for the explanation provided by Donati since it seemed the only one with any logical sense. And he had trusted a witness who, strangely enough, had appeared in person when a telephone confirmation would have sufficed.

In due course, he will report the perjury to the proper authorities: the case will certainly be reopened. For the moment, however, he will keep the information to himself, at least until he has shed light on Donati's possible involvement in the affair concerning him.

Meanwhile, Nicola Tancredi will have to explain many things to him, starting with why he lied.

As he stands up, Massimo realizes that he has not found the answer he was looking for. Whether or not there is a connection between the two investigations remains an open question, but now he is interested in other things. And then, who knows? In the end, Paolini may even be right.

CHAPTER 29

Signs advertising villas and apartments shelter the interior of the premise from the gaze of passersby – the words "For Sale" and "For Rent" paper its entire glazed wall. Only the front door shows itself in total transparency – a simple but effective ploy to invite people to cross the threshold.

Beyond the glass, Nicola Tancredi is sitting behind a desk, busy talking on the phone. From the look on his face, it must be a pleasant call. He smiles.

Nardi watches him from the street. He is undecided about the approach to take. After all, searching for the truth is a bit like venturing on an aimless journey: one knows the starting point but never the destination. Under such circumstances, there are no right or wrong paths, only those that lead somewhere. The only thing to do is to equip oneself as best one can, so as not to be caught unprepared, and to follow them.

A tempting way to proceed would be to pretend not to know, to let the liar hang himself with his own hands in the end, one lie after another. Too bad the situation lends itself poorly to credibility.

He certainly can't say he just happened to be passing by. He might as well lay his cards on the table and get straight to the point.

Without further ado, Nardi pushes open the glass door and crosses the threshold. A slight draft of air, due to the contrast with the humidity outside, accompanies his entrance.

Still caught up in the phone call, Tancredi gives him a distracted look. Time for a quick glance, and his eyes fall back down, only to rise again in the instant that follows. He must have thought it was a customer, because he shows all his surprise before his face turns somber.

"Sorry, I have to go! I'll call you back." In cutting off the conversation, he puts down the receiver, slamming it against the device. "You again?" he then continues, annoyed. "You really decided to torment me. What do you want again?"

"Are you alone?" Nardi asks, pointing to two empty desks on the other side of the room.

"My co-workers are out with clients. So! What do you want?"

"The truth."

"Huh?"

"How did things really go?"

Tancredi's expression becomes more somber. The aggressive impetus dissipates in the air, giving way to a gaping mouth from which no syllable escapes.

"I know you lied about Donati. I want to know why."

"Hey… no, wait! What are you talking about?"

"Let's go! Don't make a scene; you don't need to."

"There must be some misunderstanding. I assure you…"

Just then, a man opens the door and starts to enter.

Tancredi jumps to his feet and rushes at him, preventing him from getting any further. Without even a hint of a greeting, he says, "Look, I'm sorry! I don't know how to apologize, but we'll have to put it off for another day."

"What do you mean? We had an appointment."

"Yes, yes, I know! You're right. Unfortunately, something came up, and I have to go. If you want, I can show you the apartment tomorrow or whenever you want, but I really can't right now," he justifies himself. And before the other can answer, he raises his arm to indicate the exit.

Shortening the distance more than necessary, he pushes the customer back, almost forcing him out, until he walks away, annoyed. So he closes the door, gives the lock a jerk, and when he turns around, he leans his back against the door and lifts his head in the air.

His posture speaks volumes. There is no need to push any further. He has already given up.

So Nardi stays and watches him for a few moments, giving him time to collect his thoughts. "Well?" he finally asks. "Have you decided to tell me how it went?"

"Come on, let's talk about it over there," the other resigns.

In the back, a tiny room houses two armchairs with a small table in the middle, a TV on one wall, and a minibar in a corner. A kind of former storeroom converted into a relaxation area.

With a sigh that is anything but relieving, Tancredi drops into a chair, runs his hands through his hair, and lifts his eyes. "Am I under arrest?"

"Not yet, but you don't seem like a fool. You know you have to answer for what you've done. What you tell me now might make a difference, though."

"What do you want to know?"

"Did you agree with Donati all along? Why did you lie about him? Did he pay you, or what? Mind you! Choose your answer well, because this time I will get to the bottom of it."

"I had no other choice."

"Huh?"

"I had to protect my partner. If I didn't agree to lie, those damn people would hurt her, and I couldn't let that happen."

"So they threatened you. And who did that?"

"Some guys I'd never seen before. Friends of Donati's, I guess."

"Would you be able to recognize them?"

"Well, who knows? It was so long ago."

"Why didn't you go to the police? You wouldn't be in this mess now."

"I wanted to, I assure you. The thing is, I was afraid. And

then…" Tancredi's voice takes on a tremulous, feeble quality until it fades into a whisper.

"And then what?"

"You see, Inspector, I didn't play ball with them right away. At first, I tried to resist. Unfortunately, I soon realized that I had no choice."

Nardi presses his lower lip between his fingers as a frown appears on his face. Raising his chin, he signals to continue.

"It happened one night when we decided to go out for dinner. I had a work appointment a little late in the evening so I would have joined her at the restaurant. But when I arrived, even though I was late, she was still not there. I spent half an hour waiting for her with my heart in my throat because she was not answering her cell phone, and I didn't know what to think anymore. Then I saw her coming. She explained that she had been bumped at a traffic light. But she was fine, and the car was insured, so we went to dinner anyway. Unfortunately, the surprises were not over. When we got to the table, I got a phone call. It was one of those two guys. I still remember his sarcasm, saying accidents happen every day, and sometimes people won't get out alive. Can you imagine that?"

"Well, I'm trying to."

"As I listened to those words, I looked at the woman I loved sitting in front of me. If anything had happened to her, I could never have forgiven myself."

"So you gave in to blackmail."

"What else could I do?"

"And after that? Did they show up again?"

"Just once, to tell me how to behave. Then I never saw them again."

"Um…" Massimo is silent for a few moments, his eyes zigzagging here and there. The story seems credible, and Tancredi does not give the impression of lying. Still doubtful, though, he scans his face. "Okay. Taking your story at face value, do you have any idea why they chose you?"

"In what sense?"

"They could have been paying someone, or looking for a person whose silence they could secure. They took a big risk with you. If you had reported the fact or said one word too many, you would have spoiled their plan. So I wonder *why you*. What was so special about you?"

The other shrugs and shakes his head, showing the typical expression of someone who does not know what to answer. "Mah! Maybe they knew I wouldn't risk it," he dares. "I loved her too much to do that. I still love her to this day, and I haven't come to terms with the fact that I lost her. It's been more than a year since her funeral, and I should have gotten used to it, instead..."

"Hey, wait a minute! What do you mean, a year?"

"Huh?"

Massimo wonders if there is a grain of truth in the man's words. Did he lie at the police station, or is he lying now?

"The last time, you said that she had died shortly after the fact, six years ago. You claimed that was why you remembered the whole thing perfectly."

With a sigh, Tancredi picks up a picture frame placed next to him and brushes the glass. "Well, in a way, that's what happened," he says, as his eyes glaze over.

"What the hell kind of answer is that? If there's one certainty in life, it's death, and it certainly doesn't happen twice."

"Of course not the way you mean it. But that's how it was for me. I lost her when she went into a coma and then five years later, when she was gone forever."

Nardi opens his mouth and lifts his eyelids in amazement as the other, handing him the photo, adds, "Look how beautiful she was. It was my life."

"Angela?!"

"Uh? How do you know her name?"

To confirm that his eyes are not deceiving him, he asks again, "Was your girlfriend, Angela? Angela Brunetti?"

"But why? Did you know her?"

This revelation has caught him by surprise. He no longer

knows what to think or how to act.

It is clear that the choice of Tancredi, among so many potential subjects, was by no means a random gesture. Angela is the invisible thread that somehow connects him to Donati, whose involvement is no longer in question.

But Donati's role in the affair is still a question mark. There are too many unanswered questions about him. It is hard to believe that he could have been the architect of everything, starting with the sending of the photos. By now, he had gotten away with it; he could have stayed in the shadows. Why expose himself years later? Besides, why pick on Teresa?

"So, did you know her?"

"Huh? What? Oh, yes, yes, indeed!"

His forehead already furrowed, Tancredi shakes his head and gestures in confusion. "But how…"

"It's complicated," Nardi interrupts, reluctant to dwell on explanations. "Her mother is an old friend of mine. That's enough for you to know. Rather, satisfy my curiosity. Did Angela know about this story? Did she know about the threats?"

"No, I preferred not to tell her anything. It would have only served to worry her, and I was already doing enough of that. After all, I wasn't proud of what I had done."

Just as he imagined. In his place, Massimo would have kept his mouth shut as well. Who knows if this was also planned? Maybe the real target was Angela, and Tancredi was just the bait to get to her.

"What can you tell me about the son?"

"Uh?"

"Pier Giorgio. Do you happen to know where he is?"

"I don't follow you. What child are you talking about? She never had one."

"What do you mean? For years she has been sending her mother photographs of herself and the baby."

"Believe me, Inspector. I really don't know what to tell you. If there was a son somewhere, I never knew anything about it."

Looking at the bewildered expression etched on the other man's face, Nardi tries to collect his thoughts, but by now, there is only a lot of confusion in his head. This case is like a Penelope's web. Each unraveling knot unravels new ones, and the answers pave the way for more questions, as if there should be no endpoint.

"But did you live in the same apartment, or did you each have your own life?"

"We lived together, but, I repeat, I never saw a shadow of a child. If I even tried to touch on the subject, she would get strange and change the subject. The idea of becoming a mother didn't sit well with her."

"From the way you talk, I gather she never explained to you why."

"Oh, if I could have at least understood why, maybe I could have gotten over it. Because the idea of having a baby didn't bother me at all, but with her, there was no hope. It was like talking to the wind. Then one night, she got so angry that I decided not to push the matter any further, so I stopped asking questions about it."

"Well, I think I can answer that. Angela was a rape victim and got pregnant in her early twenties. It's hard to leave everything behind in cases like that."

"What?!"

"It's just so unfortunate."

"Oh my goodness! But how is it possible that I didn't know about this? Now I understand why there was so much paranoia. And I, who thought it was just her way of getting noticed."

"What are you talking about?"

"Her many obsessive manias. She was always checking that the door was locked or looking around when she was outside, as if everyone she met must have a reason to spy on her. She would often get up at night and look out the window to make sure everything was normal on the street. Not to mention the times she made me drive around the block two or three times before I could park. From time to time, I would suggest that she talk to a psychologist about it, but I never thought…"

"Was she always like that?" Nardi interrupts. "Or was there a particular time when she started acting strange?"

"Um!" Tancredi brings a hand to rub his chin and thinks for a few seconds. "Actually, she's gotten a lot worse lately," he finally says.

Maybe it doesn't mean anything. Maybe Angela's gestures were really those of a paranoid person. However, a question starts buzzing in Massimo's mind.

Could it be that she had recognized her attacker?

For a few moments he stares into the eyes of his interlocutor as if looking for the answer in his gaze. He is tempted to ask more questions about it, but, unable to place this conjecture in the scene, he lets the idea go as it came. "All right. I think that's enough."

Still standing on the threshold, he turns to leave. But before he can take a step, Tancredi's voice reaches him in the doorway in a wavering whisper.

"And me…?"

Massimo remains with his back turned. He barely turns his head to cast a glance behind him. "When someone you love is involved, it is easy to make mistakes. I know that very well. I won't promise you anything, but I will try to help you. If it's not necessary to mention your name, I'll see if I can keep you out of the investigation and turn a blind eye to the past."

"Thank you, Inspector. I don't know how…"

"I'm doing it for Angela. And anyway, wait until it's all over before you thank me. Like I said, I can't make any promises."

"It's already more than I expected. If you ever need anything else, you know where to find me."

"Wish you never had to see me again," he concludes. "Now I'm going to say goodbye. I have an urgent matter to attend to."

CHAPTER 30

July 13, noon

Donati lives in the southeastern part of town. From Tancredi's location, it took Nardi quite some time to reach his house. Upon arrival, he finds Lanzi lurking in his car in front of the building. He had contacted him as soon as he set foot back on the street to inform him of what he had discovered, to have the man's address sent to him, and to tell him to join him.

Busy keeping an eye on the front door, the sergeant seems not to have noticed him as he drove by, parking two cars behind him. To get him to turn around and notice his presence, he has to knock on the window.

"Oh, Chief!" he gasps from inside the driver's seat. "I wondered where you went." Getting out of the car, he adds, "I was just about to call you."

"I was in some traffic. How are we doing here? Has he shown up?"

"Not yet."

The hands of the clock do not yet mark noon.

"Are you sure he's in the house?" asks Nardi.

"I don't know. His branch manager told me on the phone that he took a few days off."

"Okay, let's try to go upstairs."

Lanzi makes his way briskly to the gate. He, on the other

hand, walks slowly, stopping every two or three steps. He scans the street in the distance, afraid that the man, if he arrives now, might recognize him and run away.

The sergeant pushes the button panel quite a few times without any response coming from the intercom. "He must have gone out," he says, pressing the button again.

"Could he have seen us coming?"

"Um! I don't think so."

A man approaches the gate. He already has the keys in his fist, but he hesitates to insert them into the slot. "Looking for someone?" he asks.

"Can you open the door for us? We're supposed to go upstairs, but there's no answer on the intercom." Nardi puts on a reassuring smile. Then, realizing that this is not enough to wipe the hesitation from the other man's eyes, he pulls his badge out of his pocket. "Rest assured; we are the police."

"Oh, that's okay then. Sorry, but these days, you know how it is. You can never be too careful."

"Yeah!"

Once inside, the man gives vent to his curiosity. "Who are you looking for?"

"A person who lives in the building," Nardi says ironically.

Annoyed, if not offended by the evasive answer, the other man frowns and falls silent. While waiting for the elevator to arrive, he limits himself to an exchange of forced glances and smiles. Then, as the car's descent begins to illuminate the shaft from the inside and the doors are about to open, he turns away from them, steps back a few feet, and begins to rummage through the mailbox.

"Do you need to go up?" Lanzi is already ready to push the button.

"Go, go! I'm in no hurry."

When they reach the top floor, Nardi waves his hand to warn his colleague not to make too much noise. Nevertheless, as soon as he steps onto the landing, he breaks the silence himself. "Hmm, bad sign," he comments, pointing to the apartment on the right with a jerk of his chin.

The door to the dwelling is ajar, and no sound comes from inside.

Lacking a regular warrant, he simply pushes the door forward. Standing motionless on the threshold, he looks at Lanzi as if asking for advice. He is unsure whether to enter or not. In the end, though, with Donati a flight risk, he hesitates no longer. He draws his gun from his holster and waves to go in.

The apartment is small. The only two doors are to the bathroom and the bedroom. The rest of the house consists of a living room with a kitchenette. It takes little to realize that no one is there.

Nardi lingers in the sleeping area, observing the wide-open closet and the clothes strewn across the bed and floor. "Looks like he packed in a hurry. He must have realized it was only a matter of time before we got to him."

"Yep, and we just missed him," Lanzi echoes from the kitchenette. "The coffee machine is still full, and it's hot."

"Damn traffic," Massimo thinks. If he had arrived a few minutes earlier, they would have caught him now.

Keeping him from mulling over the fact is the sergeant's voice that comes back to be heard: "Hey, Chief! Come here," he hears him say. "You got to see this."

"What is it?"

Standing still in the living room, Lanzi does not answer. He motions for him to come over and raises his hands to indicate the wide-open cabinet door in front of him.

Nardi steps forward reluctantly. He is still angry about what happened. The man has conned him too many times. Now, just like at the Postal Police headquarters, he has slipped out from under his nose; and who knows that he was not the guy who disappeared into the bush the night before at the abandoned cottage.

The answer to this last question comes a moment later. Just a few steps are enough.

When his gaze reaches the other side of the cabinet door, Massimo's eyes widen. A sudden gasp is followed by a brief bewilderment. "I said so!" he exclaims. "It couldn't have been a coincidence."

Taped to the wood are the photos of Teresa, Angela, and Sergio, the one of the social worker, Silvia Rigoni, and not missing those of the two tortured victims, Carlo Pietrangeli and Juliana Petrescu.

"When I think that he was sitting in front of me, I looked into his eye... what anger! We could have caught him from the beginning. I should have understood that. Now those two wretches would still be alive."

"Come on, Chief; you couldn't have known. There's no point in blaming yourself. At least the search is over. He won't go far by now."

"Oh, no! Nothing is finished. The motive is still a mystery. And without that, we are still at a disadvantage," Nardi retorts. He makes a circle in the air pointing to the photographs. "What connects these people? And what meaning do they have for him? We don't know. So if he ever plans to strike again, we have no way of anticipating him."

"But now we know who he is. If we hunt him properly, we can flush him out."

"You think so? So far, he has shown good skill. He has proven to be far too clever. He has managed to fool us all along."

The exchange of views is interrupted by the ringing of Nardi's cell phone. When he answers it and hears Paolini's voice, his mind flashes back to the scenes of this morning in a split second; he remembers how he got there and what he promised himself he would do.

Bringing a hand up to cover the microphone, he pulls the smartphone away and turns back to Lanzi. "Be sure," he whispers, "if they ask you any questions, do not mention Tancredi's name."

The other, while not understanding why, imitates him in that murmur. "What do you mean? And why?"

At this point, everything they need to frame Donati is in front of them. There is no need to implicate the man for the investigation to move forward.

"If anyone asks, we came here for the imprint on the mailing envelope, just to ask a few routine questions. Since the door was open, we got worried and came in."

The sergeant shakes his head and opens his mouth to mimic an exclamation, suggesting he has grasped his intentions.

Only then does Nardi remove his hand and decide to answer the call. "Yes, Guido. Go ahead."

"Finally! Took you long enough."

"Sorry. I was finishing up a matter."

"I wanted to let you know that we found something interesting about your case."

"Meaning?"

"Do you remember the photos found at Brunetti's house yesterday?"

"Sure. So what?"

"Do you know who appears in one of these?"

"Come on! Let's not play guessing games. I have more important things to discuss with you."

"Hey! All right, don't get excited. There is a picture of Angela Brunetti in the company of an unidentified girl. Probably a friend, judging by the shot. They were taking a selfie at a bar counter. Anyway, that's not what's important, but the fact that she unwittingly framed the man sitting two seats over, and that's Sandro Donati."

"What! Are you sure?" Massimo told him about Donati just the night before at Sergio's house, and it all ended there. Paolini doesn't even know what his face looks like. "How do you know it's him?"

"It is confirmed. Our computer analysts are trying to retrieve every kind of information they can from the photos: places, dates, and names. When I read his name, it came back to me that you had mentioned it. I called you at the office to tell you, but since you weren't there, I asked Cataldo to send me his file."

"And do you also know when the picture dates back to?"

"No, I'm sorry. Judging by her age, though, I'd say she was in her early twenties."

About the time of the abuse, Nardi thinks. In his eyes, the figure of Donati begins to become unwieldy. From the rapist to the murderer with no apparent logic. The fact leaves him baffled.

"Aren't you going to say anything? This sounds like a good turn for your investigation, doesn't it?"

"It's not *my* investigation, but it is ours."

"In what sense?"

"Do you know where I am as we speak? Right at Donati's house."

"At his house? And how…"

"He ran away," Massimo interrupts. "In return, he left us a nice little gift."

"What are you talking about? I don't understand."

"That I now have confirmation of what I thought. There were never two cases. In here are photos of everyone involved in the story."

"Are you sure?"

"I'm looking at them right now. There are pictures of them, including the two murdered people found at the Twisted Wall."

"Then don't move from there. I'll warn Stefanini to come to you with his team."

"All right. And while you're at it, contact Mellis to get an arrest warrant," he concludes, ending the call.

Lanzi has moved to the other side of the room. He looks around with his back turned.

Massimo puts his cell phone back in his pocket and returns to staring at the pictures taped to the cabinet door. His eyes rotate from one face to the next until his gaze lingers on Teresa's face.

He twists his mouth and snorts.

It is now time to bring her up to speed on the situation. He can no longer keep her in the dark about what is happening.

CHAPTER 31

July 13, afternoon

The click of the lock is like a revolver shot. It makes Nardi gasp, holding him in suspense for a moment.

As he pushes the door of the building forward and lets go of his breath, he feels the features of his face change into a mask of anxiety. He thinks it is a consequence of the stress accumulated during the previous day, in which everything had unfolded in a frenzy: there had been no time to inform Teresa.

From the moment the culprit had taken on a face, the entire task force had gone to work to begin a manhunt.

Forensics had taken possession of Donati's apartment; computer analysts, thanks to phone records and money movements, had reconstructed a map of the areas where he had been most recently; an alert had been issued to all the area police stations, as well as to the maritime and airport authorities; and investigators had circulated the man's photo among every possible informant.

Massimo, on the other hand, had been summoned to the police headquarters, where he spent most of the afternoon. After updating the police commissioner of his actions, he had been forced to attend another meeting, to inform his colleagues about the investigation in which, from the very beginning, he had been the main protagonist.

Returning to the police station late in the afternoon, he had been on the verge of making a phone call to Teresa when one too many yawns had convinced him to put it off until the next day.

Now, however, he feels the anxiety growing from floor to floor.

As if marking the notches on a thermometer, the elevator rises, reducing the distance separating him from her, and he regrets that the investigation has reached a turning point.

A stupid excuse, that of tiredness. He knows it well. The gasp from just before hid more than that.

Nevertheless, he is here now. All he can do is ignore that kind of inner discomfort and ring the doorbell.

He is surprised when the door opens. "Sergio?!" he exclaims. "What are you doing here?"

"Well, this used to be my house too, right?"

"Oh, sure, sorry! I didn't mean to..."

"Come on in."

"I just thought you were still in the hospital."

"They wanted to keep me another night for observation, but I checked myself out. It was nothing serious," Brunetti explains. Then, hinting at a shy smile, he adds, "I have to thank you. I talked with Teresa and cleared up a lot of loose ends. It would never have happened without your visit. I know it was your initiative; she would have kept me in the dark. So, thank you."

In the living room, Teresa sits on the sofa. "Finally! You decided to show up," she exclaims, not hiding her annoyance. "You promised to keep me in the loop."

"That's why I'm here."

"Is there any news?" asks Sergio.

"We identified the culprit. He seems to be responsible for everything, from Angela's rape to what happened to you the other night."

Sergio's eyes widen, Teresa jumps to her feet. "Did you catch him?" they ask in unison.

"Unfortunately, no. When we got there, the apartment was

empty. He had already fled."

"Damn it! Damn it!" she complains. "What about the photos that have been sent to me over the years? Are those his work, too?"

"It seems so."

"Who is he? Someone I dealt with when I was on the force?"

"I don't know, we haven't found anything yet. His name is Sandro Donati. Does that name ring a bell?"

Sergio and Teresa watch each other. And as their gazes question each other, mutual head shakes and chin lifts seem to say, "Not to me. And to you?"

Showing them a photo of the man, Massimo asks, "Have you ever seen him before?"

The reactions of bewilderment are repeated. The two remain staring at the face of a stranger.

Teresa's eyes become charged with rage, letting out a sense of pure hatred. "Never seen him before."

"Neither have I," says Sergio. "But I don't understand. Why would this guy target us?"

"The motive is still a mystery. And so are all the victims he left behind."

"Victims?" echoes Teresa. "You mean besides the woman killed in the hospital, there were others?"

"That's right. Have you heard of the two bodies found at the Twisted Wall?"

"Are you referring to The Missionary, the serial killer making headlines?"

"That's the one. It seems that Donati is behind these murders."

"And what would that have to do with us? It makes no sense. Already the fact that he has been stalking our family for more than 10 years seems inexplicable. But this is beyond logic."

"Less than you think."

"Huh?"

"Carlo Petrangeli, you know him, don't you?"

"He's our lawyer, a friend," Sergio interjects. "Why?"

"The man who was killed two mornings ago was him."

"Carlo, dead?!" Sergio opens his eyes wide and puts a hand to his forehead. "I can't believe it. How is it possible that no one told me anything?"

"Have you forgotten where you were that night? You were about to end up like him. It was really close."

"Oh! You're right. Then one day in the hospital. I had almost forgotten about it. Gosh, though! What bad news."

"I still don't understand, though," Teresa continues. "Are you sure you're not mistaken? Because again, this story just doesn't make sense."

"I thought so too at first. But everything seems to say otherwise." Massimo shrug and spreads his arms wide. "In his apartment we found photos of you two and the other people involved. Among those found at Sergio's house, there is also one in which Sandro Donati appears behind Angela's back, and the time seems to coincide with that of the rape." Continuing the story, he tries to convince himself in turn that this is indeed the case. In fact, part of him continues to reject the idea that the man could be the architect of it all. In any case, he has no intention of sharing his doubts. Not with them.

"But what about Pier Giorgio?" Teresa puts her hands to her chest and her tone of voice becomes more agitated. "Have you found anything that might lead to him?"

"Unfortunately, no."

"Oh my God! If it really was Donati who sent me the photos, you have to take him alive. He must know where he is."

"Um, who knows! Maybe," Massimo merely says, keeping to himself what is on his mind. Convinced that it was better to leave out a sore point, he had kept Teresa in the dark about the kidnapping story all along. And now, after talking to Tancredi, he even doubts that the grandson ever existed.

Of course, there was once a child, but he was taken away. Hard to believe that the one in the photos is really Angela's son. Easier to think of a charade staged to punish her mother. After all, she had written to her, *"He is my son. Your grandson. His name*

250

is Pier Giorgio." Words and a name that now resound like a drum.

"What do you mean? Why do you say 'maybe'?" grumbles Teresa. "If he didn't know where he was, how could he have photographed him for years?"

"I've wondered that myself."

"So what?"

"So, nothing! I can't answer that."

She looks at him biased, stares into his eyes. "Are you hiding something from me?"

"Huh? What?" he hesitates. "No, of course not. What nonsense are you thinking? I have to go now. If there's any news, I'll let you know."

As Teresa's face darkens and she returns to her seat, Sergio prepares to escort him to the door.

Massimo stops him with a wave of his hand, moves his head to point at his friend and says, "I know the way. Stay with her."

He turns, without adding anything, and walks down the hall. But on the verge of leaving the apartment, he glances behind him. For a moment, he wonders if he is doing the right thing by remaining silent. And as quickly as the question arose, he concludes that, yes, it is better to wait for the right time, when he can prove what he suspects about the existence of that grandson.

251

CHAPTER 32

July 16, morning

Three days of searching were in vain. Donati seems to have vanished into thin air. Although the police have searched everywhere for him, he is still on the run.

The thought that he might have escaped across the border put Nardi in a foul mood. The doubt haunted him all night, and then, in the morning, it even managed to make him skip breakfast. Usually, hunger drives him to rummage through the cupboard with the voracity of a wolf ready to bite. Instead, with his stomach locked in a vise, he touched no food. He barely drank a cup of coffee without tasting it.

Now he is beginning to feel some gurgling, but by now, having set foot in police headquarters, he has no time to go back and stop at a bar to eat something. He is already late for the press conference announced the night before.

The involvement of the media, decided because of the impasse, concealed the hope of getting possible reports from the citizenry. It represented a *quid pro quo* that usually got everyone to agree. In similar situations, newspapers and television were always well liked by the police. And who knows why? They, too, used to change their skin, transforming themselves from information jackals into rule-abiding professionals.

Climbing a flight of stairs, Nardi glances at his watch. Eleven-thirty passed a few minutes ago, and the meeting should have started by now. However, his pace does not seem to pick up. He continues to walk unhurriedly.

Such events always started with a slight delay. Besides, he doesn't really care. If it were up to him, he would have avoided going there; now, he would be at the police station looking for some clues to follow.

In the corridor where the conference room is located, the sight of a pair of photojournalists confirms that he was not wrong about the lack of punctuality: the two, still busy with test shots, frame here and there whoever happens to be in their way. Meanwhile, a buzz of voices emanates from inside the room, growing louder as he approaches.

Beyond the door, he sees seated journalists talking to each other, others scribbling who knows what on notepads or their tablets, some latecomers busily arranging the latest microphones on the table, video cameras mounted on tripods or slung over the shoulders of cameramen.

In the confusion, a voice rises from the chorus. It asks if there is still a long time before the start. And even though there was no answer, the crowd silences shortly after that when Paolini enters the room with two other officials and takes a seat in the middle of the table.

Behind him, four uniformed officers form a backdrop, along with the monitor hanging on the wall, the ornaments, and the symbol of the State Police.

Paolini welcomes the small audience, extends the greeting to whoever is watching from behind the screen, and then begins to emphasize the reason for the meeting, as if nothing had happened.

Seeing the almost strutting attitude with which he addresses the cameras, Nardi wonders how he can be so brazen. He finds it absurd. If his colleague feels the slightest bit of embarrassment, he does not show it.

He would not be able to do the same, not in the face of such an obvious truth. In a way, he envies his gift. For it may be true that the man likes to appear, but he is now there to announce a defeat: nothing to exult about or take credit for. But in the end, it is precisely this being a politician, even before being a policeman, that has brought Paolini to where he is. It is what has always distinguished them from each other.

"The murderer, now known as The Missionary, has been identified as Sandro Donati," Nardi hears him say. "Unfortunately, the man has eluded capture. We, therefore, ask anyone who sees him, or has information about him, to alert the authorities."

Donati's image appears on the large monitor affixed to the wall, and the cameras immediately change angles. From Paolini's half-length shot, they zoom in on the face of the wanted man.

"Is there solid evidence of his guilt?" a reporter asks.

"More than enough to link him to the murders."

"What is this about? Can you be more specific?"

"Not at this time. The investigation is still ongoing. I can only tell you that the material found leaves no doubt that he is involved."

At the sound of these words, the figure of a backpack materializes in Nardi's mind.

Found in the apartment along with the photographs, it contained a variety of notes on the victims, as well as the material used to immobilize them.

The analysis confirmed a match between the roll of tape and the glue residue found on the bodies. The same was true for the fibers of the gauze and the rope. And from the dimensions, the bruises on the wrists and ankles also matched perfectly.

Faced with this evidence, he could do nothing but put aside his doubts and accept that Donati had acted alone. From the car records, it had even turned out that he owned a black Panda. And it certainly did not take science to deduce that it was the same one used in the attacks.

With his gaze still lost in the void, Massimo returns to the question of why he did what he did. He wonders if the verses could provide an answer, or were merely a means of deflecting the investigation. On the other hand, in the absence of a motive, this series of criminal acts continues to make no sense.

When he finally turns his attention back to what is happening around him, Angela Brunetti's face fills the monitor on the wall. Paolini continues to speak, but Nardi's head is already elsewhere. Ignoring his words, he only hopes that Teresa is not watching television.

*****

Donati is holed up in an old cottage nestled in the Lazio countryside. A dilapidated, damp dump whose only virtue is its isolation from the rest of the world. No one would dream of looking for him there. The place has been abandoned for years, and the only sign of life around it is that of the wild animals that inhabit the area.

There is poor cell phone strength, so the phone has poor reception. The video comes and goes. But that does not stop him from keeping his eyes on the screen. At irregular intervals, he watches the press conference where they talk about him.

Already annoyed at how everything went wrong, he feels his anger rise when he sees the woman's face appear on the big screen in the hall. He stands there looking at her in half disbelief. He knew that he would pay for his guilt sooner or later, but he never imagined that it would happen in such a way, without even being able to reveal the truth about the matter. To think that he had even fooled himself into thinking that he could start over.

In a way, he feels cheated. It was not supposed to be this way.

Now he is hunted; he can do nothing but stay where he is, waiting for the dust to settle. But his mind is already working on a new plan.

Maybe they will catch him this time, or maybe he will manage to escape. He doesn't care. In his rage, he just wants to get revenge on those who got him into this mess.

He knew that Tancredi could not be trusted. He should have taken him out from the start. And that Inspector Nardi? He still remembers the look in his eyes during the meeting at the Postal Police headquarters. In those eyes, he had sensed danger, and he had not been wrong.

The situation itself had also seemed abnormal to him. Something was not right. Despite this, instead of listening to his instincts, he had gone ahead without thinking, underestimating his opponent and ignoring many small signs.

Ah! What a fool he was. If he only thinks back to the imprint on the bloody envelope, he cannot come to terms with it. He has taken too many things for granted, but it is too late to turn back now.

Noises coming from outside interrupt his flow of thoughts.

Fearing that he has been discovered, he jumps to his feet and goes to the window. For a few minutes, he stands motionless next to it, close to the wall. Then he sticks his head out just far enough to glance outside.

Everything seems calm, yet the tension continues to rise. His breathing begins to become labored. With his hands clenched into fists, and his jaw clenched, he feels the muscles in his body contract one by one. And, aided by the humidity, beads of sweat begin to trickle down his forehead.

The most primitive part of him wants to run away, but he is immobilized, especially when he hears the sound for the second time. Suddenly, a knot in his throat holds him with bated breath. Convinced that he has reached the end of the line before his time, he remains there, hovering, until finally, a fawn emerges from a bush. Only then, collapsing to the ground, does Donati let go. He puts a hand to his forehead to wipe away the sweat, closes his eyes, and takes a deep breath.

Thinking back to the fear he felt, he feels the anger grow even more. He glances at the mattress where a semi-automatic - a Glock 17 FS - lies. Determined to give his emotions free rein, he pulls himself up, grabs the gun, and returns to the window.

The fawn is still out there, looking around undisturbed. He takes aim, and instead of the animal, he imagines he is looking at the real perpetrators of the affair. About to pull the trigger, he sees the quadruped turn its head in his direction. It seems to stare at him with the air of a sacrificial lamb. For a few seconds, he hesitates and is almost tempted to lower his arm, but then he returns to point the gun forward and fires.

There is a wild rage in him. He keeps telling himself that, come what may, he will not be the only one who has to make amends. They will all have to pay.

They will pay dearly for what they have done to him.

***

Now over by a few minutes ago, the special service has given way to commercials. Teresa's eyes, though, are still on the television; they stare into the void that separates her from the screen. She thought she had surrendered to the evidence; instead, she still cannot accept the idea that Angela is dead.

Seeing her face in that context, without warning, was like being shot at point-blank range. Along with a whirlwind of violent emotions, that scene brought back the pain.

As if that were not enough, she is worried, or rather, afraid.

Donati is considered a dangerous individual, and in cases like this, it is easy for things to get out of control. If the police should manage to track him down, anything could happen. And she cannot help but worry about his safety.

If he were to die before he could talk, he would take all the information he has with him.

The man has taken pictures of her grandson for five years in a row. If anyone should know where he is, it's him.

It could not be otherwise.

Massimo's reluctance to admit this gives her pause; it is another woodworm that plagues her mind.

The former colleague is a man who is even too much of a

stickler. The fact that he was so vague about something so obvious is a sign that there must be more to it.

She had thought the same thing three days ago when he had only answered with a 'maybe'. At that moment, however, her hatred for Donati had gotten the better of her. Blinded by anger, she had let it go, pretending to ignore the look of discomfort on his face. As time passed, however, the doubt became more and more insistent until it became a fixed nail.

Now she can't help but wonder what information he's keeping from her.

On several occasions, she has come close to calling him to force him to talk, but the fear of what she might hear back convinced her to desist.

If she is right, this can only be more bad news. Knowing him, she would not be surprised to find that he is trying to protect her. But from what?

After so many stabs to the heart, what pain could still hurt her?

That it concerns Pier Giorgio?

At the thought, a tremor runs through her body.

Turning back to the phone, she continues to stare at it insistently. She hopes it will ring in a few moments.

She waits patiently, even though the device remains silent.

"Come on, get up! Play!" she begins to say in her head. And in anticipation, she repeats the request in bursts.

In the end, however, she has no choice but to give in. Resigned, she turns away.

It is then that she feels a pang in her stomach. A sudden spasm pushes her forward so forcefully that she is lifted an inch from her chair. It must be the part of her that would like to rebel against this passive submission.

In any case, it is all useless. Fear is stronger than her.

Although she has been tempting fate for years, never fearing the consequences of defeat, she is not willing to gamble now. If her suspicions turn out to be true, who knows if she could withstand the blow.

She prefers not to find out.

Ignoring the pain that shook her, she sits back down.

And as the mind continues to wander through the uncertainties, the eyes fall back into the void.

CHAPTER 33

Nardi was not wrong after all, Lanzi thinks. Oh, yes! After an afternoon of taking phone calls, he can't help but agree with him. That press conference was a mistake in every respect. Not only will it have helped to put Donati on alert, but it is also a waste of time. It has even slowed down the investigation, at least as far as he is concerned. Unlike the Mobile Squad – which has continued to operate in complete peace and quiet – they have been left with low-level work. It's like being in a call center, with all the calls routed to the police station.

By now, he is beginning to get tired of asking the same questions over and over again and listening to the same sounding ramblings. He has been talking to people since this morning who have lost their minds.

Even if some idiot has enjoyed giving false information, it's certain that the idea of a serial killer on the loose has created a collective fear. Suddenly, Donati has become omnipresent. It seems that everyone has seen him in one place or another.

As was to be expected, no one in authority at the conference bothered to offer any reassurance on the matter. All it would have taken was a few more words, pointing out that the killer whose footsteps they are following is of a completely different type, and now he would not have to sit there wasting his time.

However, there is no point in taking it to heart. On such occasions, it worked that way. Some things could be said, and others had to be kept quiet.

Sitting at his desk, Ettore fiddles with a rubber band, waving it between his fingers. Without stopping to huff and puff out of boredom, he keeps one elbow resting on the arm of the chair and his chin resting in the palm of his hand. He watches the phone, waiting for it to ring again, when he moves his pupils from side to side with the slowness of a sloth. He glances around for a few moments until his eyes fall back down to stare at the drawer where he keeps his notes on the case. Then he furrows his brow, lifts his eyes, and sighs.

He is disappointed by the turn of events. The idea of dealing with a serial killer had excited him. He already felt like one of those FBI criminologists who wrote books about their miraculous exploits. Anyway, the ringing of the phone, which comes back to his ears, ends this reverie.

He looks at his watch. It is almost six o'clock. "Here we go again," he thinks as he picks up the receiver. "Hello?" he answers listlessly.

Throughout the morning, he had taken the trouble to add "police" to his answer, but now he has stopped doing so, considering that calls are routed from the operations room. Those on the other end already know who they are talking to, so he has taken to saving his breath.

A male voice comes from the phone, "Yes, hello, I'm calling about that fugitive they showed on TV this morning. I saw him about half an hour ago."

"Who am I talking to? Can you tell me your name?"

"No, see… I'd rather not."

"It's the procedure. I need to know…"

"I already told the person I spoke to earlier," the voice on the other side interrupts. "I don't want any trouble. If you're interested in what I have to say, fine, otherwise I'll say goodbye."

Perfect! Now they were even starting to pass him anonymous

calls. Evidently, even the call handlers must be getting tired of this routine.

"Where are you calling from?" asks Lanzi. "Is this your number?"

"No. I'm at a gas station, and I'm using a pay phone. I told you I don't want any trouble. Are you interested in what I have to say or not?"

"Go ahead and say it. I'm listening." Ettore lets it go. After all, what does he have to lose? Talking to one person instead of another makes no difference.

"As I said, I have seen the man you are looking for. He is nearby, in an abandoned shed in the middle of the forest."

"In the middle of a forest? Ah, but!" Ettore smiles, amused. "And what were you doing there?"

"I was returning from hunting. When I heard a shot, I came closer to see who it was and recognized him."

Another idiot who doesn't know how to kill time and likes to make up fairy tales, he thinks. "Oh, I see! But it's July. Am I wrong, or does the hunting season start in September?"

"No, you're not wrong. That's why I don't want to give my name. If it were for something else, I wouldn't have called you, but since we are talking about a murderer, it seemed appropriate to inform you. However, if I have to go through trouble to do so, you can forget about my help."

A poacher! This confession of the man is like a flea in the ear; it puts every word in a new light. "How do I know you're not making this up?"

"Say, does this guy happen to have a black-colored Panda?"

"I beg your pardon?" Ettore jumps out of his chair like a spring. The press was kept in the dark about this detail. Hoping that Donati would make the mistake of not getting rid of the car, it had not been mentioned at all.

"I asked you if he drives a black Panda."

"Yes, yes, I understand. Why this question?"

"Because it was parked in front of the shed. When I realized who I was standing in front of, I didn't go any closer, but I took a picture with my cell phone and got the license plate number. Would you like me to tell you?"

"Yes, please," he replies, sure that the man is not lying. "You said you heard a gunshot?"

"That is correct. But I don't know what he was shooting at. It seemed to me that he was alone."

Lanzi immediately checks that the license plate matches. Then, with no small difficulty, he gets the location of the hut explained.

On Google Maps, he easily locates the municipal road that runs along the wooded scrubland, but then the route gets lost in the vegetation. The trails leading into the interior are not shown on the map, so he has to rely on the man's directions to circumscribe the area. "Perfect! Thanks for the information," he finally says. And putting down the receiver, he runs to Nardi's office.

***

They have been walking for about fifteen minutes now, and the sun is already out of sight. Nardi begins to fear that they are going in circles. Around him, he sees nothing but trees and bushes and clouds of annoying insects massed in the air.

He does not like forests. He has always seen them as open-air mazes. With no patterns and no landmarks, they give the impression of always being in the same place, stuck. He almost wants to give it all up and go back the way he came, but at this point, he even doubts that he can find his way back on his own.

With Paolini's team, they had met at the gas station where the report had originated half an hour earlier, and they had left the cars there.

At first, he had thought this was a good solution since, in this sparsely populated area, the unusual influx of vehicles could have alerted Donati, while the parking lot was far enough away to minimize the risk. Now, however, he regrets not choosing a closer location.

With a sigh of resignation, he continues to advance with felt-tipped footsteps. Turning to Lanzi, he asks in a low voice, "Are you sure this is the right direction?"

"We should be close." Ettore looks at the map he has printed out. "According to the directions, we should have been there a while ago."

"You said that even five minutes ago, but still?"

"Shh, be quiet!" interjects Paolini. "Guys, this could be it."

In response to this call, Massimo takes a look into the distance. And like a claustrophobic being pulled out of a confined space, he feels a weight slip from his stomach.

About a hundred feet ahead, the vegetation thins out and gives way to a clearing.

Beyond the row of bushes that separates them from the open space, he can make out a small wooden house.

The hut stands close to a rocky outcropping. Shabby wooden planks, misaligned and half falling off, give the impression of a place that has been unsafe and unused for some time. However, it appears that someone is inside. A faint light shines from one of the windows, and it's possible to see a shadowy movement.

He is on the verge of speaking but has no time to open his mouth.

"The information was right," Paolini says, turning to face him and hinting at a sarcastic smile. "The press conference was just a waste of time, huh?"

Caught off guard, Massimo feels uncomfortable and, in order not to show it, tries to pull himself together. "A stroke of luck," he says, playing it down. "What do we do now?"

"In the meantime, let's surround him. Send some of your men to either side of the shed. Tell them to keep their distance so they can't be seen. And tell them to keep radio silence. The radios make too much noise."

With a slight shake of his head, Nardi signals Lanzi to make the arrangements. Then, turning back to Paolini, he asks, "Have you any idea how to get him out of there? He's armed, as far as we know, and if we take a step forward, we'll be easy targets.

We would be out in the open."

"Don't worry; I'm not going to take any chances. He can't go anywhere anymore anyway. He will have to surrender when we tell him to come out. If he dares to fire even one shot, as soon as he sticks his head out, he's a dead man."

Hearing these words, Massimo thinks of Teresa, of her grandson. Suddenly he feels his own certainties creak. If he is wrong, if the child does really exist, Donati is the only one who can provide the answers. "We have to take him alive," he says. "We need him if we're going to get to the bottom of this investigation."

"It all depends on him."

"Let's go! You said yourself that he can't go anywhere. Sooner or later, he has to come out."

"Sure. But in the meantime, I'm not willing to get shot at."

"Nobody's telling you to do that. I'm just saying stay calm."

The exchange of banter is interrupted by the arrival of Lanzi. Careful not to be noticed, he approaches, walking with his head down. "The men are in position on both sides. What is the next move?"

"We were just talking about that," Nardi comments.

"We've already discussed it. There is nothing more to discuss. This is my operation, my decision. If you don't agree, too bad."

Paolini barely has time to finish his sentence. The sound of a gunshot unexpectedly echoes through the air, shattering the surrounding silence and causing everyone to jump in fear.

"What the hell? Who fired that shot?" cries Massimo.

"It came from inside the house," answers one of the policemen behind him.

"Damn it! I told you to keep out of sight." Paolini gives Nardi an angry look. "Well, the negotiations are over before they even started," he points out. Then, grabbing his radio, he tells the officers, "You are authorized to return fire. Move in on the flanks and get that bastard out of there, dead or alive."

"Tell him to aim low," Massimo says. "You don't have to kill him to knock him out."

When the other does not answer, he tries to insist but realizes his words are useless. Concentrated on following what is happening in front of him, Paolini has stopped listening to him. That shot has set off an uncontrollable mechanism, and now there is no way to stop it.

"Stay where you are, or I will shoot," can be heard shouting in the distance. "I will not repeat this a second time. Don't come any closer!"

Out of sheer instinct, the men slow their march slightly, looking at each other hesitantly.

One of them goes over the radio again. Looking for confirmation, he asks, "Should we keep going?"

"Yes, keep going! Don't stop," Paolini replies. "Just try to be careful. Expose yourselves as little as possible."

"You're putting men's lives at risk with your stubbornness," Nardi says. "And for what? For something you could achieve with a little patience?"

Although the words did not have the desired effect, they must have struck a chord. This time the colleague gives him a look. Short but long enough to see a strange light in his eyes. So, determined to change his mind, Massimo continues his work of persuasion, at least until a second shot rings in his ear and shuts him up once and for all.

He felt the bullet graze his head.

Suddenly, he sees the men rushing forward and returning fire, aiming at anything that moves in the vicinity of the hut. He holds his breath as one of them falls to the ground. Fortunately, the man quickly gets to his feet, starts running again, and he can breathe again.

For a moment, he lifts his eyes to thank the sky. But the relief is short-lived. Just enough time to look away, only to watch helplessly what is happening.

He wishes he could do something, intervene in some way, but the action unfolds too quickly. Before he can move a muscle, the house is surrounded, officers begin to rush in, a series of flashes of light and the sound of three or four more gunshots are added, and when it all stops, there is an unreal silence.

Convinced that the operation had the worst possible outcome, he remains motionless and silent. Quivering impatiently, he waits for confirmation, praying that he is wrong. But when the radio comes back on, even the last doubt is swept away. The man died in the conflict.

"Damn it! We needed him alive," he says in an angry voice. And with a dirty look at Paolini, he continues: "May the devil take you! You and your Gestapo methods."

Still cursing loudly, he walks toward the shed with Teresa's face in his mind like a curse.

When he reaches the door, he sees Donati's body lying on the floor. His mouth is open in a kind of silent wail, and one arm is outstretched toward the gun not far away. Despite the fact that his heart no longer has a pulse he continues to bleed, in a reddish stain that gradually soaks the floorboards.

Massimo watches the scene completely detached from it. His interest is in another detail: the man is wearing a long-sleeved shirt, just like in the headquarters of the Postal Police.

Careful where he puts his feet, he approaches the body, kneels down, and lifts the fabric from his forearm, just enough to catch a glimpse of what he is looking for.

The figure of a spider, tattooed a few inches from the wrist, confirms that Sandro Donati is also responsible for Angela's rape.

CHAPTER 34

July 17, morning, 8:00 a.m.

Sergio has been up for a while. Sitting in the living room of his house, he continues to yawn and squint his eyes as he gulps down a cup of coffee.

It is his third in less than an hour.

After this horrible night, if anyone were to ask him, he would swear that he did not sleep at all. Yes, he may have dozed off for a few minutes, but most of the time he tossed and turned in bed, thinking endlessly about the phone call Nardi had interrupted his dinner with.

Tormented by that constant nagging, the echo of his words woke him whenever his eyelids grew heavy and dropped.

"Donati is dead," he had heard Massimo say. And while he should have rejoiced at that statement, he had just stood there, his fork in his hand, staring at the plate on the table.

Unable to understand how he felt, he had simply asked how it happened and listened in silence to the answer.

And now, despite the sleepless night, he is still struggles to find an explanation for the mixed emotions running through him. As if joy and sorrow were annihilating each other, satisfaction is smothered by shame, consolation is crushed by guilt, and pleasure gives way to regret.

"Justice has been done," he wishes he could say. But he can't.

Consciousness colors this moment with a very different atmosphere than he imagined. Only now, does he seem to truly realize that his Angela will never return.

Obviously, a part of him wanted to deceive himself until the end. But unfortunately, time does not heal wounds. It only numbs them. And if, by chance, they come back to bleed, well, then it turns out that they have always stayed where they were, and they hurt even more than they did before.

He was convinced that the death of the culprit would be enough to give him peace, to at least partially compensate him for the loss he had suffered. Instead, he has the impression that he no longer feels anything. Suddenly, he feels like a barren plant, emptied to the core. Also, since nothing has changed, the disappearance of an enemy to blame has robbed him of the last foothold to which he could cling.

To dispel this feeling of apathy, he takes his last sip of coffee, puts the cup down on the table and pulls a photo of Angela from his wallet: the last one left after the police confiscated the others.

Looking at his daughter's face is enough to make him feel alive again; it makes the hatred resurface.

Raped by that animal, she will have faded day by day, consumed by pain, while he got off lightly, too lightly. Knowing that a bullet in the chest has brought him a quick death drives him mad. So, in a fit of rage, he throws the cup beside him to the ground, watches it shatter into a thousand pieces, and cries, "No! This is not justice."

Fortunately, there is still Teresa to act as a dike.

Maybe, at least with her, things will get better.

***

It is a beautiful morning. The rain that fell during the night has finally dampened the unbearable humidity of the past few days, and a pleasant wind has already blown away the clouds. In a clear sky, blue as it hasn't been in a long time, the sun is shining quietly.

Nardi has accompanied Teresa to the cemetery to visit her daughter. She did not feel like coming alone, and he could not say no.

Earlier, she had apparently planned to come with Sergio, but he backed out at the last moment because of a sudden migraine. Maybe, after the nasty bump on the head, he would have done better to stay another night in observation.

Anyway, they are here now and Massimo looks around.

A hearse has just passed through the entrance and is moving slowly with a group of people in tow. Up ahead, another funeral seems to have just ended. There are also quite a few people scattered here and there. Yet, he would be quick to say otherwise. For some inexplicable reason, all cemeteries give him this strange impression: they seem deserted, like wastelands buried in oblivion. It must be because of the many cypresses and mausoleums that make everything seem small and insignificant, starting with the very fact of existence. One is born and dies for no reason.

Absorbed in this reflection, Massimo continues to walk in silence, his gaze zigzagging over his surroundings. Then, Teresa's voice interrupts his thoughts.

"You know something?" he hears her say. "I haven't been able to set foot in a casino since this whole thing started. And, I assure you, I've tried."

"Well, that seems normal to me," he replies, turning to look at her. "You have a lot more on your mind right now."

"No, it's not that. I don't know how to explain it to you. It's like just being there makes me sick inside."

"Do you expect me to believe you would have stopped playing at any moment?"

"It surprises me too. But I think so."

"What can I say? I wish you well. The gambling has always been your downfall. If you could leave it behind, it would mean that not everything was in vain."

"You don't believe me, huh? I understand you. I've tried so

many times that I've become unreliable. But this time is different. I can feel it."

"I see you are convinced. I almost envy you, you know? I, on the other hand, have not only not moved on, but I now doubt that it will ever happen."

"Huh? What are you talking about?"

"I'm talking about the night you were attacked."

Teresa stops suddenly. She stares at him with a surprised look on her face. "I thought we said we weren't going to talk about that anymore."

"Well, now we are! Does Sergio know anything about this?"

"Where would you get such an idea? I've never told anyone. But why are you bringing it up again? It's been so long."

"For you, maybe. I have relived that scene hundreds of times. I still have trouble coming to terms with it. I killed an unarmed man and went to great lengths to cover it up. That's not something you forget."

"What is it? Do you need to feel absolved? Well, in that case, go to a priest and confess. I don't think I'm the right person." Teresa takes a couple of steps forward, bringing herself within a few feet of him. "Maybe, do you think you would have ended up behind bars if we had told it straight? At best, who knows, you wouldn't be a police inspector today. I can only tell you one thing that seems to escape you. You not only took a life that night, but you saved another. Mine. So stop agonizing over what was an accident and start thinking about living yours."

Clouded by guilt, Massimo had never looked at the matter from that perspective. He had been blind for so long that he did not realize it, but there was more than rot in his actions. He realizes it now. And for the first time in a long time, he feels an almost forgotten sensation: he feels clean. "Thank you," he says then, as Teresa's words still ring. "Maybe, I needed to hear that."

"Does that mean you're going to put this behind you?"

Ignoring the question, he flashes a smile and raises an arm, pointing to the road ahead. "Come on, let's go! We didn't come here to talk about me."

She looks at him for a moment. She doesn't seem to want to insist. They start walking again without adding anything else.

A hundred yards later, they reach the place where Angela is buried.

On a marble wall, her face is one among many.

Teresa approaches the tombstone, caresses it tenderly and lets out a soft cry.

Meanwhile, Massimo stands on the sidelines. Feeling he is in the way, he feels uncomfortable. He would like to move away from her, to leave her alone with her pain, but instead, after a while, he comes closer to her and puts a hand on her shoulder. "Be strong," he says.

Turning slightly to face him, she places her hand on his, blinking and nodding as another tear falls.

"Do you think we'll ever be able to find Pier Giorgio again?" she asks, running two fingers over her eyes to dry them.

Taken aback by the question, he wrinkles his forehead almost imperceptibly. He doubts if there is an appropriate time to tell her what he really thinks about the matter, but this is certainly not the time. So, to be as natural as possible, he lies as best he can. "I'm sure of it. You'll see! One way or another, we'll get through this."

As he finishes saying these words, his gaze falls back to the framed photograph on the tombstone. Suddenly, he opens his eyes wide and stares at the image in front of him.

"What is it?" asks Teresa.

"This picture!"

"Huh?"

"It's the same one you got two weeks ago. It's not torn, and there's no blood, but it's the same one."

Teresa puts her hand over her mouth. With a mask of astonishment on her face, she says nothing.

Massimo also shut himself in silence. Intrigued by this strange coincidence, he frowns and rubs his chin.

Is it possible that there is more?

CHAPTER 35

At the police station, life seems to have returned to normal. With little coming and going in the corridors and a total absence of noise outside, there is a calm that has not been felt for days. Except for a few voices in the distance, Nardi's office is bathed in silence, and he takes the opportunity to reflect.

Having returned about fifteen minutes ago, he sits at his desk with his gaze fixed on the window. He still cannot get the photo he saw on the tombstone out of his mind. It seems strange that Donati's choice fell precisely on that one.

It is hard to think of a simple irony of fate.

He wonders if it does not hide a deeper meaning. And if so, what might it be?

In his eyes, the only object worthy of any interest is the silver necklace. Like in a relay race, it represents a kind of passing of the baton. Sergio had bought it at the time; Teresa had received the picture showing it around Angela's neck, and he had seen it delivered to him before all of this began, resulting in his being dragged into the case in spite of himself.

But as much as it is possible to glimpse a logical thread, what undermines the argument is the impossibility of answering one question. For what purpose would Donati have involved him in his plans?

Of course, even the motive regarding the others involved remains a mystery, but as far as he is concerned, the matter is different. The search of the apartment had made it very clear who the predestined targets were, and his name was not among them. So why make him a participant?

Unfortunately, Donati will no longer be able to answer to this question, nor any others. With his death, any possibility of getting answers has disappeared.

Just thinking about it, Massimo feels the anger against Paolini growing again. His impulsive actions and lack of consideration for the consequences have practically led the investigation to a dead end, starting with Angela's son.

Does he exist? Does he not exist? At this point, he is no longer sure of anything.

After lying to Teresa for the umpteenth time, he begins to wonder whether it is the desire to spare her pain that drives him to silence or rather the insecurity that controls him.

In any case, there is no point in continuing to rack his brain. Now there is only one way to get to the bottom of things, and that is to pry into Donati's life.

On the desk, neatly arranged in a stack of files, is all the material they could find on him. So, without wasting any more time, Nardi grabs the top folder and begins to look through it, searching for any clue.

"May I?" he hears a moment later.

Looking up, he sees Ettore Lanzi standing in the doorway.

"Sure, come along. Give me a hand."

"What for?"

"I've been going through Donati's files."

"For what reason? What's the point now?"

"I need to clear up the matter of Angela Brunetti's son."

"I thought that chapter was closed as well. Last time you had said…"

"Yes, I know what I said," he interrupts, with the annoyed look of someone who doesn't appreciate objections. "But whether he exists or not, I need proof."

Lanzi nods, makes a condescending grimace, and settles into the chair. Then he stretches a hand toward the pile of documents and asks, "What exactly are we in search of?"

"I have no idea, maybe nothing. I hope something turns up. That's all."

For about ten minutes, Nardi's eyes wander unsatisfied over the pages. Each time a detail catches his attention, his gaze wanders between the lines, and he pauses to reflect. With the pen he clenches in his fist, he makes notes, underlines, and taps on the desk to mark the time. Not a single passage, however, seems to point to a concrete clue, and under the impression that he is only wasting time, he lets loose a gesture of annoyance. "The hell with it! There's not a damn thing here," he complains, hurling the file across the desk.

Taken aback, Lanzi jerks in his chair, opens his mouth, and turns to look at him. "This matter is really stressing you out," he says, after catching his breath. "Have you lost your patience already? We've only just started, and there's still a lot of paperwork to go through."

"The thing is, I'm angry. If we had taken Donati alive, we wouldn't have to stand here now looking for who knows what."

"Well, this is the way it is now. No use gnawing your guts out."

"Yeah!" Nardi replies. Twisting his mouth, he accompanies the exclamation with a resigned sigh and leans back in the chair.

Meanwhile, he sees Cataldo coming over.

With two knocks on the door, the deputy announces his presence, asks permission to enter, apologizes for the interruption, and enters the room. "The ballistics reports came in," he reveals, waving a clipboard in the air.

"Ah, okay! Give them to me, thanks."

Cataldo takes another step forward, stretching his arm just far enough. As soon as he sees the file slip out of his hand, he asks if anything else is needed, waits for the answer to be no, and takes his leave.

"Papers, papers, and still more papers. Just for a change,"

276

Nardi ironizes. With a sigh, he lets out a breath in a kind of snort and begins to read listlessly. Soon, however, he raises two fingers to rub his chin, and as he continues to read, he realizes that his expression is changing. More and more surprised by what he sees, he feels his forehead and eyebrows wrinkle, his mouth bend indecisively, one way and then another, until his teeth hold it by gripping his lower lip.

Lanzi must have noticed the sudden change. Without waiting for him to speak again, he asks, "What is it?"

"You want to know?" he shouts. "We've been tricked."

"Uh?"

"About the shooting the other night. Different shell casings were found. The caliber is the same, but the rifling doesn't match."

"What do you mean?"

"According to the ballistics guys, Donati's gun would have fired only once, at least while we were there. Only two bullets were missing from the magazine, one of which was lodged in the belly of a deer that had died a few hours before we arrived."

"Impossible! We all heard two shots. Especially the second. It came close to hitting one of us."

"Indeed. We did hear shots. But as it turned out, they were not from the same weapon. One of the cartridges was found not in the shed, but behind it, in the rocks. And the bullet from that cartridge was lodged in one of the logs behind us."

"But that means..." Stunned, Lanzi lets the sentence hang. Open-mouthed and wide-eyed, he puts a hand on the back of his head. "Oh, man!"

"Yes, it means exactly what you think. This case is far from being solved. Someone else must be involved."

"A mysterious Mr. X would have waited patiently for the explosion of the first shot and then fired at us to make us react – an ingenious trap. If Donati had pulled the trigger more than once, no one would have noticed. In the confusion, we certainly would not have counted the shots. We would have blamed him for everything."

"You used the right word, trap. I said it! The whole thing didn't add up from the beginning. A killer who seems to do everything perfectly and then falls into gross mistakes like the print on the bloody photo."

"Or like the failed attempt to kill Brunetti. Have you thought about that? The photos found in Donati's house made us think that the two cases were connected. And what if, instead, he had tried to imitate The Missionary to pin the murder on him? It would explain a lot."

"You forget about the backpack and its contents. Forensics confirmed a match with the material used on the victims. And then there's the car, the black Panda."

"Oh! You're right. I hadn't thought about it."

"Anyway, now the questions open up again. Who are we dealing with? And whether it is an accomplice or a rival, will he also be involved in the murders and everything else? Or was the other night just a way to tie up some loose ends?"

"Considering the trick he played on him, I find it hard to think of an accomplice."

"Who knows? Maybe he is a double agent. Or maybe, when he realized things were starting to go badly for him, he thought it was time to cut his ties."

Lanzi grits his teeth and pounds his fist on the desk. "It must be the same person we got the report from. I'm willing to bet on it."

"Probably," he agrees as if he doesn't care about the detail. With one elbow on the arm of the chair and one cheek in the palm of his hand, he begins to stare down at the floor. Suddenly his mind flies elsewhere. He thinks of Teresa, of her grandson, and in the meantime, he hopes that the mysterious man is in cahoots with Donati. This would mean that someone can answer questions about Pier Giorgio.

Enraptured by this thought, Nardi remains motionless for a few more moments. Even if just a little, he feels his mood rising. Taking a deep breath, he tries to give himself a boost and turns his attention back to the pile of files. "Up! Let's pick up where we left off," he says. "There's still a lot of documents to look at. It might give us a lead on the subject. There must be some connection between the two. And maybe it's in these papers."

Without replying, Lanzi continues to read. Massimo, on the other hand, picks up the file he threw away earlier and looks at the last pages he had left unread. Not finding anything of interest, he closes it once and for all and moves on to the next one.

He soon realizes that what he has in his hands is the record of Teresa's trial. Apparently, he must have gotten confused while putting it away and accidentally slipped it between Donati's papers.

Intending to put it away, he opens a desk drawer and is about to close the document when doubt suddenly seizes him. Some detail must have caught his attention, because his pupils jump frantically across the page, searching for something.

The last time, he had skimmed the transcript: just enough time to understand what had happened on that occasion. But who knows, maybe there is more. He is almost sure of it, judging by the insistence with which his eyes search the text. He must have missed some important passage.

As he continues to search, he wonders what it could be until his vision stops on a line, a name: *"Carlo Pietrangeli, defense attorney"*.

He doesn't even have time to wonder. In a split second, his attention shifts a little lower. And that's when he opens his eyes wide and in astonishment. "Oh, shit!" he exclaims.

Another name, one of the prosecution's witnesses, suddenly lifts the dark veil that shrouded the connection between the victims.

Juliana Petrescu. It was her, the woman who had argued with Teresa in the game room.

"What is it?" asks Lanzi.

"We were wrong to focus the investigation on Angela Brunetti. This case is all about Teresa Graziani."

"Why, what have you found out?"

"I reread the transcript of her trial. Pietrangeli was the lawyer who represented her, and Petrescu was one of the witnesses. I would say that completes the triangle. Add her daughter and ex-husband to the list, given their relationship, and that's it. We have a common thread between all the subjects. Except for the social worker, they are all here."

"Hmm! I don't know. Then why didn't the killer start with her?"

"Well, maybe I'm wrong, but considering the photos sent over the years, I'd say the intention was to make her suffer slowly over time."

"Let's have a look," Lanzi says, almost wary of his words.

Nardi stretches out an arm to hand him the file and stands silently, watching as he reads through the papers. Waiting for him to raise his eyes again, however, he sees a strange expression on his face. "What is it?" he asks curiously. "Did you find something else?"

"Did you notice the court order number?"

"Huh?"

"Take a look at that number," Lanzi urges, handing the file back to him.

At the top of the page, Massimo sees written, "Judgment 358/2010." However, he struggles to understand what his colleague is referring to. "Am I missing something?" he asks.

"Doesn't this ring a bell?"

"Should it?"

"Three hundred and fifty-eight. Three, five, and eight."

"The verses!" Nardi exclaims then, slapping his forehead and raising his eyes to the ceiling. "So he didn't write them just to throw us off."

"Apparently not. He may have done that too, but not only that."

"Hmm! Things are getting complicated here."

"What are you talking about?"

"The difficulty of coming to terms with it. Okay! Someone

places a special value on this ruling or what revolves around it. But what does that have to do with Donati? I don't understand it. And as for the new guy, there is no point in talking about him. We don't even know who he is. In short, it seems we're back to square one."

"Well, you said it yourself. There must be some connection between the two. Let's keep looking at the papers. Maybe it will turn up."

CHAPTER 36

July 17, morning, 11:00 a.m.

By now, Nardi and Lanzi have been sifting through the mass of documents for over an hour. Barely exchanging a few words to share some information or ask the other where he was with his research, they spent most of the time in silence.

Unfortunately, they are still groping in the dark, and the situation is beginning to become frustrating. The pile of files on the desk has been more than halved. However, no element has turned up that could lead them to the mystery man. Nothing has turned up, to be more precise. Nothing worth the slightest attention.

Tired of searching in vain, Nardi stows what he has in his hands, lets out a sigh, and directs his gaze to the other side of the window. "Shall we take a break?" he suggests, blinking a few times. His eyelids have become heavy; he struggles to focus on the building across the street.

"Uh? All right. I'm going to get a coffee. Do you want me to get one for you?"

"Yes, thank you."

Lanzi gets up from his chair and stretches his arms a little. "I'll be right back," he says, and starts to walk towards the door.

Massimo lifts his wrist to look at his watch.

"Phew! It's only eleven o'clock," he thinks, feeling his

stomach growl.

Instead of coffee, he would need a nice sandwich to satisfy his appetite. In any case, even one of the packets of crackers from the vending machine will do. He'll make do with that.

To let Lanzi know that he has changed his mind, he opens his mouth and is about to call him back when he is surprised by the ringing of the phone. Instinctively, he turns his head to the device. He looks at it for barely a second, but that's all it takes: the sergeant is already out of the room.

He wrinkles his nose and snorts, but the phone keeps ringing, giving him no time to get any worse.

"Who is it?" he asks annoyed.

"Inspector, good morning," he hears from the other end. "I'm De Marchi. Do you remember me? I hope I'm not disturbing you."

"Oh, no, you're not," he replies, assuming a more cordial attitude. "Go ahead."

"I just wanted to let you know that I found the photograph that we were talking about the last time. Are you still interested in it?"

"Yes, of course I am! Can you scan it and email me a copy?"

"Hmm... I'm sorry, I don't know how to use that technological stuff."

"I see. In that case, can I send someone to pick it up?"

"Yes! Whenever you want. Although now that I think about it, do you need it right away, or can you wait a few hours?"

"That's not a problem. Why?"

"I could ask the guy upstairs. He has the computer. He has done me the favor of sending something a few times in the past. He's not home right now, but he should be back from work this afternoon."

"Okay, then. Let's go for the afternoon."

"Very well. Have a nice day."

"Thank you. You too," he concludes. And as he puts down the phone, he hints at a smile.

It's funny. Just a few hours earlier, he would have left the office in a hurry to pick up the photo in person. But now that the spotlight has shifted to Teresa, Angela's past seems almost irrelevant to him. In the end, at least regarding the rape matter, Donati's guilt is no longer in doubt. The tattoo on his arm is proof enough. And, for sure, the DNA analysis will also confirm the match with the evidence that was taken at the time of the complaint.

"There you go!" he hears shortly afterwards.

Lanzi makes his way back into the room. With two cups in his hands, he stretches out one arm to give him one.

Massimo tries to appear indifferent. However, what comes out of his mouth is a shrill "Thank you," and he cannot hold back a grimace of disgust. Especially when he reluctantly takes a sip. With his stomach rumbling again, he spits the coffee back into the container, regrets not having the package of crackers, and sets the drink on a corner of the desk.

Embarrassed, he looks at his colleague out of the corner of his eye as he runs a hand over his chin to wipe it. To dispel the awkwardness, he says, "You know... De Marchi called me about that photo. He found it. He'll send it to me later today."

"Huh? Oh, good."

The sergeant does not give the impression that he has taken it badly; in fact, he seems not to have noticed anything. He sips his coffee quietly and, for some reason, continues to stare at the blackboard on the wall.

"What are you thinking about?" Nardi asks then.

Without looking away, Lanzi wets his lips once more. He remains silent for a few more seconds. "I was wondering how reliable are the considerations made so far," he finally answers. "If Graziani really is the linchpin of the affair, that means we started from a wrong assumption. We could easily have missed something."

"Are you just saying that or do you already have an idea in your head?"

"I was thinking back to the murder case Donati was accused of and later acquitted. We found no connection between him and the man who died. But maybe we were focusing on the wrong person."

"Are you saying that the victim could have had something to do with Teresa Graziani?"

"It is possible."

"Hmm! Who knows? Try to take another look at the file in question. See if you notice anything. In the meantime, I'll make a phone call." Massimo hastens to dial the number and, in an agitated manner, holds the receiver of the phone up to his ear. It does not matter if the sergeant's hypothesis is well-founded or not; in any case, it has set off an alarm bell in his head.

In fact, he had not thought about it until now. The mystery man is still at large, and Teresa, if she is the target, may be in danger.

The phone has rung six or seven times, but it keeps ringing. Hoping that she has simply left the house, he hangs up and calls her on her cell phone.

Impatient to hear her voice, he taps his fingers on the desk. "Come on, pick up," he repeats to himself.

"Hello?" he finally hears her say.

"Ah, there you are! Where are you? Is everything okay?"

"Massimo?"

"Yes, it's me. How are you? Has anything strange happened?"

"No, nothing. Why do you ask?"

"I called you at home and you didn't answer. Where are you?"

"Hey! Pull yourself together. What's going on?"

"I'll explain later. I'll come over and tell you all about it. Tell me where you are."

"I went back to the cemetery."

"Huh? Why?"

"For Sergio. He really wanted to come. Since he was feeling a little better, he asked if I would keep him company. We're in the car now. We were just on our way out."

"Perfect! Then don't be separated from him. Go home as soon as possible and stay there. I will join you as soon as I can."

"But come on! What's the matter? You're scaring me."

"We found out that someone else was involved in this matter. Donati may have had an accomplice. And until we know for sure, you are not safe. I hope I'm wrong, but the real target may be you."

"An accomplice?!" she exclaims. "How..."

Teresa is interrupted by Sergio, who demands an explanation.

Massimo hears the two of them talking to each other in the background.

He hears her as she makes him aware of the situation, and then he hears him as he asks her to hand him the phone.

"Hello, Massimo? It's Sergio here. Can you tell me what this is about? You said Donati was the only one responsible."

"Yes, I know, but new evidence has come to light and..."

"What evidence?"

"I don't have time now. I'll tell you all about it later," he cuts him off. "In the meantime, you guys go on home. I'll meet you there in an hour or two."

After hanging up, he breathes a sigh of relief. Having heard the phone ringing unanswered, he had already begun to fear the worst. A picture of Teresa had appeared in his mind: bent over, lifeless, her chest torn in two, a bloody cross on her forehead.

Lanzi is still absorbed in reading, but the sense of uneasiness of those moments must not have escaped him. "Are you all right?" he asks.

"Huh? Yes, yes. I'm fine. Did you find anything in that file?"

"No. Now I'm looking at the prison records."

"What records?"

"They sent them today. Cataldo must have put them there with the rest, and he probably forgot to tell you that..." Lanzi suddenly falls silent. He stares incredulously at the document in his hands. And giving free rein to his astonishment, he exclaims, "Oh, for God's sake!"

"What is it?"

"Bombshell news. Apparently, Donati had received a visit just before his release. And you can't imagine from whom."

"Come on, let's go! Who is it? Don't keep me waiting."

"See for yourself," Lanzi replies, handing over the paper and pointing a finger to indicate a name.

"Sergio?!" Massimo cannot believe his eyes. "How is that possible?"

"Well, it's in black and white. It's clear that he's involved as well."

"So the kidnapping, the attempted murder... all a set-up to divert suspicion."

"And, of course, he couldn't do it alone. He needed someone to play along with. Somehow, he must have convinced Donati to take part. He must have used him as long as he needed him, and then got rid of him when the job was done."

"But I can't understand it. Why would he..." The question sticks in his throat. Massimo jumps up in his chair and opens his eyes wide. "Oh, hell!" he exclaims. "I almost didn't think about it anymore. Teresa is with him in the Prima Porta cemetery. Hurry, hurry, alert the guards on the spot! And send the nearest patrol as well. Then be ready to go. I'll be right with you."

As Lanzi rushes out of the room, he picks up the phone again. He dials the last number in the memory but quickly realizes it is too late.

This time, the recorded voice on the answering machine answers.

CHAPTER 37

July 17, morning, 11:30 a.m.

An accomplice.

Those two words were enough for Sergio to realize his time was running out. That was why he had insisted on talking to Massimo. To find out if it had not already expired. He wanted to know if his cover had only begun to give way or if it had instead collapsed altogether.

Besides, pretending to be surprised was a good excuse to get Teresa to give him the cell phone. After the call had ended, he had turned it off without being noticed, and, as if nothing had happened, he had reached directly into her purse to give it back to her.

Now, sitting side by side in his Mercedes, they drive through the streets of the cemetery. Sergio tries to appear focused on his driving to ignore Teresa as she vents her anger and perplexity aloud. Perhaps, in the meantime, she has also asked him a couple of questions. He is not sure. He does not listen to her. He just makes a few grimaces with his lips and remains silent, distracted by other thoughts. He thinks, searching for a solution to finish what he started.

Things have not gone according to plan and at this point he can only improvise.

While speculating on some possible scenarios, he glances at

Teresa, at that fake eye that is the emblem of a principle. It calls to his mind the origins of the affair, a trace that is etched in his memory.

He remembers that it all began on an autumn evening, one of those evenings when the intense cold heralds the coming of the new season.

Having just returned from working, he was sitting comfortably on the sofa, enjoying hot tea, when he heard a knock at the door.

He wondered who it could be. He was not expecting any visitors. Besides, hardly anyone knew he lived there. He had moved into that house only a few weeks before, after another argument with Teresa had convinced him to put some distance between them.

At the thought that it really was her, the idea of not opening the door crossed his mind. Anyway, he pulled himself up and walked to the entrance.

Fear and dismay when he saw that Angela was outside, with bruises and wounds on her face and arms.

"Oh my God! What happened?" he asked in horror.

Holding her by the shoulders, he led her inside. And though he was shaken by the situation, he tried to keep his nerves in check. She was already far too upset and he certainly did not want to be the one to add to the tension.

He sat her down on the couch, made her drink some water and disinfected her wounds. All the while, he insisted on knowing what had happened to her, but she said nothing. With her eyes wide open, she seemed not to be listening to him, as if she were somewhere else.

After about ten minutes, Angela got up, went to the bathroom like an automaton and stayed in the shower for who knows how long.

When she decided to go outside, he watched her hesitantly.

He saw that she had taken off her clothes and put on the only bathrobe available. Two or three sizes larger, her slender body danced in it. She kept clutching it to herself as if she wanted to sink into it completely, and meanwhile, she would not stop scratching and pulling at her hair.

Not knowing what to do, he reached out to embrace her, but she pulled back hastily, clutched her robe up to her neck, and bent her gaze to the floor.

Sergio realized he was not wrong. Up until that moment, he had refused to listen to his intuition. He did not want to believe it. But what had only been a suspicion at first was now an obvious fact: his daughter had been the victim of a rape.

That same evening, the call from the hospital informed him of the attack Teresa had suffered and how serious her condition was. Luckily Piero was at his aunt's house, where he was going to spend the weekend with his cousins; otherwise, he would have had to call the babysitter to have her stay overnight. Leaving Angela alone in this state was out of the question.

Over and over again, he had tried to convince her to go to the emergency room, but it had been to no avail. She had not wanted to know. And the fact that he had guessed what had happened made little difference, as he lacked the courage to broach the subject and ask her for confirmation.

As long as she did not decide to confide in him, his suspicion would remain a mere assumption and there was little he could do.

Therefore, when Angela returned to her seat, all he did was to give her a dose of sedatives so that she could rest.

Crushed with helplessness, he remained silent, watching her as she sat huddled on the couch, with her thighs against her chest and her forehead on her knees, crying intermittently, biting her nails, and rubbing herself here and there.

Sergio thought it should have been her mother in that room, not him. And if he could have, he would have run to her at the hospital to ask her how to behave.

According to what he had been told, her condition was serious. Nevertheless, he decided to try to call her, hoping she would at least be able to answer and give him some advice.

So he walked over to the phone, picked up the receiver, and

started dialing her cell phone number.

That was when Angela gave him a suspicious look. Suddenly, she broke the silence and asked, "Who are you calling?" Her voice quivered; a sense of excitement was in her throat.

"Huh? Nobody, honey. I mean, I'm just trying to warn your mother..."

"No!" she interrupted. "Mom must not know anything."

"But what do you mean?" He was taken aback. Not so much by the abrupt reaction but by that order, which seemed senseless to him.

However, his question was not answered. Angela returned to the silence of earlier.

Although the conversation had ended, he continued to wonder about the reason for those words. If it had been shock that had torn them from her mouth, he might have understood, but that was not the case. His daughter had chosen to speak for a specific reason. And the fact that she wanted to keep her mother in the dark was both strange and disturbing.

He continued to wonder about this for a long time until the sedative finally took effect, and she was able to close her eyes.

Seeing her resting quietly, he had the impression that he had woken up from a nightmare. He could almost say nothing had really happened, even though the bruises on her body said otherwise.

For several moments, he stood motionless, pondering what needed to be done. When he finally determined how to proceed, he went to the bathroom to gather Angela's clothes. He put on disposable gloves and began to sort the clothes into plastic bags, one for each item. He gathered everything together into a single package and stored it safely in the closet.

He blamed himself for not stopping her from showering, but it was too late for that now. The clothes were all that was left of the attacker. If he had left any traces, they were on there.

Back in the living room, he looked at his daughter again to make sure she was still asleep. His gaze shifted here and there as if trying to run away. Moving from head to toe, it hopped from face to neck, from one arm to the other, until stopping on one hand. Sergio began to stare at it persistently. And although it seemed strange to him at first, he soon understood the reason.

It occurred to him that she must have struggled. Maybe she had scratched the man. And maybe some residue of skin had escaped the effect of the water.

He hesitated before picking up the nail clippers. Approaching the couch, he only hoped the sedative was strong enough to keep her from waking up.

With all the delicacy he was capable of, he grabbed first one hand, then the other. Finger by finger, he clipped off the tips of her nails and sealed the fragments as best he could.

When he finished, Angela was still asleep. Collapsed into a deep sleep, she gave the impression of someone who would be resting for a long time to come. It was a good time to make a quick trip to the hospital.

He did not like the idea of leaving her alone at all, but he saw no other solution. So he put on his coat, took one last look at her, and left the house.

It was already four in the morning. It was definitely not visiting time. Still, he would find a way to get in. He was a doctor, after all, and colleagues understood each other.

The whole way, he thought back to Angela's words, her request to keep her mother in the dark. He found it an absurd request, of which he still struggled to grasp the reason. In any case, he could not have talked about it even if he wanted to.

When he arrived, he discovered that Teresa had undergone emergency surgery. Although her condition was stable, she had lost one eye, could barely keep the other open, and was short of breath with several broken ribs. Even just talking caused her pain.

The doctor on duty, with whom he had managed to speak, had given him the news. After a few objections, he had allowed him to look into the room to say hello but had advised him not to tire her out.

He had no objections. He would have stayed only a minute,

the time to see the situation for himself.

Teresa was awake. When she saw him enter, she tried to say something but had no way of uttering a word.

Sergio put a finger on her lips. "Shh! Don't talk," he whispered. With the thought that Angela could wake up any moment, he wanted to get home as soon as possible. So he stroked her cheek and said, "Get some rest. I will visit you tomorrow." He left the room without even asking her what had happened.

That night he couldn't imagine how the two events were connected. He only found out five days later when Angela finally decided to confide in him.

She told him that she had been attacked by a man she had never seen before, confirmed that she had been raped, and finally reported the words that this man had spoken. *"Debts must be paid. Tell your mother when you see her,"* he had said before leaving.

Discovering that Teresa was responsible for that tragedy, he felt consumed by a blind fury. He would have strangled her with his hands at that very moment had it not been for his daughter's pleas. Despite their relationship, plagued by quarrels, shortcomings, and misunderstandings, she cared about her mother more than she had ever let on. In order to spare her from guilt, she preferred to keep quiet and endure in silence.

In spite of himself, he was forced to do the same because the lost time had now rendered any kind of contraception useless. The morning-after pill would do no good, and since Angela did not want to hear anything about abortion, he could only urge her to press charges.

From there on, the road had been all uphill.

After being discharged from the hospital about a month later, Teresa had become an unwieldy presence.

Angela had not been slow in realizing it. Back home, she soon discovered that living with her was tantamount to reliving the same torture one day after day. So she ran away. She had moved in with him. And, as hard as the first few days had been, she seemed to have made it in the end.

Who knows! Maybe she was just pretending, lying to herself to ignore the violence she had suffered. Maybe the lie was her response to pain too great to bear. Yet, looking at her, she really gave the impression of having left the story behind and started living again.

Of course, there were bad days when the shadow of that misfortune returned to hang in the air, but overall, there was an atmosphere of seeming normalcy.

It would have continued that way if that damn photo had not emerged.

On an ordinary day, Angela was fiddling with her cell phone when Donati's face suddenly appeared in front of her. In a selfie taken a few months earlier, she had recognized her attacker and, as if raped for the second time, had sunk back into the abyss. Any progress she had made had vanished into thin air.

The coup de grace came seven months later, just weeks after giving birth, with the news of her brother's death.

It was the final straw. Angela couldn't recover anymore. A few years later, she attempted suicide.

On that occasion, Sergio vowed to make all those responsible pay, starting with Donati.

He remembers spending two or three months trying to track him down. Perhaps he would have continued to search for him in vain if the newspapers had not brought his story to the fore.

He was in jail, accused of murder, and he kept saying he was innocent – a perfect situation, which had immediately given rise to the idea of using him.

The plan was simple: kill him last and then make sure the traces of the various murders led back to him.

Unfortunately the police found out about it too soon, before Teresa also paid for her sins.

Looking back on it now, Sergio almost wants to laugh.

By allowing himself to be duped like an idiot, Donati had been an unwitting accomplice. He thought he was participating in some kind of million-dollar heist, one that would change his life, while he was actually digging his own grave with his own hands.

Unbeknownst to him, he had contributed to his own demise. As in the case of the imprint left on the bloody envelope.

He didn't hesitate to accept.

He believed that drawing suspicion upon himself and then sweeping them away with a broomstick stroke was a way to provide him with an alibi and keep him away from the investigation.

For the same reason, he had not even hesitated to provide him with his own car – without knowing the purpose – convinced that, in the worst case, a theft report would be enough to get him off the hook.

And even when Sergio had sent Donati to that remote cottage in the middle of the countryside, he had trusted Sergio, convinced that he wanted to protect him from the clutches of the police.

In short, until the epilogue, Donati did not realize anything. He had no idea who Brunetti really was. And now that Sergio's eyes return to gaze at the road, he wonders if Donati was at least able to figure it out in the end.

Perhaps it was not so, but he likes to think that the image with which that man left this world as he took his last breath was that of Angela.

HELL – FINAL ACT

His eyes are keepers of a distant present, guardians of what has been and what could have been; they glimpse the ghosts of the past, a vague reflection of a reality that has ceased to exist.

He wants to cry, but there are no tears to streak his face. Only a pain that tears at his heart.

The denied future of two innocent children, the warmth of a woman, the love for life – everything has been lost.

Around him, there is only emptiness left.

Yet even there, where nothingness seems to reign unchallenged, a sound still echoes.

It is the cry of revenge. And it is announced with the melody of a telephone ringtone.

At the vibration of his cell phone, a text message informs him that the moment has finally arrived. The real culprit, the one who has turned his existence upside down, is about to pay.

And even if she will pay in a different way than planned, it doesn't matter. After all, this new ending does not bother him at all.

As the loudspeaker announces the flight to Barcelona, he suddenly feels his eyes become moist and a weight slip away.

He then looks at Pier Giorgio, smiles at him and, remembering the night he took him away with him, he runs a finger to wipe away his tears.

Soon, Angela and those two little spirits will be able to rest in peace.

CHAPTER 38

July 17, morning, 11:30 a.m.

"*...please leave your message after the beep,*" the recorded voice says.

At the sound of the *beep*, Massimo is almost tempted to speak. He wants to shout Teresa's name, warn her about Sergio, and tell her to run away.

"I should have known," he thinks. He hangs up, slamming the receiver onto the phone.

A punch on the desk rattles the objects scattered on the shelf. The blow is so strong that the paper underneath sticks to his skin.

When he pulls his hand back, the top sheet follows it for a short distance before detaching in midair and calmly floating down.

It is the sheet from the prison record. His eyes can't help but follow it in its slow relapse.

Massimo notices the date of the visit, about six years ago. It seems to suggest something to him. He has the impression of having already read it somewhere else.

Furrowed brows, upturned eyes, and a finger on the lips are the automatic reactions to uncertainty.

However, time is running out. This is not the time to think about such things. If it is not already too late, Teresa is in grave danger. So he lets it go, gets up, and sets off.

As he is about to leave his office, Angela's medical records come to his mind.

When did she attempt suicide?

He wants to rush out, yet he feels he cannot leave this doubt unanswered.

Torn, he looks down the hallway, takes a step forward, and turns to stare at the desk. "Ah, damn!" he finally exclaims, sitting back down. After all, the Prima Porta cemetery is at least a half-hour drive away. He certainly won't be the one to make a difference. He can only hope that help arrives before Sergio makes his final move.

Distracted by this worry, he rummages through the papers a little longer than he should. Then he finds what he is looking for.

He feels a kind of disappointment when he sees that the dates do not coincide. Angela's hospitalization after the suicide attempt was a few months before the prison visit.

He must have been mistaken. Perhaps he was misled by the fact that the two events had occurred in the same year. But in the end, even if the dates were the same, what difference would it have made? That detail tells him nothing. He wonders why it interests him so much. And convinced that something is escaping him, he reflects on it for a few moments.

Then, in response, his chin jerks up slightly. He wrinkles his forehead and, as if in slow motion, shifts his gaze to another file.

He realizes that he has overlooked an essential element.

Among the events of that period, there is, in fact, a third that he has not considered. The testimony that had led to Donati's release from prison, where Tancredi had played the role of witness.

According to what he had told him a few days earlier, he had given in to threats only to protect Angela's safety. But if she had already been in a coma for several months, what did he have to protect her from?

He lied. It is obvious. And the reason is all too clear. To pass himself off as a victim to hide the face of the perpetrator.

Massimo is angry with himself for letting an inconsistency slip through his fingers. However, he must admit that time has not worked in his favor. After leaving the real estate agency, he went straight to Donati's house. And from there on, events unfolded in a chain reaction. He simply let himself be swept along by the current of events.

"All done, Chief." Lanzi's panting voice breaks through his thoughts. With one foot in the room, the sergeant pauses on the threshold, ready to leave. "I've sent a patrol car and contacted on-site security. I've also reported the car to the operations center that manages the cemetery's video surveillance, so maybe they'll have a way to track it while we head there."

"No, I'm going alone. You need to go somewhere else."

"Uh?"

"We miscalculated. There were not two of them, but three. Or rather, two against one."

"What are you talking about?"

"You know Tancredi? The guy who got Donati out of jail and then handed him to me on a silver platter, remember? I just realized he's involved too."

"Why, what did you find out?"

"Nothing, but his story doesn't add up. The dates don't match the facts. I think that he and Sergio Brunetti were in cahoots from the beginning and that they planned the whole thing to take revenge on Donati. After all, they had a common motive. They both loved the same person."

"So, what do you want me to do?"

"Get Cataldo to give you his home and work addresses. Find him and bring him here. I don't want to let him get away, too."

"But just like that? Without a shred of evidence? Wouldn't it be better to wait?"

Just then, Nardi's cell phone vibrates. A short but intense sound wafts through the air.

Taking the device out of his pocket, Massimo looks at the

notification. He sees that he has received an e-mail.

The name of the sender tells him nothing, but the subject of the message does. Simple and concise, it reports just enough to understand its content. It says, "Photo - De Marchi".

Although he is now sure that he no longer needs it, he downloads the attachment to confirm what he thinks.

The photograph shows Angela in the company of another woman – presumably De Marchi's wife – and next to them, a Nicola Tancredi several years younger.

"What do you think?" he asks, handing the display in Lanzi's direction. "Can this be enough evidence?"

"What is it?"

"The photo I've been waiting for, taken at the maternity home when Angela Brunetti was expecting the baby. And the one you see next to her is our dear Tancredi. He told me he knew nothing about children."

Seeing that Lanzi has nothing more to add, he stands up and lifts his chin, motioning for them to leave. "Let's go," he urges. "You take care of him. I, in the meanwhile..." He lacks the courage to finish the last sentence. "Okay, let's go," he repeats.

CHAPTER 39

The Prima Porta cemetery is the largest cemetery in Italy. The paths inside unfold like a fan of asphalt tongues for twenty-three miles. It took a while to reach the exit.

By the time the Mercedes turns onto Highway 3 and follows Flaminia Street toward the city center, Teresa has not yet stopped talking.

Sergio continues to ignore her, but soon she notices.

"Hey! Are you listening to me?" she asks, raising her voice.

"Huh? Oh, sorry! I was lost in thought."

"But how come? Maybe someone around wants to see me dead, and you have better things to think about? You haven't changed that much, I see."

"Actually, that is exactly what I was thinking about."

"What do you mean?"

"Do you have any idea why he would go after you?"

"How should I know? Maybe for the same reason he killed that woman and Carlo. Besides, he was after you, too, wasn't he? I wonder how you can be so calm about it. Who's to say he doesn't want to finish the job? Next on the list could be you."

"That's not how Massimo thinks. According to him, you are the one in the crosshairs. Maybe you should ask yourself some questions. Before, it was just Donati, and we could even think

302

of a psychopath. But if two of them want you dead, well, there must be a reason."

"I don't understand what you're getting at."

"Nothing. It's just something that gives me pause," Sergio answers with a hint of sarcasm. He wants to wait until they reach their destination before shouting in Teresa's face what he really thinks. She has never been able to see the tragic truth. So far, remaining in the dark has protected her from her conscience, and he is eager to tell her once and for all how things really are. For now, he is content to pour a few drops of light into the foggy cluster that envelops and anesthetizes her. "Are you still gambling?" he asks nonchalantly, trying to catch her off guard.

"Uh?" A dark expression appears on her face.

"What is that look? It's a simple question."

"And now, what does that have to do with anything? Why are you asking me?"

"Oh, just curiosity. I was thinking about Piero and wondering if at least his death succeeded where I failed." Knowing the answer, he already knows that he will hurt her. "So, tell me! Was it enough to make you stop?"

"You are cruel. How can you talk like that about our son?"

"In what way? Isn't that what happened?"

Teresa looks at him sideways but remains silent.

"I see you don't want to talk about it. Well, sorry I asked." Sergio raises his hand in a sign of peace. "And what about Angela? Do you have any idea why she wanted to let you know the name she chose for her son?"

Once again, Teresa does not answer.

He glances at her and adds nothing more. Seeing her shed a tear, he hints at an imperceptible smile and goes back to watching the road.

***

Massimo barely had time to leave the police station and get

behind the wheel. A radio message reached him shortly after, informing him that Sergio's car had already left the cemetery and had been caught on camera as it turned onto the road to the city center.

However, he has not stopped, much less turned back; while waiting for an update on the vehicle's current location, he continues to drive in a northerly direction.

Knowing that the passenger side was occupied by Teresa is already a relief. But that doesn't stop the beads of sweat from dripping down his forehead or his abs from contracting into a vise grip, nor does it keep his carotid artery, which is pulsing and almost spurting out of his neck, at bay. No, a video recording, no matter how recent, is not enough to inhibit anxiety. And in the absence of new information, he feels as if every second is stretching on forever, just like the road ahead.

He refuses to admit it, but he fears that it is too late now.

Sergio is not a fool. After the last phone call, he will no doubt have realized that the noose around his neck is tightening. Even assuming he is unaware that he has been discovered, he will certainly know that he does not have much time. And that makes him even more dangerous than he already is.

If he has not acted yet, he surely will soon.

However, the way he has proceeded suggests that he had something in mind. He could have ended the game there at the cemetery, but he did not. This is why Massimo has ordered the team to intervene only if necessary. He does not want to risk pushing Sergio into a corner before his time. Seeing himself being hunted down by uniformed officers might push him to commit an extreme act, whereas he might be willing to talk to him. After all, Massimo is not only a familiar face but he was also invited to the party.

Therefore, in case of a sighting, the orders are clear: follow his movements and monitor the situation from a distance.

Nardi continues to proceed in a northerly direction with no specific destination. Periodically, he glances at the radio, hoping it will come back to life soon. And each time, he returns his eyes to the road with a disappointed sigh, biting his lip and swiveling his head from side to side.

Forced to stop at an intersection because of a red light, he distractedly watches the back of the car in front of him.

The numbers engraved on the license plate call to mind the dates on the reports. He thinks back to Sergio's visit to the prison and Angela's hospitalization. It seems that those time coordinates have taken root like the strands of a spider's web and now refuse to let go of his thoughts.

Averting his gaze, Massimo tries to shift his attention to something else, when his eyebrows suddenly shoot up and his eyes forcefully return to look forward. Struck by a sudden realization, he finally understands what he found so familiar.

It was not those events that had caught his attention, but rather what had happened a few months earlier.

The report of the rape – the day in question, to be exact – had been the real magnet.

In fact, according to the report, Angela had been raped on the same day that Teresa had been attacked. A date he certainly cannot forget because, for him, it marks the border between a before and an after.

"Strange," he thinks when he realizes the thought leaves him indifferent.

For years, he has tormented himself with the constant obsession that he shot an unarmed man. Yet, thinking about it now, he has the impression of having been little more than a victim. A victim of circumstances and the irony of fate. Because that night, in the end, has changed not only his life but the lives of so many. And like the others, he too has been part of a larger plan, a cog in a wheel that has now reached its final turn.

Now, indeed, he can see the invisible ring before him, a circle that encompasses the whole, where each point marks the beginning and the end, where the present meets the past, where the harmony of opposites creates perfection.

He is lost in these thoughts when the honking of a car horn

insistently calls him back. He notices that the traffic light has turned green again. So he shifts into gear, accelerates, and starts again. And as the car resumes its journey, he feels something detach inside him, as if a part of himself had been lost forever, abandoned at that intersection.

Shortly after that, the cell phone begins to ring.

With it in front of him, attached to the magnetic holder on the dashboard, he needs only a glance to see where the call is coming from.

"Tell me, Cataldo," he begins when he answers.

"I have the information you requested, Chief."

"Uh? Oh, right!" He had forgotten. Before leaving, he had instructed the deputy to do some research on Nicola Tancredi. "Did you find anything?"

"I would say so. It seems that the acquaintance between Tancredi and Angela Brunetti goes back a long way. Even as teenagers, they lived in the same building."

"What are you saying?"

"That's right. But there's more. He was also the older brother of Giorgio Roversi, the other child who died in the car. Half-brother, to be exact. His mother had him from her first marriage."

Massimo remains speechless. He was wrong when he thought he understood everything about the thirst for revenge and the reasons that had led the two men to ally with each other. Sure, Angela was one side of the coin, but the roots of the hatred went much deeper than he had imagined.

"Can you hear me, Chief? Are you still on the line?"

"I'm here. Anything else you want to say?"

"As a matter of fact, yes. You asked me to look at your old cases from when Graziani was still on the force. Do you remember?"

"Oh, forget it! No need to look any further now."

"Actually, I've already done that. After what happened, I thought I'd go through it all again. And by sheer coincidence, a connection to Donati came up."

"What are you talking about? What does he have to do with the investigations I've been following in the past?"

"Well, the detail goes back to when Graziani was attacked. At the time, Donati was a bouncer at a nightclub. The management has changed, but back then, the place belonged to *The Pariolino*, who, from what I saw, was your last suspect."

"*The Pariolino!*" he echoes in a whisper. Unbelieving, he watches the road disappear quickly under the nose of his car and thinks of Teresa and her fixation on the gambling. Then he makes sure there is nothing else and ends the call.

The rest of the questions on the table seem to fall like flies. Only a few remain in search of a response. He tries to rearrange the pieces, but before he can think any further, the radio crackles back to life.

Brunetti's car has been located.

The patrol that spotted it reports that it is on Corso di Francia, and the vehicle is heading towards Flaminio Square.

For Nardi, that's enough. It does not take him long to figure out where it is heading. So, without waiting for further updates, he makes a U-turn and puts his foot on the accelerator.

CHAPTER 40

July 17, noon

For the rest of the trip, Sergio has devoted himself to sifting through the topics best suited to his purpose, the ones to use once they reached their destination. After the touching of a nerve, he has had plenty of time to think. They had never exchanged another word with each other, except as they passed the Grande Raccordo Anulare ring road when she had broken the silence to point out that he had taken a wrong turn.

"You had to turn," she had corrected him on that occasion, seeing him continue straight on Flaminia Street.

"Yes, I know. But I'd like to go through a place first," he had justified himself. "It's nearby, don't worry! It won't take long."

The matter had ended there. Turning to the car window without question, Teresa had returned to her thoughts, leaving him to his.

At this point in their journey, they are climbing up Twisted Wall Avenue, less than a hundred yards from their destination, and the time to sort out his thoughts begins to shrink.

He drives with a kind of emptiness in his head, with the impression that he cannot get a single word out. The speech he had prepared up to that moment has suddenly evaporated.

But this does not surprise him. The agitation always gets the better of him when he passes through that street. That's where it all started, with Angela's rape, which happened just a little further up.

Police tape still decorates the short stretch of road, isolating a piece of land from the surrounding space.

Teresa quickly notices it and connects the dots.

"But... why are you stopping?" she asks, with a puzzled look on her face. "This is where they found the victims of that madman, right?"

"Exactly!"

"Oh, damn! And why are you stopping here? What are you going to do?"

Sergio shakes his head slightly and does not answer. To a piercing look, he adds a kind of smile before opening the door.

"Where are you going?" she shouts at him.

Continuing to ignore her, he gets out of the car, walks to the back of the vehicle, opens the tailgate, and grabs the gun he has stowed inside the trunk; the same one he used to fire at the police at the old cabin where Donati had met his death.

So far, Nicola has been the one doing the dirty work, but now it is up to him to finish the job.

Of course, things were not supposed to end this way. According to the original plan, both of them should have come out of that affair with clean hands. However, at this point, he no longer cares about the consequences.

All he wants is to get the revenge he has been craving for too long.

Covering the short distance that separates him from Teresa, he stops for a few seconds just behind her, observing her back through the car window. Eager to get to the end, he already feels a certain pleasure, yet he hesitates to act. For fear of spoiling that moment, he would like to prolong it indefinitely. But then she turns, and their gazes meet again, so he takes the last three steps. "Get out!" he commands, opening the door.

Standing sideways, he holds his right arm at his side. At first, he does not realize he is covering the weapon with his body.

"No! Not a chance," Teresa replies without flinching.

Only then, in the face of her reaction, does he become aware of his carelessness. And to make up for the oversight, he points the gun in her face, inches from her nose, making her smell metal. "I said get down!" he repeats.

"Oh, for God's sake! Are you crazy? What are you doing?" This time she opens her eyes wide and jumps onto the seat like a ball. With a jerk, she slams her elbow into the edge of the opening against the metal part of the frame – a barely audible groan of pain sticks in her throat.

"Out!" he says again, in a more commanding tone.

Overcome by fear, Teresa gets out of the car. "You... you're out of your mind," she mumbles in a feeble attempt to react.

"Oh, yes! You're right. I am mad with rage. Ever since the day you ruined my existence."

"Huh? What are you talking about?"

"Do you still not understand?" Sergio pushes her forward. "Go on! You wanted to know who it was that wanted you dead, didn't you? Good! Now you know."

"You?!" she exclaims incredulously as if she had not understood what was happening until that moment. "But you said..."

"Did you really think I could forgive you after what you did? My children! You took them from me. You ripped my life away."

"Hey, no, wait a minute!" Teresa's voice betrays a hint of pride. "Piero's death... yes, it is a burden I will carry on my shoulders as long as I have breath. You can hate me for it if you want. But you cannot also blame me for Angela's escape."

"Are you sure about this? I waited years before I made you pay. Why do you think I did that?"

Teresa turns to look at him. For a moment, the fear disappears from her face, giving way to a frown. "What are you trying to say?"

"You don't know anything. You have no idea of the pain our daughter has had to endure. You were not there to hold her hand. I still struggle to understand where she found the strength to love you. If you are alive, you owe it all to her. If it had been up to me, I would have killed you immediately."

"What?" she begins to scream. "Are you saying you knew where he was all along and kept quiet without telling me?" With her eyes blazing with anger, she lashes out at him, trying to hit him.

"I said go!" he orders, pushing her back violently and waving the gun in the air. "She's the one who wanted it, not me."

"I don't believe that. You lie!" protests Teresa as she starts to walk again. "You're just saying that to make me suffer."

"Oh, no! Believe me; it's the truth. After what you put her through, the last thing she wanted was to see you."

"But in short! What are you talking about? What would I have done to her?"

"Besides the fact that you were never close to her? You sentenced her to pay for your mistakes. You and your damn gambling habit."

"What does that have to do with anything now?"

"Oh, it has everything to do with it! It's like you raped her yourself."

"Huh?"

"Do you know what Donati, that big bastard, told her after he raped her? He told her to let you know that debts must be paid."

Those last words take Teresa by surprise. They are a punch in the gut. Sergio only has to look at her to realize it. Her emotions are palpable from the outside. And it is her whole body that speaks: the sudden jerk of her head that, like a crazy spring, twists her neck ninety degrees; the drop of her jaw; the stunned look that distorts her face. A series of details to which is added a suddenly faltering gait.

When he pushes her forward again, the pressure of a finger is enough to throw her off balance.

She stumbles and falls face down on the ground.

Lying there, she lifts her torso on one elbow, turns around a moment later, and still has the wide eyes of someone who does not believe or refuses to believe. She opens her mouth, perhaps to say something, but says nothing.

Sergio looks at her with disgust, begins to tell her the facts she is unaware of, and, between pauses, holds up her faults against her.

Before it all ends, he wants to make her suffer like she has never suffered before.

***

The Mercedes is parked on the side of the road about sixty yards ahead. Not far from the car, beyond the demarcated area, Sergio Brunetti is standing with his back turned. Teresa, however, is nowhere to be seen.

Nardi feels a shiver of cold run through his body.

Assailed by fear, he unloads the tension onto his hands by squeezing the steering wheel hard, exerting such pressure that he can feel the rubber sinking between his fingers.

Convinced that he has arrived too late, he interrupts the drive before time, gets out of the car with the slowness of one who has already resigned himself to the worst, and advances almost without reason.

Only after about ten steps, catching sight of an arm waving in the air, does he realize that the slight rise on the ground is actually Teresa's body.

On realizing that she is alive, he lets out a deep sigh. And caught between relief and astonishment, he stands there for a few moments, staring at her in a daze.

Then his mind regains its clarity, or almost. Impatient to reach the two of them, he rushes towards them, ignoring any procedure. He doesn't even bother to assess the situation.

He is caught off guard when he sees Sergio pointing a weapon at Teresa.

Fortunately, he is still at some distance and his arrival seems to have gone unnoticed. Thinking to take advantage of the element of surprise, he then draws the Beretta from its holster

312

and, careful where he steps, proceeds with stealthy strides.

But the idea of taking the other from behind is shattered before he can do anything.

Sergio turns suddenly, as if someone had alerted him to his presence. "Oh! Massimo," he begins. "Have you come to join the party?" Still keeping Teresa in his sights, he moves to the side, making sure the gun is clearly visible. "You've been clever, I have to admit," he adds. "But now it's the endgame, so stay where you are."

"Stay calm," Nardi urges him. "Nobody has to get hurt." In an effort to appear as harmless as possible, he keeps his arms down but grips the gun with both hands, ready to react at the first sign of danger.

He is still upset about the failed attempt. And what makes him angry is the certainty that he has not made the slightest noise. Sergio must have been alerted by the look on Teresa's face because as soon as she noticed Massimo arrival, she started to look at him and never took her eyes off him.

Even now, lying on the ground, she stares at him with two frightened eyes, longing for help.

"Are you hurt?" he asks her, a hint of disappointment in his voice.

"She's fine, for now," Sergio interjects. "But she won't last long. If you want to say goodbye to her, now is the time."

"Don't do it," he replies, assuming a shooting position. "Don't make me shoot."

"Do as much as you have to. I have nothing left to lose at this point."

"You think so? Look at her!" Determined to keep his aim, Nardi gestures with his head in the direction of his former colleague. "You've already achieved your goal. Don't you see? Until today, you have made her live in a nightmare, year after year. And now you have taken away her hope as well. It was the only thing she had left. The illusion that she could right her wrongs. Now she will have to live with regret. So, if you really want revenge, let her live. It will be a punishment far worse than death."

In response to those words, Brunetti's eyes shine strangely. With the tip of his tongue moistening one corner of his mouth, he smiles ambiguously. "I told you, Massimo, you are good. You would have made a good negotiator. But, I'm sorry, your nice little speech won't be enough to change my mind."

"Let's go! Killing her will not bring your daughter back."

"No, but at least then I'll feel at peace."

"Oh, I see! And, tell me, how many more will have to die before you to feel at peace? As for Donati, well, I'll be honest. Had I been in your place, I think I would have wanted him to pay as much as you. But what about the others? Silvia Rigoni, Juliana Petrescu, your so-called 'friend', the lawyer... What did they have to do with it?"

"What a coward you are!" exclaims Sergio, casting a contemptuous glance at Teresa. "Pathetic right to the end. You didn't tell him how Piero died, did you?"

She moves her eyes from one to the other. She says nothing. With a guilty look on her face, her mouth open and trembling, she seems to want to catch the words in the air.

She remains frozen in that catatonic state for several moments until, putting her hands on the ground, she attempts to stand up.

Sergio, however, slams his foot down on her back, knocking her back to the floor. "Stay down!" he yells. "Crawl like the worm you are."

"Calm down! I know all about your son," Massimo interjects. "I've read the trial transcripts."

"Then why are you asking me about Juliana Petrescu? It should be clear to you. She contributed to the events. If she had not caused problems that day, Teresa would have arrived in time to prevent the worst. Piero would still be alive today."

"What nonsense. Then you could also blame the policemen who wrote the report, couldn't you? If they had been quicker, things would have turned out differently."

"Oh! If I had a reason to do so, I would have done so, rest

assured. After all, the officers were also called as witnesses at the trial. But unlike that bitch, they did not have a smile on their faces. You didn't see her, and you can't understand. Do you know what she did during her testimony? She looked at Teresa and laughed contentedly. You know what I mean? My son was dead, and she was laughing at his mother as if she wanted to get even."

The conversation is taking a turn for the worse. Sergio starts to get nervous and his attitude is not reassuring.

Massimo quickly changes the subject. "But Carlo Pietrangeli didn't do anything. Why did you kill him?" Although he is interested in the explanations, for the moment he aims to keep the other man on his toes. He hopes that by talking, he can distract him, lower his guard and take him by surprise.

"Carlo betrayed our friendship."

"Is that all?"

"He was as guilty as the others. He was the one in charge of Teresa's defense. I asked him – no, I begged him – to make sure she lost the case so she would be convicted. Carlo wouldn't have suffered any consequences. All he had to do was be a little less zealous in his work. Instead, he chose not to care and concentrated on his career."

"There are also ideals. Have you ever thought about that? Maybe he was just a man with a conscience who wanted to uphold his oath as a lawyer. You should understand that better than most. As a doctor, you took an oath to save lives, not to take them."

"Are you trying to make me feel guilty?" Sergio lifts one corner of his mouth, the hint of a mocking smile. "Let me tell you, the only person I feel a little sorry for is the social worker."

"Oh, I can imagine! The fact that she had so little time to live must have taken away your taste for revenge."

"No. I hadn't planned to kill her. I went to the hospital with the simple intention of threatening her. I wanted to scare her so that she would keep her mouth shut if you ever traced it back to her. But it was fate that brought us together. She wanted to die.

And lo and behold, she happened to be under your jurisdiction. A perfect opportunity for my plan. So, what can I say? We helped each other, or so I like to think."

"By the way, tell me something I'm curious about. I still don't understand why you wanted to involve me in this story."

"Well, you have the answer at your feet. I imagined that your friendship would allow me to follow the investigation closely. And I wasn't wrong. Too bad it wasn't enough. You still got to Donati too soon. He was supposed to be last on the list."

"So that was the plan? To use him as a scapegoat, to make him look like the only one responsible for those deaths?"

"Exactly. But you forced me to speed things up, and I had to improvise."

So far, Brunetti has taken all the blame. He has not mentioned Tancredi's complicity, and Nardi, who is playing along, has been very careful not to mention him. After all, by now he has figured out how the events have unfolded. He just wonders which of the two was the one who physically carried out the murders.

Determined to solve this latest mystery, he is about to lay all his cards on the table when Teresa interrupts the conversation. "What have you done with our grandson?" she asks in a broken voice. Grabbing Sergio by his trouser leg, she insists: "Where is he? Please, I beg you, tell me!"

He shakes his finger in refusal. With a raise of his eyebrows, he looks at her and smiles. Finally, he opens his mouth to say something, but his breath turns to sobs.

Two police cars have just arrived on the scene.

Massimo had almost forgotten about them. Overtaking them upon his arrival, he had ordered them to stay undercover for about ten minutes.

Seeing the officers coming, he raises his hand to stop them. He did not want them to interfere before, and even less now, when tensions are high.

But although the men obey the order, each has already drawn his weapon and pointed it in Brunetti's direction.

Semi-surrounded, Sergio begins to look around uncertainly. "Well, I no longer have a choice," he says. "It seems clear to me that the end is already written."

"You can still choose to do the right thing," Massimo replies. "Put the gun down."

"Oh, no! I have no intention of spending the rest of my days in a cell."

"And how do you plan to avoid it? You see it for yourself. You can't escape from here."

"Please, Sergio!" Teresa begs again. "Tell me while you still can. Where is Pier Giorgio?"

In response to her plea, he raises his wrist and looks at his watch. "It's too late now," he then answers. "You won't catch him anymore."

"Huh? Who are you talking about? Who is it that we won't catch?" Massimo asks, confused by that last statement.

The other looks at him with the same ambiguous expression he showed earlier. "You know what? All things considered, I think I'll take your advice and let her live. That way, she'll never stop wondering what happened to our grandson."

"It's the right choice. Now lower your weapon."

"We didn't understand each other. As I said, prison is not for me."

"What's on your mind?"

"You will take care of it. You are the solution to the problem."

"Huh?"

"I'm going to count to three, and then you have to choose." Sergio moves the gun closer to Teresa's head. "Either you shoot, or I will."

"What? I don't want to kill you. But think carefully about what you are going to do. Because I will if I have to."

"Good! That means we agree on at least one thing. Are you ready? One…"

"Stop it! Don't make me do it."

"Two…"

Nardi has no choice but to squeeze the trigger.

The barrel of the Beretta is still smoking as the deflagration of the shot echoes along the ancient walls. Flocks of birds, nestled in the branches, take flight from the surrounding trees. They trill and whirl madly, chasing that echo as it scatters through the air.

Sergio is still standing, staggering. For a few moments, his head swings back and forth, his mouth hinting at a last smile, until his legs give way completely, and he falls to the ground.

In a fit of madness, Teresa jumps on his body and begins to beat him. She hits his chest again and again, almost as if she wants to bring him back to life. "No, no! You can't go like this!" she cries. "Open your eyes! Tell me where Pier Giorgio is."

"Stop it; it's useless. He's already dead," Massimo tells her.

Turning to look at him, she brings her fist to cover her mouth and shakes her head. "Why did you kill him? He was the only one who knew..." She bursts into a stream of tears that prevents her from saying anything else.

Convinced that he is boosting her morale, Nardi leans down to reveal what he has discovered about Tancredi. But just as he is about to put his hand on her shoulder, his gaze falls back on the semi-automatic at Sergio's feet.

Normally, he should be concerned with keeping the scene intact. But something doesn't sit right with him. A doubt that flashes through his mind immediately urges him to pick up the gun from the ground.

He looks at it, perplexed.

He has handled Glock 17s several times before. And he gets the impression that this one is too light.

Determined to put the thought out of his mind, he removes the magazine, but only to discover what he already suspected.

It is empty.

CHAPTER 41

July 17, noon

It's just after noon. Arriving at the building where Tancredi lives, Lanzi gets out of the car and looks up. With a bad feeling, he wonders if he will find him in the house.

Convinced that he would find him at his workplace, he had gone to the real estate agency, but only to find a closed shutter door, which was strange considering the time.

Fortunately, the apartment was not far away. If it had been on the other side of town, he would have wasted half the morning for nothing.

The building is huge, up to nine stories high. And judging from the outside, there must be at least fifteen staircases inside. That's why he drove around the block before parking. To make sure there were no other exits.

He hoped he was wrong about the number of people living there, but the intercom panels, arranged in three rows on either side of the entrance, seemed to confirm his suspicions.

He just hopes he gets lucky from the start, or he'll see double long before he finds Tancredi's last name. He almost wants to call Cataldo and ask him to check with the property records to find out the exact staircase and apartment number. But the clock is ticking, and he has no time to waste.

With a grimace of resignation, he begins to scroll through the various names.

Despite his impatience, he avoids reading too fast. The last thing he wants is to risk missing a name and having to start all over again.

It takes him a while to get to the bottom of the list. And when he doesn't find what he's looking for, he rolls his eyes and snorts.

Ready to examine the other set of intercom panels, he makes his way to the opposite side, but after only a few steps, his gaze slips inside. Noticing the porter's lodge a few feet ahead, he enters the corridor without a second thought.

The man behind the glass is not slow to speak: "Where are you going?" he asks in a suspicious tone. "Looking for someone?"

"Yes, good morning. I am Sergeant Lanzi," he replies, showing his badge. "Could you tell me the stairwell and number of Mr. Tancredi's apartment?"

The porter must be a busybody. With a curious expression, he leaves his post and goes outside. "Why are you looking for him? Did something happen?"

"Look, I don't have time. Can you please answer me?"

"Yes, of course. He lives on staircase H. Fourth floor, extension 13."

"And which side is it on?"

"On the left, the last one at the end."

"Perfect, thank you," he concludes, setting off.

He walks about ten yards before the man's voice catches up with him from behind. "Anyway, not to meddle in your business, but if I were you, I'd save myself the trouble. Mr. Tancredi is not home."

"Huh?" Lanzi says, turning around. "Are you sure?"

"Yeah. He left about two hours ago."

"Well, maybe he's come back in the meantime."

"Impossible. I've been here the whole time. I would have seen him."

"Look... I guess not, but did you happen to ask him where he was going?"

"Who do you take me for? I certainly don't bother the tenants. If they want to chat, fine. Otherwise, I mind my own business and don't ask questions."

"Yes, yes, all right. But did he say anything about where he was going?"

"Not at all! He left without even saying goodbye."

"I understand. Thanks anyway." Ready to leave, Lanzi is about to turn away when he has a change of heart. "Tell me one more thing. You said you saw him over two hours ago. Does it often happen that he's home at that time?"

"Hmm! Not really. He's usually at work. But I think he was going away today, like on a trip."

"Did he tell you that?"

"Of course not! He's not the kind of guy who likes to chat. It's just that I saw him come out with a suitcase."

"Is that all?"

"In case you're interested, he didn't even take his car. He called a taxi."

"What did you say? There! That is helpful. Thank you very much. I'll leave you to your work."

As the man re-enters the porter's lodge, Ettore hurries to take out his cell phone to call the police station.

He waits impatiently for a few moments until he hears the deputy's voice on the other end.

"Hey, Cataldo! It's Lanzi," he says excitedly.

"Yeah, Sergeant, go ahead."

"I need you to do an urgent search for me. Two hours ago, three at the most, a taxi driver picked up Nicola Tancredi from under the house. I need to know where the taxi took him. Contact all the taxi companies and find out who answered the call. You have his address. It should be easy to get a match."

"All right. I'll get right on it."

"I'm counting on it! Let me know as soon as you find out anything."

After the call, Ettore is about to contact Nardi to give him an

321

update, but then he thinks it might be better to postpone. Cataldo shouldn't take too long. He might as well wait a while.

So he returns to his car, parked across the street, gets in, and waits for the phone to ring.

Meanwhile, he keeps an eye on the entrance.

You never know. Tancredi might show up.

CHAPTER 42

The metallic voice of the loudspeaker calls the plane to Barcelona again. It announces a significant delay due to unforeseen technical problems. This has happened three times already, and Nicola is starting to get impatient, also because the plane has been on the runway for quite a while. He does not understand why they do not at least let them on board.

Fortunately, Pier Giorgio does not complain. Sitting in the waiting room, he quietly goes through his collection of trading cards.

Instead, Nicola thinks about Sergio. With considerable regret, he wonders if he has already completed the task he set for himself. That he would go so far as to sacrifice himself to see his revenge fulfilled was unplanned. It is certainly not how they had imagined it.

But in the end, Nicola is not too surprised. Nothing in his life has ever turned out the way he hoped.

With this thought in his head, he focuses his eyes beyond the glass windows to an undefined point on the runway and remains lost in the void with his gaze. His mind takes a leap into the past, jumping here and there in time, starting with the day he came to find out about the rape of Angela.

At that time, they had not been together long, but their

relationship was based on a mutual attraction that had always been there, a dormant desire that neither of them had ever given vent to.

Their love had suddenly flared up.

But what bound them together was an almost morbid love. So much so that Nicola had been sure to hate her that tragic night. He will never forget the anger with which he arrived at Sergio's house, much less the anguish with which he left.

By now, it had been a week since Teresa's apartment had been deserted. Angela was nowhere to be found and didn't return phone calls. Not knowing where else to turn, he had gone to Sergio's house to find out where she had ended up.

Unfortunately, there was no need to ask.

He saw her as soon as the door opened behind her father's back. She was huddled on the couch, her arms covered in scratches and bruises.

Anger immediately turned to fear. "My God! What happened to you?" he asked anxiously, stepping forward.

At the sound of his voice, she lifted her head, opened her mouth slightly, and stood staring at him in silence, her lips quivering and her eyes beginning to moist.

"So? What happened?"

Angela tried in vain to speak. She was unable to say anything. A grimace of pain distorted her face, and only a kind of sob came out from her throat. Then she looked away, lowered her head, crossed her arms up to her shoulders, stood up, and ran out of the living room.

He put out an arm to stop her but felt his wrist grabbed.

Sergio made a gesture of denial. "This is not a good time to talk to her," he said before releasing his grip. "At least not like this. It will take a lot of patience. And most of all, a lot of tact."

Then he began to explain why she was behaving abnormally. And the longer Sergio went on with the story, the more Nicola refused to believe what he was hearing.

Finally, he reached Angela in the bedroom. He found her lying face down on the mattress, choking back tears against the pillow.

On that occasion, he was unable to say anything to her. Feeling the hatred growing inside him, he just lay down by her side, caressing her long curly hair and crying with her.

That day, he felt overwhelmed by a real sense of helplessness. The same feeling he had already experienced when faced with his little brother's death. The same one that came back to overwhelm him several weeks later when another fact took him by surprise.

On a day that seemed not much worse than the previous ones, Angela's words caught him off guard.

"I'm expecting a baby," she told him.

Reading the terror in her eyes, he hesitated for a moment. "Huh? But do you think...?! Yeah, I mean, you don't really think that the father could be..."

"I don't know, but I'm scared."

"You don't have to be. I'm here with you. We'll face it together."

"My father says I should have an abortion. But I don't want to. The baby could be yours, after all."

"I am sure it is! I refuse to believe otherwise. You will see; the DNA tests will confirm it."

"The tests? Oh God, no! If I were to find out in the end... No, no, I couldn't bear it."

"Well then, what do you suggest we do about it?"

Angela hesitated to answer. She put her hands to her chest and rolled her eyes up and down a few times before saying, "Maybe giving the baby up for adoption would be the best solution for everyone."

"What?!" he blurted out. "How can you even suggest that?"

"I just think..."

"We're not discussing this!" he shushed her. "I'm not going to leave my son in someone else's hands."

In that child that was yet to come, Nicola saw many things. He saw his love for Angela, the memory of his brother Giorgio, the reflection of a part of himself that deserved a better future than his own. And he refused to consider the possibility of any other reality.

Unfortunately, he was not the one to decide. The last word was Angela's.

For the umpteenth time, he would have to watch passively, waiting for someone else to decide his fate. But he was no longer willing to be a spectator. Not now, when he had the chance to fight.

So, between Sergio's desire for her to have an abortion, her insistence on giving the baby away once it was born, and his desire to keep the child at all costs, the following months were a constant psychological battle.

On the day of the birth, he had to insist a lot to convince her to ask for a suspension of the adoption: two months in which she could have weighed her decision. When she finally decided to accept, he thought he had finally won. Instead, during Angela's stay at the maternity home, she became increasingly unstable.

The fear that the attacker was the one who impregnated her began to haunt her obsessively. And the mere idea of taking the tests to find out terrified her. In the end, she did not want to hear any more reasons; she opted for adoption.

Unable to accept this, Nicola decided to kidnap the child. He could not and did not want to lose him.

Entrusting him to safe hands, he kept Angela and Sergio completely unaware.

It was only several months later that he decided to tell them what he had done.

He was convinced that seeing the child again would make them feel something new, that love would find its way into their hearts, but he quickly realized that he was wrong.

Despite their tacit approval, neither of them could truly accept him. Their eyes said so. And eyes never lied.

Anyway, it doesn't matter anymore. Nothing will change what happened. Nevertheless, Nicola, coming back to reality, looks at Pier Giorgio and wonders what his own life would have been like if Angela had not held her son in such contempt.

Surely they would have kept him with them, and she would have had a reason to live. Perhaps today, they would be a happy family.

CHAPTER 43

July 17, noon

Nardi cannot take his eyes off the Glock 17. Still stunned by the unexpected turn of events, he stares mesmerized at the gun, thinking back to the strange expression he had glimpsed on Brunetti's face.

He had noticed it twice.

The first time was when he had tried to persuade him to lower the gun with a speech that he himself found hard to take seriously. And then, a few minutes later, when the other, accepting his advice, seemed to have convinced himself that for Teresa, life would be worse than death.

In those moments of tension, with more on his mind, he had certainly not paused to reflect on Brunetti's unusual attitude. Only now, seeing the empty magazine, does he understand the reason for that smirk on his face.

He had interpreted it as a sign of mockery towards himself when it must have been a smug and amused smile.

Sergio must have laughed to himself at the bizarre situation: being urged not to shoot when the idea had not even crossed his mind. Indeed, with Donati dead and the original plan foiled, nothing held him back anymore. He could have eliminated Teresa at any time, even half an hour earlier at the cemetery, but instead, he had stood still.

By now, it is obvious; killing her was no longer part of his intentions. What Nardi still does not understand is the reason for such a decision. Why did he change his mind?

Unable to find motivation, he wonders if Sergio was tired of living. Maybe that's why he had decided to sacrifice himself, probably in the belief that his death would have been a cover for Tancredi.

Who knows? Maybe he would have chosen differently if he had known that the other had already been discovered.

But it no longer matters. Teresa is safe, and the rest doesn't matter much.

Thinking of her, Massimo places the gun on the ground and turns his attention back to his friend. He sees she is still bent over Sergio's dead body and continues to despair.

"Hey, come on! Stop acting like this," he says. "There's something you don't know yet."

"Huh?" She turns her head slightly, wipes away her tears, and looks at him out of the corner of her eye.

"Sergio wasn't the only one who knew about your grandson."

"What do you mean?"

"He didn't do it all by himself. He had help."

"So what? I don't see how that changes anything, considering that you and your team also killed Donati."

"Oh no, no, I don't mean him. Donati was a mere pawn, as well as a preordained victim. Another person has remained in the shadows all this time. Someone who helped Sergio from the beginning and had the exact same reasons to hate you."

"Who are you talking about? I don't understand."

"Nicola Tancredi. Does that name ring a bell?"

"Um!" Teresa puts a hand to her mouth and wrinkles her forehead. "It sounds familiar, but…"

"I can believe it! It's no wonder," he interrupts. "He lived in your building for years."

"Mrs. Roversi's son?!" she exclaims, eyes wide open and mouth agape.

"Yes. The half-brother of the child who was in the car with your son."

Teresa's expression shows no sign of change. Still in disbelief, she looks straight ahead and remains silent.

"He and Angela had a relationship," Massimo continues. "We know that by the time she was pregnant, they had already been seeing each other for quite some time. And they have not been separated since. I think he was the one who kidnapped your grandson, maybe to prevent him from being given to the foster family. And even if I can't prove it, I'm convinced Sergio knew everything."

"Even if they had a love affair, it doesn't mean he is involved in this story, let alone that he knows where Pier Giorgio is. How can you be sure?"

"Oh, there's no doubt about his involvement. You don't know this, but in the past, Donati was in prison, accused of murder. He was still awaiting trial when the charges were suddenly dropped. He became a free man overnight. And you know who made that happen? Sergio and Tancredi. I imagine they must have offered to give false testimony in exchange for his complicity."

"But then we have to act! Do you have any idea where he might be?"

"Yes, don't worry. I have already sent someone to take care of it. By the way, give me a moment so I can inquire if there is any news."

Getting up, Nardi moves a few feet away and starts looking for Lanzi's number in his phone book.

Meanwhile, amid the buzz of voices around him, he hears that someone is already in radio contact with the police station. Without much interest, he lifts his eyes just a little, just enough to notice the presence of two female officers in the group.

Bringing the cell phone to his ear, he approaches the nearest one, nods his head in Teresa's direction, and says, "Think of her for a moment, please. Get her away. It's not a good idea for her to stay there."

The policewoman barely has time to give him an affirmative look in reply; as she opens her mouth to speak, the sergeant's voice echoes from the device, and he silences the woman by raising a hand and then turning his back on her. "Hey, Lanzi! So, any news?" he asks. "Any luck finding Tancredi?"

"Unfortunately not, Chief. It seems he has left. Not to be a bird of ill omen, but I'm afraid he managed to escape."

"What?!"

"When I arrived at his house, he had already left an hour ago. The doorman of the building saw him leave with his luggage and take a taxi. I was able to track down the taxi driver who picked him up, and according to him, he took him to Fiumicino Airport. But Cataldo just checked the passenger list, and there is no reservation in Tancredi's name."

"Hmm! I doubt he went there to watch planes land. Maybe he obtained a fake document to bypass the security checks. Where are you?"

"On my way back to the police station."

"Good. Then spread his photo to the authorities on-site," Nardi concludes. "I'm on my way too. See you there."

Now it's clear to whom Sergio was referring to when he said they wouldn't catch him anymore. He had begun to watch the time and had orchestrated that performance, all for one purpose: to buy Tancredi precious minutes.

Determined not to waste any more time, Massimo has already started walking toward the car, but then he remembers that Teresa is right behind him.

This time he cannot keep her in the dark. And given the urgency, he has neither the desire nor the time to make up an excuse. So he turns and starts to call her. He will take her with him.

CHAPTER 44

July 17, afternoon, 12:50 p.m.

Upon arrival at the airport, Massimo parks the car without much ceremony. He stops in front of the entrance doors in an area marked no parking reserved for public transportation vehicles.

A border police officer, seeing him getting out of the car, approaches him and shouts, "Hey, you! You need to move from there. Don't you see the signs? It's a no-parking zone."

"I'm Inspector Nardi," he replies, showing his badge. "I'm on duty. And I'm in a hurry."

"Oh, my apologies! Can I be of any help?"

"Yes, thank you. Could you show me to your offices? I need to speak with a security manager."

"Of course, follow me."

The man holds up his hand to show the way, and Nardi, starting to walk, waves for Teresa to follow.

As soon as he enters, Massimo begins to look around, scanning the faces of the people nearby and casting a few glances off into the distance. Like every day, though, Fiumicino Airport is teeming with people. Finding Tancredi will be anything but easy.

On the other hand, in this crowd it would be a challenge to find any random person, including Lanzi, who should be arriving shortly. Therefore, while the officer continues to lead the way, he decides to send a message to the sergeant to let him know where to meet.

When they arrive at the offices, the policeman shows his palm to signal them to wait. "Just a minute," he says. Turning to a colleague, he announces their presence by asking him to call the supervisor. Then he says goodbye and goes back the way he came.

"Do you think Tancredi is still here?" asks Teresa in the meantime.

"Well, I hope so."

"And what if he has already left?"

"Let's take it one step at a time," he suggests. "There's no point in worrying unnecessarily in advance."

Moments later, another uniformed man appears in the hallway and walks toward them at a brisk pace.

When he reaches them, he looks at Teresa with a smile, extends his hand to Massimo, and asks, "Inspector Nardi?"

"Yes, pleased to meet you. And you are?"

"Airport Superintendent De Vito. I was already informed of your arrival. I've been waiting for you."

"Ah, good! I'm looking for…"

"Relax, Inspector, I already know everything," interrupts the other. "Come on! Let's go to the operations room. We're trying to locate your man. Nothing has turned up so far, but if he's here, we'll find him."

The three of them walk into the room where security activities are coordinated.

On the back wall, which is completely covered by high-resolution screens, several shots of the areas of the airport, both inside and outside, appear.

"As you can see, my men are combing the entire airport," De Vito points out.

"How long have they been at it?"

"About ten minutes."

"And will it take long to complete the search?"

"Well, with any luck, we could be done soon. Otherwise, I don't know. Anyway, don't worry. We've distributed his photo to the boarding gates and put all personnel on alert. So if he's inside, he can't go anywhere."

"Understood?" Massimo says then, turning to Teresa. "Now, the best thing you can do is sit quietly and wait."

She seems about to argue but has no time to open her mouth. At the sight of Lanzi crossing the threshold, he turns completely around and walks over to the sergeant. "Ah, there you are!" he exclaims. "I was beginning to wonder where you had disappeared to."

"I did my best to be quick."

Without even introducing him to the superintendent, Nardi waves him out of the room. "Come on, let's go! We can't be of any help here. We might as well take a look around." He is about to leave when he looks back at De Vito. "Can you get us some radios?" he asks. "So you can keep us informed."

"And what about me?" Teresa interjects.

"You stay here!" His dry tone leaves no room for a reply.

Anyway, no one has time to add anything else. One man throws his arm up in the air, waves his hand to attract attention, and says, "Hey, hey, maybe we've got something."

"Huh? What is it?" De Vito asks, making his way to his station.

"A cleaner seems to have recognized Tancredi from the photo the agents showed him."

"Where?"

"At Terminal 3. Exit 8 of Concourse C."

"Let them know we're coming," Nardi blurts out. And before De Vito can turn around, he is walking briskly toward the door. "Come on, let's go!" he says to Lanzi.

Overcome by impatience, he does not even bother to reprimand Teresa, who has already begun to follow them without hesitation. Glancing at her, he barely raises an eyebrow to hint at a grimace of disagreement, then crosses the threshold and walks straight ahead.

Positioned in a secluded spot, two airport security agents are talking to a young man. He can't be more than twenty, maybe even younger: one almost wonders if he's of age. But judging by his work clothes, he seems to match the person they were talking about in the operations room: the cleaner.

When Massimo is only a few feet away from them, he skips the preamble of introductions and breaks into the conversation. "Is he the witness?"

Obviously annoyed by the interruption, the older policeman turns and gives him a sideways glance. "Inspector Nardi?"

"Oh, yes!" he confirms. "Sorry, it's the rush. So? Is he the one who recognized Tancredi?"

"Yes. He claims to have seen him half an hour ago."

"And where is he?" asks Teresa immediately.

"Hey!" Massimo points his finger at her. "You wanted to come, and I let you, but don't make me regret it." Unnerved, he stares at her for a few moments before looking away. Turning to the agent, he points to the mug shot in his hand and asks, "Can I have it?"

As soon as the man hands it to him, he lifts it in the air and brings it up to the cleaner's face. "Are you sure this is the same person?" The young man's childish expression does not inspire much confidence, and he wonders if he is just trying to get attention. "Is it just a resemblance, or would you be willing to swear it's really him?"

"No, no! It's the same guy, no doubt."

Nardi stares at him for a few seconds; he seems sincere. Still, he insists, "Are you really sure? We don't have time to waste."

"Yes. Absolutely! Hard to be wrong. I've never seen a man so pale. With two pointed canines, he could play the role of a vampire."

This last detail sweeps away all doubt.

The waxy complexion was what had also struck him when

Tancredi had crossed the threshold of his office at their first meeting.

"But was he alone?" asks Teresa.

With a sideways glance, Nardi is about to scold her but the cleaner anticipates this and replies, "No, he was with his son, at least I think so. A boy of ten or twelve."

"And where did you see them?" Teresa insists.

"There, at gate 13, while they were announcing the flight to Barcelona."

Everyone turns to look in the direction indicated by the young man.

The gate in question is practically deserted. There are only two female gate agents joking and laughing on the other side of the counter, but there is not a trace of travelers in sight.

Tancredi could be in the air by now. Teresa has already figured it out. Because her expression suddenly changes: her eyes go wide, her face pales.

Sensing her anxiety, Massimo puts a hand on her shoulder. He feels her tremble. So he says: "Come on! Let's go get some information."

"You wait here with him," Lanzi instructs the agents before leaving in tow. "We might still need him."

The two women soon become aware of their presence.

Seeing them approach, they stop talking while forced smiles on their faces replace the spontaneous expressions they had just moments ago.

One of them steps forward and asks politely, "May I help you?"

"Yes, we are looking for this man." Nardi identifies himself and places the photo on the counter. "Did you happen to see him during the boarding procedure?"

"Hmm! I don't think so."

"Are you sure? Take a good look."

With a slightly annoyed expression, the woman takes another glance at the picture before confirming her answer with a nod of the head.

"And what about you?" he then asks her colleague.

Having remained on the sidelines until then, she takes a few steps forward, grabs the sheet from the counter, and replies, "Let me see."

A moment later, she raises an eyebrow and waves the piece of paper. "Oh, yes, yes!" she exclaims. "He was with his son. A nice little boy. I checked their boarding passes myself."

"Is the plane still on the runway, or has it already taken off?" The question is purely a formality. Massimo already imagines the answer, and he is not surprised when he hears the woman say, "I'm sorry, it took off about twenty minutes ago."

Teresa, on the other hand, rests her elbows on the counter, sinks her forehead between her palms, and begins to despair. "Oh God, no!" she cries. "Tell me it's not true."

"And why are you crying now?" he complains. "You should be happy. It couldn't have gone better."

"Are you making fun of me?"

"What? Do you think I would joke in a situation like this?"

"What do you mean?"

"Oh, damn it! This whole thing has really messed up your brain. You can't think straight anymore."

"Seriously! What the hell are you talking about?"

"Hey, calm down! And try to think. They're on a plane. Where do you expect them to go?"

In response to his words, Teresa leans back against the counter. Tilting her head back, she places one hand on her chest, covers her forehead with the other, closes her eyes, and finally breathes a sigh of relief.

"Besides, they're only going to Spain, certainly not to a country without extradition," Lanzi points out. "We'll arrest them when they land."

"Yes, yes, I understand. I hadn't thought of that." Now relieved, Teresa hints at a half-smile.

Nardi, for his part, is eager to leave. "Lanzi, I'm going back to the police station to inform the prosecutor and the commissioner. You take care of the rest. Go back to De Vito and contact the Spanish authorities to make the arrangements."

"Who is De Vito?"

"Huh? Oh, right!" he exclaims, remembering how he dragged the sergeant away upon his arrival. Without any introduction. "He's the superintendent and in charge of the operations room."

"Ah, I see! Okay, then. I'll go right away."

As the sergeant leaves, Nardi returns to the two agents.

"Okay, we're done here. You can let him go," he says, referring to the cleaner. And as he extends his hand to the worker, he adds, "Thanks for your help. You've been very helpful."

Clearly pleased, the young man reaches out to shake hands, smiles triumphantly, and puffs his chest like a proud rooster.

"I bid you farewell. Good work," Massimo concludes. Leaving him to enjoy his moment of glory, he heads for the exit, waving to Teresa to join him.

Once outside the airport, he breathes a sigh of relief.

Finally, this ugly affair has come to an end, this time for real, and the closing of the doors behind him almost seems to underline it.

Despite everything, Teresa appears silent and troubled, which is a bit strange. Although, considering what she's been through, it's understandable.

"Aren't you happy?" he asks, just to distract her. "Soon, you'll be able to hug your grandson."

"Yes, of course. It's just that I don't think I'm ready."

"What do you mean?" he replies, starting to walk toward the car. "This is what you wanted, isn't it? Besides, you are the only relative left now, and it will be up to you to take care of him."

"Yes. But I don't know where to start."

"You'll probably get custody without any trouble."

"Oh, that's the least of my worries. The problem is that I never thought I would actually meet him. Yeah, well, before he was just a face in a photo, but now... What will I say to him when we meet face to face?"

"If I were you, I wouldn't worry about that. You'll see! You'll find the right words at the right time."

"The truth is, I'm afraid. I know practically nothing about him. What if Sergio turned him against me? Who knows what he might have told him all this time."

"I'm sorry, Teresa, but I can't help you with that. I think you'll have to find out for yourself." Massimo has already opened the car door and put one foot inside; when, straightening up again, he puts on his sunglasses, leans one arm on the car roof, and adds, "I can tell you one thing, though. I envy you and would gladly trade places with you. You know my story. You know how badly I wanted a son. If I had to choose between a living son who hates me and a dead one who can never do that, well, I would choose the first option a hundred times over."

With those last words, he gets behind the wheel of his car, showing no desire to continue the conversation. He doesn't even urge Teresa to get in; instead, he patiently waits for her to do it herself.

It is bitter to realize how life always holds in reserve the exact opposite of what one desires. And when the object of others' unhappiness could be the source of our own happiness, the situation becomes even sadder.

Not wanting to dwell on this, Massimo turns the key and accelerates. He revs the engine four or five times, trying to drown out his thoughts with the roar, but to no avail. Eventually, he resigns himself, shifts the car into gears, and starts driving back.

CHAPTER 45

July 17, afternoon, 1:00 p.m.

During the takeoff, Nicola had not taken his eyes off the window. With his gaze fixed on the other side of the glass, he had continued to watch the runway, which grew smaller and farther away, the succession of cultivated fields that covered the ground like a vivid checkered blanket, and then roads and vehicles, buildings and domes and monuments.

Suddenly, everything flowed away quickly.

A liberating feeling, one he had felt in those moments.

The city flowed beneath him, and the past slipped away with it until it was lost in the boundless blue of the open sea.

But only now, as the clouds have swallowed everything, does he really feel that he has broken the chains that enslaved him.

Soon the world will reveal itself again, but with the freshness of the unknown, with new lands, new roads, and new horizons. Everything will be different. Not even people will be the same, and he will no longer be himself. He will be a man without a past and with a future to discover.

Although he will carry the emptiness of loss, he is comforted by having found peace. Finally, time will be able to heal the wounds, and he will be able to begin to live again.

He would like to stay like this forever, to continue dreaming in the midst of the soft, whitish mantle of water vapor that envelops the plane. Instead, he is suddenly torn from his thoughts. He feels his pant leg pulled.

"Hey, Dad!" Pier Giorgio calls to him. "But do we really have to go?"

"Huh? What do you mean? Aren't you happy? Now we can live together. We'll have a house all to ourselves, and we'll be together every day."

"Yeah, but… what about my friends?"

"Oh! I bet you'll make new ones in no time."

"And what if I don't like living there? Can we come back then?"

"Trust me! Where we are going is a wonderful place. Once we get there, you won't want to go back."

"But if I don't like it, will you promise to take me back to Auntie?"

"We will see. For now, try to get some sleep," he concludes, ruffling the child's hair and simulating a reassuring smile.

Pier Giorgio's gaze reveals a certain anxiety. Nevertheless, he seems to trust him and closes his eyes. And resting his head on Nicola's arm, he holds him tightly with both hands, almost afraid of losing him.

He holds him in return, making him feel his presence, and seeing him fragile and defenseless, he feels a pang in his heart. Aware of the deprivations the child has suffered since before his birth, he thinks back to the night he had taken him from the institution.

To keep him safe, he had entrusted him to a distant cousin - Aunt Aurora, in Pier Giorgio's eyes. She, who had never been able to have children, had not hesitated to help him in her desire to fulfill her own dream.

A false birth certificate had allowed the baby to grow up in a semi-normal state, although there was little or nothing normal about his existence.

He and Angela visited him only on weekends or special occasions. And although Angela tried to appear natural, there was always an invisible line she couldn't cross.

But as far as Pier Giorgio knew, they were his real parents.

Pier Giorgio had often asked for explanations as to why he had to live with his aunt. He never missed an opportunity to ask what job was so demanding, preventing them from caring for him like normal parents.

It had never been possible to give him a good reason – at least not one he could understand.

Even now, as he sleeps innocently, he cannot imagine the truth. And he will never have to know.

Nicola will do whatever is necessary to guarantee him the happiness he deserves, but to do so, he will have to make sure that this dark side of his past remains buried. Therefore, just as he was born and raised in a lie, so he will continue to live in a lie.

After all, what difference does it make? The dividing line between truth and falsehood is a moving boundary where the absolute truth continues to layer itself infinitely. It just depends on which angle you look at it from. And he knows from experience that sometimes it's better to look from the wrong side. For when the truth is as sharp as a guillotine blade, ignorance is the only salvation.

He won't let that sharp axe fall on Pier Giorgio. He will be the one to protect him.

With this thought, he turns his gaze back to the window.

It is then that he notices that the clouds have parted to make way for a blue sky and blindingly bright sun. The light is so intense that he has to squeeze his eyes shut to bear the sight of it.

They're almost there. Spain is close, and he is eager to reach his destination. He doesn't know what the future holds for him, but those reflections of light seem to herald a better tomorrow.

And he is confident; he wants to believe.

From now on, life can only smile on him. After all, it owes him that much.

BOOKS BY JACQUES OSCAR LUFULUABO

INSPECTOR NARDI MYSTERY-THRILLER SERIES

- ***SHADOW OF PUNISHMENT*** – (Readers' Favorite 5-Star)

- ***ENIGMA OF THE MISSIONARY***

THE LAST SPIN

AFTERWORD

Thank you for reading *Enigma of the Missionary*. I hope you enjoyed this novel.

If you'd like to be notified when my next book comes out, as well as alerted of free book promotions, join my community.

* Follow me on my Amazon Author page

* Follow me on Facebook: OscarLufuluabo.Autore

* Follow me on Goodreads: Jacques Oscar Lufuluabo

AND PLEASE...

If you have a moment, I'd really appreciate a review on Amazon, no matter how short. Honest reader reviews help others decide whether they'll enjoy a book.

Thank you again, dear reader, and I hope we meet again between the pages of another book.

Printed in Great Britain
by Amazon